T0053931

ABOUT THE AUTHOR

William Keeling is a former foreign correspondent of the *Financial Times* who exposed a multi-billion-dollar corruption scandal in Nigeria that led to his summary deportation. He eventually left journalism for chocolate, becoming co-owner of the historic chocolate company Prestat, but is still plotting his return to the true home of jollof rice. Like his late uncle (referred to in this book), he has a creative mind. He lives and writes in Somerset.

Belle Nash and the Bath Circus is the second in his series, *The Gay Street Chronicles*.

THE GAY STREET CHRONICLES
VOLUME 2

Belle Nash
and
the Bath Circus

William Keeling Esq.

16
EnvelopeBooks

Published 2023 in Great Britain by EnvelopeBooks
A New Premises venture in association with Booklaunch

EnvelopeBooks
12 Wellfield Avenue
London N10 2EA

Cover design by Stephen Games | Booklaunch

A CIP catalogue record for this title is available from the
British Library

ISBN 9781915023117

Edited and designed by Booklaunch for EnvelopeBooks
EnvelopeBooks 16
www.envelopebooks.co.uk
www.gaystreetchronicles.co.uk

What a chimera, then, is Man!
What a novelty, what a monster, what a chaos,
What a contradiction, what a prodigy!
Judge of all things, feeble earthworm,
Repository of truth, sewer of uncertainty and error,
The Glory and the Scum of the Universe.

Blaise Pascal, philosopher
1623–62

For my dear friend
Andrew 'Mr Fabulous' Reid
who, a king among men, truly is fabulous.

FOREWORD

A S READERS OF the first volume of *The Gay Street Chronicles* will know, some years ago I received a letter from a solicitor informing me, or so I supposed, of my death. It was not I who was dead, however, but my uncle and namesake Dr W.B. Keeling, a relative who lived in Gay Street in Bath.

My uncle had bequeathed me a Queen Anne silver toast rack and a small trunk of undisclosed contents. As a keen consumer of toast, I was delighted with the rack but it was the trunk that changed my life. In it were numerous letters, diaries and records from the nineteenth century as well as a host of muddled manuscripts written by my uncle, reflecting his enthusiasm for Bath's rich history.

My uncle was an amateur historian and his writing focused on a man who had once lived in Gay Street and served as a city councillor: Mr Bellerophon Nash (1796–1864), commonly known as Belle.

According to my uncle's research, Belle Nash was a flamboyant public figure, unashamed—like my uncle—of his bachelor status. This was in an era when sexual relations between men were a criminal offence, although Belle Nash was afforded some protection through his family name. The famous Beau Nash, very probably his grandfather, was the Master of Ceremonies who had made Bath the social hub of England a century earlier.

My uncle uncovered Belle Nash's close friendship with Mrs

Gaia Champion (1795–1873), who was appointed magistrate of Bath (the subject of Volume 1 of the *Chronicles*) at a time when posts of public authority were the preserve of men. In modern parlance, Gaia Champion was a feminist outlier and she and Belle Nash supported each other's determination to cut a swathe through the conventions of early nineteenth-century Bath society.

Their efforts to confront bigotry, in particular, did not go unchallenged, however. Misogyny, homophobia and racism were rife, papered over by a veneer of English gentility, even in that most genteel of cities.

Intrigued, I believe, by the absurdity of bigotry, my uncle sought to bring Belle Nash and his friends to life, although at what point he wrote *The Gay Street Chronicles* is not certain. No attempt was made in his lifetime to publish his work and, sadly, not all his writings have survived. On a later visit to his house, I found more than a few pages lining a cat-litter tray. Such was the nature of the man and of the historian.

What remains I, a mere journalist by trade, have tried to reconstruct and now publish as Volume 2. The year is 1835 and after a four-year period of exile, Belle Nash has returned to Bath, where he is immediately embraced by familiar friends. But all is not well, for Belle Nash is a changed man.

William Keeling Esq. (nephew)

A PECULIARLY LONG
PREFACE
IN FIVE CHAPTERS

CHAPTER I

The Amazing Mrs Nonsuch

I T WAS NOT the first time that a Bow Street officer had made enquiries at Jaunay's Hotel in Leicester Square, an establishment renowned for its distinctly theatrical, often foreign-sounding patrons. Stretching across three grand terraced houses, the hotel had a small portico designed to impress the cultivated Londoner. Less so, however, London's new rough-neck force of bobbies on the beat.

Detective Inspector Decimus Dimm, an unprepossessing middle-aged man with red cheeks and rustic sideburns, stepped up to the portico with accustomed determination, only to have the hotel doorman block his way.

The doorman in question was short and stout, although it was not his physique or the elegant cut of his uniform that made him stand out. Rather it was his face: lips embellished by red lipstick, eyelashes extended with the liberal use of coal dust and grease.

'Afternoon, Sir. How may I help?' the doorman enquired.

'I require entry, of course.'

'Ah, how many of our visitors say that!' the doorman replied, with the suggestion of a smirk. 'In your case, however, I fear you ask too much.'

'I'm a detective inspector,' Dimm responded, dimly. 'From Bow Street. That means I embody the Law and I'll thank you to make way.'

To his surprise, the doorman remained unmoved.

'I see that you wear a Peeler's blue swallow-tail coat, Sir, with a high collar to protect you from garrotting, but sadly you do not meet the dress code of the establishment.'

Before Dimm had a chance to object, the doorman stepped forward and inspected the material of his jacket, then stepped back with the expression of disdain adopted by all stout men who wear mascara.

'As I thought. Your jacket is made of serge. A nice-enough weave but we require something fancier: a silk chiffon cravat, perhaps, or a Calais lace kerchief. You display neither of these, I regret. Other men may enter; you may not.'

The two men appeared to have reached an impasse, but Dimm was not used to being stymied by coal dust and grease. He pulled a small notebook out of a pocket and flipped it open.

'I insist you tell me your name at once.'

The doorman was happy enough to oblige.

'I call myself Beauty, by daylight. Beauty of the McBeautys of Bellarena. In Ireland.'

Dimm winced and, pocketing his pencil and pad again, reached down into the tails of his coat. 'Now here's the thing, whatever your name is. Either you stand aside or I'll hit your head hard with this newly issued wooden cosh that I'm entrusted to carry. What's it to be, then?'

Faced by Dimm's truncheon, the doorman quickly relegated the importance of sartorial elegance and stepped to one side.

'Of course, Sir. Who at Jaunay's do you wish to see?'

'The manager,' replied Dimm. 'Where can I find him?'

The doorman pointed through the glass panes of the double doors towards the far side of the lobby.

'Straight through. You can see the door to ... '

Dimm pushed his way past.

' ... her office. For the manager, Sir,' said Beauty, as the front door slammed closed, 'is a woman.'

ON ENTERING THE lobby of Jaunay's, a guest would typically stop to admire the lobby's elegant Chinoiserie wallpaper, its gilded furniture and the air perfumed with rose water. Dimm, however, was not such a person, and he made straight for the manager's office to catch its occupant unawares.

Any hope he had in this regard, however, was misfounded, for the manager, Mrs Nonsuch, had a nose for trouble. She could smell a policeman, especially one of Dimm's rank and intelligence, from afar.

As he entered the office, Mrs Nonsuch rose and Dimm found himself confronted by a redoubtable lady whose nature was reflected in her surroundings. He was not the first to gawp at the sight of an iron hoop, hung on a wall, flecked with dried blood and dried divots of human flesh—relics of those whom the fair lady had bowled her hoop at in the past.

Hoop-bowling had been a competitive sport at the dame school to which the teenage Mrs Nonsuch had been sent. No one who had attended the summer sports day would forget the anguish of the once fleet-footed, sixteen-year-old Lady Amanda Cavendish as the Nonsuch hoop had splintered her kneecaps whilst she was demonstrating the quadrille; or the pain felt by Miss R. Grainger, whose left ear was unexpectedly torn off by the hoop whilst rehearsing 'Cupid's Kindness', one of Ludwig van Beethoven's *26 Welsh Songs*, outside the parish almshouses, for a fundraising gala the following day.

'And who do you have the sadness to be?' Mrs Nonsuch demanded, her dark eyes staring with furious intent at Dimm. 'Not a guest of Jaunay's; that fact is as plain as a codpiece. Not with that jacket.'

As is often the case with men when faced with women of character, Dimm felt a wave of inadequacy wash over his pre-existing inadequacy. Mrs Nonsuch's assertive tone, broad shoulders and bloodied iron hoop were surely reason enough, but there was something else about her that troubled him.

'This is the second time this afternoon that my apparel has been bequestioned,' said Dimm, defensively. 'I am a Peeler, Madam. A detective inspector from Bow Street and I wish to enquire about a certain criminal whom your establishment is currently entertaining as a guest.'

Dimm's request was met with a glower; it was not Mrs Nonsuch's habit to betray the privacy of Jaunay's residents.

'I hardly think you'll find anyone here who's a criminal. This is Jaunay's, founded in 1800 by Louis Brunet, an *associé* of the Prince de Condé and other aristocrats exiled from their beloved France by the Revolution. We have a reputation, Mr Dimm, for social distinction as well as *la cuisine française*.'

Dimm, however, was a simple man who preferred jellied eels over French cooking. 'It's for me to say who's a criminal, Madam. We have reason to believe that the man I'm after is staying here. Now be good enough to let me see the register of guests, Ma'am.'

As Mrs Nonsuch trudged grumpily into the back office, Dimm's eyes followed her. Though now at Bow Street, he had started his career in the West Country, where he had been taught by the magistrate to regard all women with suspicion. And, to his eye, there was something strange about Mrs Nonsuch.

A moment later, the hotel manager returned with the register and laid it open on the desk for Dimm to inspect. Dimm passed a calloused finger down the names of guests, flicking back through the pages one by one over the previous two months.

'I'm confident that you'll find nothing amiss,' said Mrs Nonsuch, forcefully. 'We are a highly respectable establishment.'

Dimm raised a hesitant eye.

'I see nothing yet, but that doesn't surprise me. The man we're looking for is devious in the extreme and is likely to be using a pseudonym, although by the looks of it ... '

He twisted the ledger around so that Mrs Nonsuch could read the entries.

' ... your register is filled with many suspicious names. Look at them, Madam. Many are hard to pronounce. That usually means they're foreign and foreigners are always suspect, what with their strange accents and fancy manners.'

Mrs Nonsuch snorted. 'Our foreign guests are all men of impeccable reputation. We currently have the eminent French philosopher Monsieur Blaise Pascal staying with us, although he is without his friend and colleague, the dramatist Jean-Baptiste Racine. Among the other residents are British actors who have adopted stage names, making them not foreign but professional.'

'They sound foreign,' said Dimm, 'and that's enough for me, Madam.'

'Then let me relieve you of your scepticism,' said Mrs Nonsuch and she pointed to a name in the book. 'The popular Russian dancer Svetlana Krasko is none other than Maeve Cooley from Shoreditch; and Miss Kitty Pineapple, who sadly died in Room 106 a fortnight ago, was proved by the coroner to be the Earl of Dumfries.'

Dimm's eyes widened.

'A peer of the realm? Pretending to be Miss Pineapple, you say?'

'Indeed—or was it the other way round? I cannot recall.'

Mrs Nonsuch sat back in her chair.

'Too often, Sir, how we are perceived is superficial or irrelevant. At Jaunay's, we welcome all our guests without prejudice. As, no doubt, should the Law ... '

Dimm grimaced.

' ... and the Church,' added Mrs Nonsuch, judging that she needed to raise the ante, 'for are we not all God's creatures?'

Realising that the manager was getting the better of him, Dimm decided to reassert himself and slammed the register closed, hoping to impress by a show of masculine force.

'Four years ago, the criminal in question was exiled to the West Indies by a justice in Bath and barred from returning to British shores until a week hence. Should he already have returned to

London, as we have grounds to believe, he will be exiled a second time, and this time more harshly, as the Law rightly demands.'

'The West Indies!' Mrs Nonsuch laughed. 'How very dramatic. Or do you mean the East Indies? Or perhaps the North or South Indies? To which Indian islands was he exiled?'

Dimm's voice turned to a growl. 'Do not seek to distract me, Madam. The Law is not to be trifled with and nor am I.'

But Mrs Nonsuch was not so easily threatened.

'To assist you, Officer Dimm, you must divulge the name of him whom you pursue.'

'Him whom?' said Dimm, for whom grammar was a weakness.

'Yes, him whom. I cannot say if the miscreant is staying under Jaunay's roof if I do not know the man's identity.'

Dimm opted for another display of male eloquence and pounded the desk with a fist. This woman was intolerable!

'You know, I'm sure, to him to whom to I'm referring!'

'To him to whom to?' queried Mrs Nonsuch.

'Yes, to him. Who.'

'Detective Inspector Dimm, I cannot read your mind nor imagine the many names of those who might appear on your Most Wanted list.'

'I refer to Bellerophon Nash, of course! Otherwise known as Belle Nash, the well-known Bathonian finger-twirler.'

Having said which, Dimm immediately cursed and slapped his forehead with a hand. It had not been his intention to reveal the name but this devil of a woman had outwitted him. As for Mrs Nonsuch, she did not hide her pleasure.

'Ah, dear Mr Nash of Bath!' she exclaimed, clapping her hands. 'The grandson of the great Beau. Why, of course, we know Mr Nash! He has been a guest at Jaunay's many a time and oft.'

Dimm struck the desk again, but this time in triumph, and looked around the office as if Mr Nash might at that moment be hiding behind a cabinet or a side table.

'I thought as much. My greatest foe! It's thanks to him and his

8

lady magistrate friend that I lost my job in Somerset. Where is he?'

Dimm's jubilation, however, was short-lived.

'Mr Nash has been a guest, but not for many years,' said the lady manager. 'I believe the last time we saw him was in 1829. Exile would explain his absence, though if he's due to return to England soon, that is good news indeed.'

Dimm slumped back with his head hung low.

'Not here? That is a blow ... if what you say is true.'

'Do not question my integrity,' said Mrs Nonsuch, leaning forcefully across the desk. 'Look me in the face and tell me that I'm not a fine, upstanding, honest woman.'

Dimm looked up. He wrinkled his nose in displeasure. He pursed his lips. Damn all women of authority. If Mrs Nonsuch were a man, he told himself, he would have cuffed her!

He hissed, 'Very well, Madam, but I'll be watching Jaunay's. And, if you change your mind, it were best you sought me out.'

'Indeed, Detective,' she replied, 'I'd be happy to sort you out. But for today, I bid you farewell.'

Moving from behind her desk, she showed the officer out and then turned sharply to a bellboy.

'What a vile and stupid man. Tell Beauty never to allow him into Jaunay's again. But first get out the rose water to clear the stench of ignorance from the air.'

'Yes, Ma'am.'

'And kindly inform Monsieur Blaise Pascal when he collects his key that I need to see him on a matter of urgency.'

A s DIMM STEPPED out again onto the busy sidewalk, he took a moment to peer back at the edifice of Jaunay's.

'There's something going on in there,' he whispered to himself. 'Something mucky that I can't put my finger on.'

Looking back at him with a grin of satisfaction was Beauty the doorman, who appreciated what Dimm failed to understand: that Jaunay's provided an insight into the future. The door that he guarded was the gateway to a remarkable establishment where anything was possible—a pointer to a world without boundaries, a world in which doormen might wear lipstick, East End maidens might be Russian dancers and lords of the realm feel free to dress as stocking-clad coquettes.

A world in which, dear reader, if you had not guessed it already, a talented woman, born to an English plantation owner and an enslaved African mother, could manage a London hotel.

Well, almost: for let us not forget that the year is 1835 and that those who had been cruelly enslaved, though now 'freed', remained indentured—required to earn their freedom from 'owners' whom Parliament had deemed worthy of compensation.

Mrs Nonsuch's success, therefore, was not easily achieved. Despite her resourcefulness and intelligence, or because of them, she had been ostracised by polite—and sometimes impolite— society. As the once fleet-footed Lady Amanda Cavendish had explained to her whilst recuperating on a *chaise longue*, 'My legs may be in splints but I'm still a lady and you're still a *mulatta*.'

Meanwhile, in her office, the hotel manager poured herself a glass of rum and studied her reflection in a mirror, seeing back a handsome woman of determined mind. She looked about the room, at an oil painting of her father on a wall and at a charcoal drawing of her mother on her desk. Jaunay's was more than a refuge to her. Jaunay's was her world.

The rum was sweet and she smiled, remembering the words that she had whispered back into her opponent's ear: 'You deceive yourself, poor Amanda. This country is as much mine as yours; and there is no one at the dame school who wishes to learn the quadrille, whereas my bowling skills are now admired by all. As for whether you're a lady, that empty honour bestowed on you by birth is but a mirage, for you're no lady. You're a ... .'

And here discretion draws a veil over the epithet launched by Mrs Nonsuch at young Amanda Cavendish, except to say that it had much the same impact as her hoop had done earlier.

NOTES

My uncle's willingness to mix fact and fiction can be seen at its height in the opening chapter and presents a minefield for the dedicated historian:

- Jaunay's Hotel was located in Leicester Square and was favoured by moneyed 'bachelors', including the public outcast William Beckford, one of the wealthiest men of his age.

- The bowling of iron hoops was the most popular pastime of children in this era and iron hoops had customarily to be confiscated by the police in London streets because of the injuries caused to pedestrians.

- I have found no evidence of the life of Svetlana Krasko (formerly Maeve Cooley) nor of the double life of the Earl of Dumfries as Kitty Pineapple. Nor, regrettably, of Mrs Nonsuch, who appears to be entirely the product of my uncle's prodigious imagination.

CHAPTER II

In the Absence of a Friend ...

T HE AFTERNOON SUN shone warmly in the sky over Bath, its rays cascading off the honeyed stone of the royal city's famous crescents. Among the many homes that its softening light illuminated was Number 24, Somerset Place, situated high up on Sion Hill, the grand home of Mrs Gaia Champion, the first lady magistrate of Bath and the woman who, in 1831, had ended the Bath career of then Special Constable Decimus Dimm.

In Gaia's living room, the hostess and her three guests had removed themselves to a green baize table, leaving the remnants of afternoon tea scattered variously around the room. Through the large sash windows, the tower of Bath Abbey could be seen a mile to the south, a distant reminder of Christian morality standing in stark contrast to the immoral behaviour of the four ladies.

'Good fortune shineth! That's another trick to Miss Prim and myself,' announced Gaia who, like her late and adored husband Hercules, was skilled at dice and cards.

Two of her guests, Lady Passmore of Tewkesbury Manor and Margaret Pomeroy of Lansdown Hill, had long faces. Her ladyship looked particularly put out. In her carriage before they had arrived, she had told her constant companion, and in the clearest possible terms, not to suggest a game of whist. In her ladyship's opinion, card playing was a deplorable pastime, the more so when you lost, as she habitually did.

'You're no good at it, Mrs Pomeroy. You and I always play as a

12

team and we only ever lose. You don't follow the cards and you get the suits muddled up,' she had snapped.

'If you say so, Lady Passmore of Tewkesbury Manor,' Mrs Pomeroy had dutifully replied, 'although I have of late been taking lessons from Mrs Hill, the wife of the Quaker minister.'

'Taken lessons from a Quaker? Fie, Mrs Pomeroy, you might sooner quiz the angels about alcohol! You have all the sense of a turnip.'

As might have been expected, the past had proved a reliable guide to the future. Twenty minutes into the tea party and, overexcited after eating too much cake, Mrs Pomeroy had blurted out, 'Shall we not now play a game of whist, ladies? I love whist. I will partner Lady Passmore of Tewkesbury Manor. It is time we executed our revenge for our previous loss. And for the one before that. And the one before that. And ... '

'Mrs Pomeroy!' Lady Passmore had barked. 'Enough. We none of us require a history lesson, unless it lead us to the realms of greater virtue.'

The fourth lady, Phyllis Prim, was Bath's premier knitter and she had quickly supported the proposal. This was odd, because she had a nervous disposition and cards were madly exciting and could set her heart beating thirteen to the dozen. But Miss Prim had a second ailment, namely a stipend too small to cover her expenses. It was true that Miss Prim paid no rent to her family for her Gay Street residence, and that the wages of her Tamil cook, Mrs Mulligatawny, and her absent maid, Millicent, were similarly provided by others. But there were still expenses that required access to cold, hard cash.

Miss Prim had learnt that playing cards with Gaia against the talentless duo of Lady Passmore and Mrs Pomeroy entailed no risk whatsoever. As such, it provided a guaranteed source of income, the supply of which was always much needed in the wicked town of Bath.

'Let us,' she had said. 'I'll play with Mrs Champion, if I may. I

13

need more wool for my knitting. I'm making a nightgown for Mrs Mulligatawny and I'm down to my last few balls. Would anyone like to look? I have it here.'

Miss Prim had reached for a knitting bag that was never far away, leaving Lady Passmore conflicted. The choice was to lose at cards or suffer an intolerable hour listening to more of Miss Prim's knitting stories—the time she had slipped a stitch and had to unravel an entire smock when she'd got to the gusseted crotch; or the time she had inadvertently jerked a ball of wool out of her bag at the home of her friends, the Hoares, where it had run down three staircases, tripping up two footmen and a chambermaid and strangling a cat before anyone noticed; or the time ...

'It's most inappropriate to show off one's knitting at a tea party,' Lady Passmore had admonished, 'but, sweet heavens: you're knitting a nightgown for your cook? Who is the servant in your household, Miss Prim? Never have I heard the likes!'

'But look!' Miss Prim had cried, pointing to her knitting bag. 'Take a look at my balls.'

'I have no interest in how many balls you have,' Lady Passmore had huffed, 'but you have the advantage of me, Ma'am. If the only alternative to displays of knitting is cards, then cards let it be.'

And cards it was. Having now played and lost several hands, Lady Passmore was wondering whether pleasure could ever be derived from life again; and how it was that, as a quartet of highly refined women, they had fallen into such an ungodly habit as gambling—the ungodliness of which was proved by her always losing.

'That's tuppence to Miss Prim and me, so far,' declared Gaia.

'Tuppence!' cried Lady Passmore.

'Oh dear,' whispered Mrs Pomeroy. 'Did I throw away an ace?'

'We're stopping right now,' ordered her ladyship.

The directive, however, did not go down well with Miss Prim.

'Only tuppence. A few more hands, please. I've agreed with the Mineral Water Hospital to knit ... oh ... .'

Lady Passmore's already straight back straightened further, bringing Miss Prim to a dead halt.

'No, Miss Prim,' said her ladyship curtly. 'I'm not of a mind to subsidise further your provision of clothing to the servant class. I kindly suggest, if Mrs Champion permit it, that we return to our tea and engage in genteel conversation of a kind more appropriate to those of our class and standing.'

Their hostess nodded and the friends returned to the sofa and chairs. Gaia rang a bell and soon John Pritchard the butler arrived bearing tea and fresh cake, which Gaia distributed in fair part to her guests, Mrs Pomeroy receiving a large slice while Miss Prim, who was unnaturally thin, received something closer to a crumb.

'A Genoese!' remarked Mrs Pomeroy. 'Full of whipped cream, I see. How delicious!'

'I don't know if I could,' said Miss Prim, who had yet to recover from the cessation of whist. 'You do spoil us, Mrs Champion.'

Lady Passmore huffed and then harrumphed. The loss of tuppence had soured her mood.

'I fear we spoil ourselves and not in a good way,' she said, the little finger of her right hand extended in righteous pique as she held her teacup.

'What an interesting insight, Lady Passmore of Tewkesbury Manor,' said Gaia, trying to ease the tension. 'What lies behind your observation? Would you venture a conversational sally?'

Lady Passmore adopted the haughtiest of expressions from her armoury of haughty expressions.

'I wonder,' she began, 'why we gamble. As a child, I was taught by my governess to avoid vice. The woman would be turning in her grave if she knew what we were up to. Really, I feel this sinful indulgence must stop. After all, one of us already suffers from gluttony,' and she stared at Mrs Pomeroy, whose mouth was full of the Genoese cake.

'I beg ... ,' started Mrs Pomeroy, unable to continue for the whipped cream.

Gaia made a valiant effort to lighten the mood.

'Dear me! Genoese cake as a source of evil! What other vices might we succumb to, I wonder?'

'Knitting!' her ladyship declared, emphatically. 'Especially to launder one's ill-gotten gains!'

'Ooooah,' whimpered Miss Prim, as she endeavoured to swallow her crumb. 'I haven't sought to gain anything, I assure you. Mrs Champion, please ride to my rescue and tell me I haven't.'

Fearful that Miss Prim might throw a faint, Gaia decided the time had come to intercede.

'Please, ladies. That's enough! You have a valid point, of course, Lady Passmore of Tewkesbury Manor. Society must be alert to vice. But the problem is not Miss Prim's knitting or the game of whist.'

'Bless the Lord,' said Mrs Pomeroy, now finishing her mouthful.

'That is a relief,' squeaked Miss Prim.

'Then what is it?' demanded Lady Passmore, who required more than a few platitudes to cease her attack.

Gaia momentarily held her counsel, lest what she wanted to say add to their discord. Unwittingly, however, she had left herself no option but to speak.

'The problem, dear ladies, is this: for the past several years we have been without our beloved friend Mr Nash to entertain us. We have had a void in our lives and one that we have struggled to fill. Whist is one means; Miss Prim's knitting is another. Eating Genoese is certainly a third, judging by our relish of it.'

The statement struck a chord. It was undeniably true that ever since their close friend, the former city councillor, had been exiled to the British West Indies, their tea parties had not been the same. He was the glue that had held them together and his loss had been keenly felt.

The reason for his exile was, however, highly contested and had not been settled by the ladies in all the time that he had been absent.

'And who was to blame for our loss?' said Lady Passmore, with a rush of righteousness, for it was Gaia who, in her first case as magistrate, had ordered his banishment. 'Four years exile in Grenada you set, and what for? Improperly collecting soil samples from Royal Victoria Park! How could you have done that to good Mr Nash?'

Gaia acknowledged the deed with a heavy heart. In truth, she had made the order to save her friend and his then companion, Herr Gerhardt Kant from Königsberg, from being tried for another, more serious, crime: that of love between men, and in a public park to boot. Also, the journey to Grenada was one to which Belle was already committed. His aunt had unexpectedly inherited a plantation on the island and, coming from a family welded to liberal values, Belle had been mandated to enable the enslaved to go free.

Ordering his exile, therefore, was an expedient solution that Belle had himself supported, but all the while secrecy had been required. None of the detail was known to the other ladies. To them, it was Gaia who was to blame for the loss of a friend and no other explanation was possible.

Gaia said, 'You do me an injustice, Lady Passmore of Tewkesbury Manor. When, in due course, Mr Nash returns, he can explain the true circumstance of his exile. Until then, I accept that I, and our own friendship, will carry the burden of your doubt.'

All four ladies fell quiet. Gaia had spoken well and with poignancy. Lady Passmore lowered her teacup so that she, too, might now speak with dignity.

'It is true that on all other matters, bar dear Mr Nash, your conduct has been exemplary, Mrs Champion. As magistrate, you have attacked corrupt practices with gusto unparalleled, and we all recognise the service you have performed. As you say, when Mr Nash returns, we can put the past behind us. But on that subject, now I bethink myself, is not the term of his exile all but concluded?'

On this, they were in near agreement.

'I make it a week on Tuesday that the exile ends,' said Mrs Pomeroy hopefully.

'I thought Wednesday,' said Miss Prim. 'I am knitting him a jumper as a welcome home present, though I am not sure what size it needs to be. Maybe Mr Nash has expanded in the years he has been away. I hear that sugar ... '

'Never!' asserted Mrs Pomeroy. 'Not our Mr Nash. Not in body or in soul. He will always be the same.'

Gaia, however, with whom Belle corresponded most frequently, shook her head, for she feared that, when it came to his mind, their friend was very much changed. His early letters had contained passages of unusual distress that she had kept from the ladies. But of late, he had not written at all.

She said, 'I confess, dear ladies, that I have not received a missive these six months now. But neither have I heard that he is ill or in any way incapacitated. Let us hope he is well.'

As was her style, Lady Passmore wanted more than hope.

'Please remind us of the contents of his last letter,' she pled.

Gaia nodded.

'As you will remember, Mr Nash created a "free" plantation, ahead of slavery's abolition, and last year transferred title of the land to the workers. In his latest letter, he spoke of the other plantation owners' fury that his action might set a precedent that the Law would make them follow. To protect himself from any act of vengeance they might visit upon him, dear Mr Nash decided he had to escape from the island, though whether he also planned to return pre-emptively to England, in defiance of the Law, I cannot say. Any parting will have been made with a heavy heart, for he has, in his words, "bonded" with the local community.'

The ladies contemplated the news, before seeking an explanation for there being no more recent letter.

'How long does the sailing back to England take?' asked Mrs Pomeroy.

'About twelve weeks,' replied Gaia.

'Then that is the reason there has been no letter,' Mrs Pomeroy declared. 'He has been unable to post one these past three months, because he is on board ship.'

Mrs Pomeroy's logic, however, was flawed.

'If only that were the case,' responded Gaia. 'But letters take the same time to sail the ocean as people! If we were to receive a letter from Mr Nash saying he was leaving in a week, he would arrive in Bath one week after the letter, not three months.'

Mrs Pomeroy frowned.

'Are you sure about that?'

'Entirely sure.'

The ladies once again fell silent as they digested the science of time.

It was Miss Prim who spoke next.

'What then, Mrs Champion, would explain the lack of correspondence?'

It was a question for which there was no easy answer.

'Maybe a boat carrying a letter has sunk,' Gaia said in a low voice. 'I'm sure it can be nothing worse.'

The words were said without conviction, and they exposed her true thoughts: that her dearest friend Belle, who as a Bath city councillor had enabled her to secure the position of magistrate, might never return. That the boat on which he travelled had been lost to the oceans. That he had succumbed to a tropical disease. Or that a foul, yet unexplained, human deed had befallen him.

She was not alone in her fears.

'What should we do if he is lost? What if ... ' stuttered Mrs Pomeroy.

A tea party is an occasion designed for pleasure. But not on this day. Unexpectedly, Gaia found herself wiping away a tear.

'Life has a cruel habit of requiring that we carry on, regardless of loss,' she replied, thinking of the death from cholera of her husband, Hercules, five years earlier. 'The start of the Season is only a week away and the highest in society will be descending on Bath. Families will fill the great houses of the city. Music will emanate from the Assembly Rooms. Whilst we might mourn if we choose, the rest of the city will be gay.'

There was no appetite among the ladies for gaiety.

'Whilst respecting the rights of my fellow aristocrats,' said Lady Passmore, 'I, for one, will not attend an Assembly Room function this Season unless Mr Nash returns. In his absence, I shall spend the winter alone at Tewkesbury Manor, wearing black crêpe.'

The room fell silent, except for a whimper from Miss Prim. There was no need for a spoken consensus. Without Belle as their companion, the impending Season in Bath would be devoid of meaning. It was painful enough that his possible demise had now been voiced out loud.

The tea party had become a wake. Mrs Pomeroy wiped a last morsel of cake from her mouth. Miss Prim reached for the comfort of her knitting. Lady Passmore glowered. As for Gaia, her heart beat as a drum of sorrow.

'Hear me, Belle,' she silently cried. 'Hear my ache. Hear my sadness. Come back to me.'

NOTES
* Whilst the despicable trade in fellow humans in the British Empire was ended in 1807—and slavery in England had been ruled illegal in 1772—slavery in the dominions was not abolished until 1833. Even then, freed slaves in the British West Indies were required to remain on their plantations as indentured apprentices to 'earn their freedom', a practice not ended until 1838 (and not until the twentieth century for the slaves of some other nations). For this reason, the latter date is regarded in the West Indies as the year British slavery ended.
* In the eighteenth and early nineteenth centuries, Bath became the favourite playground for Britain's aristocracy. The period

of their attendance, known as 'the Season', ran from early December until mid-June, and contributed to a doubling of the city's population to 60,000. Its success was due in large part to Belle Nash's grandfather, Beau Nash, who was the city's greatest Master of Ceremonies.

CHAPTER III

The Despicable Coin

I T WAS FORTUNATE that Police Officer Decimus Dimm, of the Bow Street Runners, was not a man of letters or he may have questioned how it was that Monsieur Blaise Pascal, the famous French philosopher, had come to be staying at Jaunay's Hotel a full 173 years after his death.

As for the staff at Jaunay's, respect for their guests' privacy was paramount and it was not for them to question the veracity of Monsieur Pascal's identity.

After all, everything pointed to his being French: he wore a provincial Basque beret, waxed his moustache, stank of rose-petal perfume and spoke English with a comical accent notable for its insistence on adding an 'h' to the front of words that did not have them, and removing the same letter from the front of those that did.

'Good afternoon now, Monsieur Pascal,' said Beauty the doorman, who had yet to move from the front steps. 'Although it's a miserable day, even by London standards, to be sure.'

Whilst keen to get inside, Monsieur Pascal nevertheless halted his advance. He peered up at the doorman, whose mascara—thanks to the thick, wet rain—had run down his cheeks.

'*Mais oui, c'est* hawful,' the philosopher replied. '*Vraiment terreebl*.'

Beauty was in a chatty mood.

'Are you returning from a late lunch?'

'*Oui*. Halthough *le* food *anglais*, *eet ees* ... well, even worse *zan ze wezzer*.'

The doorman held the entrance door open, then remembered Mrs Nonsuch's strict instructions from earlier in the day.

'Monsieur Pascal, I nearly forgot: Mrs Nonsuch asked to see you. Something urgent. You're to go straight to her office, so you are.'

Monsieur Pascal hesitated, the blood draining from his face. The word 'urgent' worried him.

'But why? I mean *pourquoi?*'

'Maybe something to do with a visit from one of our Bow Street friends this morning,' the doorman replied. 'She wasn't in the best of moods when he left. I got it in the neck for allowing him inside. Unpleasant fellow he was, right enough.'

It was therefore with trepidation that the celebrated seventeenth-century philosopher entered the hotel and walked through the lobby to the manager's office. To make matters worse, the receptionist gave him a nod of recognition, but no smile—a *froideur* that reminded him of the walk to the headmaster's study when a schoolboy, guilt-ridden and pensive with the certainty that a caning was in store. It is a feeling that can stay with a man until long into old age, an emotional dread, often accompanied by an emptying of the bladder when triggered by moments such as these.

He knocked tentatively at the open door.

'*Bonjour*, Madame Nonsuch. May I come in?'

Mrs Nonsuch looked up from her desk. She had been impatient for this meeting.

'Please, Monsieur Pascal, close the door and take a seat.'

He moved into the office and gingerly sat down, eyeing the battered hoop and the baton that went with it. That baton would make a formidable tool to beat a boy with, he thought—even worse than the split billiard cue that his own headmaster had used to instil discipline.

'Monsieur, we had a visit from the Bow Street police today,' said Mrs Nonsuch sharply. 'Your name came up.'

'*Oh là là. Sacré bleu.*'

'*Sacré bleu*, indeed,' agreed Mrs Nonsuch.

Monsieur Pascal's look of worry deepened.

'But why *mon nom?*' he double-checked. 'That is *incroyable*. And not just because *eet eez*, has you say, a *palindrome:* "Mon Nom"—*oui?*'

Mrs Nonsuch leant back in her chair. It was, she decided, time for Monsieur Pascal to come clean about his posthumous life.

'For the moment, Sir, you are only one of many foreign names on our register of guests and today's visitor was not the brightest. But should he return and ask me how it is that a dead French philosopher is staying at Jaunay's, I confess, Sir, to being unsure how I should reply. *Comprenez?*'

Monsieur Pascal blinked.

'Dead, you say? *Moi?*'

'*Mort*, I say. *Vous.*'

Monsieur Pascal considered for a moment whether to take off into the warren of alleys that surrounded Leicester Square but ended up, like any good Frenchman, shrugging his shoulders in a theatrically Gallic manner.

'*Je suis désolée*, Madame Nonsuch. Maybe I ham alive, *peut-être* I ham dead. But please remember, "Contradiction is not a sign of falsity, nor want of a contradiction a sign of truth," if I may quote a line from my own *Pensées*.'

'The *Pensées* of 1670?' asked Mrs Nonsuch, who was better informed than many hotel managers are today. 'Remembering a saying, Sir, does not transform you into Blaise Pascal.'

The man in the chair was downcast.

'It doesn't?' he asked, squirming.

Mrs Nonsuch leant over her desk and for a moment the *soi-disant* Blaise Pascal feared he might be slippered or worse. Instead, the hotel manager addressed him in an unexpectedly soft voice.

24

'Monsieur, I have known from the moment you arrived twelve weeks ago who you are, but it was not my job to say. Now, however, it is time to discard your disguise and reveal yourself as Mr Bellerophon "Belle" Nash, citizen of Bath, formerly city councillor and lately, so I understand, returned from the West Indies.'

There was silence in the room. The guest turned as white and startled as a shorn sheep on a Welsh mountain in mid-winter. He looked around the office for support but there was none. There was only Mrs Nonsuch on the other side of her daunting desk. Slowly, he lifted a hand and removed the beret from his head.

'You have seen through me, Madam,' said Belle Nash for, indeed, it was he. 'Rather than fooling you, I have been fooling myself all this time. But what gave me away? I thought my beret and moustache were foolproof.'

With the truth established, and Belle Nash now exposed, Mrs Nonsuch relaxed. She became less of a monster, more like a caring matron.

'Dear Mr Nash, it's a common mistake of men to believe that women do not read or take an interest in intellectual pursuits. As an admirer of Mary Wollstonecraft, I am a keen student of both English and French philosophy. Imagine, then, my surprise at seeing Blaise Pascal registered as a guest.'

Belle nodded.

'Your philosophical expertise was my weakness.'

'The beret was, *ow you say, amusant*—but not sufficient to cover your appalling French accent.'

Belle was hurt and surprised by the criticism. He had, after all, lived for three months believing his disguise to be impenetrable.

'My accent?' he said meekly. '*C'est mal?*'

'*C'est diabolique, monsieur.* I have heard French delivered better on the stage at Drury Lane. You speak the language of Voltaire and Rousseau like a German comic—and there are precious few of those.'

This brought a smile of sadness to Belle's lips. The Germanic

25

twang was undoubtedly the result of a tumultuous year spent sharing his life in Bath with his Prussian companion, Gerhardt Kant, who himself had had to live disguised as Belle's Prussian second cousin twice removed, to shake off suspicion about their relationship. It was irresponsible Gerhardt who had landed him in Gaia Champion's court. And now, four years after their friendship had ended, Gerhardt had proved his undoing once more.

'I surrender to your tender mercies, Mrs Nonsuch,' said Belle with an ironic grin. 'Do what must be done. Hand me over to Bow Street, if you must. I do not wish to bring disgrace to Jaunay's reputation.'

He put his arms on the table, wrists together as if waiting to be handcuffed. But with a sweep of her own right arm, Mrs Nonsuch pushed them away. Then she laughed, a raucous laugh of deep-throated splendour.

'Hand you in?! I think not, Mr Nash. Jaunay's is here to serve its guests, not to hand them to the police. No, no. What we do is open a bottle of fine rum and discuss your predicament together. I want to hear everything that you've been up to. You can start by telling me about your time in the West Indies, which is my birth-place. Are people still misbehaving themselves on the islands?'

SEVERAL GLASSES OF fine West Indian rum had been downed by the time Belle Nash finished explaining his 'exile'. The afternoon sun had set, the Chinoiserie on the office walls had begun to shimmer in the lamplight and Belle's cheeks had taken on a rosy hue.

'By all the gods, Mrs Nonsuch, this rum is the nectar of Dionysus. I feel like Aristides, back from ostracism—except that I am not legally back.'

'The rum is a cut above Pusser's to be sure,' said Mrs Nonsuch, who was also showing signs of being tipsy. The alcohol, in the way that vinegar removes grime from an oil painting, had brought out the colour of her Caribbean voice.

'It has been an ordeal disguising myself from you, Ma'am,' said Belle, who had always enjoyed his stays at Jaunay's. 'At times I have thought myself a worse schemer than Dolos, god of trickery.'

'I too,' Mrs Nonsuch laughed. 'Was I not his female counterpart Apate, spirit of deception? We are of a kind. But now that you are yourself again, pray, Mr Nash, tell me more about your time on the islands. I was six when my parents brought me to England. My memories of Barbados, where I was born, are few.'

Belle was grateful for her words but felt distant from the man he had been hitherto. Four years on a plantation had scarred him.

'I wish my time on Grenada was spent barefoot, running through the blue surf,' he replied. 'But the sand and soil of that sorry island are red with blood. Your parents were wise to bring you to England before you could understand the vile misery that slavery inflicts. I had feared the worst, but what I saw was beyond my worst imaginings.'

He bowed his head, his body shaking involuntarily as he looked to the floor.

'My mother's family still lives there,' said Mrs Nonsuch. 'Cousins, uncles, aunts. I want to know what you found. How badly have they suffered?'

Belle reached out for the glass of rum with a trembling hand. His eyes brimmed with tears.

'My aunt inherited a plantation that she declared must be "freed", a decision with which I wholeheartedly agreed. I did what I could, Madam. At the earliest opportunity, I gave the ... the ... '

He paused.

'You hesitate, Mr Nash.'

He whispered, 'I do not wish to demean my fellow men and women with the term.'

'Say it, Mr Nash! The term exists. We cannot wish it away from history.'

With a sense of shame, he relented.

'I gave ... the *slaves*, Mrs Nonsuch ... their freedom—for in

27

this evil world I found that it was mine to give. And, in so doing, I attracted the hatred of the other ... the other ... '

Once more he found the challenge too great, but again she commanded.

'The other *what*, Mr Nash? Do not hide that word either. It is the reverse of the same despicable coin.'

' ... I attracted the hatred of the other ... *owners*. What I witnessed there was—oh my, Mrs Nonsuch! That we should create a world of owners and slaves, divide ourselves by our colour, maintain that division through shackles, torture, rape and murder, through floggings and behandings. And for what? For sugar, that is all. And for rum.'

He pointed at the half-empty bottle before them. Mrs Nonsuch twisted the glass she had been nursing between her fingers before speaking.

'I drink this rum not for the pleasure but to remind me of the blood and sweat of my mother's family, who were stolen from their African homes to harvest cane for the white overlords in the Caribbean.' Then she laughed dryly and said: 'Not that drinking rum is without pleasure, of course.'

Belle shared a reluctant half-smile and sat back.

'That's true. It is an irony that the sweetness of sugar and the delight of fine spirit should be the product of so much evil.'

They each drank a further tot in unison, a synchronicity of souls. Mrs Nonsuch looked at him square across her desk. Whilst Belle had spoken of the horrors he had witnessed, she guessed that there was more to his angst.

'You have told me but half the story, Mr Nash. I can see it in your eyes. What else happened to you on the island?—for there was surely something.'

He nodded and drank heavily from his glass, which Mrs Nonsuch refilled.

'In truth, Madam, it is less than half the story. A mere third by my calculation, for in Grenada, like the fool I am, I fell in love with a young man named Pablo Fanque, to whom I had granted freedom. He worked in the plantation office and was as bright as a button. When it came to numbers, he added and subtracted like quicksilver but beyond this was a heart of kindness that defied the gross inequities he had suffered in life.'

Mrs Nonsuch sipped at her own rum. She was accustomed to hearing stories of heartbreak from the bachelor guests at Jaunay's —being a sympathetic ear had become part of her role as manager—but Belle's tale was one of unusual complexity.

'I take it that your love was not one of mere infatuation.'

Belle shook his head vigorously.

'It was not. He forgave me my sin. Provided me redemption from my guilt. And for that more than anything else, I loved him.'

She leant forward across her desk.

'And did he love you in return?'

It was a question, of course, that cut to the point, one that would tear at the fabric of any mind, and Belle paused before answering.

'I do not doubt that he had affection for me. But love? I cannot answer on Pablo's behalf. Even after the gift of freedom, how could he love me? I could not disown my unwanted past as his ... owner; nor would he disown his as that of a ... a slave. I have struggled to determine how things stood between us and concluded that one cannot love in such circumstance.'

To his surprise, Mrs Nonsuch disagreed.

'Not so. My father loved my mother; and she him.'

The matter of her parents was not one that Belle had considered.

'In truth?'

She nodded.

'In truth. Both are deceased, but in life, Sir, they loved each other with a rare intensity.'

Her statement allowed Belle to reconsider his own experience.

'Then the most I can say is that I wish to believe that Pablo loved me,' he declared. 'What is certain is that he also had an unbreakable bond of loyalty to his half-sister, a girl named Mercy. He was much distressed. The poor maid worked in the household of the manager of the largest estate in Grenada. The plantation was notorious for the very worst of practices.'

The face of Mrs Nonsuch hardened.

'Who owned the plantation?'

Belle's face, already grey, took on a deathly pallor.

'Lord Servitude, an absent aristocrat who has never left these shores: a peer who owns plantations across the islands and who has opposed abolition, and encouraged others to oppose it, with all his might. For two years, his estates in Jamaica have been managed by his son, the inappropriately named 'Honourable' Cecil, for never has there been such a dishonourable wretch. It was to his household in Kingston that Mercy, without her consent, was sent. I could not stay in Grenada for fear of death—and my dear Pablo would not join me in England until he had secured Mercy's return.'

'You feared death?'

'Daily,' confirmed Belle. 'Transferring title of the land to the workers spurred men such as Cecil to threaten my life, and so I ran. And no doubt they reported as much to the authorities here in London—hence my need for a disguise. Never have I felt so bereft. I spent the three months at sea mourning Pablo's loss. I saw his face in the spray of the ocean. I sensed his arms reaching out to me in the squall of the winds. I yearned for him to be with me again, to touch me, but he was nowhere. It was as if he had died.'

Belle wept openly as he spoke. Mrs Nonsuch understood the reason for her guest's distress but still she pressed, adjudging that there was more to come.

'That is not the whole story, Mr Nash. Like the young man who you loved, I, too, am good at numbers. You are two-thirds of the way through your tale. As we finish this bottle of rum, so you must conclude.'

Belle emptied his glass and offered it for a final refill; Mrs Nonsuch emptied her own before obliging.

'Mrs Nonsuch, you are a keen observer, Ma'am, and I am a hesitant storyteller. Very well, then. I returned to England before my sentence of exile had expired, and therefore with a bounty on my head. And then the most extraordinary event occurred, as if concocted by blindfold Tyche, capricious dispenser of good and ill fortune. Having docked in London and taken a room at Jaunay's in the name of Blaise Pascal, I reacquainted myself with our great capital, and in particular frequented its theatres and circuses. Among these I visited Astley's Royal Amphitheatre in Lambeth to watch the jugglers and tightrope dancers. Imagine my surprise, then, when the proprietor, Mr Ducrow, announced a display of equestrian skills and into the arena, standing astride four horses, there rode none other than ... '

Belle stopped.

'Who?' asked Mrs Nonsuch, who liked every detail of a story to be spelt out. 'Don't hold back, Mr Nash. And don't tease. I do not wish to outpace you in your telling of your story. Say it all, plain and clear.'

She was in for a treat.

His eyes widened with amazement as dark rum pulsed through his veins.

'Atop the horses, majestic as a prince, was none other than the man I had left behind. Pablo Fanque, Mrs Nonsuch. It was Pablo Fanque!'

NOTES
* Blaise Pascal (1623–1662) was a French mathematician and philosopher. As a teenager, he designed and built mechanical calculating machines before focussing his mind on projective geometry and probability theory. His works, including *Lettres Provincials* and *Pensées*, combine philosophical insight with wit. He never married and lived with his sister.

- Mary Wollstonecraft (1759–1797) was an English philosopher and advocate of women's rights. She wrote the first great feminist treatise, *A Vindication of the Rights of Woman*. She died from infections following childbirth, having survived two attempted suicides. She was the mother of Mary Shelley.
- Astley's Royal Amphitheatre opened on Westminster Bridge Road in 1773 and survived under various names for 120 years. A typical programme included jugglers, gymnasts, contortionists, tightrope walkers, a 'military' band and skilled equestrians.
- Pusser's Rum was the 'overproof' rum made for the Royal Navy, in accordance with Admiralty Regulations. Its alcohol content by volume was a whopping 75%, compared with the standard 40%.

CHAPTER IV

The Great, the Good and the Vile

P LEASE FORGIVE YOUR humble scribe for a brief interruption. Has Pablo Fanque of Grenada truly and miraculously appeared in London dancing on a horse? And is Belle Nash now safe from the grasp of Detective Dimm?

Even to speak of these events, and those to come, we must first immerse ourselves in history, and specifically that of the city where—with Liberty's fair wind—our hero will shortly arrive to meet four ladies. So, return to your desks, dear pupils, and open *Historia Anglorum*, by Henry of Huntingdon, and let us learn about the Royal City of Bath.

Bath's history can be traced back to Prince Bladud of Wessex in 860 BC. As a young and handsome man, he had been sent to study in Athens and had returned with a benefit and a curse. The benefit was that he had acquired an understanding of Socrates. The curse was that he had succumbed to an alien disease to which his Welsh origins had given him no immunity.

Bladud's good looks had been ruined by a dermatological infection, possibly *rosacea*, with its pus-filled lumps. But his discomfort was not terminal. On his return to his father's kingdom, the prince passed some hot springs and, seeking relief from his ailment, he took a dip. He emerged with his skin blemish-free and word quickly spread of the water's healing qualities.

To paraphrase *Historia Anglorum*, '*Satis principi Bladud, satis omnibus*'—what was good enough for Prince Bladud was good enough for all!—and demand for the healing waters grew. The scabrous were joined by the kingdom's hypochondriacs and the hypochondriacs were followed by druidical witchdoctors and the druidical witchdoctors were followed by conmen and the conmen were followed by a legion of alcoholics, gamblers and nymphomaniacs—and so Bath as a spa city was established.

Good health and lechery might seem unnatural bedfellows but not when mixed with prodigious quantities of gin and claret, and the application of mercury to the genitals, a fact understood by Beau Nash—the grandfather of Belle—who was appointed Master of Ceremonies of Bath in 1704. Attracted by Nash Senior's glamorous marketing, the law-abiding and the syphilitic of Albion alike flocked to Bath. They came in ever greater numbers for the Season, and brought their equally syphilitic families, with whom they filled the magnificent terraces and crescents that Beau and his colleagues built on Bath's many hills.

AND SO, WE return to our story in the year 1835 by way of a bachelor living in Bath named Lucius Lush. Young Lucius, known to many of his friends as 'Luscious', was a fine-featured, fey fellow whose mind was filled by the opportunities that the Season presents. Master Lush was clerk to Belle Nash when the latter was a city councillor, and during the four years of Belle's absence had provided his services to Magistrate Gaia Champion as her clerk-in-court.

There should be no doubt that Master Lush was a loyal and efficient worker, but for half of the year he was bored, for it was only during the Season that the city came to life. And so it was that, faced with another dormant day at court, Master Lush had what can only be called an entrepreneurial epiphany. He was struck by a commercial idea of such magnitude that he would have shouted 'Yippee!'—more probably in Latin ('*Euge!*'), though not impossibly in Ancient Greek—had he not simultaneously felt so weak that he could not stand.

'Master Lush, what ails thee? You look most peculiar,' Gaia had noted when she espied her clerk on the floor by his desk.

'I have had an idea,' he had replied.

'Oh reckless youth,' Gaia had teased. 'Leave ideas for your elders. Little good ever comes of novelty in a neo-Classical culture such as ours.'

'I intend to publish a book listing all the families taking up residence in Bath for the Season, with their addresses.'

Gaia had looked quizzical. 'You have aspirations to become a postmaster?'

'I will be serving the needs of society,' Master Lush had said proudly. 'It will be a social almanac. Who's in; who's out. I will make my fortune from it.'

'You are a whimsical fellow and you will conjure many other amusing ideas while working in my office. But for now, I cannot do without you as my clerk. So, please, raise yourself from the floor and take hold of your quill.'

Gaia's opinion on Master Lush's idea had changed, however, after bringing it to the attention of her friends at one of her ladies' tea parties.

'A social almanac?' Lady Passmore had hooted; 'it's a preposterous idea.'

'I venture that people will like it,' Phyllis Prim had responded, standing her ground for once. 'Everyone in society wants to know who everyone is. And young Master Lush is a handsome young man. It's very hard to disagree with handsome young men. I have spent most of my life trying to find one to disagree with. Impossible! I think I shall knit him a counterpane.'

For her part, Mrs Pomeroy had sided with Miss Prim.

'Undoubtedly, it will be successful.'

Gaia, intrigued, had pressed Mrs Pomeroy to say more.

'Because people will love reading about themselves. Anyone with an entry in the book is bound to purchase a copy—even those who decry its vulgarity.'

Gaia had nodded. What Mrs Pomeroy had said made perfect sense.

'I agree,' Gaia had replied, ignoring Lady Passmore's stern expression, 'although I am not convinced that Master Lush has yet found the right title for it. Or the best companion to help him in his efforts. He is relying, for assistance, on the eccentric Mr Quigley. And the title that he has chosen for the book is ... '

F AMILIES RESIDENT IN *the Royal City of Bath for the Season, Their Children and Other Interests*,' said Master Lush with a flourish.

'It's much too long. I can't remember it all,' replied Arthur Quigley, the octogenarian music master of the Abbey School for Boys whom Master Lush had roped in to help with the great enterprise.

It was true that the older man's memory was not what it had been in its youth, although he could still remember most of the notes of Bach's six violin sonatas and partitas, humming to himself encouragingly when he got to a note that eluded him. It was also true that his memory could be rapidly improved by a visit to Sally Lunn's for a warm Bath bun with soft butter and strawberry jam. His hopes had been raised, therefore, by the news that Master Lush had invited him to North Parade Passage, the home of the tearooms since 1680, which was even further back than Mr Quigley could remember.

At eleven o'clock, as planned, Master Lush arrived to find the music master already waiting.

'Dear boy, how thrilling to see you. My, in what finery do you appear before me. Adonis himself could not look better.'

'Thank you,' said Master Lush, who had removed his clerk's wig but otherwise remained in his court clothes. 'I've come from work. Magistrate Champion has granted me the day off.'

'I marvel that there were no cases for the great lady to hear. Perhaps she is making this wicked city a better place after all.'

Master Lush blushed. He had an admission to make.

'Don't tell Mrs Champion but I asked a favour of Special Constable Evans yesterday evening. I've been struggling to visit all the necessary houses to complete the almanac. With Mr Evans's help, for the first time in living memory, there are no cases for the court!'

Mr Quigley was delighted.

'Excellent, boy! No doubt you learnt well from your time with Councillor Nash, bless his memory. He and I used to meet regularly at the tearooms here. I presume you're familiar with them. As we have time on our hands, maybe we could ... '

Master Lush, however, was not to be distracted.

'I learnt much as Mr Nash's clerk, in particular how to put work before pleasure. The book must come first.'

Mr Quigley's face, already characterised by an abundance of hanging skin, fell.

'Oh, but I thought ... What's the name of this book again?'

'*Families Resident in the Royal City of Bath for the Season, Their Children and Other Interests*.'

'No, it's too long,' Mr Quigley said again. 'No one will remember it—unless they have a cup of tea inside them, and a soft warm bun with butter and jam. Then, maybe ... '

Master Lush was having none of it. Every penny of his savings had been put aside for publication and none for tea.

'No, Mr Quigley. First, we must earn our keep. I can see that you have come dressed for the part in your elegant Savile Row suit and your top hat of beaver felt. And you have the military medal from your time in India, no less.'

Master Lush's calculated flattery worked. Mr Quigley's eyes glistened with pride. He inspected his reflection in the glass of a shop window and saw himself exactly as the clerk had described. He saw the tattered silk dressing gown that he habitually wore over his torn riding breeches as indeed a suit from Savile Row, and the tea cosy that he always wore on his head was indeed a magnificent top hat. As for the pewter spoon that was pinned to his gown and may or may not have seen service in India, he was sure that no finer medal of gallantry had ever been displayed.

'Dear boy, I am attired to impress aristocracy. Lead the way.'

'You look wonderful, Mr Quigley, and ready for action,' Master Lush announced, before outlining the plan for the day. 'There are three streets remaining where we must make enquiries: Brock Street, The Circus and Gay Street. I'm allocating you Gay Street and I am taking Brock Street and The Circus for myself. You haven't forgotten the questions that need to be asked at each house, have you?'

The music master looked blank.

'Now wait a moment, young sirrah. Did we want to know whether the mistress of the house takes her tea with lemon?'

'Not on this occasion, Mr Quigley. What I need you to note is the surname of the family that is resident in each house; also, the Christian names and titles of its members, especially those who are eligible for marriage. Please enquire also as to the location of the family's principal seat or estate; and ascertain as much as you can about their background. For instance, do they derive their wealth from land or commerce?'

Mr Quigley did his best to look confident.

'Yes, of course, young Lush. Eminently straightforward.'

Master Lush smiled and allowed himself to feel reassured. The almanac would be a famous success.

'We are ready to start,' he said, gently taking hold of the old man's hand and leading them away from North Parade Passage, past the Pump Rooms and towards Milsom Street. Progressing up the hill, after a gentle five-minute stroll and a repetition by Master Lush of the day's necessary instructions, they arrived at Gay Street.

There, they separated to start their work.

With a spring in his step, Master Lush followed Royal Avenue to the far end of Brock Street, from where he could work his way back to The Circus. Full of energy, he rang the doorbell of the first house and waited. The door was opened by a maid.

'Hello and isn't it a fine day?' he said to the girl, whilst fluttering his eyelashes and allowing the sunlight to cast off his high cheekbones.

The maid stepped outside and looked at Master Lush.

'You're right. You're, I mean it's ... a beauty.'

Master Lush followed what was a well-rehearsed routine.

'I expect you've been stuck indoors getting the house ready for the Season. There's a family from out of town arriving in the next week, I wouldn't wonder.'

'There most certainly is,' the girl acknowledged. 'A rich family from Herefordshire.'

Master Lush offered his most engaging and innocent smile.

'And who might they be?'

Meanwhile, matters were not proceeding quite so smoothly in Gay Street. Mr Quigley had left a trail of confusion in his wake when a footman mistook his questions as intimate advances and an elderly widow assumed he was lost and wanted directions.

His current victim was a frightened maid who told him, 'We don't commune with tradesmen here. Or people what don't dress or wash proper.'

'I'll have you know, little miss,' Mr Quigley rejoined, 'that this is a Savile Row suit. As for my personal toilette, I can assure you that I take a bath once a month, whether I need one or not.'

The door was closed firmly in his face.

'Well, I never. The maids of today have no manners at all,' he reflected, before moving along the terrace to Number 40.

Number 40. He studied the number closely. There was something familiar about it. Was it the number of piano sonatas that that parvenu Beethoven had written? No, that was thirty-two. Or string quartets, maybe? No, that was sixteen.

He rang the bell whilst deep in thought. Why did forty seem so familiar? Inside the house he heard footsteps approaching and the turning of a latch. His mind was now working its way through Johann Sebastian Bach's children and wondering how many were also named Johann. Were there forty of them, perchance? No, there were eleven sons and five were called Johann. Mind you, both of Bach's brothers were named Johann, as was Bach's father and his father's twin brother. He had just counted nine Johanns when his train of thought, such as it was, was broken.

'Hello, Mr Quigley, what can I do for you?' came a familiar voice.

There was a lady standing at the door peering at him with a puzzled expression that left Mr Quigley agog.

'Saints and sinners, you look exactly like Mrs Mulligatawny, Miss Prim's cook! I'll pass by her house later and tell her there's an imposter in the city. She lives near here.'

The woman let out a sigh of despair, firstly because she *was* Mrs Mulligatawny and did not like being called an imposter, and secondly, because she was *not* Mrs Mulligatawny, never had been and never wished to be, but because the inbred people of Bath—with the notable exception of Gaia Champion—were unable to pronounce her real name, Miss Aagalyadevi Balasubramaniam, she had ended up being known by the moniker of a soup. A proud Tamil lady (and an excellent cook), she had learnt to return each insult with a jibe, but the English were so stupid that few, if any, ever picked up on it.

'Potatoes, Mr Quigley,' she replied in kind.

'Potatoes?' the music master said, feeling at even more of a loss. Then remembering that he was on Master Lush's errand, he asked, '*Potato*. Is that the surname of the family that resides here? Or the source of their wealth?'

Mrs Mulligatawny was flummoxed.

'Swedes, if you'd rather, Mr Quigley,' she responded curtly, choosing a new vegetable as her riposte.

'They're Swedes?! Why did you not say so before, dear Madam? And why are you disguised as Mrs Mulligatawny?

'I am not disguised as Mrs Mulligatawny, Mr Quigley. I *am* Mrs Mulligatawny. You are standing outside Miss Prim's house. Number 40 Gay Street. You have been here for tea many times. Your friend Mr Nash used to live next door before he went to the Caribbean.'

So that was why he recognised the number forty! Nothing to do with Bachs named Johann or sonatas by Beethoven. And what had the imposter said? Something about tea.

'Did you mention tea, Madam?'

'I did.'

'And buttered buns?'

'Served the way you like them.'

Mr Quigley clapped his hands in delight and made his way into the house.

'So good of you. One builds up a hunger knocking on doors. And a thirst. I will tell Mrs Mulligatawny all about your kindness to me.'

MEANWHILE, MASTER LUSH had completed his visit to Brock Street and had entered The Circus, than which there are few finer sights in Bath. The Circus is a circle of the most elegant Georgian houses made up of three identical crescents, beautiful not just in their proportions and the colour of their stone but in their details. Their curved façades represent an idealised image of Roman town planning and are ornamented with three tiers of paired columns, capped at each level by Doric, then Ionic and lastly Corinthian capitals. Decorative friezes made up of mythical and nautical symbols adorn the houses, and roof-top parapets sport giant stone acorns. Every time Master Lush entered The Circus he would stare at its magnificence in wonder. Thus, he decided, lived Julius Caesar and Mark Antony. Thus lived Virgil and Quintilian.

Each crescent had the appearance of a single palace, in spite of the regular punctuation of front doors. This grand architectural fiction greatly preened the egos of The Circus's grand residents, who at one time included Prime Minister William Pitt and the artist Thomas Gainsborough. That wealthiest of men, Clive of India, lived at Number 17—before cutting his own throat, his vast fortune unable to save him from the curse of mental despair.

Master Lush worked his way methodically around the houses, starting at Number 1, his bonny-faced demeanour serving him well, and prompting each set of servants to reveal excited details of the grand families and personages due to arrive during the next month.

'Viscount Melbourne and his family ... '

'The handsome American actor Ira Aldridge ... '

'Lord and Lady ... '

It was with a sense of impending finality and fulfilment that Master Lush reached Number 33, the last of the houses, but was put off by the sight of building works taking place on the upper-most floor. Wondering whether the improvements might be concluded before the family arrived, fair Lucius decided that the house must be empty, and started to turn away, when the front door was opened slightly by a thin lady beyond her middle years, with hair pulled back from a high brow and a face so sharp, it could have been used for chopping wood.

'What brings you a-spying on the grand folk?' demanded the harridan. 'I seen you from my window, knocking on all the doors. You's not to be trusted is my guess. You're got up smart but my hunch is, you're no more than a common beggar.'

If the woman had not already struck a fear diabolical into the heart of our eager young publisher, the emblem on the frieze above her head, of a coiled snake waiting to strike, convinced him that behind this particular front door, terrible Hades lay concealed.

Not wishing to be outdone, however, and determined that his almanac should be complete, Master Lush stood his ground.

'Madam, I am nothing more than an honest publisher of an

42

almanac documenting who is resident in Bath for the Season, and I collect names, not handouts. Perhaps, Ma'am, with the building works being done upstairs, Number 33 will be unoccupied this year. If so, I pray you forgive my intrusion, for I had not wished to cause alarm.'

'You're a presumptuous young article,' sneered the termagant. 'What, Number 33 without a family? Stuff and nonsense. You think I keep house for nothing? This building will soon welcome the finest of men. What you see are the preparations for his lordship's arrival.'

Master Lush peered beyond the woman and into the entrance hall of the house, where a stygian light revealed workmen putting up new and garish wallpaper.

'Gold,' he noted. 'To match the opulence of your master.'

'Purple and gold,' commented the housekeeper. 'That's how his lordship likes it.'

'Of course,' said Master Lush, jotting down his discovery in his notebook. 'Purple: the colour of Holy Orders; and gold for the birth of our Lord Jesus. Forgive me for asking, but what is his lordship's name? He is an archbishop, I presume.'

The woman snarled at Master Lush.

'An archbishop! His lordship is of a higher order altogether. There's no harm telling you his name, I suppose. You'll learn of it soon regardless. It's the great Lord Servitude who'll be living here. And my name's Mrs Neech, if you want to take a note. That's Neech as in Leech but with an N.'

The blood drained from Master Lush's face, caused not by the housekeeper's name but that of her master. Like every subject of the King William, he knew Lord Servitude only too well by reputation.

'Lord Servitude, you say,' he responded, wondering how he could compose an entry in his almanac for such a man. 'Goodness. And is he accompanied by family?'

The woman's mouth curled up at the sides.

43

'His son, the Hon. Cecil, is to arrive shortly in Bristol from Jamaica, to be with his lordship for the Season.'

'Yes, of course. A son, you say. The Hon. Cecil. And does he have a wife and children of his own?'

'All in good time,' snarled the gorgon. 'The Hon. Cecil is the most eligible man in the kingdom, and when he desires a wife of high-enough status, he shall have her—like that!' and she clicked her choppy fingers.

'Marvellous, marvellous,' beamed the young entrepreneur, warming once again to his task. 'And, finally, if I may be so bold to ask, Madam: does his lordship have any business interests? I ask only to provide a little background for my readers.'

Mrs Neech's hands curled around the edge of the door, the muscles and tendons in her arms tightening. Her dark eyes glistened with venom.

'Slavery, of course. It has been, and always will be, the business of the Servitudes. It brings in a fine income.'

'Despite the abolition?' stammered Master Lush, reduced anew to profound discomfort, for he abhorred slavery and had delighted in its passing.

'Despite and because of,' shouted the fishwife, unashamed. 'Slavery, what brought order to society. Slavery, what made this country great. Slavery, what separated the races into their natural hierarchy. Slavery, what rewarded the brave and disarmed the unworthy. Let slavery prevail!'

Master Lush stepped back into the street. He wished to protest but felt suddenly weak and disempowered. How did one fight back against the certainty of malice? Evil seemed to know so well its own mind, and its best lines. The young clerk wondered what his mentor, Belle Nash, would have said and wished that he might return soon from Grenada. Then, cursing his own cowardice, he turned and, in quickstep, fled.

NOTES

- There were thirty-two piano sonatas and thirteen string quartets written by Ludwig van Beethoven. As for the Bach family, there were two dozen members of the Eisenach branch named Johann, largely because first names in Germany were as loose and imprecise as surnames. To identify someone, one more often used nicknames or second and third names. Thus Carl Philip Emanuel Bach would have been known as Emanuel rather than Carl. The most famous Johann Bach, Johann Sebastian Bach, had twenty children and not only named five of his sons Johann but two of his daughters Johanna. Uncles, cousins and second cousins were similarly named. There were three other branches of the Bach family with a further thirty-two Johanns across the same generations. It was almost as if the first name served as an introductory surname.

CHAPTER V

The Second Christening of William Darby

A ND SO TO the final chapter of this Unusually Long Preface, the purpose of which has been to set the scene for dramas yet untold—and at the heart of such drama lies human affection: the affection between friends bound together by tea, warm buns and melancholy; and the affection of lovers, those strange beasts who share their souls in the belief, so often misplaced, that they know each other. Of which a case in point for Belle Nash was ...

'Pablo Fanque! He's come to London!' exclaimed Mrs Nonsuch who, after half a bottle of rum, was an eager listener. 'He did love you and love crosses oceans! I knew it, Mr Nash. But how did he make the journey from Grenada ahead of you? And how, in so short a time, did he become a circus performer?'

'Ah, trust a woman to fall into such a trap,' replied Belle, now wiping away tears. 'I, too, wanted the romance to be true, but my eyes had deceived me. For all the world, he could have been Pablo Fanque's twin but the circus artist was not my lover. Instead, he goes by the name of William Darby of Norfolk.'

Mrs Nonsuch could not hide her disappointment. How much more perfect it would have been for the real Pablo Fanque to be riding the stallion!

'William Darby of Norfolk? So not the same person at all. Yet he could be Mr Fanque's twin, you say?'

The disbelief was evident in her voice.

46

'Oh, most definitely, Ma'am. The two men could be Taiyewo and Kehinde, so similar are they!'

Mrs Nonsuch laughed. She was hooked, once again, by the tale.

'You certainly know your African lore, Mr Nash,' she said. 'How might that be?'

'From my time in Grenada, Ma'am. There were workers on the plantation who had been stolen from their homes west of the mighty River Niger. They told me of their traditions and their gods, including Shango, the god of thunder and lightning: their Zeus!'

Mrs Nonsuch clapped.

'Then you could not be accused of not knowing one African person from another.'

'Please, Madam. The man I saw was Pablo's age and likeness but he was no relative. It turns out that Darby was born in Norwich.'

'Darby was born in Norwich?' Mrs Nonsuch scoffed. 'Or do you mean that Norwich was born in Derby? I'm having difficulty keeping up.'

'Madam, his father was brought to England from the Gold Coast but, sadly, has not been a presence in his son's life. The mother is from Norwich. Whilst African in appearance, the lad is Norfolk through and through.'

Mrs Nonsuch's expression now softened as her eyes widened. What at first she had deemed implausible she now accepted as true. Belle was a man of integrity and she was touched by the obvious depth of his affection. She also liked a good story and from long experience as Jaunay's manager, she knew there were few stories to pull the heartstrings more than a bachelor romance.

'To know so much, you must have spoken to him,' she said, correctly. 'And what came of your conversation?'

Belle finished his glass of rum and placed it beside the empty bottle.

'Naturally, like Echo and his mountain nymphs, we conversed.

But first, I marvelled as a man whom I thought was my lover rode into the ring, jumping from stallion to mare. The skill! The dexterity! The litheness of his body! Imagine my ecstasy. In a moment I was on my feet in the audience, my arms aloft, crying, "Pablo! Pablo! *C'est moi!*" But so focussed was he with the horses that my efforts to attract his attention failed. His act finished, he galloped from the arena, unaware of my presence.'

Mrs Nonsuch bit her lip in eager anticipation.

'I left my seat as the ringmaster, Mr Ducrow, introduced Mr Ki Hi Chin Fan Foo, the human spider from the Orient. I must tell you that Mr Foo is a wonder to behold, a man, like Haydn's tiger, so flexible that he can sit on his own head—but I had to find Pablo.

'A distance from the circus tent are the caravans in which the performers live, and there I found him, removing his coat. Naturally, I fell upon my beloved and embraced him with a wild hug and an even wilder kiss.'

Mrs Nonsuch half-whimpered with excitement.

'And did he respond?'

Belle's arms fell to his sides.

'Not with the passion I had anticipated. The man I knew as Pablo said, "Bless me, Sir, but that's not right" and pushed me firmly away. I stood there aghast, wondering how a love requited on a Caribbean island should end up unrequited in Lambeth. Could the world be so fickle? And then it dawned on me: Mr Darby was not my man. Not the man I wanted him to be. I was embarrassed beyond measure. I made my excuses, of course, explaining my amorous behaviour as the unfettered affection of a French philosopher and, to lend substance to my excuse, telling him my name was Blaise Pascal.'

'And ... ?'

'He laughed, said that no harm had come of it, and invited me into his caravan for a toddy, stating that it was not every day that he was visited by a French philosopher.'

'So, he believes you to be Blaise Pascal?' she queried.

Belle nodded.

'Indeed. Since then, I have returned to Astley's most evenings to watch him perform. In addition to bareback riding, he also walks the high wire. Heaven, how I nearly cry, for one slip and he might fall and die! After the show, we converse in his caravan or, onwards, at a Lambeth bar. Whilst he is not Pablo, in the soft lamplight of The Crown & Anchor I feel that there is a mutual ... . You understand, don't you, Mrs Nonsuch? After all that happened in the Caribbean, I yearn for him to be ... '

Belle sank his face into his hands.

'You cannot imagine the pain I suffer, Madam. One moment, he is Darby of Norfolk; the next, I imagine him to be Pablo with the hills of Grenada behind us and tropical birds in the trees and the taste of mango on our tongues. Advise me, dear lady. I believe I am going mad. What am I to do?'

They fell into a silence which hovered in the air until broken by a sharp knock on the office door. Without invitation, Beauty the doorman entered.

'Begging your pardon, Ma'am, I have just seen a group of Peelers gathering at the top of the square, led by Officer Dimm. I'm thinking they may have spotted our guest and be preparing an assault on our premises.'

The mention of the former special constable from Bath caused an immediate reaction in Belle.

'Decimus Dimm! The very scoundrel with whom I battled four years ago. If I am caught within this week, I shall be exiled again. I fear I am doomed!'

Mrs Nonsuch rose, her mind made up in an instant.

'Courage, Mr Nash. Pick up your overcoat and beret and leave through the kitchens at the back. Have you sufficient money to take the post chaise to Bath?'

'I do. But what of my account here?'

'You are a trusted guest. We will forward your belongings and you will settle your account once you are safe. But for now, hurry before Dimm and his men besiege us.'

Mrs Nonsuch pulled Belle by the hand from her office, past the reception desk and down a flight of steps to the kitchens. Above them, she could hear whistles being blown and then the voices of Peelers as they pushed their way into the hotel lobby. She guided Belle past stoves of sizzling pans to the tradesmen's entrance where, exiting into the dank drizzle of a London evening, Mrs Nonsuch turned to her guest.

'You will prevail, Mr Nash. Evil must be fought and love must be secured. If Mr Fanque is lost, Mr Darby may yet fill the void. Tread carefully, but do not lose him. Go to Astley's, tell Darby the truth and then run to safety. Do not wait, Sir: run, before you are discovered!'

Belle understood the urgency but stopped a moment to give thanks.

'I will never forget your kindness, Mrs Nonsuch. And I will repay you everything, I promise. For now, good lady, *au revoir*.'

Belle kissed her on the hand and, obeying her instructions, threw on his overcoat, pulled the beret over his head and sped by foot down the alley. Mrs Nonsuch watched as he turned a corner and disappeared. Then she returned upstairs, wondering if she would ever see her Blaise Pascal again.

A T THE FIRST opportunity, Belle exchanged his unusual Basque beret for a more common Tilbury hat and stopped by a barber to have his moustache refashioned. He would have accepted the offer of cologne but contented himself with a hot flannel, for time was of the essence.

He was soon in Whitehall and, with every step, distanced himself further from Jaunay's. This did not stop him, however, from looking over his shoulder every ten yards to check that Dimm was not following.

At the House of Commons, he joined the crowds and carriages

that crossed Westminster Bridge and headed for Astley's Royal Amphitheatre, where he spent the evening hiding beneath an elm tree lest his now familiar face be recognised by any of the regulars. In the cold and the rain, Belle watched as the artists moved in and out of the great tent. There was the aged prize fighter Tom Shelton, who did his best to flex what remained of his muscles, and the Ridley Brothers, a pair of clowns whose antics tickled the crowd, though they were not a patch on the much-loved W.F. Wallet.

There followed a display by somersault artists and tightrope dancers, after which William Darby was called to perform. Single-handed, he readied four horses, pulling them side by side into a line. Then, with the agility of a cougar, he leapt onto their backs, a whip in his right hand, the reins in his left, and drove them into the tent, receiving a great 'Hurrah!' on his arrival.

Belle wished he could watch the act but having seen it fifty times or more was able to track every detail in his mind. Then, as the performance reached its conclusion, he broke from the cover of the tree and made his way towards Darby's caravan, while the crowd called out for more.

Concentrating on keeping the wind and rain out of his face, Belle failed to notice a man approach who also had his head bowed toward the sodden earth. The two collided and both went sprawling to the soggy ground.

'Get away from me, Dimm!' he called out, believing he was being arrested.

But when he looked up, instead of West Country sideburns, he saw the painted eyes and pigtail of a man from China. It was, he realised, Mr Foo, the human spider.

'G'wan with ye, now, ya bowsie!' snapped the startled spider, who jumped up, hid his face and hurried towards the circus tent.

Confused by the encounter, Belle pulled himself to his feet.

'Mr Foo, I do beg your pardon. I didn't mean to ... ' he declared too late. Then, looking down at his muddied overcoat and trousers, he added, 'O hell, what a sight I am!'

51

It was a situation that might have left him in despair were it not for the warm Norfolk voice that filled the air.

'No need for 'ee to worry about yon Mr Foo. Tha' man's made of India rubber, remember!'

In his excitement, Belle nearly slipped a second time. His spirits rose and a smile broke across his face.

'Pab—I mean Mr Darby, what a joy to see you!'

Darby stepped forward and placed a firm hand on Belle's shoulder. He was radiant with the success of his act.

'Loikewise, Monsieur Pascal, though tha' lookst in a roight state. Tha'd best follow oi to moy caravan to get cleaned up. Taint proper for a gentleman like thi'sen be covered in mud.'

Five minutes later, with his overcoat removed and his breeches stripped off, Belle found himself by a brazier, steam gently rising from his undergarments. Over his shoulders was thrown a blanket that smelt of sweet William and between his hands he held a mug of hot spiced cider.

In ordinary circumstances, Belle would have been a picture of contentment, but tonight he was a hunted man, and his ears rang with the words of Mrs Nonsuch: 'Tell Mr Darby the truth.'

Opposite him Darby reclined spread-eagled in a chair, his limbs stretched out, his shirt open to the chest, sweat from his exertions glistening on his skin. He had ridden four horses simultaneously whilst leaping between them and he basked in the self-confidence that only the very skilful can enjoy. Belle tried in vain not to stare.

'You're very kind, Mr Darby,' he said meekly. 'This cider has restored me. I am a new man!'

Darby smiled.

'A new man with a new accent, Monsieur Pascal, unless oi'm very mistaken! Is there summat tha'st been hoiding from oi? Oi 'aven't 'eard 'ee talk this way afore.'

'Ah—I do believe I am found out.'

Darby's smile widened.

52

'Oi believe thou art, *Monsieur*. Or should it be "*Sir*"? Do tell: Oi'm a Norfolk man moyself; oi likes plain talk!'

'Mr Darby, you will take me for a knave, for I have not been fully open with you these last months, but I must now shake off all deceit. The truth is, I'm not a Frenchman. I know, after all this time, you may find that hard to believe.'

"'ard to believe?' The circus man started to laugh and then laughed louder and louder until he fell off his chair and lay on the floor, hugging himself as he roared.

'Th'ast knocked oi over wi' a feather, Monsieur Pascal. Oi'd not guessed for a moment tha' wuzn't French!'

'Nor is Blaise Pascal my name, Sir,' Belle confided further, uncertain quite where he stood.

'Not Blaise Pascal?' Darby howled, rocking back and forth. 'Oh, now oi is roight shocked!'

'Mr Darby, I am unsure whether you are outraged or mocking me. I have not wished to deceive, only to protect myself.'

'Ah, Monsieur Pascal,' said Darby, pulling himself together and climbing back into his chair. 'Tha'st a fine one. But as tha'art in the mood to share secrets, oi've one for thee too. Oi've known for long enough that thou wuzn't who thou saidst. Tha' canst not 'ave been, what with your *terreebl'* accent, and so—tha'll forgive oi for spoying—oi followed 'ee back to th'an lodgings one noight, to learn who tha' really wast.'

Belle was startled.

'And what did you find, Sir?'

'Oi spoke to yon doorman at th'hotel. Beauty, 'e calls isself, oi believe, or Jasmine, or Columboine, dependin' on the time of day. He told oi that tha'art Councillor Bellerophon Nash of the City of Baath. He'd heard tha'd been exoiled a few yearn back.'

Belle's surprise turned to shock, not so much at the failure of his disguise as at the doorman's indiscretion.

"'Tis true. To the other side of the Atlantic. To Grenada. Did you pay the doorman for the information?'

'Dismiss that worry from thoi moind,' said Darby, waving the thought away. 'Beauty's a good man. Oi merely gave 'im the oiye, the way yew bachelors do, and 'e spilt the beans. He couldn't tell oi whoiy tha'd changed tha' name but 'e said it was fair common among Jaunay's guests. Said the Earl of Dumfries loiked to be called ... '

Belle spluttered into his cider.

'Enough,' he implored. 'You know my true identity—and yet my deceit did not worry you. Did the doorman say anything else?'

Darby took time to answer. He could see that Belle was perturbed and needed calming.

'He said thou'art a gentleman oi could trust.'

In nine kindly words, Belle's confidence returned.

'In what manner?'

'To advoise me. And to return a favour to a friend, should a friend requoire it.'

Belle's heart began to race.

'What sort of favour, Mr Darby?'

Darby leant forward. During all the time that he had known of Belle's identity, he had longed for the moment when they both could drop their guard and reveal themselves. Darby did not know why Belle had been exiled, nor why he had disguised himself on his return, but he had convinced himself that Belle was a man of honour and authenticity, and one who could make his dreams come true.

'Dowen't get me wrong, Mr Nash. Oi'm happy in moy own skin and oi'm doing well enough at Astley's but oi want more. Oi feel trapped—that's the way of it.'

'Trapped?' said Belle. 'How so?'

'Oi wants to be moy own man. Run moy own circus. Oi's 'ad enough of Mr Ducrow cracking 'is whip. His circus is stuck in Lambeth. No one knows us except them as seeks us out. Oi wants to take our acts around the country. Bring us to a woider audience. Get us better known.'

'It sounds like a wonderful ambition, Mr Darby. But how do you think I can help?'

His question was met with a disbelieving look.

'Of all the people in thur country, thou shoulds't understand. Everyone goes to Baath! Men of wealth and consequence, all bound for entertainment. Oi wants to go to Baath too, with a travelling circus of moy own. Takings will start to droy up here in Lambeth in't next few months. Why not capitaloise on the Season? And oi thought that having been a councillor, tha' might'st assist me in moy enterprise.'

Belle looked at William Darby and saw a man eager to succeed. There was, beside his extraordinary skill on horseback, an energy and ambition that cried out to be supported. And beyond this, for Belle, there was love, if not for the man before him, then for the man he so resembled, left behind in Grenada.

'My influence has waned, Mr Darby. I once lived like Crassus in a fine house on Gay Street, but no more. I had position, but that too is past. I still have friends, and could discuss your proposition with them, but we would need to understand all the practicalities of staging a circus, for there is bound to be opposition from my former enemies, and you must understand also the extent to which my hands are tied. For reasons too absurd, I am temporarily a wanted man and must continue to hide for the next five days. Perhaps you could assist in that regard.'

Darby chuckled. The circus troupe was full of questionable characters, so that hiding one more for five days could be achieved without effort.

'Easily done. Tha' shalt make this caravan thoine home. Wuz there a second problem?'

'That, when you arrive in Bath, I cannot admit to knowing you.'

'What?' said Darby, now surprised.

Belle raised his hands to placate his new friend.

'So far as the world is concerned, I am at this moment still sail-

55

ing on the high seas, *en route* back from the Caribbean. My boat is due to dock in Bristol next week. As such, I cannot have been to Astley's and cannot have made your acquaintance. And having known me as Blaise Pascal, for which necessary subterfuge I beg your forgiveness, you must forthwith call me "Belle".'

'Not "Mr Nash"? Oi'd be 'appy to do so, Sir, but dost tha' not foind "Belle" too familiar, loike?'

'It must be,' Belle insisted.

'Then oi'll do as tha' sayest. Be that all?'

Belle hesitated. He was fearful of the absurdity of what he was about to ask.

'In private, I may call you William,' he began, 'but not in public. For, in the eyes of the world, you shall be ... '

Darby growled.

'Be careful, Sir. Oi must warn 'ee, oi's moy own man and no one's servant. And never their ... '

Belle looked alarmed.

'No! Mistake me not for a ... I only ... Oh dear, Mr Darby, to realise your plan, in public you must assume another's identity. It is a lot to ask but I cannot assist you in any other way.'

It was a strange request and Darby looked troubled.

'Tha'rt sayin' oi'm no longer to be William Darby of Norfolk? Tha'rt expectin' me to give up moy name and oidentity? Oi can't. Moy celebrity as a performer, for what it is, is built on both, Sir. The crowds come to see William Darby, not some other.'

'I would not ask were it not vital, William. And what I shall propose is a good name—a fine name,' replied Belle, seeking to reassure. 'It belongs to ... '

The name caught in Belle's throat. For a moment, he looked at Darby and saw palm trees in the distance and a blue sea lapping at white sand. It was a vision blurred by tears that gathered in his eyes.

Darby leant forward to dry his eyes.

'No need for tears, Mr Nash—or Belle, as tha'd 'ave me say.

Just tell me the name, if thou can'st, Sir, and whoiy oi must adopt it.'

Belle whispered, 'It is the name of a dear friend, like you, William ... '

'Tell me.'

' ... a man called Pablo Fanque.'

'And whoiy?'

Belle lowered his head and muttered a private prayer: 'Sweet goddess Eleos, have mercy on my soul.' Caught between his desire for himself and his strategy for William Darby, he knew not what to express nor how much to hide.

'Mr Darby—William—through my letters to friends and associates in Bath, the name of Pablo Fanque is already known to those closest to me, for he too was closest to me in Grenada. If you become him, I can the more easily facilitate your entry into Bath society, for I can then introduce you as a beloved companion and intimate from my years of exile abroad. If not, then you arrive in Bath as someone unknown to me, and I fear your passage will be the harder.'

Darby considered Belle's request. Though strange, there was sense to it, for it seemed to offer his best chance to win over Bath's most privileged and thus to break free of Ducrow. What Belle had left unspoken, but of which Darby was not ignorant, was his need for love of a kind still outlawed by society. The circus man thought a moment longer.

Then, with the lure of success so great, each held out a hand to accept the terms. As they reached for the other, the words of Mrs Nonsuch echoed in Belle's head.

'Maybe Mr Darby can fill the void.'

She had spoken with the best of intentions ...

'Maybe Mr Darby can fill the void.'

... but her words would unleash the fiercest of storms. As the men shook hands in agreement, a crack of thunder sounded overhead. It was Tyche, capricious dispenser of fate, not Eleos, goddess of clemency, who had heard Belle's plea.

Their fingers touched—William and Belle—and into the furious void they fell.

NOTES
- William Darby (1810–1871) was a renowned nineteenth-century equestrian and tightrope performer born in a Norwich workhouse to an African father and an English mother. My uncle's assertion that he took the performing name Pablo Fanque is true and can be seen on posters of 1837, shortly after which he performed for Queen Victoria in his own circus.
- The greatest clown of the nineteenth century was almost certainly W.F. Wallet. The so-called Ki Hi Chin Fan Foo was a popular contortionist. The famous Tom Shelton was a bare-knuckle fighter of the era.
- In Yoruba tradition, the first-born twin is called Taiyewo and the second-born Kehinde. In the Yoruba religion, twins are believed to have supernatural powers and to be under the protection of the god Shango. The Yoruba empire straddled modern Togo, Benin and Nigeria (west of the Niger river). Its ancient capital Katunga, or Òyó-Ilé, had a population thought to have exceeded 100,000 people.

PART ONE
'THE GLORY'

Love knows no limit to its endurance,
No end to its trust,
No fading of its hope;
It can outlast anything.
Love still stands when all else has fallen.

Blaise Pascal

CHAPTER VI

Return of the Prodigal Son

I S ANY MEMBER of the public attending court today?' asked
Gaia Champion, who had come to wonder whether Bath had
entered hibernation, so few were the number of hearings and
so limited the public interest. Lucius Lush peered into the
courtroom through a peephole window in an adjoining door.

'Just one person present, Ma'am: Miss Prim, in the front row,
knitting.'

Gaia sighed at the mention of Phyllis Prim.

'I remarked to her that the court has been quiet and she
threatened to come along. The click-clack of her needles drives
me to distraction but she means well and it will be nice to have a
friendly face in court for once.'

Master Lush was not a man to take affront easily, but ...

'I had not realised, Ma'am ... '

Gaia quickly recognised her mistake.

'Other than yours, of course, Master Lush,' she added. 'I
would be lost without you. Right, let us face the day while Apollo's
friendly beams light up our path. From Special Constable Evans's
report, a straw thief has been apprehended. I anticipate a defence
ornamented with rustic logic. Shall we go in?'

It was not a question but a command. Master Lush moved
across the office and opened the door to the courtroom. He
enjoyed making the most of his entrance—a highlight of his day
—and, in a voice loud enough to be heard in Milsom Street, to

declare, 'Be upstanding in court for Mrs Gaia Champion, Magistrate of the Royal City of Bath!'

Miss Prim, though a spinster, was not of such advanced years as to be hard of hearing. Concentrating on the garter and fine rib stitches for her shawl, Master Lush's announcement startled her.

'Ooooh,' she cried, spilling her balls of wool to the floor.

Master Lush rushed forward to retrieve them.

'A thousand pardons, Miss Prim. I should not have declaimed with such vigour.'

Behind them, Gaia took up her position on the magistrate's bench and did her best to suppress her amusement.

'When the clerk-of-court has finished scrabbling about on the floor, could he spare the time to inform the special constable of our presence?'

Master Lush returned the balls of wool to Miss Prim and scampered to the back of the courtroom. His dignity challenged, he went into the lobby and, a moment later, returned.

'On his way, Ma'am, along with the accused,' he said hurriedly, before retreating to his writing desk. Breathing heavily, he reached for a quill to record the session.

A few seconds later, Special Constable Evans entered with a dishevelled, middle-aged man who was badly in need of a wash and a new set of clothes. The accused looked about the court with a sorry expression and accepted a helping hand into the dock. Miss Prim resumed her knitting.

'Good morning, Special Constable Evans,' said Gaia, looking at her notes. 'And is the defendant a Mr Henry Coxe of no fixed abode, but formerly of Peasedown St. John?'

The special constable took off his hat and stood to attention.

'Yes, Ma'am.'

'And on what charge is the defendant being held?'

'Theft, Ma'am,' said the policeman, adding, 'of straw. A bundle off the back of Mr Cardew's cart.'

'One bundle, do you say, Special Constable?'

62

'Yes, Ma'am.'

Gaia tried to hide her disappointment. She had hoped for a crime of some significance, the loss of a winter's worth of bedding, perhaps, or a theft involving affray or offences against the person. Truly, the city had hit a lull when the day's only case was a stolen bundle of straw. Nevertheless, it was a sign that, under her magistracy, crime in Bath was on the decrease and, besides, she had pledged to treat all cases with an equal duty of care.

'Very well. First, will the accused please confirm that he is Henry Coxe, formerly of the aforesaid Peasedown St. John and still of no fixed abode?'

Henry Coxe nodded through a thick, matted beard.

'That's me, Ma'am.'

'And do you acknowledge that you stole the straw, Mr Coxe?'

'I do, Ma'am.'

Sitting on the front row of the public part of the court, Miss Prim kept up her rhythmic knitting—click-clack-click, click-clack-click—and attended closely. She could tell from the accused's eyes that he was a criminal; he looked furtive. As ever, she was impressed by how promptly Gaia got to the nub of a case. And how often the guilty revealed their guilt under her incisive questioning.

'And why did you steal the straw?' Gaia asked.

Henry Coxe, who had expected to be sentenced without further ado, paused before replying. The logic of his case made perfect sense to him; would it make sense to others? 'To keep myself warm, Ma'am, last night having a chill about it. I sleep rough, close to the canal, and I wanted to make myself a bed.'

Gaia studied the vagrant. As a woman, she felt pity. As a magistrate ...

'And where is the straw now?'

The guilty party worried that he might have committed a more serious, unknown offence. The pace of Miss Prim's knitting quickened. Click-click-clack.

'Took it with me to Pulteney Gaol, Ma'am. Them mattresses in gaol, they've seen better days, what with the lice and filth. Just like me.'

Gaia could not resist a half-smile, and Miss Prim briefly paused.

'Is it true, Special Constable Evans, that the stolen straw is in the gaol?'

Evans took a step forward.

'Yes, Ma'am. Mr Cardew allowed the accused to keep the straw but insisted that I carry out the arrest to deter Mr Coxe. It's not the first time he's stolen straw from Mr Cardew ... '

'It gets damp after a few days,' interjected Mr Coxe.

' ... and he's a-tiring of it,' explained Evans.

Gaia raised a hand. She had heard sufficient on the crime. There was, however, one more piece of information she required to make a judgement.

'Mr Coxe, before I pass sentence, what was your profession when, in happier times, you resided in Peasedown?'

The eyes of the vagrant became watery as he recalled his past.

'I was a hedger, Ma'am. I laid hedges. But it was hard work and I drank to deaden the aches and pains, and my wife wouldn't have me in the house on account of it. Said that she'd married a man and ended up with a flagon of cider and I dare say she was right. Cider's what lost me my family, my home and my occupation, Ma'am.'

Miss Prim shook her head. How easily was the working man led astray!

'I see,' said Gaia. Stories of broken men and wrecked marriages were a staple of the court and she had taught herself to harden her heart. On the other hand, what was the point of a legal system if it could not reform the felonious and raise up the downtrodden?

'It seems to me, Mr Coxe, that you need a roof, a job and a change of clothing, if you are ever to mend your ways.'

Gaia looked over to Miss Prim, who made a mental note to fit another jumper into her knitting schedule.

'I am sentencing you to be held over for a further two days in Pulteney Gaol, to keep you out of mischief, Mr Coxe. During that time, I will make enquiries of the City Corporation about its need for park labourers. That, I surmise, is your only road to redemption. If they do not need you, you will be sent to a workhouse. That is all. Take Mr Coxe away. Although before you go, Special Constable Evans, is this truly the only case for the day?'

'Yes, Ma'am,' the policeman replied apologetically. 'There appears to be an unnatural respect for law and order in the city at this time. I find it worrying.'

Gaia laughed.

'Well put, Special Constable Evans. I am sure that a healthy disorder will shortly return.'

And without further comment Gaia rose and descended from the dais as the canalside vagrant was taken back down.

Alert to her departure, Master Lush jumped to his feet and shouted, 'All rise ... ' Then, as he saw Miss Prim shake her head, he concluded quietly ' ... for Mrs Gaia Champion.'

Once Gaia had left the courtroom, Master Lush went to check on Miss Prim.

'Is that it for the day, Master Lush?' she enquired.

'I fear so, Miss Prim. It was hardly worth your coming.'

'It was all over in an instant,' she agreed. 'And I was so hoping to finish this shawl today. Would Mrs Champion mind, do you think, if I stayed a while longer? I was quite settled in and the light here is good for knitting.'

Master Lush reached out and touched Miss Prim on the arm.

'Of course, Miss Prim. This is a public court and you have every right to remain. Make yourself at home. And may I be permitted to bring you a cup of tea and a biscuit whilst you continue your knitting?'

It was just what Miss Prim had hoped to hear. She was always so well looked after by Master Lush when she came to court. Such a polite young man.

'How very kind of you, Master Lush. Tea and a biscuit would be most pleasant. Very little milk and one spoonful of sugar, if you would.'

Master Lush nodded and left Miss Prim wondering how on Earth the clerk could remain unwed. Perhaps he needed an elegant scarf to catch a lady's eye but did she have enough wool? She looked in her bag to assess her diminishing stock. On current demand, another game of whist against Mrs Pomeroy and Lady Passmore could not come soon enough.

A LTHOUGH HER APPOINTMENT as magistrate had cast her into the public realm, Gaia had had many years of experience of Law prior to her selection. Her late husband Hercules had been a prominent solicitor and, behind the scenes, she had worked closely with him. Now on the bench, she prided herself on keeping up with the never-ending changes in legislation.

While Master Lush prepared Miss Prim's cup of tea, Gaia busied herself studying the new Poor Law Act passed by Parliament the previous year. It had been designed to reduce the public cost of caring for sorry souls like Henry Coxe through the establishment of workhouses but it was an irony, she considered, that one year after abolishing slavery in its overseas dominions, Parliament should be condemning the domestic poor to another form of servitude.

Gaia turned her chair to a window that looked over Pulteney Bridge and the River Avon. Having spent the previous ten minutes listening to the click-clack-click of Miss Prim's knitting needles, she now listened to the sound of the busy city and the rushing of water. It reminded her that, regardless of the text of the law, her role was to protect all people, including the disadvantaged.

'I had better find you a job, Mr Coxe, or the mattresses in gaol will be the least of your problems,' she muttered to herself.

Behind her, a door opened and the tinkle of cups on a tray alerted her to Master Lush's return. Without breaking her gaze, Gaia motioned with an arm and said, 'Put the tray down on the desk, Master Lush, if you please. And help yourself to a cup, if you're thirsty.'

'If you say so, Ma'am. You are, as ever, the epitome of kindness,' came the reply.

It was not the words but the voice that prompted her to turn— a voice that made time stand still, a voice that she had longed to hear for four years, one she fought to remember in the face of worsening fears—its melodic cadence creating a change of mood so profound, it was as if perpetual winter had been swept away.

She spun her chair round and sprang to her feet, and there, lit by the window behind her, was her closest friend.

'Belle!' she cried, dropping The Poor Law to the floor, throwing her arms in the air, unable to articulate her joy. 'Hah! Belle ... oh Belle ... oh Belle! It's you!'

He stepped forward and they embraced, the firm grip of each other's arms tightening, their minds flooded by memories of love, friendship and trust. Gaia thrilled at the playfulness of his eyes, the upturn of his mouth as he smiled—even, almost imperceptibly, the fragrance of his skin. Rarely had she felt such joy.

'You're alive! And you're here!'

'Yes, dear Gaia!' he replied in kind, then letting her go so he could perform a Scotch reel. 'I am alive and straight off the boat from Bristol. And, Madam, I have missed you more than Orpheo missed his dear Eurydice, when taken from his side by the viper's bite, more than Ovid missed Terentia after being banished by Augustus, more than ... '

'Oh Belle! Forsooth!' laughed Gaia, and looked for a chair to offer him. 'Let us take tea together, for I see that Master Lush has armed you with all the necessaries.'

Belle laughed. How perfectly English, he thought, to manage ecstasy, as well as grief, with tea.

67

'I met Mistress Lucy in the corridor and relieved him of his duty,' he explained.

'You still like sugar?' Gaia asked, smiling, as she poured his tea and remembered his sweet tooth.

'Bright Helios has shone down fiercely on me during my four years in the Caribbean,' he replied, 'and brought both wisdom and discomfort to many of my former joys. But in my tea, yes, I find I cannot forsake my weakness for sugar.'

'And more widely, Belle? You are still sweet in nature, I hope,' she laughed, determined to keep the conversation light.

He smiled but did not answer her question directly, staring instead through the window at the distant sky.

'I have much to tell you, Gaia, of what I have witnessed. Not all of it is sweet, Madam. I wish it were.'

'You do have much to tell,' she agreed, handing over the tea-cup on its saucer. 'We have heard nought from you for six months and were worried. Did you not care to write?'

'Did you not receive notice of my return?' he asked, feigning surprise, even though telling the smallest of untruths to Gaia hurt him. 'Then I fear that the postal system is not the same as it was in old Ralph Allen's time. I will have strong words with the new postmaster general when I see him. I expect a bag of correspondence was spoiled by seawater and molasses. But no matter, for I am here.'

For a moment, Gaia stayed silent. In such instances, time spent in a friend's company means more than the words that may pass between them. Then she spoke.

'I would ask whether you have visited Gay Street but your house is now sold. It breaks my heart to see others living where you once made your home. But despair not, dear Belle. In the hope that you would return, I took the liberty of renting for you a house on Bathwick Hill. The road is named Sydney Buildings and lies beside the canal. It is not a match on Gay Street, I confess, but it is an elegant house with a pleasing aspect.'

68

Belle's eyes filled with tears, relieved at Gaia's kindness in securing accommodation for him. His heart would remain in Gay Street but he was thankful for a new home.

'The view across the river to the abbey is splendid,' Gaia added, reassuringly. 'I do not think you will be displeased.'

'You are a good friend to me, Ma'am.'

'Not at all. In a while I will have Master Lush walk you there. Looking at the dirt on your face and your hair and your clothes, I venture that you need to attend to yourself. You are as grey as a spectre.'

'I am!' he laughed. 'And the house: does it, too, need fair Hygieia and her broom?'

Gaia smiled.

'Hygieia can remain in Olympus for now. The house is in good condition and your collection of *Königliche* porcelain is in place. The rooms will need airing, of course, the stove lit and the dust-sheets removed.'

'I long to be there. My old bed again, after four years!' Belle declared, sipping at his tea.

It was the second time that Belle had mentioned the length of his exile. Gaia could not let it pass. It was, she decided, an issue to be confronted at the earliest stage.

'Belle, I must ask: do you blame me for your exile? Certain ladies do. It has been heavy on my conscience and grown heavier with time.'

It was a topic that he knew would be raised. It was one he had spent many an evening pondering, both in Grenada and all the weeks on board ship.

'We both know that it was my decision more than yours, and circumstance provided no alternative,' he replied, purposefully. 'Without exile, I would surely have been hanged for my bachelor ways. The exile saved my life and that of dear Gerhardt Kant too. Not to mention the sacrifice I made for Mistress Lush. There is no blame to be apportioned.'

Gaia was grateful for his response but there were others who needed to be enlightened.

'Belle, I must ask that you repeat that to Lady Passmore and Mrs Pomeroy. They have not excused me all this time.'

He nodded, unsurprised.

'I see. So, you have never explained ... ?'

'No. The ladies gossip and my position as magistrate would have been imperilled by any rumour that I assisted you.'

Another sip of tea salved his wounds of regret.

'Then I shall host a tea party at Sydney Buildings a few days hence. That shall be the occasion to explain the truth. I am sure there is no injury that a crafted word cannot set right.'

Gaia was pleased with the answer. The issue would soon be in the past.

'An excellent idea,' she adjudged. 'And the more reason for you to go now to your new abode. Prepare the tea party without delay. Lady Passmore will forgive neither of us if she is made to wait!'

At the mention of Lady Passmore, Belle felt a small wave of foreboding. One of the few things to keep him awake at night was fear of her ladyship's displeasure.

'I understand. But I must be allowed a few days first to settle.'

Gaia nodded: it was a reasonable request.

'Of course, you must make yourself at home,' she replied. 'In that regard, let Master Lush assist in opening up the house.'

'But is he not busy, here?'

'Not at all. The court has been unusually quiet. In fact, the clerk has been busying himself publishing a social almanac for the Season and ... Oh, enough of that, it can be discussed another time. Of more relevance, where is he I wonder?'

Belle looked to the door. He knew where the clerk was. And he knew who was with him.

'Mistress Lush is waiting outside ... '

'Then we must ask him to come in.'

Belle cautioned, ' … where he is entertaining a fellow traveller from Grenada.'

Gaia now hesitated. From his letters, she knew Belle had be-friended Grenadians but had imagined that he would return alone.

'A fellow? Then you travelled with a companion? You had mentioned in your letters a certain friend, but … '

Belle stood up, suddenly uncomfortable in his skin. His nervous eye twitched in agitation.

'Yes, a young gentleman from the island. Someone I wish to introduce to you.'

'A young gentleman?'

In her heart, Gaia had known that the passing years would bring change and that her friend would not return wholly the same. But, perhaps driven by her own desire, she had not con-sidered the form such change might take. In the silence, the click-clack rhythm of Miss Prim's knitting in the courtroom could be heard. She rose, understanding that further hesitation was not in order.

'Please, Belle, introduce me to the gentleman.'

He walked to the door and opened it. Stretching out a hand, he beckoned his companion to come forward, and the fine figure of William Darby entered her office.

'I am delighted to introduce … '

Belle paused, as if weighing up the facts before making a commitment.

' … my cousin from the island, Mr Pablo Fanque.'

Gaia did her best not to appear startled, not at the nature of the man who had entered—he was every bit a gentleman—but at the implied relationship between them and at Belle's nervousness. This was more than mere friendship, then. In the background, Master Lush also entered and stood to one side.

'A cousin?' Gaia repeated, comprehending the bachelor code. 'And an intimate? It is a pleasure to meet you, Mr Fanque. Bath welcomes you to its bosom.'

71

William stepped forward to take her hand.

'It's roight excoiting to be in Baath,' he replied gaily. 'Oi's long dreamt of comin' 'ere. Been meanin' to for years.'

Surprised by William's arrival—and by the unexpectedly East Anglian lilt of his voice—Gaia gave her inquisitive mind full rein.

'May I declare my gratification that our royal city is so famed in the West Indies that you have yearned to see it. And your accent, Mr Fanque, is not one I had imagined common so far across the Atlantic.'

Belle intervened. Once the lies start, they often come in quick succession.

'Grenada is a melting pot of accents,' he agreed. 'The plantation had a foreman from Norfolk and, the next thing you know, the entire population had adopted it. You'd have thought the whole island was born in Great Yarmouth!'

'Well, I never,' commented Gaia, wisely choosing not to enquire further. 'Master Lush, kindly go with Mr Nash and Mr Fanque to Sydney Buildings and spend the day assisting them in opening up the house. I will send word to Somerset Place for a maid to help.'

'Yes, Ma'am,' replied Master Lush, happy to help and delighted to be at the centre of affairs. 'Although might I first take a cup of tea and a biscuit to Miss Prim? She stayed on in the courtroom to knit. I offered her tea some fifteen minutes ago.'

Belle raised his hands with joy at the news that Bath's premier knitter was nearby for, after Gaia, of all the ladies, he adored Miss Prim the most. With Miss Prim, unlike Lady Passmore, there was nothing to fear, and she had been a considerate neighbour in Gay Street.

'Miss Prim! I thought I heard the clacking of knitting needles. I must see her at once. Pablo, you must meet her too. She is the dearest of creatures.'

On the long coach journey from London, Belle had occupied the hours talking about his many friends. He grabbed William by the hand, and familiar with the layout of Gaia's office, he led him straight to the door that gave entry to the courtroom.

'Belle, less haste ... ' said Gaia, but to no avail as her friend and his companion disappeared. With foresight, she added, 'Master Lush, attend them—quickly! Miss Prim has a fragile disposition, and seeing Mr Nash with Mr Fanque may come as a ... '

Her advice came too late. Belle's eagerness to introduce William had got the better of his normally sound judgement. Miss Prim was a woman who struggled with surprises and none proved greater than the emergence of a friend who, after so many years, she had struggled to believe was still alive.

'Miss Prim,' announced the dusty apparition, 'I do hope you still remember your erstwhile and most esteemed admirer, Mr Bellerophon Nash of this city.'

'Oaah!'

The click-clack of the knitting needles ceased abruptly.

'And this is my dear cousin ... '

'Oaaaaah!'

The squawk was followed by the sound of a body collapsing to the floor, followed closely by a pair of knitting needles and a ball of wool.

' ... Pablo Fanque.'

NOTES
- Ralph Allen (1693–1764), the postmaster general in Bath in the early eighteenth century, became one of England's richest men by acquiring licences to deliver post from London to the regions. He subsequently acquired quarries around Bath and made a second fortune selling the stone used in the construction of Bath's Georgian buildings.
- My uncle has Gaia draw a link between the Slavery Abolition Act 1833 and The Poor Law of 1834. The first entailed a huge cost to the government; the second was an act of economic austerity. There may well have been a link. To

compensate slave-owners for their loss of 'property', the government raised a £20 million loan—£22 billion in today's money—which was equivalent to 40% of the government's annual budget. So great was the loan that it was not fully repaid until 2015.

CHAPTER VII

The Perfect Setting

IT HAD NOT taken long for the windows of Belle Nash's new home in Sydney Buildings to be opened, the rooms aired and the stove lit. Lucius Lush had been a marvel gathering the dustsheets, William Darby had carried furniture hither and thither, whilst the maid from Somerset Place had scrubbed clean every pan in the kitchen.

This had left Belle free to reacquaint himself with his collection of *Königliche* porcelain. He had picked up each beloved piece, holding it to the light, remembering the detail of every design, from the soft brush strokes of the Rococo to the firm lines of more recent Neo-Classical tastes.

Although the house was not as grand as that of Gay Street, it was by no means modest. Large sash windows looked over the waters of the Kennet & Avon Canal beyond to the river, the abbey and the city. At a distance, on a far hill, Belle could just make out the home of Gaia Champion on Somerset Place.

In the drawing room, Belle had William align each piece of furniture with his memories of Gay Street. And what memories they were! The rosewood table on which he would arrange plates of cake and finger sandwiches; and the gilt-framed mirror oft used by his previous companion, Gerhardt Kant who, above all else, loved to be reminded of his own reflection. Indeed, for a second, Belle had imagined the face of Gerhardt in the glass.

Once all was in order, Gaia's maid had been sent home and the three men had shared a bottle of port, toasting their domestic achievements. It was only once Master Lush had bade farewell, and the stars started to shine in the clear night sky, that Belle finally experienced the longed-for moment: a night in Bath, in his own bed, with his body entwined with that of …

Of whom?

As William slept between the sheets in the moonlight, Belle studied the man beside him. In that halfway state between sleep and consciousness, he believed that he was with Pablo Fanque, that the trauma of being forced apart six months earlier had been a dream and that love, as the saying goes, had triumphed.

It was with this thought that he fell asleep.

The next morning the two men woke invigorated and within an hour were walking into the city to secure breakfast. Belle led the way, taking them across the canal and past the allotments of Bathwick Hill towards the river.

'Tha' lov'st Baath, roight enough,' said William, staring at Belle. 'Oi've ne'er seen a man so happy.'

Belle had a bounce in his step and replied with a broad smile.

'This is one of the best days of my life, William. To be in Bath, in the bright sunlight of early December, with the beautiful surroundings of its hills—and to be here with you, introducing you to my friends. Truly, it's perfection.'

William laughed.

'Perfection, tha' say'st? That's not what oi'd call moy introduction to Miss Prim yesterday. Thur poor lass fainted full away.'

It had, indeed, been a moment of high drama, but nothing that a bottle of smelling salts hastily dispensed by Gaia could not cure.

'She soon recovered,' said Belle. 'She always does.'

William, however, was alert to other risks.

'Without wantin' to alarm 'ee, Mr … Belle … not all tha' friends will accept so readily tha' story that oi's Pablo Fanque from Grenada. Oi comes from the Fens, not from Mount Gay. Mrs Champion looked roight curious. As well she moight.'

Belle nodded. Gaia had indeed been suspicious.

'Then we must work the harder. The truth must not come out.'

William remained unconvinced and Belle noticed his companion dragging his feet as they entered the floodplain.

Belle asked, 'Is it shame that you feel? Tell me. You are plainly ill at ease.'

An eyebrow was raised.

'Shame. From what cause?'

'From the pretence of being another man. Or is it the name—Pablo Fanque?'

'There's many a circus artist what's taken a fancy name, Sir, so oi 'as no complaints in that regard. And "Pablo Fanque" has a pleasin' ring to it. Oi loikes the name.'

Approaching the river, they turned right towards Pulteney Bridge. On the far bank loomed the east front of the abbey.

'I shall do everything to assist you, William, in your endeavour,' said Belle, trying to encourage his companion. 'This morning we will inspect sites for your circus—but first, let us purchase a slice of breakfast pie from Mrs Crust.'

The man from Norfolk licked his lips.

'That sounds loike a capital idea.'

'Also, William, do not forget that we are in consort and that, so far as the world is concerned, we are cousins, to boot. Remember that.'

William laughed and shook his head.

'Tha' and oi, cousins! There's none so queer as folk. Ha! Oi never knew the meanin' of that phrase before, but oi does now!'

F OR ANYONE LOOKING for excellence in West Country food, Mrs Crust's Pie Shop was to pies what Sally Lunn's Tearooms was to buns. Quite simply, none made a pie as fine as Mrs Crust. Among her choice ingredients she selected venison from Dyrham Park and wild garlic from Rainbow Wood on Widcombe Hill. She also understood that the pastry of a pie is as important as the filling and made her famous shortcrust with proper beef dripping.

With Mrs Crust there were no half-measures, either in her work or her conversation. She had baked at length for the seasonal influx of visitors, trade had been brisk and she now had a rich seam of gossip. By the time Belle opened the door to her shop, Mrs Crust already knew that he had returned to Bath in the company of a Caribbean relative.

'Why Mr Nash, I do behold it's you,' she declared as he entered the premises. 'And this is your cousin who I'm told comes from an island a little to the south-west of the Bristol Channel.'

Belle opened his arms in delight.

'Dear Mrs Crust, it is good to see you after all this time. And, yes, this is Mr Pablo Fanque from Grenada, who is my cousin no less. Pablo, please say hello to unarguably the most important person in Bath, and author of the best pies in Somerset.'

William bowed and Mrs Crust blushed, and Belle noticed that he had despatched his lie with greater confidence than with Gaia.

'We've missed your wit, Mr Nash. And your custom. Both are welcome back in our fair city.'

In response, Belle leant forwards and studied the impressive array of pies, admiring their warm tones of golden brown and the sweet fragrance that filled the shop.

'Your welcome is my principal joy, Mrs Crust, but I can see that others have become as devoted to your wares as was I before my absence. As fair Hestia is my witness, your pies are so agreeable, they sell themselves. For many a visitor to Bath, your shop is their first port of call and I surmise that shrewd Mercury has smiled on your enterprise.'

Mrs Crust enjoyed a compliment as much as she did a wholesome meal, and she beamed with pride.

'We have seen a fair number of luminaries enter these portals, that's true enough, though not Mr Mercury. But I hear word that Viscount Melbourne is in the city again.'

78

'Willy Lamb?' smiled Belle. 'A base fellow, indeed; I never condemned Lady Caroline for her treatment of him. I might have done the same myself. And is he still home secretary?'

'Sir, he is our prime minister!'

'No!' gasped Belle. 'Then these are ill times. But, Madam, if he is a frequenter of your fine establishment, I must try to forgive him for his other lapses!'

The proprietrix of pies laughed.

'I won't. Not on certain matters anyways. He came by the shop last year and, if my memory serve me right, bought a slice of apple pie. I told him, "Buy a second slice and you'd have my vote, if women were allowed it!"'

Mrs Crust was never one for holding back.

'And what did he reply?'

'He paid me for the pie, left faster than a jackrabbit and hasn't been back since. I'm not sure he appreciates a lady with an opinion.'

'Nor any what seek freedom from oppression,' added William, entering the conversation.

Mrs Crust shook her head.

'No, Sir, not like the actor that everyone's been talking about who's at the Theatre Royal for the Season. The handsome one with the deep voice. He comes in here like clockwork at ten each morning. Fair likes my chicken pie, that one does.'

Belle was behind on the theatrical news.

'In the name of Dionysus, of whom do you speak?'

'You know, Sir, the famous one who's been in the papers.'

Belle tried to remember the names of renowned actors.

'William Macready?'

Mrs Crust shook her head.

'Not Macready, though he was here a couple of years back. Now he's a one for pigeon pie, he is. No, the one I'm talking about is the American fellow who's been causing a stir. He kissed what's-her-name on stage.'

79

Belle looked blank and was helped by William, who whispered a name in his ear.

'Desdemona?' Belle repeated, looking at William in surprise.

The pie-maker nodded.

'That's the lass. She gets around, they say. Kissing a man on the stage! Where will it end? But what is the actor's name? Oh, if it isn't right on the tip of my tongue. The young ladies don't stop talking about him. He's like ... .' She stumbled. 'Like your cousin, there, Mr Nash. A gentleman of ... you know ... .'

At which point William intervened.

'Oi've heard of that actor that tha' mention'st, Mrs Crust: Mr Oira Aldridge. He come from New York City, though his family, loike moy own, originates from Africa.'

It was Belle's turn to blush.

'I am all ignorance,' he stuttered. 'Forgive me, Mrs Crust. I have been away these past four years and Mr Aldridge's name has not been conveyed to my attention.'

Though true, it was a poor excuse and he immediately cursed himself for it.

'But your cousin's been away his whole life,' Mrs Crust pointed out, 'and he knew him.'

William laughed.

'Oi does,' he replied. Then, seeing Belle's befuddlement, he explained. 'Mr Aldridge played Othello in London laast year and caused a roight stir. He decoided to follow Shakespeare's script to thur letter and kiss fair-skinned Desdemona. It caused such a scandal, the company had to close the run!'

Mrs Crust clapped her hands.

'That's right,' she said excitedly. 'Can you believe it? Not the kissing, I mean. There's nothing wrong with a good kiss. But the kiss of an African gentleman! I wish I were that lucky! There's too many ignorant people in this world, that's my opinion—which, come to think of it, was what I told Viscount Melbourne last year, for he was not a friend of abolition, if I might be so bold. But unlike Mr Nash here, you seem knowledgeable about our goings-on, Mr Fanque. If you don't mind my asking, how come you knows so much when you've been a-living on that island of yours?'

It was a good question and one that put Belle on edge. William had been right to suggest that others would question the pretence that he was from Grenada. It was to their good fortune that William kept his composure.

'Oi 'as the honour to be in a similar line of work, Ma'am. Not an actor loike Mr Aldridge, for there's no theatre in Grenada, but, believe it or not, we'd a circus on the island with acrobats, jugglers and 'osses. Oi 'elped run it and oi got to hear news of the world of en'ertainment from travelling performers. There's few what don't enjoy the sharin' of whispers.'

'Well, I never,' replied Mrs Crust.

'Indeed,' said Belle, glad to embrace the untruth.

'And tis moy intention,' declared William, making the most of the opportunity, 'with the help of Cousin Belle 'ere, shortly to bring a circus to this fair city of Baath.'

Mrs Crust clapped her hands again.

'That sounds a wonderful idea, Mr Fanque. A circus! We've not had one of those in years. Oh, Mr Nash, you are full of surprises. You've been back less than a day and already you're planning an extravaganza. And what a nice man your cousin is. Now that we have met, I can see the family resemblance. You're two peas of the same Nash pod, you are. I can't wait to tell the rest of my customers that a circus is coming to Bath, in faith I can't.'

AFTER LEAVING THE pie shop, Belle and William had taken advantage of a bench in Queen Square to eat their pie, after which Belle honoured his promise to walk William round possible sites for the circus. They set off first to Royal Victoria Park, which on first inspection seemed the most obvious location, with its large central meadow flanked by an arboretum and ornamental ponds.

'This is one of three locations I have in mind,' said Belle. 'What do you think?'

William, however, was unconvinced. To his more experienced eye, the park had its disadvantages.

'It's a fair distance from people's homes and the paths at night will be dark, especially now winter is comin'. People are afraid of the dark. One bad incident and the circus would face ruin.'

'That's true,' Belle concurred. 'And at present there's a city ordinance that bars entry to the park after dusk.'

It was an ordinance that Belle knew only too well, its having been the cause of his arrest four years earlier. Not that he had even been in the park; he had been in Gay Street in bed!

The guilty parties had been his then companion Gerhardt Kant, who had been introducing Master Lush to the night-time pleasures of the arboretum. To save the clerk, Belle had declared in court that it was he, not Master Lush, who had been with Herr Kant. Gaia had then found the two of them guilty of collecting illicit soil samples, thus allowing both to escape the more serious charge: carnal relations between men, then punishable by hanging.

But Royal Victoria Park was not Belle's first choice. In truth, he had only shown it to William so that his new companion could better understand the geography of the city, and to provide a contrast to the next two locations.

'One down, two to go, then,' said Belle. 'Let us continue.'

They exited the park and emerged at the western end of Bath's most famous street, the Royal Crescent.

'And here is my second choice.'

Like many a first-time visitor, William stopped and gasped in amazement at the grand sweep of John Wood the Younger's design, the façade of the immense houses and their huge Ionic columns climbing high into the sky.

'Oi'd heard that Baath was beautiful,' William marvelled, 'but this is top drawer, roight enough.'

'The Royal Crescent is a wonder to behold,' Belle agreed. 'But what do you think of its grassy parkland?'

Below the houses lay a semi-spherical lawn that adjoined a widening field on which sheep grazed. The two were divided by a ha-ha, a near invisible ditch that ran below the eyeline and kept the sheep from invading the lawn. It was a ditch into which many a night-time reveller, and not a few sheep, had fallen. William inspected the lawn, then shook his head disconsolately.

'In moy estimation, Belle, the tent would fit the curve of the crescent. Problem is, the ground slopes. See, a circus needs flat ground for th'acrobats and 'osses to perform. We'd have to level it, and oi don't imagine the residents would welcome that.'

'Oh dear,' Belle sighed. 'That strikes two from the list. I'm not sure my third proposal will fare any better.'

They walked the length of the crescent, looking out across the valley southwards toward the dizzying heights of Beechen Cliff and westwards to the stately home of Prior Park. The landscape could hardly have been better imagined by that illustrious artist John Constable. It was no wonder that Bath was celebrated.

Leaving the Royal Crescent, they entered Brock Street, where a few days earlier Master Lush had been gathering information for his forthcoming social almanac.

'How far is the third site?' asked William.

'No distance at all. But let us curb our hopes for all I have left is the poor relative to the former two.'

Belle pointed to the far end of Brock Street. William looked up and an expression of intrigue crossed his face.

'More magnificent 'ouses,' he said.

'As you would expect,' agreed Belle, with a yawn, seeking to underplay his careful orchestration of their stroll. 'They come thirteen to the dozen, do they not? Typical of Bath. Quite dull in some regard.'

There was, however, nothing typical or dull in what William saw, even if the distance only afforded him a partial view. His pace quickened, his hand breaking from Belle's as he moved down Brock Street, his excitement growing by the yard as more and more of The Circus came into view.

From a distance, Belle said casually, 'The houses form a perfect circle around a considerable lawn. But is it large enough to site a tent? In that question, Sir, I cannot venture an opinion. I can only advise that a short distance away, on the far side of the lawn, are the Assembly Rooms, where the foremost of Bath's visitors go each night to gamble, dine and dance.'

William had now reached The Circus and within an instant was dancing a jig, spinning around in delight, overcome by joy.

'Belle, Sir, Mr Nash! Cousin! It's roight perfick!'

Smiling after his great reveal, Belle advanced to the end of Brock Street and crossed the road to join William.

Thrilled, the younger man asked, 'This ... this ... I wants to call it a square but it's not. It's a circle—a wonderful, perfick circle! Dear friend, what name dost tha' give this place?'

Belle laughed.

'In that regard, Mr Darby, or Cousin Pancho as I should say, it is even more fortuitous than Archimedes might have conceived. It is called The Circus.'

William's mouth dropped open.

'This is a joke, Sir.'

'Not at all, my friend. It really is called The Circus.'

William could no longer contain his emotions. He could see the future: a circus within The Circus, the great tent standing proud, the crowds jubilant as they watch tightrope artists and clowns performing, and all under his leadership and direction.

'Tis meant to be,' he cried. 'Never will a circus have a more perfick setting. Oi'll bring to the citizens of Baath entertainments beyond their imagination: oi'll give 'em the greatest acts on Earth, whether they deserve them or not. They'll get hoss-dancin' and acrobats and jugglin' and toight-ropes. Today, Cousin Belle, "Pablo Fanque's Circus" is born!'

Overwhelmed with joy, William took hold of Belle and hugged him close.

And with that hug, Belle's landscape changed. The Palladian architecture of Bath was replaced by the palm trees of the Spice Isle, the rooks and pigeons of Somerset by the parrots and cockatoos of Grand Anse Beach. And there he was in the arms of the man he loved—Pablo Fanque—their cheeks together, the hot sun warming their souls, two hearts beating as one.

Free, at last, of the torment they had witnessed. Of the chains ... the beatings ... the shackles ... and the blood.

THE ARCHITECT JOHN Wood described houses of The Circus as built for 'the elegant, the civilised and the deserving'.

They were not words that obviously described the brooding figure whose bulky form looked out from a first-floor window at Number 33. Splayed legs extended from wide hips. Matching the barrelled torso was a pumpkin-sized head topped by a mass of dishevelled hair. As he surveyed the lawn with sullen eyes, he growled, then shouted a command.

'Mrs Neech! Here! Now!'

Behind him, the figure of the cold-blooded housekeeper emerged from a dark corridor.

'Yes, Your Lordship. I am here.'

As throughout his life, the ugly narcissist desired an audience.

'It's an outrage. Yesterday we learnt that a blackamoor actor is to be our neighbour for the Season. And now in full public view here's a Negro fellow and an Englishman hugging each other. I warned that Christian decency would be injured if slavery was abolished. That the delicate morals of English society would be put at risk if the races were allowed to mix. Now see my words materialise before us.'

Mrs Neech moved forward and looked through the window.

'Disgusting, My Lord,' she said, sharing his distaste at the sight of William and Belle. 'A complaint should be raised with the city magistrate. It should be against the law.'

Lord Servitude turned to the housekeeper.

'You sing my song to the note, Mrs Neech. Let me consult my son, the Hon. Cecil. Call him for me.'

Mrs Neech nodded, but then raised her head to the floors above.

'Yes, My Lord. I would. But the Hon. Cecil is currently with the maid that he brought from Jamaica. She has been locked in her room—the one with the barred windows—whilst he reminds her of the bedchamber duties that she is expected to perform at his command.'

Lord Servitude smirked.

'Is that so?' he said. 'I thought I heard a whimper from above. After the long sea journey, the young man deserves his pleasure. And there's nothing that stirs the soul more than the sound of a plantation maid whimpering. Ha! That's true, Mrs Neech, isn't it?'

The housekeeper nodded and turned to depart, to wait in the corridor until called on once more.

'Yes, My Lord. No finer sound. From her and all her kind.'

NOTES
- The two most famous British actor-managers of the early nineteenth century were William Macready (1793–1873) and Edmund Keane (1787–1833). Ira Aldridge (1807–1867), however, surpassed them as an actor of international renown. He filled theatre houses in North America, Britain (including London, Edinburgh and Bath), Ireland, Prussia and Russia.
- William Lamb, 2nd Viscount Melbourne (1779–1848), served as private secretary to the young Queen Victoria but was involved in various political scandals. His first term as prime minister was brought to an end after only four months

by King William IV though he served for another six years after being reappointed five months later. He was a dedicated opponent of the abolition of slavery, which he called 'a great folly', and became a focus of public ridicule when news of his wife's affair with Lord Byron, the poet, became known in 1812.

CHAPTER VIII
The Tea Party

TWO DAYS LATER, Belle Nash was in a state of high tension. In the drawing room at Sydney Buildings, William Darby and Lucius Lush had been busily preparing his 'welcome home' tea party and had only just laid out the finger sandwiches, cakes and biscuits when Belle requested that they remove all the plates so that he could polish the rosewood table one more time.

'I cannot risk giving Lady Passmore of Tewkesbury Manor any reason to complain. She may be furious that I have not paid a visit to her since my return. Dust on the table would make matters infinitely worse.'

After an application of beeswax, Belle agreed to sit down and stop fussing, much to the two younger men's relief. As the tea party had approached, his state of agitation had worsened. He had made outrageous complaints about the cutting of the sandwiches, which he considered insufficiently precise, and insisted on sticking knives into the cakes to test their texture. Now, at last, he was quiet, a man absorbed in thought, his head turned to a window but his mind looking entirely inwards.

He had been away from Bath, he reminded himself again, for four years and much had changed. New buildings had risen up, of course, but people he knew had slumped. The gravity of time had inevitably expanded waistlines, pulled eyelids lower and nurtured liver spots on the once fine faces of old acquaintances.

Having not seen Lady Passmore or Mrs Pomeroy for so long,

he feared that they might no longer know or trust him—in short, that they might consider him an imposter to his old self. And what if Lady Passmore found the new Belle unamusing? The thought filled him with dread and he wiped his brow with a kerchief.

Rising to his feet, he crossed to the gilt mirror that hung between the two windows of the drawing room and inspected his cravat. Here, at least, there was no fault: cravats were ageless and would always be in fashion, as long as they were well tied and secured with a jewelled pin. Then his eyes moved to Master Lush who, behind his shoulder, was manoeuvring a cake upon its central axis, judging that it might be better presented when rotated between eighty-four and eighty-five degrees.

'What do you think, Sir?' the younger man asked. 'Lady Passmore will notice if it's not exactly right.'

Belle crossed to the table to inspect the cake.

'The end result is perfect, Lucy, but I fear that you erred in one respect. It is well established that cakes may only be rotated clockwise, in like manner as the passing of the port bottle.'

'Is that so?'

Master Lush was hesitant. Belle nodded solemnly.

'As decreed by the goddess Fornax. But question Lady Passmore on the matter when she arrives, if you wish. Now, where has dear Pablo gone?'

Master Lush corrected his *faux pas* by rotating the cake 360 degrees to the right, noting, having done so, that it now seemed identical in every detail to its previous aspect.

'Mr Fanque is in the kitchen, checking that the water is on the boil,' the clerk said. 'He seems remarkably relaxed at meeting Lady Passmore but I suppose he has never met her!'

The remnants of blood drained from Belle's face.

'And she has never met him, more to the point,' he said, before checking his fob watch. 'There could be fireworks. Oh dear. Ten minutes to go. If I guess right, the ladies should be entering their carriage at this moment.'

89

B Y TRADITION, GAIA Champion, Lady Passmore, Mrs Pomeroy and Phyllis Prim always travelled together by carriage
when all had been invited to a social gathering. It allowed
them to enter the mood of the event before arriving at their
destination. It was clear, however, that as they collected in the
hallway of Number 24 Somerset Place, the mood for this
particular tea party would be far from convivial.

Belle had good reason to feel nervous, for Lady Passmore
nursed an excessive belief in her own eminence and took offence
at any hint of a slight.

'It is simply unacceptable behaviour by Mr Nash,' she stated to
the assembled company. 'It has taken him three full days to invite
us to tea. It is no way to treat friends. It is what comes from living
on the wrong side of the river.'

'Lady Passmore of Tewkesbury,' started Gaia, ' you are unfair,
Madam. I have already explained ... '

'We have all heard your explanation, Mrs Champion,' ranted
her ladyship. 'That Mr Nash required time to open the house and
to settle in his cousin. All of which would be good and true were it
not for the fact that he has found the time to gallivant. Chatting to
Mrs Crust. Taking a walk in Royal Victoria Park. Dancing a waltz,
by all accounts, in The Circus. We've heard the gossip before
we've seen the man.'

Gaia tried to douse the fire of Lady Passmore's ire.

'And why should he not do such things?'

'Yes, why shouldn't he, Lady Passmore of Tewkesbury Manor?'
Mrs Pomeroy added. 'I'd love to dance a waltz if someone should
invite me.'

Gaia was grateful that Mrs Pomeroy had come to her aid but
her efforts to douse the fire were fruitless.

'Because you and I are his friends!' beseeched Lady Passmore.
'Mr Nash stopped by Guildhall to greet Mrs Champion, where he
chanced on Miss Prim. But what about us? We should have been
seen first, being senior in rank. Really, after just four years in the

Caribbean, he seems to have forgotten his manners. I shall have to have strong words with him this afternoon.'

Exasperated, Gaia signalled for the front door to be opened. Their departure could not be delayed any longer.

'Please don't, Lady Passmore of Tewkesbury Manor. Lecturing Belle at his own tea party would be an unkindness. He has not meant to cause offence and it will give the wrong impression of us to his cousin, Mr Fanque.'

The mention of Belle's companion further riled Lady Passmore.

'The wrong impression! And who is this Mr Fanque? The Crown Prince of the Colonies?'

Gaia reluctantly led Lady Passmore out of the house, leaving Mrs Pomeroy and Miss Prim to follow at a distance; if the big beasts were to fight, the smaller creatures of the forest could at least enjoy their own company.

Mrs Pomeroy whispered to Miss Prim, 'I confess, I am looking forward to seeing the cousin. I imagine he must be like Herr Gerhardt Kant. As cousins, they are all members of the same family, are they not? Tell me, is he terribly handsome?'

Miss Prim dithered.

'I barely saw him before I fainted,' she replied. Then, thinking of the powdered wigs beloved by Belle's Prussian cousin, she added, 'he looked less like a sheep than Herr Kant.'

They stepped onto the wide pavement of Somerset Place, where Gaia's splendid carriage awaited them.

'I do hope Lady Passmore doesn't make a scene,' said Mrs Pomeroy. 'If she does, we will have to find a distraction. Whist, perhaps.'

Unexpectedly, Miss Prim took hold of Mrs Pomeroy's hand and held her back. The mention of whist had triggered a deepening need. The spinster's other hand gripped her ever-present knitting bag with vice-like rigour.

'Yes, we must play whist,' she pled. 'Even though Lady Passmore may object, it would be so refreshing to have a game. Will you ask Mr Nash? I am sure he'll agree.'

MRS POMEROY EXCELLED at performing more than one task at a time: most notably, she could eat a slice of cake and an éclair simultaneously, without any effort at all. On arrival, she duly asked Belle whether they might play whist whilst blushing at the sight of William. The cousin from Grenada was indeed handsome to her eye.

Keen to please, Belle agreed to play cards, only to find Lady Passmore objecting in the strongest possible terms. Though he retracted the offer at once, all was lost, and what could have been a joyful reunion of friends soon started to resemble a Wesleyean prayer service.

Miss Prim withdrew into her shell and said barely a word. William poured tea and Master Lush passed round plates of food, but gone were the light-hearted quips of old. Instead, the guests sat looking at each other as pugilists do, waiting for the bell.

Ting-a-ling-a-ling.

Once cakes had been eaten and tea sipped, Belle followed tradition by standing to welcome his guests.

He said, with faltering levity, 'Of all the things that I missed most in my time far away in the shadow of the Americas, it was our tea parties. Ladies, permit me to perform the role of Philophrosyne, sister of Euthenia, Eupheme and Eucleia and goddess of hospitality, by welcoming you to my new home at Sydney Buildings. With your presence this becomes, indeed, a home—for a home is not a home without honoured guests.'

The laudable statement, however, did not satisfy Lady Passmore, who made clear her displeasure at the tardy nature of the event.

'It is, of course, our privilege to be received by you, Mr Nash —latterly of Gay Street—and to meet Mr Fanque, whom we understand is latterly of another Gay Street, or of Mount Gay, or places thereabouts, and who has been the talk of the city these past days. How extraordinary it must have been to discover that you possessed a cousin in Grenada, Mr Nash.'

Belle suppressed the urge to panic and placed his trust in the thin fabric of his deceit.

'Indeed, Lady Passmore of Tewkesbury Manor. Although no more extraordinary than for Mr Fanque to find that he had a cousin in me—ha ha!'

William attempted a smile. His loyalty to Belle was once again being tested.

'Tis a surproise indeed,' he agreed. 'But a pleasant enough one, of course, to find that oi be a part of the Nash family.'

Everyone sipped their tea, hoping that the thunder of the Tewkesbury storm had passed. It had not.

On rolled the clouds of Lady Passmore's grumbling. 'And in what way, Mr Nash, is Mr Fanque related to you and to your nephew Herr Gerhardt Kant? I see from observation that they are not siblings; nor do they share accents: one Germanic, the other strangely of the Broads.'

'I was wondering the same,' said Mrs Pomeroy unhelpfully. 'Perhaps you have the answer, Mr Fanque?'

William most certainly did not and, with a gesture, passed the question back to Belle, who thought, 'If I am by necessity to lie, I must do so with a straight face.'

With as much confidence as he could muster, he said, 'Different sides of the family. Gerhardt was my late older sister's first child from her late first husband. Pablo is my late mother's late brother's first wife's child from a romantic liaison with Pablo's father. Both late.'

Lady Passmore huffed.

'People have a habit of dying in the Nash family. It's a wonder, Mr Nash, that you're still with us.'

Belle nodded solemnly, whilst wondering if Odysseus had ever been thus challenged.

'Indeed, Your Ladyship. The Nashes have had more casualties than Pompeii and our mausoleum overfloweth. But enough of my miserable *familia* for a day. We have fine food to enjoy. Another slice of cake, perchance?'

The offer provided a respite and Master Lush did the honours.

'Not for me, Master Lush,' responded Miss Prim weakly. 'I have already enjoyed half a slice and am thus quite full.'

By contrast, Mrs Pomeroy's side plate was empty.

'The filling of strawberry jam is delightful,' she commented, taking two pieces.

Master Lush then nervously approached Lady Passmore.

'More cake, Lady Passmore of Tewkesbury Manor? You have no reason to fear, for the cake was rotated clockwise.'

Lady Passmore gave the young man a stern stare of the utmost disapproval.

'You've clearly lost your wits,' she said, waving the plate away. 'Although we knew that already, given the hare-brained almanac you're compiling. By what title does it go, again?'

Master Lush's bottom lip quivered.

'Families Resident in the Royal City of Bath for ... '

'Resident!' interrupted Lady Passmore. 'Since when have the Season's visitors been residents, I ask you? They are visitors, Sir, and you are visiting an oxymoron on us, if ever I've heard one.'

Visibly upset at the comment, Master Lush did well not to tip the remaining cake into Lady Passmore's lap. Unsettled by her clerk's distress, Gaia spoke up on his behalf.

'You are in the wrong, Lady Passmore of Tewkesbury Manor. I, for one, believe the almanac will last for many years. Master Lush, when are we to expect publication of *Families Resident in ...* erm ... ?'

Master Lush had turned away from Lady Passmore with tears in his eyes.

'Tomorrow, Ma'am. The printer has assured me that the first copies will be ready in the morning.'

'I shall undoubtedly subscribe to a copy,' Belle offered promptly. 'I have no doubt that it will prove an essential guide.'

The almanac's most avid supporter, Mrs Pomeroy, did her best to swallow her piece of cake. She, too, wished to add her support.

'Sho shwall I,' she added, trying not to spit out jam-laden crumbs. 'I cwan't wait to shee my name in pwint alongfide that off the pwime minishter.'

Lady Passmore decided to test the depth of opposition by sounding out William.

'What about you, Mr Fanque? Would you be so kind as to share with us your view of Master Lush's strange enterprise?'

The room fell silent. A weak man would have panicked but William was not a weak man. Indeed, having spent the last twenty minutes in the ladies' company, he felt he had got the measure of them. And whilst Lady Passmore was certainly as intimidating as a circus lion, William was used to holding his nerve. Having suddenly become the focus of the room's attention, he made use of the opportunity. After all, he had his circus to promote.

He placed his teacup on a side table and spoke with clarity.

'T'would be moy privilege, Lady Passmewre of Tewkesbury Manor, to be granted an opinion, having lived moy early loife as a slave with no opinion thought worthy of askin'. Now, 'avin' won moy freedom, oi embrace th'opportunity to vent me thoughts and to know that they counts for almost as much as those of moy former masters. Indeed, if oi should one day earn sufficient to acquoire a property, oi will then also have earnt the roight to vote, and be able to exercoise moy opinion on matters of state—a roight yet denoied to them of the fairer sex, regardless of toitle.'

The room fell silent, teacups in limbo.

William continued, 'Oi aint yet seen Maaster Lush's book, moind. Whoilst oi must, therefore, withhold comment on its contents, oi wholeheartedly applauds th'endeavour, which oi hopes will also be tha' response when oi brings moy own fair enterprise to Baath.'

The ladies looked at each other.

'Another enterprise?' squeaked Mrs Pomeroy.

'Oooah,' whimpered Miss Prim.

William nodded.

'Cousin Belle, please share with these 'ere ladies what oi did back in Grenada—and what, with tha' help, oi'll shortly be doing in this 'ere city.'

Heads turned to Belle, who coughed in the hope of buying time, fiddled with his cravat and then adjusted his sleeves, very slowly. But there was no avoiding the need to provide an answer.

'Yes, of course. I had forgotten that the ladies were unaware. How foolish of me—ha ha! My cousin Pablo ... well ... as it happens, he ran a circus on the island. And a jolly good circus at that.'

The ladies were bewildered, for none had ever heard of a circus in the West Indies before.

'A "circus"?' squawked Lady Passmore. 'Like a Roman circus, with chariot races and gladiators and the killing of barbarians? My apologies, Mr Fanque, if I speak plain.'

'Are you certain?' asked Mrs Pomeroy. 'I would never have thought ... '

'Not a Roman circus, Ma'am,' said Belle, drinking ever deeper from fantasy's trough. 'An African circus, part of a nomadic tradition that crossed the oceans with the slave ships.'

'On those terrible ships?' asked Gaia. 'It sounds most unlikely.'

'Yet true,' Belle insisted. 'Like so much of African history, it is largely unrecognised by us Europeans but kept brilliantly alive by Pablo in honour of his ancestors. It runs in his blood, so much so that he wishes to bring such a circus to our own city. And, indeed, he will—within the month.'

'Within the month?' asked a disbelieving Lady Passmore. 'Is yours to be a one-man act in the Assembly Rooms? How novel.'

William held his nerve.

'Not at all, Lady Passmewre of Tewkesbury Manor. Moy circus

will 'ave dancing 'osses, toight-rope walkers, clowns and a human spoider.'

'"A human spider"?' repeated Lady Passmore. 'He sounds quite repellent. Will he have eight legs and ooze slime?'

'Oi 'ave written to circus performers all across England,' William persisted, 'and together we shall raise a tent in Baath.'

Silence returned. The introduction of William as Belle's new companion had been surprising enough. That he was to erect a circus tent and fill it with jugglers, equestrian displays and dare-devil artists seemed neither inviting nor respectable.

It was Gaia who spoke next, not with disapproval but with a tone of caution. She knew Belle well and, in her heart, sensed that something was awry.

'It sounds terribly exciting, Mr Fanque. But forgive me for asking: do you have permission for the circus? As I am sure Belle has told you, entertainment for the Season is subject to approval by the City Corporation. At this late date, a public notice will be required too. There is a process for such things.'

As it happened, Belle had not mentioned any such requirement, leading William to give his newfound relative a disbelieving look. Gaia caught it, fixed her attention on Belle and motioned him to the door.

Belle gulped.

'More hot water for the tea? Excuse me whilst I locate the kitchen.'

'Let me help you,' responded Gaia, rising. 'If you would excuse us, for a moment.'

In the hallway, Belle fidgeted from one foot to the next.

'It's all going rather well, I think,' he said, looking furtively back at Gaia.

'You know it's not,' Gaia snapped back. 'It could only be worse if you had invited Mr Quigley to play his violin. As he grows older, he is starting to sound like a jackdaw. You, meanwhile, are starting to sound like a jackass.'

Belle had forgotten how fearsome Gaia could be.

'You don't think it's going well?'

'What on Earth are you up to? You have hardly stepped ashore and you're already cooking up trouble. An African circus? In Bath? Have you lost your mind, Belle?'

Belle tried to stand tall.

'Pablo is a wonderfully skilled performer. He rides horses, you know. Four at a time. Bareback.'

'Bareback? In public? In Bath?' shrieked Gaia. 'Who would be bareback? Mr Fanque or the horses? You risk social outrage. I should have to exile you again.'

Belle blushed at the threat.

'It has been Mr Fanque's dream to bring a circus to Bath for many years and I said that I'd support him. Admittedly, I had not considered the requirements of the City Corporation, but ... '

'I suspect you didn't choose to. You oversaw entertainment for ten years at Guildhall. How could you forget? You'll need permission from the responsible councillor and then pray there are no objections, a prospect I consider highly unlikely. If it ends up in my court for a ruling, I may have to find against you.'

Belle had rarely seen Gaia more agitated.

'But Madam, do you think someone will object?'

'Of course. This is Bath: someone always complains. Where are you thinking of building this circus? Have you found an architect? You can't use Mr John Nash: he died six months ago. Who will design this new colosseum, with its cages for wild animals and channels for the letting of blood? Belle, the city will be up in arms.'

Belle felt the full force of that sinking feeling that so often accompanies the words, 'It seemed like a good idea at the time'.

'Not a colosseum, Ma'am. Just a big tent. I thought we might erect it in The Circus. You see? A circus ... in The Circus! It seemed a good ... '

Gaia raised her hands to her face.

'O Belle! Don't you know who's resident in The Circus this

year? The abominable Lord Servitude and his deplorable son, the Hon. Cecil.'

Belle looked at her aghast.

'Servitude! And his poisonous spawn! But Cecil's in Jamaica.'

Gaia shook her head.

'Like you, Sir, he has returned. And his father is in boisterous mood, forever out for a fight. My advice would be to steer well clear of both of them and, if opposed, concede. Is this ridiculous circus so important?'

Belle took a moment to consider his options. It was true Lord Servitude would be a formidable opponent, but …

'I cannot disappoint my cousin, Ma'am. At the very least, I must do what I can for him. He is a true friend: the Damon to my Pythias. Who in the Corporation oversees entertainment?'

Gaia hid her grimace in a smile.

'The ancient Chairman Camshaft. A goodly man but now confined to bed. The word is that he has lost his mind, though you may recall that it started to go missing long since, and he may soon be dead.'

Belle shook his head. The Fates—Clotho, Lachesis and Atropos—appeared to have changed their allegiance.

'I will go to his house in the morning. With good fortune he will agree. I shall sacrifice bulls and pour libations, and implore good Hermes to intercede and blind the Servitudes to the public notice.'

Gaia sighed. Too often Belle's impulsiveness had been his undoing in life and she did not want the same fate to befall him again—not, at least, so soon after his return.

'Time will tell,' she said. 'For now, return to the drawing room and entertain the guests. I will collect the water from the stove.'

Belle looked despondent as he walked slowly back to the drawing room. Gaia, of course, was right. Entertaining his guests should be his priority. Miss Prim required cheering; she had barely uttered a word since arriving.

But then he stalled. For Gaia was also wrong. If opposed in his ambition to secure the circus for William, he would not concede.

Standing in the corridor, he closed his eyes and whispered, 'Lord Servitude, I have seen what you and your family do—the misery that you inflict—and I know what you are. But you're not in the Caribbean now. You have no army of slavedrivers and whippers here. You're in Bath. And so am I. We shall see who has the upper hand.'

NOTES
- The prudish John Wesley developed a particularly pious form of Protestantism. When Wesley first preached in Bath in 1739, the meeting was interrupted by Belle's grandfather Beau Nash, who declared, 'Your preaching frightens people out of their wits.' Unfortunately for Beau Nash, the congregation sided with their preacher.

CHAPTER IX
Of Fact and Fiction

A T THE END of the tea party, Belle Nash had secured a
further few minutes alone with Gaia Champion whilst the
ladies gathered their cloaks and bags. He wished to learn
more from Gaia about the well-being of Chairman Ernest Camshaft of the City Corporation.

Before his exile to Grenada, Belle had exploited Camshaft's
poor eyesight and enfeebled mind to have Gaia appointed magistrate, a post never held by a woman. Now, it seemed, a further act
of persuasion—if not of outright subterfuge—would be required to
secure the old man's permission for the circus.

'The word in Guildhall is that Chairman Camshaft is bedbound,' Gaia had reiterated, 'and conducts his business between
the sheets.'

'Sounds messy,' Belle had replied. 'I hope he uses a bedpan.'

It was a joke that had lacked an appreciative audience.

'Do you wish for my advice or not?'

'I apologise, Ma'am. Please continue.'

'Like the dear ladies,' Gaia had explained, 'the chairman may
be ignorant of the events that led to your exile—in particular that
you were nowhere near the Royal Victoria Park that dreadful
night. You claimed to be there to save his great-grandson Master
Lush from prosecution. If the chairman knew that, he might look
favourably on Mr Fanque's circus.'

'Well, he might,' Belle had agreed, before his face fell. 'Which reminds me: I was to explain to the ladies over tea that you were not to blame for my banishment. Shall I ... ?'

'Not now, Belle,' Gaia had advised. 'There will be time enough when Lady Passmore is in a more forgiving mood.'

THE NEXT MORNING, Belle assured William that everything would be fine and that they should design, print and circulate posters for the circus without delay. Belle then placed in his satchel a document—a contract of permission for the circus to perform—that he had prepared the previous evening, even whilst knowing that acquisition of the chairman's consent might depend more on chance than guile or goodwill.

'Not, of course, that guile would go amiss,' he thought as he crossed Pulteney Bridge. 'Or a piece of Mrs Crust's pie, come to think of it. Or ... '

He stopped and, to the surprise of onlookers, kicked at a lamppost.

'Do not let yourself be distracted! Not even by Mrs Crust's fine pies,' Belle chided himself. 'For Pablo's sake, you must make this circus happen!'

The walk to the Camshaft residence in Rivers Street—misnamed since it was halfway up a hill—took twenty minutes. At the house, the window shutters were closed but Belle pulled the front doorbell and, after a short wait, the door was opened by a butler.

'Good day to you, Mr Nash, and welcome back to Bath. May I take it that you have come to see Chairman Camshaft?' the servant asked.

Belle smiled for he recalled the butler's name.

'I have indeed, Mr Hoskins,' he said, 'and thank you for your welcome. It is well received.'

The butler bowed.

'Yes, of course, Sir. Chairman Camshaft sometimes speaks of you. Not so much in recent times, however, given his poor health, but let me show you inside.'

Belle stepped into the house and was led by the butler up to a bedchamber. On the way, the rooms he passed were dark and the air inside them still. The clutter of life that one anticipates in a home was all but absent.

'The windows are shuttered tight as a coffin lid,' he thought.

In the bedchamber, an oil lamp provided a light that, though weak, was sufficient for Belle to see. There, in the bed, lay Chairman Camshaft, apparently asleep.

The chairman had always been of slight frame, almost too thin to cast a shadow on a summer's day, but what Belle now saw was a fraction of that man. His face had a sickly pallor; the body beneath the sheets might, on touch, have crumbled into dust. And yet, remarkably, there was evidence of life. With skin so thin as to be translucent, on the old man's neck Belle could see blood weakly pumping through a vein.

The butler positioned a chair by the head of the bed and beckoned Belle to sit. Then, with a graceful bow, he left the room.

Belle stayed silent for a minute, looking at the older man who had for two score years chaired the City Corporation. In his prime, he had been nicknamed the 'Head of State' by Guildhall wags, which struck Belle as apt even now, albeit for a different reason. The bedsheets were drawn up so high that only his head, propped up on three pillows, was visible.

On the top of the head, Belle noted, was a pair of spectacles. Then, almost imperceptibly slowly, the chairman's eyelids opened and a weak voice spoke. It was the voice of a kindly man.

'Who's there? Gentle Sir, oblige me with your name.'

Belle leant towards the bed.

'It is I, Belle Nash, your former colleague and councillor. I have come to wish you well.'

Chairman Camshaft was silent and for a moment Belle feared that mention of his name had prompted no recollection. The nonagenarian's memories, however, simply took time to emerge, rising slowly to the surface.

'Nash, of course I remember you. The Master of Ceremonies. You were quite a dandy. What times we had, eh? The dancing! How we loved to dance.'

Belle smiled.

'That was Beau, my grandfather, Sir. You're remembering when you were a very young man. I am Belle Nash. You may recall that I took charge of Princess Victoria's visit to the city a few years ago.'

The cogs of the chairman's mind moved slowly forward seven decades.

'Belle Nash, of course. How could I forget? Shortly after that visit, you caused a stir with your bachelor ways. Was not my great-grandson Lucius involved? That young man attracts trouble more than he attracts the ladies, I fear.'

Belle attempted a soft laugh.

'I fear that we bachelors often attract trouble. Not that we mean to, of course.'

A small and slightly mischievous smile now cracked across the chairman's face.

He whispered, 'Lean close, Nash. I have a secret to tell.'

Belle obeyed and moved his head to within inches of the old man's lips.

'Here I am, Sir. What is it?'

The chairman whispered, 'Between you and me, I could have been a bachelor myself until I met my wife. I got drunk at a ball and took a shine to one of the Pitts. Nothing came of it, and then soon after I married Audrey. Marvellous woman. Never told her, and neither should you. It's our little secret, dear boy.'

Belle placed a soothing hand on the chairman's bony shoulder.

'You need have no worries on that account, Chairman. I am the very soul of discretion. And how is Mrs Camshaft?'

The chairman's smile deepened.

'Busy as ever. Out walking the dog, I expect.'

Belle laughed as he recalled the name of the Labrador.

104

'General MacCarthy? He's still alive? He was a fine dog.'

The chairman's eyes now burnt bright as candles.

'Still rutting the neighbour's spaniel when he's not here with me,' he said. Then, all of a sudden, to Belle's consternation, Chairman Camshaft started to flip his head from side to side. 'By gad, he's upon me. You're a lively beast. Get down, MacCarthy. Stop licking my face. Stop it, I tell you. I say, Sir, he's a joyful thing.'

Belle looked to the door for assistance but the butler was nowhere to be seen. Unsure of what to do, he made a play of pulling the invisible dog away.

'Sit MacCarthy! Good boy,' Belle exclaimed, which seemed to have the desired effect, and the bedbound head returned to its previous position.

The chairman closed his eyes and his breathing, which had become hurried, calmed.

Then his eyes opened and he called out his wife's name.

'Audrey!'

'Not here, Sir. She's out walking ... '

'Couldn't go on without her, Nash. She's a tower of strength. Gatekeeper and adviser. Knows a charlatan when she sees one. Fine judge of character.'

At that moment, Belle caught sight of himself in a vanity mirror and wondered whether he himself was such a charlatan. He hoped not but what he did not need was Mrs Camshaft challenging him. He decided, therefore, to move to the business at hand.

'I do not wish to impose myself, Sir, but there is a reason for my visit. I have a paper for you to sign regarding entertainment for the Season.'

The chairman screwed up his eyes.

'Rather late in the day, isn't it? The events were signed off weeks ago. The only thing lacking, I recall, was a croquet tournament.'

'Croquet?' Belle said. 'What is that?'

105

'Oh, it's all the rage in Ireland, apparently. Some kind of French game. You swing a mallet between your legs and try to smack your ball into another ball. Perfect sport for bachelors, I imagine, Sir. Come to think of it, perhaps you could organise it.'

Belle stifled a laugh. Though tantalisingly close to death, the chairman's wit remained alive. Then Belle gasped as he realised the opportunity that the chairman's offer presented.

He seized the moment. Reaching into his satchel, he bought out the contract of permission for Pablo Fanque's circus and held it in front of the chairman's face.

'Indeed, we can't let the Season pass without a croquet tournament,' he said, pretending to check the document. 'And by good fortune I have the paperwork to hand. Let me see. Yes, definitely a croquet tournament, and on The Circus too. All it requires is your signature.'

Belle handed over the paper and the chairman squinted at the text.

'Remarkably quick, Nash. Well done,' he opined. Then he asked, 'Can you see my spectacles? I'm forever losing them.'

Belle looked at the eyeglasses on the top of the chairman's head.

'Unfortunately, not,' he lied.

'Have to do without, I suppose. Let's see. The Circus. Yes,' he agreed, as Belle pointed at some of the words while obscuring others with his sleeve. 'That all seems quite in order. Tell Hoskins to bring me a quill and ink. But remember that you must post a public notice. A bore, I know, but you are late in your request and everything must be above board.'

Belle groaned inwardly. Now he did not know whether to give thanks or to curse. On balance, he decided, thanks were in order, if he could get the document signed.

He was about to call the butler when, as if by magic, Hoskins appeared with the necessary equipment. With practised precision, the servant lifted the bedsheet and placed a freshly dipped

106

quill into the chairman's right hand, and a signature was duly scrawled at the bottom of the document.

'There, Sir,' the butler said, handing the document to Belle. 'If your business is concluded, I can see that Chairman Camshaft is tired and in need of rest.'

With gratitude, Belle took the paper.

'Of course.'

Belle would have taken his leave without delay had the old man not held him back.

'Two more minutes with you, Nash. In private,' he ordered. 'Then I can sleep.'

Once more, the butler left the room. Foregoing the chair, Belle now knelt by the bed.

'What is it, Sir?'

Chairman Camshaft took his time as he gathered his words.

'A glass of water, my boy. My mouth is dry. I need moisture on my tongue to speak.'

Belle lifted an adjacent glass of water to the chairman's mouth and helped him drink, then took a flannel and wiped his lips.

'Is that sufficient?'

The chairman nodded and spoke, this time in a more lucid manner than before.

'It is true that my mind comes and goes, along with my eye-sight and my understanding. But one thing I have not forgotten.'

Belle took hold of the old man's hand.

'Which is?'

The eyes of the chairman looked directly into his.

'At your trial, you saved my great-grandson's life by taking the blame for his tomfoolery. It was he who was in the park that night with that Prussian nephew of yours, not you.'

Belle dropped his head. The mystery as to what Chairman Camshaft knew of the event had been answered.

'It matters not,' Belle replied. 'I did the right thing and I have no regrets.'

107

The chairman, however, had more to say.

'It matters to me a great deal. Young Lucius could have hanged for doing no more than I had minded to do with Pitt. As for me, in return for your noble act, I remained silent. And, in so doing, I was wrong.'

Listening to the words, Belle felt a sudden surge of anger.

'It was not you who was wrong, Sir. It is the law.'

The old man shook his head.

'Both. Politicians create the law,' he whispered. For a moment he drifted away. Then, tightening his hold on Belle's hand, he said, 'It has been good to see you, Nash. I wish you well for the future—including whatever it is that I have put my signature to.'

Belle laughed as he rose to his feet. The chairman's mind was evidently not as enfeebled as it appeared. And then Belle shed a tear, for he knew that this was the last time he would see Ernest Camshaft alive. He kissed the old man on the forehead, then retraced his path to the hall, where he was met by the butler.

'Your business is concluded, Sir?'

'Successfully, Hoskins, yes. The chairman has done all in his power to assist. And may I say, I am sorry to have missed Mrs Camshaft on my visit. Please pass on my regards to her. The last few years must have been a terrible burden to her.'

His statement prompted a reaction. Hoskins took a step back and did what butlers do when they have something serious to impart: he stood ever straighter.

'I regret to inform you, Mr Nash, but Mrs Camshaft passed from this world three years ago. The chairman retired to bed shortly after. Her death was the cause of his current malaise.'

The news stunned Belle as he tried—as all mankind must do—to understand the mix of fact and fiction that is the human mind. He could have been there for some time had the butler not opened the front door; it was the air of a cold easterly wind entering the house that brought him back to the present. Blinking into the light of day, man to man he shook the major-domo's hand.

108

'I must go. The chairman commands me to put up a public notice without delay. It is bureaucracy and we must all bow to its demands.' He stepped into the street as he waved farewell. 'I wish you a good life, kind Hoskins.'

'And to you, Mr Nash, Sir,' the butler replied, raising a white-gloved hand in response. 'And to you.'

NOTES

- Brigadier-General Sir Charles MacCarthy (1764–1824) has a place among England's long list of worst military commanders. He met his end in the Gold Coast (modern Ghana) when faced by an Ashanti rebellion. Not only did the Ashanti army not flee after MacCarthy had his band play *God Save The King*, it transpired that his barrels of spare gunpowder contained not powder but macaroni. MacCarthy and his division of 500 men were duly slaughtered.

- My uncle has certainly drifted into fantasy regarding the Pitts. Assuming Ernest Camshaft was born in 1740, he would have been nineteen years older than Pitt the Younger and thirty-two years younger than Pitt the Elder. There is debate as to the younger Pitt's preferences in matters of intimacy. He never married, preferring to dedicate his life to politics, and enjoyed the company of young men. He had a youthful friendship—and an intense falling out—with William Beckford, perhaps the most notorious and wealthiest gay man of the era.

CHAPTER X

The (Dis)Hon. Cecil Servitude

T HIS MORNING, GAIA Champion, though notable for her intellectual clarity, was a woman of unsettled mind. As Belle Nash left Rivers Street after a successful morning's work, she sat in her Guildhall office cogitating. What perturbed her was not the drunken brawl in the street that had upset court proceedings; the foul-mouthed participants had already been arrested and been despatched to Pulteney Gaol for a week. Rather, it was the memory of Belle's little tea party the day before.

After the business of court was concluded, Gaia had given Lucius Lush permission to leave, for he was eager to collect the first copies of *Families Resident in the Royal City of Bath for the Season, Their Children and Other Interests* from the printer. Now free of her clerk, Gaia mulled over the previous afternoon's events. To aid her, she opened a tin of ginger-nut biscuits.

She had no wish to characterise the mood between her friends as one of enmity but there had undeniably been discord among them. And over what? For years, the ladies had paid homage to Belle in his absence: the reading of his letters from Grenada had been the centrepiece of many of their gatherings. Yet now that he had returned, they could not find goodwill.

There were, she decided, two possible explanations. The first was that they were fighting for his attention, like hens for a cockerel, and were perhaps even jealous of his new cousin, Mr Pablo Fanque, to whom Belle was evidently very attached, but such an explanation demeaned them as women. Each had her own motives for behaving as she did, and though these motives might be irrational and unharmonious, they were nonetheless truly felt rather than the product of girlish infatuation. For fie!—the ladies were all in their middle years!

She took another bite at her biscuit.

The second explanation was that Belle's return exposed them to issues that they had habitually avoided in the past and that left them discomforted. Whilst the ladies could tattle until dawn about the foibles of Bath society and the cost of ribbons, there were other topics that they never addressed, preferring even to play whist, with all its accompanying vices.

On the question of slavery, for example, Gaia had read various writings by Olaudah Equiano and Ottobah Cugoano, freed slaves who had arrived in London in the late eighteenth century and gone on to campaign for abolition, writing in the newspapers and giving public talks. Gaia applauded their efforts but the ladies had never discussed the issue of slavery as a group, perhaps on the grounds—nurtured by men—that politics was unfeminine and indelicate. With the arrival of Pablo Fanque on Belle's arm, the ladies had been thrown into a social setting for which they were wholly unprepared.

Having demolished her first ginger-nut biscuit, Gaia reached out for a second.

As a magistrate, being well informed and holding enlightened opinions were both matters of necessity, and she now felt that she should have ensured that her friends were similarly well equipped. After all, in a society where women were denied a public vote, it mattered even more that they were able to develop and express opinions behind the scenes. They might thereby even influence the men who captained the ships of state.

'What one does not discuss, you cannot expect to understand,' she said to herself. 'Oh Gaia: what a fool you have been. One's first duty is to challenge ignorance, not condone it.'

What must Belle have thought of them all? He had battled hard and honourably in Grenada to create a free plantation. He had suffered the threat of death from plantation owners for giving title to the soil that his workers had sweated on.

And, in return, his friends ate cake.

Then she remembered her conversation with Belle the previous day. She had suggested that if Lord Servitude, the worst of the plantation owners, were to protest at Pablo Fanque's circus, then Belle should reconsider his plan. How cowardly she had been!

The more she pondered, however, the less likely it seemed that Belle would heed her advice. He would not bend easily to the likes of Lord Servitude, for her friend would fight to the last for what he believed in.

She bit into a third biscuit.

'You had better be prepared,' she told herself. 'With Belle back, life in Bath is about to get complicated.'

G AIA WAS NOT the only lady that morning with a troubled mind. In a similar state of agitation, although for a very different reason, was Phyllis Prim.

It might seem odd for Miss Prim to be so troubled. Her modest stipend let her live in comfort in a house in Gay Street, that most celebrated of addresses. She was looked after by a cook, Mrs Mulligatawny, and by an often-absent maid named Millicent who liked to spend her time gossiping with other errant maids. Her good fortune, however, did not prevent her from being lonely.

Her family rarely visited Bath. They did not dislike the city but they could not abide Miss Prim's wittering. For the same reason, for ten years she had not been invited to her childhood home of Brandon Hall; her relatives' fear that she might outstay her welcome by a month—or several months—was too great.

In the absence of family, it was knitting that gave her a purpose in life. If a new-born required a shawl, or a gamekeeper a pair of woollen gloves, Miss Prim would knit them.

She was democratic in her approach to her work. Any need for a woollen garment was to be satisfied, regardless of the gender, age, class or race of the recipient. Indeed, needs had been met even when they did not exist, for nothing would stop her rising to challenges, whether real or imaginary. Among Bath's knitting sorority, Miss Prim was famed as 'The Human Metronome' in honour of the consistent and rapid clack-click-clack of her needles, and some wits, whose knowledge of music was limited, suggested that François Couperin and Domenico Scarlatti had composed their harpsichord music with her in mind.

Unfortunately, as the young John Stuart Mill could have advised, the problem with infinite supply is its exorbitant cost.

Whilst her monthly stipend was adequate to cover the running costs of the house, it was insufficient to pay for all the wool she consumed, which this week had produced fifty pairs of bed socks for the House of Bedlam; the expense of last week's jumpers for the chimney sweep and his five siblings had seen to that.

Miss Prim should, of course, have shared her problem with her friends. By keeping it a secret, the burden had become intolerable and had left her badly in debt.

The wool shop she frequented, Mrs Wellow's House of Wool on George Street, had been generous in its credit but charged Miss Prim, who understood little of financial affairs, a usurious rate of interest. Over time, her debt had ballooned and she had needed all her winnings from whist simply to service the penal interest charged by Mrs Wellow. Lady Passmore's disapprobation of cards had now caused this secondary source of income to dry up, leaving Miss Prim in trouble.

Such was her stress and inner turmoil that Miss Prim's mind finally gave way. At the moment when her crisis struck, the dear lady was in the library at the rear of the house, where the morning light was best. Elsewhere in the house, Mrs Mulligatawny was checking the fire grates that the maid Millicent had failed to clean. Attuned to the sounds of the building, the cook suddenly became alert to the fact that the regularity of Miss Prim's knitting needles had suddenly broken down.

Clack, clack. Clickety-clack-clickety. Click click click click click! Clack-click. The metronome, it seemed, had gone awry.

'That's not right. That's not right at all.'

Mrs Mulligatawny gathered up her skirts and hurried to the library. When she entered the room, what she saw exceeded her worst expectations. Miss Prim sat in the corner, perspiration pouring from her brow, her fingers whirring as she produced a garment that only an unhinged mind could produce.

'Madam, what are you doing?' the cook cried. 'Stop, Madam. Stop!'

A helpless Miss Prim looked up in despair.

'I can't, Mrs Mulligatawny. The bed socks for the lunatics must be done.'

The cook rushed forward.

'Carrots, Madam. Can't you see what you're doing? You're sewing bed socks into a shawl!'

Miss Prim stopped, blinked and held the garment away from her.

Mrs Mulligatawny was right. Protruding from a haphazard shawl were half a dozen socks. Horrified by what she saw, Miss Prim started to weep, her frail body convulsing from exhaustion— and from all the as-yet-unfulfilled promises of knitwear that she had made, and the debts she had accumulated, and the shock of Belle's return, and the surprise of meeting his unlikely cousin, Pablo Fanque.

The burden of life had suddenly become too much.

'Oooah,' Miss Prim spluttered. 'What have I done, Mrs Mulligatawny? What have I become? I've knitted Satan's shawl. I am doomed! Oooooah!!'

And she fainted.

CONTRAST NOW THE wearisome concerns of middle age with the ebullience of youth. Whilst Gaia was analysing life's woes and Miss Prim was being administered another dose of smelling salts, Master Lush was full of hopes and looking forward to the day. He was with William Darby, which further improved his mood for the two men had forged a fellowship in the white heat of Lady Passmore's ire.

In conversation after the tea party, they had agreed to meet at Master Lush's printer the next morning, and to share the excitement of seeing the very first copies of *Families Resident in the Royal City of Bath for the Season, Their Children and Other Interests*. Master Lush's hands shook as he picked up a copy of the book. It was all he could do not to cry. It was, he imagined, how a mother must feel holding a child in her arms.

'Sir, it's magnificent,' he told the printer. 'It is everything I wanted it to be. All I need to do now is to sell it.'

Meanwhile, having interests of his own, William took the opportunity to discuss posters for his circus and the printer, who, unlike some in Bath, was a decent man, gave him a favourable price.

'I should be delighted to do the job for you, Mr Fanque,' said the printer. 'As for you, Master Lush, here are twenty copies of your book in hard cover and I'll have bound a further eighty copies in two days' time.'

The twenty copies weighed considerably more than Master Lush had expected, and he was grateful for the assistance of William, who was strong as an ox and carried them with ease.

'Thank you, Mr Fanque; I'm most obliged,' Master Lush said, before explaining his intentions. 'I purpose to give away these twenty copies to those families who will esteem them the most, in the expectation that when they will talk to others of the publication, news of it will spread like wildfire. Then other families may buy the remaining stock through Lackington's Bookshop on Quiet Street at a fair price.'

'That seems a grand plan,' agreed William, encouragingly.

'See here on the frontispiece, I provide details of Lackington's. I will break even on the cost of the printing if I complete the sale of the eighty books. Then, on the next print run, I will turn a profit.'

William slapped Master Lush on the back. It was good for him to be with someone of a similar age and ambition. Good to be out of the house too, away from Belle and his unsettled disposition.

'Congratulations are in order, Maaster Lush. Let Fortune smile on tha'n efforts.'

'And on your circus too, Mr Fanque. I marvel that you should be bringing one to Bath so soon after arriving in England. If I may ask, how have you been able to gather up all your performers?'

William wished he could provide Master Lush an honest answer but he continued to respect Belle's line.

'There's naw almanac for circus performers, Sir, least of all for bearded ladies, what is a rare species. Over the years, oi've collected names and when oi finally made plans to travel across the seas with Mr Nash, oi wrote 'em all letters asking 'em to make themselves ready.'

'Golly!' said young Lush excitedly. 'And when will these performers be arriving?'

'Oi got word this mornin' that they'll shortly be camped by a town called Chipp'n'am, some fifteen moiles or so from 'ere. Oi shall travel there in a couple of days. But first, tha' books, Maaster Lush.'

'Indeed! And if we're aiming for the top, this is the place to start!'

The two men were by Marlborough Buildings, close to where William had first set eyes on the Royal Crescent.

'The buildings lose none of they's grandeur being viewed a second toime,' William said. 'Baath is a grand city.'

'A fine one, Sir,' replied Master Lush, checking a notebook and pointing to a house. 'Let's go to Number 4 and leave a copy

116

there. It is occupied for the Season by a family of textile merchants from Yorkshire. They have four daughters who are bound to tell others about the book when they see it.'

As the two of them reached the house, Master Lush pulled on the bell and was greeted by a maid.

Master Lush recognised her from his earlier visit, and she him.

'It's Lizzie, isn't it?'

'Yes, Sir. Good morning, Sir. Are you looking for Mr and Mrs Hawthorn?'

'No need to disturb them, Lizzie, but I'd be obliged if you'd hand them this book. It comes fresh off the press.'

The girl looked nervously at the unsolicited gift.

'Off the press, Sir. What kind of press is that?'

'The printing press, Lizzie!'

'And was they expectin' it, Sir?'

Master Lush was caught on the hop, having expected the maid to deliver his charge without any fuss.

'It's an almanac of the Season for visitors to Bath entitled *Families Resident in the Royal City of Bath for the Season, Their Children and Other Interests*.'

The maid gulped.

'Could you say that again, Sir? I didn't quite catch it.'

'*Families Resident in ...* 'He stopped and pointed to the cover. 'The title's here on the front.'

The maid looked at him and the book blankly.

'Beggin' your pardon, Sir, but I wasn't taugh to read. Them's just words to me. That's why I'm a maid.'

'But ... '

'And I don't know if I can take it off of you. It might not be proper.'

While Master Lush paused to consider what to do next, William stepped into the breach.

'Don't worry about not knowing the meaning of all the words Maaster Lush uses,' he said; 'oi doesn't know 'alf of them moyself!

'—but oi daresay we both recognoise the colour of money,' and with that he waved a coin in front of the maid. 'Master Lush would esteem it a favour if tha' would'st koindly take this 'ere book and put it on a table where Mr and Mrs Hawthorn will foind it.'

The maid curtseyed, nervously, having never spoken to a dark-skinned man before but very much liking the look of his money.

'Yes, Sir. I most certainly will,' she replied, pocketing the coin and taking the book.

As the door closed, Master Lush turned and curtseyed at William.

'Yes, Sir. I most certainly will,' he said, repeating the maid's words, and the two roared with laughter.

Master Lush then returned to William a coin from his own pocket.

'There go my profits, Mr Fanque! Will we have to bribe every maid to take the book?'

'Not everyone will droive the same baargain,' William replied, 'although tha' should'st maark her response to the toitle. She couldn't get 'er tongue round it.'

'She was a maid,' said Master Lush. 'The almanac's designed for her employers.'

'Mayhap,' said William, 'but in the circus trade, we takes note of 'ow the audience reacts. Now th'art in trade too, tha' might'st learn from this and consider another toitle for tha'n almanac.'

'I fear you're right,' said the budding publisher, after a moment's reflection. 'Something shorter, maybe. More memorable.'

'A toitle to make them as are named in the almanac feel good about theirselves, and make those not named feel envious,' William concurred. 'As it happens, oi thought of a fair toitle this mornin'. But before oi imparts it to 'ee, let's we hand out a few more copies and see how they fares.'

They distributed three more books to houses on Royal Crescent before heading north to St James's Square. From there, they planned to ascend the hill to Somerset Place and Lansdown

Crescent before returning south to distribute the last books in The Circus. It was a journey, they estimated, that would take them an hour.

This meant they would miss Belle's own visit to The Circus. Belle had returned to the site of the intended spectacle—Pablo Fanque's Circus!—to fulfil his own obligation of putting up the public notice that he had paid a printer a pretty sum to produce quickly.

If William and Master Lush had been there too, perhaps the misery inflicted on the Caribbean girl, who remained locked in the barred attic room of the Servitudes's house, might have ended. Mercy was her name and younger, keener ears would surely have heard her cry for help. Followed swiftly by her scream of anguish. But not cloth-eared Belle who, with string provided by the printer, was struggling with the mundane task of tying the public notice to some railings ... .

L IKE MANY WHO post public notices, Belle wished that his might remain hidden lest someone read it and object. Having surveyed the scene, he decided that the railings surrounding the green would do best, and that the most obscure spot would be one that faced one of the three streets.

Not only did Belle not want the notice to be seen, he also wished not to be seen posting it. On both counts, he was to be disappointed, for his presence in The Circus had already been noted by Lord Servitude who, as was his wont, stood at his drawing room window looking out onto a world that he considered his own. Within an instant, the peer had summoned the housekeeper.

'Mrs Neech, that louche fellow we saw the other day dancing with a piccaninny: he's back. Look. He's attaching something to the ironwork across the road. When he's gone, go and see what it is. I don't like the look of him.'

'Yes, Lord Servitude,' said Mrs Neech, staring in distaste at Belle.

By chance, Belle had also been seen by Mercy from her attic room. Unlike Lord Servitude, she did not look out on the world with a sense of entitlement, for her room was a gaol, and whilst it offered a view of Bath's most elegant houses, the grandeur of their architecture did not in any way elevate her but only enforced her wretchedness.

In her short life, she had suffered more hardship and abuse than any human should know: cruelty, deprivation, hard labour, beatings, hunger, thirst and—even as a child—the unwanted attention of white men in Grenada. Then, having entered womanhood, she had been sent against her will to Jamaica to serve the Hon. Cecil as his enslaved concubine. And thence to Bath.

Not for Mercy the benefits of abolition.

At the moment when Belle came into her view, her melancholy had grown to such a pitch that her fingers were trying to loosen the window bars that held her captive, so that she could hurl herself out onto the street below and, she hoped, die.

And then she saw Belle. He had his back to her now but, for a second, she had seen his face and thought she recognised him: pasty-faced, weak in body, ridiculously attired—like so many white men—but familiar all the same. Was he not someone she knew from the West Indies, maybe even a friend of her own half-brother, one of the rare Europeans who had stood apart by decrying his fellow plantation owners?

Whilst her actions might endanger her, she was determined to attract the man's attention. In desperation, she put her head to the bars and cried out into the midday air.

'Sir! Up here. Please help. I am held captive!'

Belle, however, was intent only on tying the notice to the railings and was not aware of her call. He looked around at people who walked nearby but not up high to where, with her arms stretched through the bars, Mercy was confined.

She called again but, weakened by her long sea voyage and by the daily abuses visited on her, her voice barely carried.

She was heard, however, by the Hon. Cecil, who had been lying on his bed on the floor below, pleasuring himself with Euripides's *Medea*. At the sound of Mercy's voice, he was up on his feet, pulling up his breeches, reaching for the keys to her room and leaping up the stairs, two by two. He quickly unlocked the door, crossed the small room and violently pulled Mercy from the bars.

Unlike his father, the Hon. Cecil was a thin man on whose narrow shoulders and long neck sat an elongated square head. Black hair was tightly combed across its plateau the way that Nanny had taught him. Nanny had taught him many other things too, none of them good.

'You're a wicked girl,' he hissed, his fingers choking her throat. 'And worse than that, ungrateful. I had the Christian kindness to bring you first to Kingston and now to England, and all you do is misbehave. If I had thought of releasing you from this bedchamber to enjoy the freedom to roam our house, I repent now of any such tender feeling. You will remain locked in this room until you have proved yourself duly submissive. And make no mistake, if you squeak from that window again, I'll chain you to your bed.'

Then, withdrawing his belt from his breeches, he lashed her across the shoulders and arms.

Mercy wept, shaking, terrified.

'Please, Sir. Please don't do that. Don't be doing that no more.'

She screamed in anguish but the Hon. Cecil did not relent. He struck her to the floor.

'You're a heathen girl unworthy of the Lord. As God is my Saviour, you are my slave and I your master. Your mother may have named you Mercy but you'll be getting no mercy from me.'

NOTES

- James Lackington (1746–1815) was born in Somerset and revolutionised the book trade. Before his time, booksellers habitually destroyed books to keep supply low and prices high. Lackington adopted the reverse strategy, buying books in volume and selling cheap while declining to provide credit to customers. His vast bookshop was in London's Finsbury Square but he would have frequented Bath.

- Medea was the brilliant, manipulative, psychopathic wife of Jason the Argonaut. A woman scorned, in various versions of her tale she kills a princess, her own brother, an uncle and most famously, in cold blood, her two helpless infant children.

CHAPTER XI

Saints Crispin and Crispinian

TWO DAYS HAD passed and Belle Nash reclined exhausted in the drawing room of Sydney Buildings. The week since his return to Bath had been a whirlwind of activity. What with Phyllis Prim's fainting, and his agreeing a site for the circus with William Darby, and Lady Passmore's haranguing of him at his own tea party, and his tying a public notice to some railings, he had barely had a minute to himself.

He had spent the last forty-eight hours with William, placing announcements of the circus about the city. Since there had so far been no public objection, Belle had also accompanied William earlier that morning to the peculiar space in Bath now known as Bog Island, where coaches to neighbouring towns were boarded. It was time, William had decided, to join those of his Astley's colleagues who were now encamped at Chippenham, awaiting the final leg of their journey to Bath.

William needed to ensure that the troupe members were fit and ready to perform. He also had the task of explaining to them that, as their impresario, he had adopted a new name: Pablo Fanque.

'How readily do you think your troupe will accept your new identity?' Belle had asked, nervously.

William had smiled, for there seemed to be a simple answer.

'They'll welcome it, oi'll be bound. For an African, oi've a dull English name whereas them circus people, they loikes their names weird and fantastic. Calling myself Pablo Fanque makes me sound more loike one of them!'

Belle, however, had not taken kindly to the comment.

'Pablo Fanque might sound weird and fantastic to you, Sir, but to me he is flesh and blood—someone I love, and as real to me as ... as you.'

The Norfolk man had hesitated. He had been mistaken about his being an easy answer, for there were no easy answers with Belle. Worse, William was no Ira Aldridge and he was finding the role of Pablo Fanque far from straightforward. It might be easier, in some respects, were he not another man's *Doppelgänger*. Then, at least, he could *play* the part rather than *be* the part.

And did he and Pablo really look alike? Belle had no portrait of his Caribbean counterpart. The substance of the claim lay solely in Belle's unsettled mind.

'In which case, oi 'ave much to live up to,' William had replied, determined to keep the peace.

Which happened to be, thought Belle, as he lay on his silk-covered chaise longue, the burden of his own life. Even as a child, he had felt the need to live up to the Nash name: to honour, if not match, the reputation of his celebrated grandfather, Beau Nash, who, through the strength of his personality, had inspired the construction of Bath as a Palladian pleasure dome.

He recalled, however, that Beau had not been universally admired. For every person who had complimented him on his achievement, another had excoriated him as an attention-seeker and arriviste.

'Am I thought of the same way, I wonder?' Belle whispered. 'Maybe Gaia is right and I am just toying with life. Making a nuisance of myself by being a bachelor. Stirring society's pot by falsely claiming a Caribbean cousin. Asserting contrarian values so I can strut like a peacock through the city.'

The thought, however, brought him a half-smile that now blossomed into a laugh.

'But if it brings Pablo and a circus to Bath,' he said out loud, rising to his feet, 'it cannot be all bad. I may mourn Gay Street, for never was there a finer home, but I have a more-than-decent roof over my head and my unparalleled collection of *Königliche* porcelain still to admire. So I shall look on the bright side—and with that thought, I shall pour myself a midday gin.'

THE AIR SEEMED particularly fresh and the sun blissfully warm to William as he stepped down from the coach after the three-hour journey to Chippenham. The distance from Bath was not so great but the state of the highway was poor, with potholes the depth of buckets waiting to catch the coach's wheels and jar the passengers' spines.

His fellow travellers disembarked with the usual chorus of disapproval about the journey, cursing the coach company, local officials and government ministers for their incompetence and lack of respect for the wayfaring citizen. The coachman had heard it all before and, with a shrug, he headed for an adjacent inn.

William stepped onto the pavement, shaking the dust of the journey from his coat. Although he had never set foot in Chippenham, he had been told precisely how to find the common land by Belle, who would visit the town to see his aunt, Mrs Sarah Rous. With a spring in his step and a satchel slung over his shoulder, William headed east along the high street before turning north. It did not take him long to find his colleagues, who were resting after their journey from London.

The Ridley Brother clowns were frying a feast of gammon on a campfire. Waiting like a prize bull for his portion was the aged prize fighter Tom Shelton, whose reputation, like his stomach, had sagged badly in recent years but he still knew how to make women swoon in the front row.

Further behind was the troupe's retinue of jugglers, high-wire dancers and acrobats, some of whom were practising the vaults, leaps and somersaults that so amazed the crowds.

Finally, at a distance to one side, was the contortionist Ki Hi Chin Fan Foo, who was busily tying himself in knots.

Mr Shelton was the first to see William and stood up to welcome him, grimacing with the pain that standing brought to his knees.

'Mr Darby is here!' he bellowed. 'People gather round! Mr Darby is here!'

Everyone ran forward, the gammon left in the pan to spit, as hands were shaken and backs slapped. It took a few minutes for the excitement at his arrival to calm down but, even then, the mood was elevated.

'When do we start for Bath, Mr Darby? Is everything in order?' asked the Ridley Brothers in unison.

William held up his hands. He understood that words of leadership were required. His colleagues had put their trust in his hands, and with that trust their means of income.

'All is arranged, all is arranged,' he declared. 'We opens the circus within the week. A soite's been chosen and the bills 'ave been posted.'

'Do you have a copy we can see?' asked one of the acrobats, while the others applauded. 'I cannot wait to jump my first somerset in Somerset!'

'Of course,' William replied, reaching into his satchel. He had anticipated the request and had chosen this moment to share his new name. 'But before that, oi 'as an announcement to make. Yew rapscallions is always telling oi that "William Darby" uz the dullest of names and one unfitted to the dazzle of the Big Top.'

'Darby of Norfolk, merchant of potatoes!' jested one of the Ridleys, to the laughter of others.

'Cruel, Sir, cruel!' William grinned, 'particularly when oi tells 'ee that oi 'as taken tha'n criticisms to heart. On the advoice of a patron from the city, oi 'as taken upon moy'self a new name and character.'

As the company all let out comic 'oohs' and 'aahs', William

produced from his satchel a copy of the poster, which he unfurled for all to see. 'Yew will notice, moy foine fellahs, that across the centre is an oriental human spider. Tha'll recognise tha'self there, Mr Foo. And here at the top are depicted performers balancing on a toight-rope: these are yew, gentlemen. And down this soide is our famed prize fighter—tha'sen, Mr Shelton—and the Ridley Brother clowns, whom I still cannot tell one from t'other after all these years. And then, down the other soide, our acrobats vaulting through an 'oop of foire. Above and below, dear friends, are your names and a description of your wondrous skills. And in the centre, ahem, moyself, your 'umble ringmaaster: Pablo Fanque, the Magician from the Caribbean!'

A little to William's disappointment, the performers focused all their attention on their own names and portrayals, caring not a jot what William called himself—until a voice spoke out and changed the tone. It was Mr Foo.

'Pablo Fanque's Circus? In da name of de Holy Further and all de saints, who the bejasus is Pablo Fanque?'

All fell silent, their eyes on William.

'T'is a stage name, Mr Foo, such as th'an own, and it'ull make us money. Nor is it a matter for debate: the decision is made. From today, William Darby is dead and yew will all refer to me as Pablo Fanque, as if oi wuz a free man with a noble soul, recently arroived from the spoice island of Grenada. Does everyone understand? If not, oi advoises 'ee to take the next chaise back to Mr Ducrow in London.'

Silence. The troupe had rarely, if ever, seen William display anger and in that instant he earned their respect. His word was not to be challenged. A new impresario was born.

Then Annie, a trapeze artist who doubled as a stable lass, stepped forward.

'Would you like to see your horses, Mr Fanque? I know they'd like to see you.'

William gladly took up the invitation. He handed the bill to Mr

Shelton, and while the others gathered round him to take a closer look, William followed the lass to an enclosure in which four horses were grazing: three mares and a stallion, all black. He was elated to see them. Whatever the troubles and complexity of the world, in these animals there resided calm and harmony.

Whether by instinct, sight or smell, they became alert to his presence and cantered over to welcome him. The first to arrive was the stallion.

'Hey, Osei, how art tha', moy man?' William said joyfully, the horse swaying its head in acknowledgement as he stroked its cheek. 'And how are the ladies: Idia, Nzinga and Beatriz? Yew 'ave survived the journey well, moy ladies. 'As yew missed me?'

The mares gathered around William, nuzzling their noses into his shoulders and neck.

'Not just them. We've all missed you, Mr Fanque,' said the lass behind him.

'Truly?'

Turning to the girl, he saw that they had been joined by the Ridley Brothers.

'To be sure,' the clowns both said. 'We've left Mr Ducrow for good. None of us wants to go back to Astley's. You're our king now, Mr Fanque.'

William bowed.

'Well—'and me a sword and oi'll knoight yew all. Ain't that what kings do?'

Annie the stable lass clapped with joy.

One of the Ridleys declared, 'Please, Mr Fanque, leap onto Osei and make a speech like Henry at Agincourt!'

'That's right,' cried the other. 'For St. Crispin's Day is only a week or so past!'

It was said in good humour but to their surprise, the brothers found themselves admonished. William had been taught the saints by his mother and, with a stern look, he wagged his finger at the clowns.

128

'Oi'll have you not mention St. Crispin again, if tha' please, Mr Ridley. He sits not well with oi.'

The faces of the fraternal jesters fell.

'Have we caused you insult?' they asked.

Although William waved away their concerns, his face remained grave.

'Not with intention, so oi takes no offence. But no more of St. Crispin. Let us return to the camp and ready the caravans. Tomorrow, we saddle the hosses and make our way to Baath. The royal city awaits.'

T HE AFTERNOON WAS ending and Belle was on his third gin when the doorbell rang at Sydney Buildings.

There is something about gin that alters the senses. With the first glass, Belle's mind had drifted back to past times in Bath. He had imagined that he could hear his former companion Gerhardt Kant making strange clucking noises as he powdered his wig. On the second glass, he had been transported back to Grenada and the challenges he had faced to end slavery on his aunt's plantation. But by the third glass—or was it the fourth?—slavery was over and he was in the arms of Pablo Fanque under a cloudless sky filled with cockatoos.

Had he drunk more gin, the cockatoos would have flown through his front door. Instead it was Master Lush who stood before him. Belle felt a surge of joy. How wonderful that the young clerk with his prepossessing features had come to see him. How fortunate that there was gin in the house!

'Mistress Lucy, go into the drawing room and look out of the window for cockatoos. I think they're laying eggs.'

Master Lush gave Belle a dubious look.

'You're speaking gibberish, Mr Nash.'

'Kipper fish, Lucy? How dashed funny you are! No, they're cockachoose, Sir. Chotackoos. Ah, I can't get my tongue round their dashed name but they're laying eggs. Look out!'

'You have been drinking, Mr Nash,' said Master Lush, entering the drawing room and espying the bottle of gin.

'Maybe a glass,' Belle admitted, giggling. 'Maybe several. But Pablo's gone to Chipp ... Chipp ... chips and ham and I was feeling dry. Do you feel dry, Lucy? Why don't you wet your whistle?—there's a glass—or let me wet it for you!'

The clerk held the bottle up to the light.

'That's quite a thirst, Sir. I had intended to pour you a splash before breaking the news but you appear to have poured yourself a flood already.'

Belle walked uneasily to his chair and sat down with a thud.

'What are you on about, man? You're talking in riddles. What's the news?'

Master Lush considered pouring himself a glass but decided against.

'There's no easy way of saying this, Mr Nash,' he said. 'I was walking home from Lackington's bookshop, where I was checking on sales of the almanac and ... '

Children Having Baths with Residents, and other Sins.

' ... and I passed by places where the bills for Mr Fanque's circus had been placed. And I must report that they are there no longer. They appear to have been all torn down.'

Master Lush fell silent as Belle tried to absorb the news. Through the fog of gin, he knew what Master Lush had said had merit.

'Torn down? Why would anyone tear them down?'

'Indeed.'

At that moment, the doorbell rang again.

'Ring, ring, ring! Who's there, i' the name of Beelzebub?' exclaimed the host. 'This is a popular house tonight. I had better find more gin.'

As Belle went to a cabinet to collect a new bottle, Master Lush went to the front door. To his surprise he found Gaia Champion waiting on the other side.

'I was expecting Mr Nash, not my clerk,' she said brusquely. 'What are you doing here?'

'I am here to inform Mr Nash that the bills advertising the circus have been torn down, Ma'am, but I don't think he took in my words. Gin has got the better of him.'

Master Lush's news did not surprise her. The moment she had anticipated, when life in Bath would become complicated, had at last arrived.

'Should I leave, Ma'am?' asked the clerk. 'Perhaps you have private business to conduct.'

Gaia shook her head.

'No. Please stay. You may be able to assist.'

'Of course, Ma'am. In what way?'

'By making tea.'

'By making tea, Madam?'

'The problems for Messrs Nash and Fanque multiply by the hour,' Gaia said, placing a hand on her clerk's shoulder. 'In response to the public notice, a complaint regarding the circus has this afternoon been lodged by Lord Servitude and his son.'

Master Lush's heart sank.

'Is Mr Fanque's enterprise doomed, then?'

Gaia shrugged.

'Not necessarily. To ensure fair judgement, the complaint must be heard before a court.'

Master Lush's mouth fell open.

'Our court?'

On a different occasion, Gaia might have laughed, but from the drawing room she could hear the clink of a glass of gin and the words of a song being sung:

'*Rock-a-bye baby on the treetops…* '

Gaia looked her clerk firmly in the eye.

'I had always considered it *my* court, Master Lush, and was not aware that you had an equal claim upon it. Now tell me, how inebriated is Mr Nash?'

131

Embarrassed, Master Lush gave her his estimate.

'Five glasses, I'd say.'

'Then make plenty of tea, for Mr Nash is not my only concern this night, and I must shortly be on my way. I received a message from Gay Street that Miss Prim is poorly and has requested the priest. I must see her as a matter of urgency. So, into the kitchen with you and make the tea.'

It was close to dark in Chippenham, the light of the setting sun matching the dying embers of the campfire. The habit of drinking gin was not unique to Bath and the troupe that had celebrated William's arrival had also enjoyed a little too much spirit. They would be travelling to Bath nursing sore heads, and William, a troubled mind.

The mention earlier in the day of Saint Crispin had unsettled him. As a child, his mother had told him the story of Crispin and Crispinian, a pair of twins who in Roman times had endured torture for their Christian faith.

The child had anticipated a happy ending, for the brothers had survived being thrown into a river by the wicked governor of Gaul with millstones around their necks. But William's mother went on to reveal that having experienced one miracle, the boys did not enjoy a second. The Emperor's sword had seen to that, severing their heads from their bodies in his rage.

The story had always troubled William and as was his custom when troubled, he sought out the company of his horses. Dew was forming on the grass as he crossed to the enclosure. He made a low whistle through the night-time air and, within a few seconds, Osei had trotted up beside him.

'Hello, moy man,' he said, stroking the stallion's mane and feeling its warmth. 'Oi 'as much to tell 'ee, Osei. Particularly of a man who loves me, or would wish to, for he thinks oi be the twin of 'is lost companion.'

The horse shuffled its feet.

'"Do I love him in return?" tha' ask'st. Well, Osei, Belle is a good man who 'as moy deep affection and respect. But 'is mind is troubled. He carries within 'im a past oi fears to share.'

The horse gently neighed.

'Come closer to oi, Osei. Oi 'as more to impart, but be sure to keep it to tha'self. Not a word to the ladies, dost hear?'

William moved his mouth closer to the stallion's ear.

'In my 'eart, oi worries that, by some strange spell, Belle be roight: that oi be twinned with Pablo Fanque, if not in blood then in spirit—that he and oi be Crispin and Crispinian reborn. Stay close to oi, Osei, and protect oi. For Saint Crispin's fate may be moyn own.'

NOTES

- Bog Island lies between Bath Abbey and the River Avon and was the site of two Georgian public toilets, as well as being the current destination for some coaches. A 'bog' is a colloquial term for a toilet although, given its proximity to the river, the area would also have been a literal bog in times past.
- William Darby had named his horses after major figures of African history. Osei Tutu (1670–1717) was the first Ashanti king in what is now Ghana. Ana Nzinga (1583–1663) was Queen of Ndongo, in current Angola. Dona Beatriz (1684–1706) was a prophet who taught that Jesus and other early Christian figures were from the Kongo empire, straddling today's Congo, Angola and Gabon. Idia, finally, was a warrior queen of Benin, in what is now Nigeria.
- The source of Belle's 'Knock, knock, knock' misquotation is the drunken Porter in Shakespeare's *Macbeth*.

CHAPTER XII

Bibles and Truncheons

T HERE IS RARELY a good time for a hangover. A dark room, fresh air and ice all help to quell the pain. By contrast, what compounds a hangover is the requirement to break bad news to someone you love. Worse still, when that someone is also experiencing a hangover.

'There's been what?!' cried William Darby, distraught, his head pounding from the previous night. 'Is that thee, Belle, or t'last night's liquor screamin' in moy brains?'

William had already suffered an unpleasant morning, a winter downpour leaving him wet and bedraggled. He had brought the circus troupe to the village of Batheaston, then advanced alone to confirm that all was in order.

'There's been a hitch,' repeated Belle Nash, trying to summon up some trace of authority.

William was aghast.

'An 'itch! Is that what tha' call'st it, Belle? Oi don't call it an 'itch, Sir. Oi calls it ha catastrophe.'

The pitch of his voice was too strident for Belle.

'Please, William, calm yourself. We both of us are suffering the penalty of last night's carousing and you cannot be too much surprised. We knew there were procedures to follow and risks attached. Gaia told us as much.'

The statement did little to soothe his companion.

'Oi knew,' said William dismissively, 'but oi expected 'ee to

134

'ave cleared the way for us. Few people ever complain about circuses. Circuses is loved!'

At this point, Belle foolishly attempted levity, which, let it be put on record, like tightrope walking, should never be attempted with a hangover.

'Bath is a fickle place,' he joked. 'If the Romans had built a vomitorium here, people would have told them that retching was un-English.'

William responded with unamused silence.

Belle coughed, then continued, 'Anyway, it is not Romans and vomitoria that we have to contend with but Lord Servitude and his miserable son, though some may see the two as connected.'

The identity of their protagonists shocked William into cold sobriety.

'Did oi hear thee aright?' he asked. 'Lord Servitude, who demanded compensation for those what owned slaves: is he the complainant?'

Belle nodded.

'The very same.'

'The one man above all else what people with dark skin and sound moind most abhor?' continued William. 'This is the demon what 'as seen fit to complain about moy circus?'

Belle nodded again but raised a finger.

'Indeed—although a small correction, if I may. Lord Servitude *and* his ungodly son, the Honourable Cecil. They are co-complainants. The evil spawn of his father has recently returned from the Indies. Master Lush was told that he is looking for a bride.'

William looked confused.

'The Honourable who?'

Unlike William, Belle's head was yet to clear. In an alcoholic fug, the ghosts of Grenada preyed on his mind.

'Cecil Servitude. To whose Jamaican household your sibling Mercy was sent as a maid,' explained Belle, still unaware of Mercy's onward passage to England as the Hon. Cecil's slave concubine.

135

'Mercy?'

'Your half-sister.'

William's confusion turned to irascibility.

'What art tha' jangerin' about, Man?'

'Pablo, how could you forget?' replied Belle, shocked. 'Mercy was taken against her will from Grenada to Kingston. It was the reason you stayed behind when I fled—in the hope that you would be re-united.'

Too late he realised his mistake. It is often said that the drunkard may see two people where there is but one. Those with a hangover, Belle could now attest, can see one person where there are two.

'William, my friend, Sir—I am sorry. I mistook you for Pablo again. Last night's spirit still has me in its grip. We are alike in that regard.'

The Norfolk man was of a mind to tell Belle that they had absolutely nothing in common, but he knew that this was not the time for division. He merely commented, 'Oi 'ad hoped that abolition moight serve as the poultice to English bigotry. Yet the Servitudes floy the flag for slavery still—and set their faces against our honest enterproise.'

Belle sighed.

'The truth is, William, we're caught in a snare. To the magistrate's court the complaint must go. The hearing is tomorrow.'

The explanation caused William to raise his hands in supplication.

'But won't yon Mrs Champion rule in our favour? There are no just grounds to the action.'

Belle, however, was circumspect in his reply. He had been guilty of raising false hopes before and did not wish to do the same again. He mopped his forehead and spoke plainly.

'Gaia will rule according to the law but she will also need to maintain public order. The Season in Bath is not the time for political conflict and if the Servitudes choose to turn society against us, she will be hard pressed to favour our cause. Which means, William, that we need to have a plan.'

William's shoulders slumped.

'The hearin' is set for tomorrow, tha' say'st. Then we're as good as defeated.' A tear gathered in the young man's eye. 'Moy circus comrades, presently camped just two moiles away, trusted oi and now they be lost.'

Belle closed his eyes. He would have to think fast. He had asked William to play a part in exchange for a reward and now had let that reward slip from his grasp. No one but he could clear up the mess. Opening his eyes, he took hold of William's hand and led him out of the drawing room.

'Where are we going?'

'To the kitchen, of course. When a plan is required, eggs, toast and tea must be served. Come.'

I T REMAINS A mystery of science—one that defied Newton no less than it defied Archimedes—how eggs, toast and tea have the power to counteract the distillate of juniper and turpentine, and yet, miraculously, they do. Half an hour later, the two men were sufficiently bright-eyed to start constructing a plausible plan.

'The first rule of engagement, as glorious Athens's first citizen Pericles understood, is to consider our opponent,' explained Belle, his elbows on the kitchen table. 'On what grounds do the poisonous peer and his son base their complaint? I ensured the public notice was short on detail.'

'Unloike the poster,' noted William, reaching into his satchel to produce a copy. 'The poster was full of matter.'

'Ah! The circus bill! Spread it out on the table,' said Belle, pushing their plates to one side. 'Let us see what offence it could cause. And, more importantly, what we can use to our advantage.'

William spread out the bill and together they studied it.

'There's old Mr Shelton, depicted in 'is underpants. That

moight've upset the sensitivities of a few of Baath's more delicate souls,' said William.

'But not Lord Servitude,' replied Belle. 'No, I suspect this description of you as *the Magician from the Caribbean* comes nearer the mark. It sounds like an innocent phrase but it is one that would rile a bigot.'

William blinked in disbelief.

'Tha' could'st be roight, there. But oi'll not hoide moy'self nor moy ambitions.'

'Nor should you,' said Belle, reaching out a hand. 'We shall consider what else there is.'

After a minute, Belle licked his lips and tapped a finger on one of the performers on the poster.

'An oidea 'as occurred to thee, oi thinks,' said William.

'Indeed it has,' replied Belle, the cogs of his mind whirring. 'About this man, I have a question. Dependent on your answer—and the behaviour of an aunt of mine—we may have our play.'

Belle asked his question and received the answer he desired. William, however, sat back in his chair confused.

'An aunt? Tha'st lost me, Mr Nash.'

His confidence rising, Belle stood up and grasped his companion's shoulders.

'In time, all will be revealed, Good Cousin. For now, however, let us get on with our day. You must return to Batheaston and tell the troupe to delay their entrance to the city.'

William stood.

'And thee? What holds the day for thee?'

Belle looked at his companion with serious intent.

'I have social engagements that I cannot ignore. I wish it otherwise, but such is the life of a Nash in Bath.'

A few minutes later, they left the house and went off in different directions: William to the troupe in Batheaston and Belle to the centre of town.

138

B ELLE'S SPIRITS WERE boosted by a sense of purpose, for having a plan in life is a wonderful thing. He crossed Pulteney Bridge and walked the short distance to the post office, where he handed over a letter addressed to his aunt, Mrs Sarah Rous of Chippenham, and passed a coin to the postal clerk.

Next on his agenda were his social engagements, which were not as onerous as he had hinted to William. His first engagement was with Arthur Quigley, his old music master, at Sally Lunn's Tearooms. Afterwards, he planned to visit Phyllis Prim, now recovering in her sick bed in Gay Street. Like Gaia, he believed that Miss Prim would in fact live to a hundred years but superior breeding required him to pay his respects—although he also had a less than superior ulterior motive for the visit.

As Belle approached Sally Lunn's, he congratulated himself on a plan so well conceived that it justified indulging in a feast of warm Bath buns, soft butter and quantities of strawberry jam.

Whilst not wishing to promote unduly the merits of baked dough, there is something comforting, decent and civilised about the Bath bun. Break it open whilst it is warm, spread the butter and confiturial conserve into its sweetish, sensuous centre and men, women—nay, children too—will find themselves transported to a world of perfect harmony. Hurrah for Sally Lunn's!

It was with genuine pleasure, therefore, that Belle entered the tearoom and saw among the packed tables Mr Quigley, who was wearing his standard garb of pyjamas, tattered overcoat and tea cosy, the last of which served as his hat. The octogenarian was ready and waiting, a large linen napkin tucked into the neck of his night-time apparel.

'Young Nash, there you are! I say, isn't this fun? Sharing tea at Sally Lunn's again. By all the gods, I've missed you.'

'I think you've missed the buns more,' Belle remarked, as he shook Mr Quigley's hand and joined him at the table.

'I won't deny it, Sir. I have encouraged others to invite me to tea but with very little success. A belief in fine manners bypasses, it seems, today's youth. Even Master Lush proved disappointing in that regard. Delightful fellow in nearly every way but he leaves much to be desired in the bun department.'

'I'm sorry to hear that, Mr Quigley. I'll have words with him,' replied Belle, settling into his seat and inhaling the fragrant air of the tearoom. This was what life was about, he thought to himself.

As for Mr Quigley, he seemed satisfied now, having expressed his gripe about Master Lush.

'Tell me, Nash: what have you been up to? I hear you have a charming new cousin. I saw a picture of him on a circus bill and he's quite the catch. Reminds me of the Chevalier de Saint-Georges, conductor of a symphony orchestra in Paris. Have you heard of him?'

'On occasion,' said Belle, who had been told about the great chevalier every time that he and Mr Quigley had met.

'I was in my twenties, discovering the joys of Paris, when I came across him,' Mr Quigley explained for perhaps the hundredth time. Tremendous fellow. Came from Guadeloupe. Handsome as a lion. Fabulous fencer. Knew his way around a violin too.'

'Remind me how you met him, Sir,' asked Belle politely, filling in the time before the buns arrived.

'An excellent request! I shall. It was like this. I won a place in his orchestra as a third violinist. I felt very honoured. I asked him for personal lessons but sadly he was a ladies' man. To console me, he bought me an absinthe and advised that I stroll down to the Bois de Boulogne at dusk. What a conductor, I say! So easy on the eye.'

Belle laughed nervously, aware that those at the next tables were within range of their conversation. He had forgotten the peril of communing with Mr Quigley in a public place. Fortunately, at that moment, their buns and tea arrived.

'Have a Bath bun whilst it's still warm, Sir. And let me pour the tea.'

Mr Quigley, however, would not be distracted. After one sip of tea and a mouthful of bun, he was back in the disreputable Bois de Boulogne.

'And can you guess, Sir, whom I met there that evening, parading his wares among the French oaks? Chevalier d'Éon in perfumed ruffles and a gown. "Was he male or female?" you may ask. Never did find out. Prodigious legs, though. I could have died for one touch of them.'

Before he could continue, a man sitting a few feet away turned his head towards Belle with a sneer.

'I would ask you, Sir, to entreat your friend to lower his voice. His clothes are offensive and so is his speech. Some topics are unsuited to Christian company. I wish to drink my tea unsullied.'

Belle nodded.

'Of course, Sir. My sincere apologies.'

Mr Quigley, however, was not so compliant.

'Do not pander to the man's ignorance, Nash,' he muttered loudly. 'I speak of nothing that was not written about in Hellenic writings.'

'Mr Quigley, please. Let us enjoy our tea.'

The old man huffed and glared at their neighbour, who now got up and moved his chair, to be further away.

'If we must change the subject, let us talk about your cousin, Sir. How is his circus? I love a circus.'

It was at this point that Belle made a terrible mistake. Relieved that they were no longer discussing the intimate anatomy of Chevalier d'Éon, he changed the subject to Lord Servitude and the problems he and his son were causing.

'So now we have a fight on our hands, I'm afraid. Servitude and his spawn have objected.'

'Lord Servitude!' cried Mr Quigley, jumping to his feet. 'How I despise that man. He's a monster, Sir. How dare he object to a circus?!'

It was a question that received a swift reaction from a couple seated at another table.

141

'I advise you to keep your political opinions to yourself,' said the man. 'Lord Servitude is a champion of fairness and justice, a man whom we much admire. He has led the fight for compensation. The money we received for our slave has paid for our Season in Bath. Is that not right, my dear?'

'We could have been ruined, had not Lord Servitude spoken up for our interests in the House,' his wife piped up.

'Compensation!' intervened guests at another table. 'What a disgrace. Parliament should be compensating our dark-skinned brothers and sisters, not funding the holidays of their former owners!'

Such arguments rarely end well.

'No compensation?' responded the other man's wife. 'Like good Christians, we follow the practice of the Church. And why should we not get compensation? We didn't work hard all our lives to have our slaves taken away for nothing.'

A second abolitionist joined in the fray.

'You didn't work hard, Madam? I believe you. Look at the size of you. I can't imagine you ever doing a thing for yourself if a lackey could be found to do it for you.'

It is, of course, the recognised duty of husbands to defend their wives' honour, even when those wives have none.

'Slurs and insults!' declared the husband, rounding on the assailant. 'See how abolitionists speak. No argument; just invective. It's shameful. The slaves have their freedom and we deserve remedy for our loss. Argue your way out of that, if you can!'

'You speak of argument!' cried the irate abolitionist. 'Your argument begins and ends with yourself. That is why the Jacobins in France turned to violence. It was the only argument their enemies understood.'

'What, like this?' called out a new entrant to the dispute, and flung a Bath bun across the tearoom, hitting the abolitionist square on the forehead. Fortunately, Bath buns are incapable of doing great physical damage and so the abolitionist picked up the bun and, with a more practised arm, hurled it back across the room. Within moments the air was thick with buns as former slave-owners and abolitionists fought it out with their weapons of dough.

Sometimes, Belle now decided, the best plans are those expedited with haste. Seeing that Mr Quigley was arming himself with his own bundle of buns, Belle pulled the old man to one side.

'Pardon me, Nash. It is time to take up arms,' he said, shaking Belle off and starting to sing the Marseillaise:

> *Aux armes, citoyens,*
> *Formez vos bataillons,*
> *Marchons, marchons!*
> *Qu'un sang impur*
> *Abreuve nos sillons!*

'Mr Quigley, Sir. With respect to your revolutionary passions, the situation is turning nasty and you must leave younger men to fight. As for me, I cannot risk being here when the constabulary arrive.'

With reluctance, Mr Quigley allowed Belle to lead him to the door, although not without lobbing two more buns across the room as he went. He slipped a third into his overcoat for an evening snack. Once outside, the two moved swiftly out of North Parade Passage.

'That was a spirited affair,' said a sprightly Mr Quigley. 'Oh, I feel the old fight surging through my veins:

> Oh! pleasant exercise of hope and joy!
> For mighty were the auxiliars which then stood
> Upon our side, we who were strong in love!

Where next can we go to man the barricades?'

Belle, however, had in his diary a second social engagement.

143

'Nowhere, Sir. Not for me, at least. I must visit Miss Prim in Gay Street. The word is that she has called the priest.'

'Sensible lady, Miss Prim.' Then the old man's eyes lit up. 'Shall I join you? She has an excellent cook who bakes a good bun.'

'I'd prefer not, Sir,' said Belle, shaking his head. 'I have an important task to complete. But walk with me to Gay Street, if you will.'

'So long as we can chat along the way.'

It was a compromise accepted by both parties. Taking each other's hands, they passed by the abbey and made their way from Abbey Church Yard to Milsom Street. As they ascended the avenue, they met a crowd dressed in their finest clothes, holding Bibles for evensong. Then whistles sounded and through the churchgoers ran three special constables armed with truncheons, heading to Sally Lunn's.

'Bliss was it in that dawn to be alive, but to be young was very heaven,' chirupped Mr Quigley and Belle laughed. The old man had spunk.

Bibles and truncheons—welcome to modern-day Albion, thought Belle.

NOTES
- Chevalier de Saint-Georges (1745–1799) was born Joseph Bologne in Guadeloupe, the son of a wealthy French planter and an enslaved African maid with whom his father had fallen in love. Father and mother moved to Paris and Saint-Georges developed into a man of extraordinary talents: the leading fencer, violinist, composer and conductor of his generation. In the French Revolution, he formed and commanded an all-Black regiment, the Légion St. Georges.
- Chevalier d'Éon (1728–1810) was an androgynous diplomat, spy and fearsome swordsman. He spent many years in London as the French *chargé d'affaires* and was pictured dressed as a

woman fencing Chevalier de Saint-Georges at Carlton House in 1787. The London Stock Exchange ran a betting pool on his true gender.

- I believe that my uncle based the character of Lord Servitude on George Hibbert (1757–1837), a Member of Parliament and a brilliant propagandist who campaigned for compensation for slave-owners. The country's leading abolitionist was William Wilberforce (1759–1833), MP for Hull, whose so-called Clapham Sect met on Sundays at the Holy Trinity church in Clapham, London. In the same church, on the opposite side of the aisle, sat Hibbert.

- At the time of Abolition, close to a hundred Church of England clergymen personally owned slaves. The Church itself owned two plantations in Barbados through a missionary agency, the Society for the Propagation of the Gospel. Its slaves were branded on the chest with the word 'Society' to discourage runaways. The Church was paid £8,823 restitution by the Crown in 1833 for the 'loss' of 411 such 'possessions'.

- An amateur and an imperfect historian, my uncle made a worthy attempt to ensure the language of *The Gay Street Chronicles* was in keeping with the period. The columns of his manuscripts are filled with notes, for example: '*racist*. Etym., first rec. use 1903. Must find alternative. Aaargh! Bigot? Xenophobe? Contemptuous, small-minded ass?'

- The lines of poetry that Mr Quigley quotes are from Wordsworth's poem 'The French Revolution As It Appeared to Enthusiasts At Its Commencement', which was written in 1804 and later included in his autobiographical masterpiece, *The Prelude*.

CHAPTER XIII

A Day in Court

T HE NEXT MORNING, Gaia Champion was in need of tea, following a court hearing that would long stick in her memory.

'What did they think they were doing, Master Lush?' she asked, as she supped the soothing cup of Assam that her clerk had just brought her.

In the four years of her magistracy, Gaia had heard cases of drunken brawls galore. But to have a dozen respectable householders all in her dock at the same time for complicity in a bun-fight was beyond anything she or anyone in Bath had seen before.

'And at Sally Lunn's, of all places!' she said, sitting down to gather her wits. 'Apart from anything else, it was an insult to Bath's most celebrated *pâtissière.*'

Master Lush busied himself tidying papers.

'The topic of slavery undoubtedly tipped the balance,' he advised.

Gaia nodded and looked at the clock on a cabinet.

'Which may well be the subtext of our next case: the complaint by the wretched Lord Servitude and the Hon. Cecil against Mr Fanque's circus, a case that sadly brings dear Belle back to our court. Goodness, it's like he's never been away.'

The same thought occupied Belle Nash's mind as he checked his pocket watch in the lobby of the court. Neither William Darby nor Lord Servitude had yet arrived but the lobby was overflowing. Word of the hearing had spread and Bath citizens in great number had arrived to watch the proceedings unfold.

Belle listened to the general chatter.

'I like the sound of this case immensely,' said a fashionable lady carrying a chihuahua. 'Lord Servitude is always good value!'

'And he is opposing a circus man from the Caribbean, as well as Bath's Mr Nash,' her friend added. 'What with Mr Aldridge performing at the Theatre Royal, it seems there's an African invasion this Season.'

To Belle's right, a group of women from Phyllis Prim's knitting sorority chatted among themselves. Then, seeing him, one of the ladies stepped forward to greet him.

'Dear Mr Nash, how happy we are to have you back in Bath after your adventures abroad. But have you seen Miss Prim? She's often in court and we were counting on her being here today.'

Belle blinked.

'You flatter me, Madam. I too am glad to be back. But no: I regret that Miss Prim's malaise keeps her yet in bed.'

Belle's admirer was disappointed to hear the news.

'So unfortunate. She will be missing the best hearing in years. But God speed you, Mr Nash. Magistrate Champion has just levied fines for the mistreatment of Bath buns. She is in the mood today, make no mistake.'

Belle blinked some more.

'I will be trusting in more than luck,' he said with a small bow. 'I wish you a pleasant day, Madam.'

He uttered the words with a degree of confidence. Whilst victory was not assured, the visit to Miss Prim the previous evening had been more than satisfactory. For once, her gossipy maid Millicent had been at home and Belle had regaled her mistress loudly enough to be sure that Millicent heard everything. So long as the postal service to Chippenham was reliable too, there was a fair chance of success.

147

Belle's eye then caught a commotion in the crowd. On the far side of the lobby, Lord Servitude and the Hon. Cecil had arrived, followed at a distance by William. The start of the contest was upon them.

A LL RISE IN court for Magistrate Champion,' cried Master Lush, adding, after a pause, 'I repeat: "All rise." The hearing will not start until *all* have risen.'

That everyone attending court must stand is a tradition that confirms the status of the presiding magistrate, and this was especially important in the case of Gaia, the country's first and only female magistrate. It was vital that all present recognise her not as a woman, whose authority some might otherwise have doubted, but as their superior, in terms of her knowledge of the Law and her power to pass down judgements.

As Gaia entered the court, she saw that Lord Servitude had remained seated.

'Trouble with his hips?' Master Lush suggested, tactfully.

'Or that a woman will be sitting at the bench, more likely,' Gaia replied.

She now ascended the dais and, from the position of her chair, looked down upon the courtroom. Not for the first time, she carried within her a conflict of emotions. Days such as this, when the court was full, signalled that something in the city had gone awry. But she also felt pride that it was she who had been granted the power to judge on the matter at hand.

'You may sit,' she announced, 'but you must also stay quiet. I see that the public benches are full and I want you to know that you are all most welcome. The court, however, is not a place for social conversation. We are here to understand a dispute between two parties: Mr Pablo Fanque, sponsored by Mr Bellerophon Nash, who has applied for a licence to bring a circus to Bath; and Lord Servitude and the Hon. Cecil Servitude, who oppose him. I will hear both sides and rule on the validity of the licence. In this

148

regard, I should make clear how this court operates. The court is objective. I shall listen to matters that pertain to the case and to the case only. I am uninterested in politics and neither party should elevate what is a dispute over a licence into a political issue. You have been given fair warning.'

The courtroom fell quiet.

Gaia continued, 'And so, to the case itself, gentlemen. Certain facts are not in dispute. A licence was sought by Mr Nash for Mr Fanque to bring his circus to Bath. The request came outside the normal period for consideration but was approved by Chairman Camshaft of the City Corporation. In instances where licences are approved late, a public notice is required. Objections are then heard by the city magistrate.'

Gaia paused to provide all in court a moment of reflection. Then she leant forwards towards the crowd.

'I remind you once more of the need for good order. I have already fined a dozen men and women this morning for unruly behaviour and I shall not hesitate from meting out far harsher punishment to anyone—and I do mean anyone—who shows contempt for this courtroom. You will note that I have two special constables in attendance, and there are more on hand if required.'

She pointed to the special constables who stood to the side.

'Let us proceed. Mr Fanque, please take the stand.'

Belle had watched Gaia with a mixture of delight and respect. Following his securing of the magistracy for her, she had brought his own career as a councillor to an end, but it had been a sacrifice worth making. She was not only born to the role; she *owned* it. Though many members of the public were already itching to comment on the proceedings, none dared test Gaia's patience. The court was hers to command and none doubted it.

Responding to her request, William rose to his feet with a determined air.

'Stand beside, but not in, the dock,' Gaia told him. 'No one is on trial here today. Please tell me your name.'

Though asked the question by Gaia, it was to Belle that William looked.

'Pablo Fanque,' he replied.

'And your occupation?'

'Circus impresario, Ma'am.'

'And what does that role entail?'

William pulled back his shoulders.

'Oi manages the circus as well as perform,' he explained. 'We 'as to have skills of our own to earn our artistes' respect. Oi walks the toight-rope and juggle but oi is best with the hosses. Them's dance to my instruction, the *waltz* bein' their latest trick, and oi somersaults on their backs as they canter.'

There were gasps from the benches—people's imaginations had been sparked—and it was to the benches that William now turned.

'Oi've not got all the skills. Oi can't clown about loike the Ridley Brothers. But thems can't roide bareback on two hosses like me, nor walk a toight-rope in their big shoes!'

There were further gasps and laughs that Gaia allowed, though her gavel lay at the ready.

'And what is the history of yourself and the troupe? Sufficient, it seems, to have won Chairman Camshaft's approval for the circus through the offices of Mr Nash.'

William nodded.

'Mr Nash 'as been most helpful, Ma'am. Pablo Fanque's Circus is a new venture but most of the troupe, other than me, was recently employed by Astley's Royal Amphitheatre in London. They'll put on a real treat for Baath when we open. A real treat.'

Gaia made a couple of notes, then she looked across at William.

'Mr Fanque, that will be all for the moment. Unless Lord Servitude or the Hon. Cecil Servitude have questions?'

Belle watched as Lord Servitude and his son—both slouched in their chairs—made dismissive gestures with their hands. Belle considered William's to have been a brave and controlled performance and they shook hands as William returned to his seat.

'They wuz too damn froightened to question oi,' his companion remarked, beaming.

'I'm not so sure,' was Belle's measured reply. 'Lord Servitude is no fool. He wants centre stage when he speaks.'

At that moment, Gaia turned to the peer.

'Lord Servitude, please take the same place beside the dock. You are a well-known public figure so I shall dispense with asking for your name and occupation.'

Lord Servitude adopted a casual gait as he walked the short distance to the dock but simultaneously used the moment to impose himself. He spoke with an orator's voice, one accustomed to making public speeches.

'No, Madam Magistrate, if that is your title. I insist on being treated like any other man. For is this not an English courtroom where all are equal? My name is Lord Servitude. And my occupation?'

He reached his spot, then spun on one heel to face his audience.

'As a peer of the realm, I have no trade but am much preoccupied with the economic value of slavery throughout our great empire. As you may be aware, but I wish to put on record for the benefit of this court, I was, and remain, an opponent of the abolition of slavery, which I consider the gravest mistake this country has made since surrendering the Thirteen Colonies of North America. I now campaign for justice for those fellow citizens who, like me, had their property seized by Parliament, thereby destroying our capacity to increase the nation's wealth. If I am to have an occupation, you may now call me a Champion for Compensation, though hitherto, in the days before abolition, I was a Champion of Commerce.'

It was a masterly performance in which he used the right to speak to promote his cause. Up until that moment, Gaia's control

151

of the court had been complete. Now, suddenly, her courtroom fell into uproar, exactly as Lord Servitude had intended. Behind him, the Hon. Cecil smirked as angry claims and counterclaims were shouted on the public benches.

'Good man, Servitude,' said one smart voice. 'Why should Parliament take away our property? I paid good money for our slaves and I expected to get full value from them. If God hadn't wanted us to have slaves, He wouldn't have populated the world with them.'

'Quite right,' said one of the city's cobblers, who had come to see the fun. 'What else is Africa if not a continent full of slaves, all ripe for the plucking? We all know that, but Parliament has been taken over by fools. They don't represent us no more. Democracy is dead!'

'Hypocrite,' a third man was shouting. 'Don't you dare claim to be a champion when you represent nothing but your own self-interest.'

'Exactly,' added a fourth, who published political tracts and prayerbooks for missionaries. 'You claim to represent justice when in fact you stand for injustice. You are a disgrace, and when the Lord looks down upon you, He laments that He ever gave you birth.'

In response to this commotion, Gaia rose from her chair and slammed down her gavel but it took eight hefty blows before silence was restored. In the meantime, she had not been an idle spectator.

'Special Constables, you are to arrest that man there, two in from the aisle on the third row. And the man standing two rows further back. Oh, and the woman with the chihuahua ... '

In total, Gaia had ten people and a dog taken to Pulteney Gaol for later sentencing. There was shock amongst the remaining members of the public, many of whom had only retained their liberty by chance. With a semblance of order now returned, she faced down Lord Servitude.

'I made perfectly clear, Lord Servitude, that the matter before this court was the licence and nothing but the licence, and that I would not tolerate the entry of politics into the proceedings.'

'But Madam Magistrate,' Lord Servitude protested grandly, 'I was merely describing my occupation. I had no intention to cause a ruckus. The outcry simply shows that people are jittery and that the presence of Mr Fanque and his circus in the city has worked them up into a state of unrest.'

'And why should people be jittery, Lord Servitude?' said Gaia, aware that she was taking his bait.

The peer smiled as he took control of the argument, and pointed at William.

'One moment this man's a slave on the other side of the world, serving the empire and defending our interests against the French. The next moment we remove his shackles and he's over here, exploiting our civic freedoms so he can construct an arena for mayhem—for you know the licentiousness that circuses encourage.'

There was a murmur amongst the public, both for and against these words. Lord Servitude now held up his hands.

'I have no argument against Africans, Ma'am—many of my finest servants were brought from Africa to the West Indies to provide the sugar for the tea that so many of us enjoy. And that was their destiny in life, and one they adapted to happily, to the benefit of all. But what of this Mr Fanque? He may look cheerful enough with his watermelon smile but, Ma'am, he is no longer in anyone's employ, which means that no one now monitors him, as we monitor our slaves, so why should we trust him? That's the question that must be asked. As we witnessed a moment ago, many of Bath's citizens are uncomfortable with his presumption in coming to Bath and trying to take advantage of our goodwill. He is, Madam, an unknown quantity. On that basis, it cannot be reasonable to license him to perform—we cannot have our population living in fear—and thus my complaint should be upheld.'

As magistrate, Gaia did her best to appear impartial. Her role was to remain above the fray. She looked across to Master Lush who, as clerk of court, was making notes.

'Let the records show that the basis of Lord Servitude's complaint is that the population of Bath are fearful and jittery of Mr Fanque; and that, allegedly, Mr Fanque is not to be trusted.'

'Exactly,' said Lord Servitude. 'My son, the Hon. Cecil, has more evidence, and is yet to speak, but your record is correct.'

With that short statement, and before any questions could be asked, he resumed his seat, like Caesar, in triumph.

Now it was Belle's turn and Gaia beckoned him forward. Having taken up position by the dock, Belle set his mind to meet the challenge. His commitment to Pablo Fanque, and to justice, must be unshakeable. He breathed deeply to calm his nerves.

'Your name, please.'

'Mr Bellerophon Nash, commonly known as Belle. I have recently returned from the West Indies, having been formerly a councillor of this fine city.'

To one side, an agitated Master Lush scribbled with a quill. The hearing was not going well, in his opinion. By whipping up public resentment, Lord Servitude had created the justification for his complaint.

'And you, Mr Nash, are an acquaintance of Mr Fanque from your time in the Indies?' Gaia asked. 'Is that correct?'

Belle nodded. On such a truth, a fiction could be spun.

'Yes, it was there that Mr Fanque came to my attention. When the enslaved on the islands rightly won their freedom, I suggested he bring his extraordinary talents to England. He contacted performers from Astley's, a well-established circus across the River Thames in London, and his new circus was formed. As Mr Fanque has described, it will be a treat for the city.'

'And as to the nub of the complaint,' said Gaia, 'that Mr Fanque is to be mistrusted and feared, what of that?'

Belle turned to the benches and looked deep into the public's

154

collective eye. Like Cicero in the forum of Rome, he seized the moment.

'Noble citizens of Bath, we live in a time of change, a marvellous modern world in which we enjoy all the fruits of human invention. We have more choice than ever before—of food and clothing and reading and machinery—and with that choice comes freedom. We know more, and have opinions and are free to speak our minds. That is the basis of our democracy, and at us other nations marvel. We are an inspiration to the world. Should we then deny such liberties to others? Surely, it is our obligation to take this gift and broadcast it afar, not hug it to ourselves. Liberty brings change, of course, and some men are fearful of change. Lord Servitude, whom you heard speak just now, is fearful of change because it means that he must change. Some may sympathise; I do not. Should the fate of nations be held back because one man cannot adapt? Should slaves be trapped forever in conditions of depravity because one man will not change?'

A sound of light applause came from the public benches.

'You see before you Mr Pablo Fanque, a freed man. Lord Servitude questions whether we can trust him. Why should we not? He is a man and wishes to succeed. Which of us does not? He has come to Bath to succeed. Which of us has not? We trust the great Ira Aldridge from America to hold our minds captive on stage as he plays King Lear. Mr Fanque is no less a phenomenon. I know Mr Fanque and can attest to that. Chairman Camshaft granted him a licence and he can attest to this. You see before you a man with burning ambition yearning to be fulfilled—an impresario of the future, the embodiment of the freedom we all crave. Bath will be the birthplace of his career and will be thus honoured to eternity. The complaint should be dismissed.'

Having concluded his statement, Belle returned to his chair. The public had absorbed his words and remained quiet, sensing the decision was on a knife edge. Indeed, it seemed to all that it would likely hinge on the testimony of the Hon. Cecil.

The horrible boy now rose to his feet and took his place by the dock. In one hand, he held a large sheet of paper, rolled up. With the other, he held a pair of spectacles, which he now applied to the bridge of his nose as if he was a man of intellect.

'My name is the Honourable Cecil Primus Rectus Servitude and my father owns plantations on the islands of the West Indies,' he declared, before being asked.

'Indeed,' said Gaia. 'And your father suggested you had further evidence regarding the trustworthiness of Mr Fanque.'

The Hon. Cecil pulled back his slender shoulders.

'Not against Mr Fanque directly. Despite investigation, there is little information on Mr Fanque, who appears to be a man of no reputation whatsoever. But against the troupe he leads, I have made the most harrowing discoveries. I have learnt that Mr Fanque's performers recently camped in Chippenham on their journey from London.'

Gaia looked over to William for confirmation.

'Can you validate that?'

'Yes, Your Honour. Them wuz in Chipp'n'am for three days before movin' west to Baatheaston,' confirmed William.

'And your point, Sir?' Gaia asked the Hon. Cecil.

Like his father before him, the son now had his moment.

'My point, Madam, is that their stay coincided with a series of burglaries wherein the culprit, not yet apprehended, was a China-man.'

Gaia was unimpressed.

'I do not think, Sir, that Mr Fanque's fate in Bath hangs on the petty crimes of a gentleman from China. Please explain yourself.'

'It will be noted from this circus bill,' said the Hon. Cecil, unfurling the roll of paper that he had in his hand and adjusting his spectacles, 'that a Mr Ki Hi Chin Fan Foo, a human spider from the Orient, is a member of the troupe—a man from China, the land of opium, rice and foot-binding. It is evident that he is the burglar and that he uses the circus as cover for his larcenous activity. Could he do any of this without the knowledge of Mr Fanque? I think not. And yet our great city is to invite these criminals into its very heart. People's safety is at risk, Madam Magistrate. I rest my case.'

For a moment, visitors on the public benches seemed about to protest loudly again, but Gaia pre-empted their outbursts with a hefty blow of her gavel.

'These are serious accusations, Sir, and ones that the court cannot take lightly.' Gaia turned to William. 'Mr Fanque, please confirm that you have a Mr Foo within your troupe.'

William stood.

'We do, Ma'am. And oi attests to his good character. He has been much maligned by this gentleman.'

Gaia nodded.

'Your words are noted, Mr Fanque, but your own good character has been brought into question by the complainants.' She returned her gaze to the Hon. Cecil. 'In support of your accusation, do you know of a witness who would recognise Mr Foo as the burglar in question?'

The Hon. Cecil had come armed with the information.

'A Mrs Sarah Rous of Chippenham,' he said smugly. 'Mrs Rous was the victim of a burglary a few days ago and had sight of the thief. I have her home address to hand, Madam.'

'A Mrs Rous, you say ... ,' replied Gaia.

Sniffing a plot in the making, she cast an enquiring eye at Belle, who looked back at her in a blissful innocence that masked the radiance he felt inside.

'Well done, gossipy Millicent!' he wished to cry. 'What a gal you are!'

His plan was working and the Hon. Cecil, puffed up with his own pomposity, had no intimation of the trap that Belle had sprung.

'Very well,' Gaia declared. 'My clerk will send a message immediately, requesting Mrs Rous to attend court tomorrow. At that time, Mr Fanque, you will return with Mr Foo. I will then investigate the issue raised by the complainants today. This hearing will re-convene at midday.'

With a final blow of her gavel, she rose from her chair.

'All stand for Magistrate Champion,' declared Master Lush, stepping out from his desk to open the door that led to her office.

In the courtroom, Lord Servitude and the Hon. Cecil shook hands, delighted with their morning's work. A short distance away, Belle was similarly pleased, although William had not enjoyed the accusation that he ran a criminal cabal.

'We've got them where we want them,' Belle said. 'Victory is within sight.'

'Ar't sure, Belle?' said William. 'Tha's yet to explain to me thoy plan. Who is this Mrs Rous? How did Lord Servitude's son get 'er name? And how will she serve our cause, rather than theirs?'

'Go back to Batheaston, William,' said Belle, confidently. 'And tomorrow, don't just bring Mr Foo. Bring them all. The entire troupe should bear witness to Pablo Fanque's triumph!'

I N HER OFFICE, Gaia threw her peruke on the floor, frustrated at the way the hearing had turned out.

'They're all playing at games in there. You agree with me, Master Lush, do you not?'

It was not a question—and Master Lush was not in the habit of disagreeing with her.

'I do. Something is undoubtedly afoot.'

He picked up the wig and gave it a sympathetic stroke, as one might pet a cat.

Gaia began to pace the room. It irked her when key facts were withheld. And in her opinion, dramatic interventions were for the theatre, not the courtroom.

'I don't trust any of them,' she concluded, 'and that includes Belle. I fear that he has lost his mind. And what are the Servitudes doing naming Mrs Rous? If I recall, she's Belle's aunt. She's the one who inherited the plantation in Grenada that Belle went out to set free. Don't the Servitudes know that?'

'I believe not,' said Master Lush, astutely, 'and I suspect it's rather important that they don't.' He finished petting the peruke and returned it to the wig stand. 'Thankfully, as the aunt lives in Chippenham, she wasn't named in my almanac, and so the Servitudes are none the wiser.'

The mention of Master Lush's book brought Gaia's pacing to a sudden halt. It was several days since she had last enquired after the almanac and now it was published. Such discourtesy would not have happened if Belle, Mr Fanque and the Servitudes had not distracted her.

'Master Lush, I am remiss. I should have asked earlier: I expect the residents of Bath are flocking to buy your valuable publication. *Bath Families and their Interesting Children Residing Throughout the Season*, was it not? I hope I remember its title aright.'

'It does well, Ma'am, and all the better for a change of name.'

'A change?'

'It was Mr Fanque's idea. He said my title was over-long and that titles should be short. I am yet to see him ride a horse but he has a knack for promotion. After the title change, Lackington's bookshop requested a second print run at double that of the first.'

Gaia clapped her hands excitedly. She always enjoyed a friend's good news.

'That's splendid, Master Lush, and deserving of praise. A positive contribution from Mr Fanque too. So, the almanac is a success! Tell me, what is the abbreviated title that has worked such wonders?'

Master Lush was delighted by the compliment and prepared himself to reveal all.

'Simplicity itself, Ma'am, but also a play on words. That's what makes it so clever. It's ... '

NOTES

- The American War of Independence lasted from 1775 to 1783 and might have been settled amicably had Great Britain allowed America's Thirteen Colonies to be represented in the British Parliament. Having been rebuffed, the colonies declared their independence in 1776 as the United States of America, a declaration which brought the French, Spanish and Dutch into the conflict on the side of America, leaving Britain entirely estranged in Europe, apart from the German state of Hesse. The war was ended by the Treaty of Paris, which involved not just the surrender by Great Britain of the Thirteen Colonies but transfers of land as far afield as the Caribbean, India and West Africa.

CHAPTER XIV
The Great Reveal

NEWS OF THE events in Gaia Champion's court spread like quicksilver through Bath. Maids of grand houses were soon gossiping to footmen, whose words were conveyed by butlers to Bath's many families in residence. By sunrise, even those in the Poor House were talking of how the arch-criminal Hi Ho Bing Bang Boo, lately of the Shanghai underworld, was to be arraigned before Magistrate Champion. Their reports, which became more and more inaccurate the more they were repeated, were the first example in England of what became known as Chinese whispers.

If the courthouse had been full for the first day of the hearing, it was overflowing for the second. William Darby wisely arrived early with the circus troupe, who merrily entertained the crowds outside Guildhall, with the Ridley Brothers in full clown attire. With William was Ki Hi Chin Fan Foo.

The Ridleys drew a crowd of spectators, some of whom broke away when the American actor Ira Aldridge appeared. Mr Aldridge had heard word that his name had been mentioned in support of Pablo Fanque. Having suffered discrimination of his own, he determined that he would assist the cause, and was amused to see that his presence was greeted with general swooning and excitement among the younger ladies.

Belle Nash was delighted to see his own friends turn out too. A chaise and four decanted Lady Passmore, accompanied by Mrs

Pomeroy. Also in attendance was Arthur Quigley, who had pinned on his dressing gown a line of pewter spoons.

Belle went to greet him.

'Good morning, Mr Quigley. My word, you're in dapper form today.'

'I thought I should make an effort for you and young Mr Fanque, Sir. I'm sporting my Waterloo medals,' replied the music master, pointing to his spoons. 'Hell of a battle. Damn near lost the Landolfi to a cannonball.'

'A close-run thing, indeed,' agreed Belle, who had heard variations of the story as often as tales of Mr Quigley's meeting the Chevalier de Saint-Georges. 'Do go in, Sir, and take a seat while such are still available. Ah, dear ladies, what a delight that you're here today,' he added, turning to greet Lady Passmore and Mrs Pomeroy. 'On which side of the aisle do you wish to repose yourselves: the bride's or groom's?'

Mrs Pomeroy broke into titters.

'Oh, Mr Nash, how you always stay light-hearted is a miracle of our time. Bride's or groom's! You always tickle me so!'

She stopped laughing on receiving a disapproving look from Lady Passmore.

'Control yourself, Mrs Pomeroy. This is a court of law, not a music hall,' said her ladyship, before turning to Belle. 'We are on your side, Mr Nash, but you should place us somewhere discreet. Lord Servitude pursued me in my debutante year and I do not wish my rejection of him then to antagonise him now.'

'Of course,' Belle replied, glancing behind the two ladies. 'But is Miss Prim not with you? I had expected her to be in attendance.'

'Miss Prim has been unwell ever since you returned to Bath,' replied Lady Passmore, her haughty chin rising by ten degrees. 'Now convey us to our seats without delay, if you please. I feel like a commoner standing in this lobby.'

Belle grimaced and quickly found them a suitable place at the back of the public gallery. He then took his own position at the front of the court. Sitting alone, his nerves grew more inflamed. To distract himself he thought of Miss Prim but that merely brought on an attack of guilt. When he had visited her two days earlier, he had focussed on attracting the attention of her maid, Millicent. Perhaps Miss Prim really was ill.

Further thoughts were vanquished by the sound of the midday bells from the abbey. The hour was upon them and Belle was joined by William. Close by, Lord Servitude and the execrable Cecil took their seats. Belle noted with surprise that Ira Aldridge had chosen to sit directly behind Lord Servitude. The American, it seemed, was a man who liked to get close to his enemies.

Belle turned to the door through which Gaia would come. Set into it was a peephole window, no more than six inches square, within which was framed the excited face of Lucius Lush.

Belle took a deep breath. Destiny was upon them.

I S THE COURT busy?' asked Gaia, straightening her wig with the help of a small mirror.

'Packed, Ma'am!' Master Lush replied. 'And we are joined by a member of the theatrical aristocracy.'

Gaia suspected Master Lush of playing a joke on her.

'The theatrical aristocracy? Who on Earth can you mean? Maria Foote, Countess of Harrington? I saw her perform the part of Miss Letitia Hardy in *The Belle's Stratagem* at Covent Garden ten years ago. Or George John Bennett who played Romeo and Cassius there too? But fie!—you cannot mean Henry Gattie who played Vortex in *A Cure for the Heartache* for I heard he had retired to open a cigar shop in Oxford just two years hence.'

'None of those, Ma'am,' said Master Lush, who felt suddenly out of his depth. 'No: one of the acting fraternity currently gracing the boards in Bath.'

'The law so takes up my time that I am out of touch, Master Lush. Tell, of whom do you speak?'

'Ira Aldridge, Ma'am!'

It now dawned on Gaia that her clerk was being truthful.

'Not possible. The American? Here?'

'See for yourself.'

As Gaia stepped forward to the peephole window she saw, almost breathing down the neck of Lord Servitude, the famous actor. He was exactly as the newspapers had described, with the dashing good looks so beloved by the fairer sex. For an instant, Gaia wondered whether he might be attracted to a more mature woman, applied a dab more make-up, then pulled herself together.

'Pray, how am I looking, Master Lush?'

'Most elegant, Ma'am.'

'Then it is time to ring up the curtain. Please enter and ask the court to stand.'

T HIS TIME EVEN Lord Servitude stood and all in court were silent. Gaia realised, however, that good decorum might not last—Lord Servitude and the abominable Cecil would see to that—so she quickly reminded both sides of the purpose of the hearing and the reason for the adjournment.

'Yesterday, the Hon. Cecil accused the contortionist Mr Foo of being responsible for a series of robberies in Chippenham. If true, questions must be asked as to whether the circus is a crimin-al enterprise.'

Lord Servitude and the detestable Cecil nodded in eager agreement.

'To clarify matters, attending the court today is Mrs Sarah Rous of Chippenham, a victim of a burglary who caught sight of the thief. And we have Mr Foo, who has come to the court of his own free will to clear his name. We shall now proceed. Special Constables, please bring in Mrs Rous and Mr Foo.'

All heads turned as Mrs Rous and Mr Foo entered. Gaia directed them to stand in front of her but at a distance apart. Belle felt a shiver go down his spine as he looked at the newest participants in the drama. It was, he knew, on their statements that his own future happiness depended. Instinctively, he tightened his grip on William's hand.

Belle stared at his aunt. He had not seen her for four years, before travelling to Grenada to free the slaves on the plantation that she had unexpectedly inherited. He knew her to be a good woman, but could she be relied upon? Perhaps, as a bachelor, he misunderstood womankind. Some examples, he had heard, could be fickle. After all, the core of his knowledge derived from a lecture provided by his father when he was six.

'When it comes to the female sex,' Belle's father had explained, 'there are ladies and there are women. Ladies include your mother and your aunts. Women are harder to explain. You might wonder as to the difference, Sir, but all will become clear when you grow up. Right, I'm glad to have cleared that up. Wasn't looking forward to it but we got through it, didn't we, boy? You can go back to the dolls' house if you wish.'

It was with these words in mind that Belle now studied Mrs Rous, dressed in a floral silk dress, her hair neatly tied. As an aunt she was a lady but he would more readily have described her as a woman—an elegant woman. Oh, it was all so confusing.

Despite his father's assurance that with adulthood he would come to understand what in childhood had been mystifying, Belle found his aunt impossible to read. He knew her as a person of liberal mind and strong resolve, but her deciding to free enslaved Caribbean families might not predispose her against Lord Servitude and his malodorous son in court.

'Please confirm that you are Mrs Sarah Rous from Chippenham,' requested Gaia.

'I am,' came the reply in a soft but clear voice.

At his desk, Master Lush made notes with his quill.

'It has been suggested by the Hon. Cecil Servitude, a complainant in this case, that your home in Chippenham has recently been burgled.'

Mrs Rous did not answer immediately. Instead, she turned to look at the Servitudes with a mixture of suspicion and disdain.

'I dislike gossip but, yes, it is true that I was burgled. There seems no end to it.'

Unusually, Gaia hesitated.

'There seems no end to *what*, Mrs Rous? Burglaries or gossip?'

Mrs Rous smiled.

'We have been assailed with gossip since Adam set up home with Eve in the Garden of Eden,' she replied. 'I was referring to the burglaries. It started with the bread, then the butter and most lately the milk. It really is most vexing.'

For good reason, Gaia looked troubled. In his seat, Belle smiled. His aunt—a Nash lady through and through—was playing her part to perfection.

'Explain a little more, if you will,' Gaia asked. 'You mention butter and milk. Were not monies stolen? Or jewellery? Paintings? Furnishings? Fine wine?'

To everyone's surprise, Mrs Rous put a hand over her mouth to cover up a short laugh.

'Goodness, no! I suppose my money might be useful but I doubt that the thieves in question would have any use for a brooch or a necklace. As for paintings or furnishings, where would they put them?'

A sense of confusion now took hold, for nearly everyone in the courtroom had imagined the type of dramatic thefts hinted at in the odious Cecil's narrative of events.

'You seem to know, Madam, exactly who your burglars are,' said Gaia. 'Are we talking about a tribe of Chinese contortionists, newly resident in Wiltshire?'

'Chinese contortionists?' laughed Mrs Rous. 'No, Madam, I refer to the town's street children, of course. They live behind the coaching inn and beg for pennies from the travellers. When they run short of provisions, they take to stealing from doorsteps. I have instructed the delivery boys to bring everything indoors but they will not follow directions. Perhaps they're in cahoots with the urchins—who can know?—but what is one to do? The children must eat, I suppose, and we have a weak-willed magistrate in Chippenham, unlike Bath.'

Gaia suppressed a smile.

'I see. But do you know of other, more serious burglaries?'

Mrs Rous shook her head.

'No, Madam. The coach travellers, of course, are reminded to take care of their luggage, but otherwise Chippenham is a quiet town. Our peace is rarely disturbed.'

As the public laughed, Lord Servitude and the repulsive Cecil shuffled uneasily. The deposition was not what they had anticipated.

Gaia continued, 'As for the Hon. Cecil's claim that you identified the thief of the latest burglary as being from China, do you have any comment?'

Mrs Rous took the question in her stride.

'That's the gossip at work. A lady at the haberdashery said she had seen a man of oriental appearance drinking milk on the High Street. She was amused because the cream had turned his long moustache white. "Maybe it was he who stole your milk," she said. We both of us laughed as we all know it's the children.'

Gaia nodded. She was reaching the end of her questions.

'Finally, Mrs Rous, have you ever seen this gentleman, Mr Foo, before?'

Mrs Rous looked directly at Mr Foo.

'No, Ma'am. I have never seen him before.'

It was a comment that brought further laughter in court. Having nothing further to ask, Gaia passed the questioning to Belle and William but both declined.

'Chippenham's reputation for law and order is restored,' Belle quipped. 'May divine Themis take up residence there. We have no wish to take up Mrs Rous's time any further.'

The Servitudes, however, had no option but to fight back. After a brief confabulation with his father, the loathsome Cecil took to his feet.

'Mrs Rous,' he declared, 'the burglaries may not yet have extended to possessions more valuable than milk but it stands to reason that every thief has to start somewhere. What did Autolycus steal, I wonder, before appropriating King Sisyphus's herd? By which I mean ... '

' ... that minor crimes may lead to major ones,' Mrs Rous replied. 'But no major crimes have befallen Chippenham in recent times.'

The Hon. Cecil narrowed his eyes.

'It is noteworthy, though, that the suspicion of the lady at the haberdashery should first fall upon a man from China.'

'I do not think so,' responded Mrs Rous.

'And, by your own description, though there has been an escalation of burglaries, a possible thief is identified but is neither questioned nor arrested. Instead, licence is sought for him to make his way to Bath to perform in a circus!'

For the first time, Mrs Rous looked flustered.

'I can only say that I have never seen Mr Foo before. And I doubt that he is the same ... '

Belle's aunt, however, was drowned out by the unutterable Cecil, who had no time for awkward women.

'Should we trust him, Madam, this mysterious Mr Foo?' he cried. 'Can we trust anyone from China, a land bedevilled by mysticism and opium? It is the contention of Lord Servitude and myself that we cannot—we must not—as will be the contention of others in this court of democracy and free speech, who wish their voices to be heard.'

It was an unmistakeable call to arms and one that was immediately answered by those present who sided with the Servitudes.

'Tie him up!' came the first cry. 'You can't trust Orientals.'

'Ladies, hold onto your purses.'

168

'They're worse than Africans.'

'Indians!'

'Frenchies!'

Gaia slammed down her gavel. Hard. The inability of people to keep their mouths shut never ceased to amaze her. Immediate action was required.

'Special Constables!' she commanded. 'Restore order. Pulteney Gaol will be filled this day.'

WITHIN TEN MINUTES, a dozen members of the public had been removed. During the mêlée, Belle had gripped William by the arm, persuading him to hold fast and not become involved. He had done the same in Grenada when urging Pablo to choose his battles wisely. Ira Aldridge, too, had judiciously held back, when fired with the urge to punch both Servitudes.

With order restored, Gaia set about admonishing the Hon. Cecil.

'I warned your father and let this be a final warning to you. My role is to provide a fair hearing to your complaint, which requires good order. Foment trouble and you, too, will be a guest of Pulteney Gaol.'

'But Madam Magistrate, I ... '

Gaia was not to be challenged.

'Silence. You have had your say. Mrs Rous, you may return to Chippenham with the court's thanks for journeying to Bath at such short notice. Now that order is restored, I will ask questions of Mr Foo.'

The Hon. Cecil took the admonishment in his stride. In fact, he looked quietly pleased. He had illustrated weaknesses in Mrs Rous's statement and, by inviting the court to protest, had reminded Gaia that public order should inform her decision.

As for Belle, the endgame had begun.

His aunt had played her part to perfection and the fact they were related had not been revealed. As Mrs Rous left the courtroom, his attention turned to Mr Foo, a man whom he had last seen while lying on his backside in the rain in Lambeth.

Mr Foo's features remained unchanged: the same pug nose, black hair, theatrical eyes, a suspicion of mascara and a moustache with two tendrils that framed a shaven chin. But what struck Belle most, in the clear light of the courtroom, was Mr Foo's thinness. A red, black and gold changshan jacket hung from his shoulders around a body so slight that it might have been made of air.

Belle noticed also that his brow was beaded with sweat. Mr Foo had good reason to be nervous, having been subjected to physical threats by the Servitudes's supporters. The pressure on him, however, was far greater than that, for William had demanded that he reveal the secret upon which his livelihood depended.

It was time for Gaia to begin her examination, which she introduced by asking the simplest of questions.

'For the purpose of the court, would you prefer to be referred to as Mr Foo, or as Mr Ki, as, I believe, is the custom in your country?'

It was not often that Gaia's first line of enquiry yielded spectacular results. On hearing Gaia's request, Mr Foo began to squirm, his shoulders and arms resembling the actions of a disturbed crab.

'Ah well now, Ma'am, dat's a question all roight.'

'And what is the answer?' Gaia asked.

'De ting of it is, Ma'am, oi cannot rightly be sayin' now,' Mr Foo added.

Gaia gave him a stern look.

'Well then, will you confirm that you are Ki Hi Chin Fan Foo, the contortionist pictured on the poster for Mr Fanque's circus?'

This question seemed to please Mr Foo more.

'Oi am dat!' he cried, throwing out an arm. 'Dat's who oi am, for sure.'

Gaia's expression, however, turned quizzical. The answer, though definite, seemed inconclusive—as did Mr Foo's accent. Though no expert on Chinese dialects, Mr Foo's had more than a touch of the Celt about it.

'Then why is it I cannot wholly believe you, Mr ... Foo?'

The contortionist began to squirm again, like a schoolchild forced to tell on a friend.

'Ah, Mr Fanque,' he implored. 'Could you be after helpin' me out now, Sorr? De question's too hard, so it is. I don't want people a-laughin' at me.'

Everyone in the courtroom was silent. Belle's eyes darted from Mr Foo to William and Gaia to see who would speak next. It was William who seized the mantle, rising to his feet and stepping forward. Belle was mesmerised by the scene. It was the final act of the drama that he had put in play.

'If oi may, Ma'am,' said William.

'I think you had better,' Gaia replied. 'Whatever Mr Foo is struggling to divulge needs to be told.'

William took a deep breath, for what he was about to say broke a sacred code of trust in the circus world.

'The truth is, Ma'am, that us circus people uses names to suit our act. No one wants to see John Smith on a toight-rope. Some in the trade go further and change the country of them's birth. It's all innocent, of course. The necessities of the profession, done to support the magic of the circus.'

'I see,' noted Gaia, who had started to understand the substance of Belle's plot. 'And in this instance ... '

William indicated to Mr Foo, who continued to shuffle uncomfortably on his feet.

'In this instance, whilst the Hon. Cecil would wish moy colleague to be Mr Foo and would have 'im be Chinese, the fact is that the greatest contortionist on Earth is ... '

At this point, everyone's attention was on Mr Foo, who had placed a hand across the top of his head. He now proceeded to lift the silk hat he was wearing and with it a wig of black hair to which it was attached, thus revealing a bald scalp. Then he neatly plucked off the tendril moustache and wiped away the mascara from his eyes.

He revealed, 'I have de honour to be Mr Declan Finucane from Dublin, Ma'am—a proud Irishman plying his trade as Ki Hi Chin Fan Foo. People pay good cash to see me dressed as a man from China, sure enough. Dey wouldn't do that for a Dobliner, now. Dat's how it is.'

There were gasps of astonishment as Mr Foo's true identity was revealed. The man from China, bar the changshan jacket, had completely disappeared. As for Lord Servitude and the objectionable Cecil, they had turned pale. Defeat was all but assured, for even Gaia, though it was unbecoming of a magistrate, had descended into a fit of laughter and was waving the gavel above her head to keep her balance.

'Oh, Mr Finucane, I totally understand. An apology is owed. Make-believe lies at the heart of entertainment and this hearing has done you a disservice. I only hope the accompanying publicity will boost ticket sales, so that the damage to your income is restored.'

Her comments sparked jubilation among members of the circus troupe. It was clear that their show would go on. Gaia, however, held up her hands in a request for silence. She straightened her wig as she prepared to speak.

'Even when the result is clear, procedure must be followed: a summing up is required. After hearing the testimony of witnesses, I find no evidence of Mr Fanque's circus being a threat to public order. In support of my finding, I declare that the crimes alleged by the complainants to have occurred in Chippenham did not occur, nor was Mr Foo identified as a thief by Mrs Rous. It transpires, moreover, that Mr Foo is not from China but from Ireland. And finally, that while the Hon. Cecil Servitude stated that there is reason to distrust people from China, he provided no evidence to support this claim. My conclusion, therefore, is that the licence of the circus has been properly issued. This hearing is closed and I wish you all a good day.'

Having made her summation, Gaia swiftly left the dais, followed by Master Lush, who cast an eye over his shoulder to the courtroom behind. The celebrations had begun in earnest. Belle and William were hugging each other tight and quickly brought Mr Foo into their embrace. Behind them, a juggler had taken six clubs from a bag to begin an impromptu show. As the rear doors of the courtroom were opened, two of the troupe did triple backward somersaults down the central aisle. And Ira Aldridge pumped his arms in the air as he shared in the triumph.

As the supporters of the Servitudes slunk away, their critics voiced their scorn.

'You're a fool, Lord Servitude. A slave to your own craven prejudices.'

'Tricked by a Dubliner. Fancy that! Shanghaied by an Irishman!'

'Where are you from, Lord Servitude? Constantinople most likely, for you strut like a prize turkey.'

'You'll be the dishonourable Cecil now!'

As for Belle, he had not felt such pleasure in years.

'We did it, Pablo! We did it!' he cried.

William smiled as the tears flowed. His lifelong dream had become a reality.

'Oi got me circus—and defeated Lord Servitude into the bargain. What could be better?'

'What, indeed?' thought Belle, as the two men hugged.

For what could be worse?

NOTES
* Whilst it would raise questions of cultural appropriation and racism today, Pablo Fanque's Circus Royal (as it became) did have an Irish contortionist disguised as a Chinese man. He

went by the circus name of Ki Hi Chin Fan Foo. So successful was his disguise that in about 1850 two Chinese tea merchants in Glasgow took Mr Fanque to court. Having been denied access to their 'compatriot', they accused Mr Fanque of holding Mr Foo captive, requiring his true identity to be revealed in court.

CHAPTER XV

Thunder and Lightning

B ELLE NASH, AS anticipated, had found Mrs Rous waiting for him in the corridors of Guildhall.

He had fallen into her arms, thanking her profusely for her support.

'You are the best of women, dear aunt.'

Mrs Rous had laughed, pushing him away.

'Sweet nephew, a small fib in court is a small price to pay to defeat Lord Servitude. I already owed you a debt of gratitude for dispensing of that evil plantation in Grenada and was overjoyed to receive your letter this week. I had hoped to repay you for your kindness and now I have.'

Belle had kissed his aunt's hand and, soon after, had seen her to her carriage. Having waved her goodbye, he now took William Darby by the hand and led him off to The Dog & Duck, along with the circus troupe, Lucius Lush and a posse of abolitionists.

A WORD OF ADVICE from an old hand: always choose a Friday for a night out, especially if you plan to frolic to excess. The young and exuberant can pass off a Friday night's immoderation as the start of a triumphant weekend. The older and wiser can quietly lie in bed the next morning and spend till Sunday recovering. Either way, Friday is the week-night to choose.

Thus it was to our heroes' good fortune that the trial concluded on a Friday, for there was much for them to celebrate. Pressed to buy a few rounds at The Dog & Duck, Belle stayed in the public bar until long past midnight, sharing draughts and drams and a few pipes of tobacco and several pinches of snuff, listening to a tiltering Tom Shelton recount how he could have beaten George Maddox in the ring, if only ... if only ... if only ... .

And so, to Saturday morning, with each person facing the day as best he might.

Belle and William woke with pounding heads but soaring hearts. Master Lush opened his eyes to find a somersault artist named FlipFlop asleep beside him. Mr Foo found himself contorted in the embrace of an Irishman who knew nothing of China. And the Ridley Brothers both woke up remembering the same joke but not its punchline.

Gaia Champion, who had avoided the inn and had received word of Phyllis Prim's continued frailty, made plans to visit Gay Street.

As for Lord Servitude and the repulsive Cecil, they rose early from their beds to feast on a full breakfast of gammon, mutton pie, fried eggs, sausages, bacon, horseradish and black pudding before spending hours wallowing in anger and self-pity. As ever, their housekeeper, Mrs Neech, provided a sympathetic ear to their catalogue of moans. It was, she agreed, a dark day indeed when people of independent mind disparaged the Servitudes's greatness of spirit.

B ELLE AND WILLIAM had an altogether healthier breakfast—porridge—and an altogether more wholesome conversation.

'I spoke with Mistress Lush at the inn,' said Belle. 'He tells me that the success of his almanac is thanks, in large part, to a title that you created.'

'Oi merely spoke as oi found,' said William. '*Families Resident in the Royal City of Bath for the Season, Their Children and Other*

Interests was a terrible toitle. Too many words. Impossible to remember.'

'What did you suggest instead?'

William smiled at the memory, for he had first pulled Master Lush's leg.

'Oi offered him *Smug Superior Gentry who Impose Their Sense of Entitlement on The Rest of The World.*'

'No?! And did he believe you? He's an innocent boy. It's part of his charm.'

'Oi think he did, for he looked sorrowful and disappointed and told oi, "That won't sell, Mr Fanque! At least, not to its intended audience."'

Belle laughed and asked, 'And how did you put him out of his misery?'

'Oi come clean and told him his best option: *Landed and Lauded.* It's a play on words, d'you see? Lauded, as in ... '

Belle clapped.

'Quite brilliant! If the circus is half as brilliant, we'll have two successes on our hands!'

The impresario nodded.

'And now, Belle, let's be finishin' the remains of our breakfast for we need to visit the lawn this mornin' and take measurements. Oi must know 'em before oi lays out the tent.'

SOME THIRTY MINUTES later the two partners departed Sydney Buildings, and Belle looked up at the sky. It was a bright and cold winter's morning but the weather was set to turn. Away on the horizon, dark clouds were gathering and those with an eye for a storm would have seen them and felt unease.

The same was true for relations between the two men, not in the falsehood of their being cousins but in the tenderness of their affection. They had been jolly enough at breakfast but the time was not far off when their temper would descend into mere pleasantries.

In theory, there is little between bachelors that a bowl of porridge and a spoonful of sugar cannot cure. William's victory in court, however, had given him his circus and thus fulfilled his primary purpose in befriending Belle. As for Belle, he had awoken with the mistaken belief that their victory had won him happiness. In his mind, possession of the circus licence had completed the transformation of William into Pablo Fanque.

For the moment, however, the two men remained in ebullient mood and unaware of their divide.

'Of course, oi never doubted tha' plan, not for an instant,' said William, 'but indulge me for a moment and tell me 'ow it worked.'

'Gossip is a creature whose beating heart is the household maid,' laughed Belle, finally granting William entry to his web of deceit. 'The maid with the latest information is always held in highest esteem, and when it comes to being a babbler, there is no better maid in the West Country than Miss Prim's Millicent. It is her need to tittle-tattle that explains her frequent absences from Gay Street.'

William nodded.

'Oi follows 'ee, Sir. Then what?'

'I knew that she and Mrs Mulligatawny have keen ears,' Belle smiled. 'They always hide in corridors and spy on my conversations when I visit. So long as Millicent was at home, it was certain that any intelligence I imparted would find its way up Gay Street and to The Circus within minutes. So I chose a time to visit when I was sure that Millicent would be at home.'

'But 'ow couldst tha' be sure it would reach the Servitudes?'

'I spoke plainly with Miss Prim!' explained Belle. '"My dear Miss Prim," I said, "the last possible person who can know of the burglaries in Chippenham, or the identity of the thief Mr Ki Hi Chin Fan Foo, or of the latest victim being Mrs Sarah Rous at Number 23 The Beeches, is Lord Servitude. We must keep this dangerous knowledge to ourselves."'

William laughed.

'And the maid took tha' bait! But how much faith didst tha' 'ave that tha'n aunt would play 'er part when tha' wrot'st to her?'

'I was all but certain that she would acquiesce,' Belle replied, whilst eyeing a passing cloud that had covered the sun. 'Aunt Sarah is a woman of firm principle. I explained my love for Pablo Fanque and wrote that we can enjoy no freedom so long as Lord Servitude and his ilk are set against us. Freedom, like equality, is not a half-measure. My aunt knows that.'

They were approaching Pulteney Bridge and William was suddenly struck by a thought.

'Not only do oi now carry the name of Pablo Fanque but it is tha' love for 'im that won me me circus.'

Belle reached back and made to pull William forward.

'You have more than his name, sweet William. You *are* Pablo now. Flesh and blood, you stand before me.'

In the distance, thunder rolled.

T HE TWO MEN continued their walk past Guildhall and on to Milsom Street, and thence up the well-trodden path to George Street and Gay Street—oh, how Belle missed Gay Street!—before emerging into The Circus. As they climbed Milsom Street, the gathering clouds thickened and a chill descended. Belle studied the sky; Bristol was sending a storm their way.

'Let's hope the rain holds off or heads south to Radstock. I don't want anything to spoil our day,' said Belle.

English weather, however, is rarely accommodating. As they turned into George Street, the first drop of rain, thick and heavy with intent, fell. Pedestrians wore worried faces. Caught out by the sudden change, their footsteps quickened. The tempo of Bath had picked up a notch.

It was with some surprise, therefore, that Belle saw—despite the rain—a queue of women waiting in a line in George Street. As others pushed by, the women seemed listless, like beggars, their shoulders hunched.

179

Belle's first impression was that they were preparing to enter a workhouse, although there was no workhouse on George Street. Then, as he and William passed by, he noted the name of the premises they were waiting outside—Mrs Wellow's House of Wool—and saw that each woman carried a knitting bag.

A few steps later, they had reached the junction of George Street and Gay Street.

'Does not tha' friend Miss Prim live close by?' William asked.

Belle looked down the street to Number 40, and to his adjoining former home, before looking back at the distressed women outside House of Wool. He felt unsettled and not just by the rain.

'Belle?' William said, wishing to have his question answered.

'What? Oh yes, we might pass by her house later. Miss Prim remains unwell and I must visit her again. But, judging by the sky, we should first hurry to complete your work before the rain starts in earnest.'

'Thank 'ee,' agreed William, wiping a raindrop from his brow. He shivered as the temperature dropped by another degree. 'To The Circus, then, without delay!'

T HOUGH DENIED THE company of Belle, Miss Prim had another of her friends beside her, although there were signs that the friend was flagging. After thirty minutes by the bedside, Gaia Champion was tiring of the patient's wittering woes.

It had become clear to her that Bath's foremost knitting spinster was suffering an ailment not of the body but of the mind. The matter that bothered her, however, remained unknown, and, despite her best efforts at investigation, Gaia had failed to elicit an explanation.

This left Bath's magistrate frustrated and concerned.

It troubled Gaia in particular that Miss Prim was not knitting, for on other occasions when Miss Prim had been struck low, visitors typically left with a pair of gloves. Mrs Mulligatawny had confirmed that Miss Prim last touched her needles the previous week. Indeed, the knitting bag had been left abandoned on the bedchamber floor.

Gaia had done her very best to tease, entice and cajole Miss Prim to reveal the cause of her distress but the only response had been a shaking of the head and a variety of bird-like noises.

Allowing herself an interval from her bedside vigil, Gaia now rose from the chair to collect the knitting bag. If a knitting bag were capable of emotion, Miss Prim's appeared disconsolate and unloved, and it seemed only right to reunite it with its owner.

Miss Prim recognised Gaia's purpose and, for the first time in the visit, spoke with clarity.

'No, Mrs Champion. You must leave the devil's bag alone.'

'The devil's bag?' said Gaia, greatly alarmed. 'My dear Miss Prim, whatever can you mean?'

Ignoring her host's warning, Gaia picked up the bag and was immediately disquieted. Wool is voluminous and Miss Prim's bag was normally packed with a dozen balls or more. But on picking it up and looking inside, Gaia saw that there was ...

'Half a ball only? Miss Prim, these are deep waters.'

'Oooah,' replied Miss Prim, who saw a determined look come into Gaia's eyes.

For a moment, Gaia considered calling Mrs Mulligatawny and subjecting her to a battery of questions. Instead, she opted for an even more aggressive approach. On occasion with friends, one must be cruel to be kind.

'My dear Miss Prim,' Gaia began, in the manner of the magistrate, 'it is evident to me that you are hiding something of the greatest import and that your hiding it is making you unwell. I understand that there are sensitivities you wish to protect, and a risk of embarrassment in your revealing them, but Miss Prim, I care more that you regain your health, and for that to happen you must be truthful. Nothing more is to be achieved by my wiping your brow a moment longer, or in having others fret about your well-being. Tell me now: why have you just half a ball of wool in your knitting bag?'

Miss Prim found the energy to protest.

'Mrs Champion, I cannot,' Miss Prim pled, her thin arms flailing. 'And you mustn't push me. You know not what you ask.'

But the initiative was Gaia's and she would not back down.

'I can and I will. If you refuse to cooperate immediately, I shall on this very hour summon Dr Griffith of The Paragon to attend to you.'

Dr Griffith was notorious in the city for an approach to medicine that was both eccentric and startlingly unsuccessful.

'Not Dr Griffith of The Paragon!' cried Miss Prim, understandably agitated.

'Yes, Madam, Dr Griffith of The Paragon. And I shall order him to apply his poultice of bran and goose fat to you.'

Miss Prim looked at her friend in dismay. She had sworn never to reveal the debt she owed to Mrs Wellow's House of Wool. The shame of others knowing, she deemed, would be too great to bear. But now she was faced with the alternative of being covered in bran and goose fat.

Given the choice between the two, Miss Prim's instinct for self-preservation kicked in. Her right arm, no longer flailing but firm as a pikestaff, stretched out in the direction of George Street and pointed precisely to where Belle had seen the line of distressed women. Miss Prim was evidently not alone in having allowed her love of knitting to drive her into penury.

'It's the House of Wool!' she cried. 'That is the nether realm of my undoing!'

T HE RAIN NOW falling on Bath was egalitarian in its persistence, as liable to drop on the head of Viscount Melbourne as on his footman, and splattering the attic windows of the maids' bedchambers no less than the panes of the grandest drawing rooms.

This was, however, not a cleansing rain. It sat heavy on the windows, perhaps held by the year's dust that had collected on the glass. It muddied the view of the outside world, turning the clear outlines of passing pedestrians into tearful blurs.

Rain carries memories. Poor Mercy, locked in the top floor room of Number 33, The Circus, heard the raindrops drumming on her tiny window and remembered the great tropical storms of the Caribbean, of sheltering in her grandparents' porch watching sheets of rain, a waterfall from the sky that turned the path outside into a red river of mud.

She looked through the bars that kept her a prisoner. A few days earlier, she had imagined seeing a familiar face in the street below. After the Hon. Cecil had released her from his grip, she had remembered the man's name: Belle Nash. Since then, however, her doubts over who she had seen had grown and her hopes had faded. In her enslaved life, she had only experienced pain. As a child she had been beaten by the plantation managers, and on reaching maturity, abused. Though she wished for a miracle, it was not in her nature to believe that any such happiness could ever come her way.

Nevertheless, the driving rain drew her to the closed window again. She looked up to the sky as lightning broke and a crash of thunder roared. Nature in all its fury was in full cry. She felt her grandfather on his porch pull her close for protection.

'Come here, gal,' he had said, holding Mercy in his embrace. 'You'll be safe with me.'

Mercy followed the lines of rain as they fell to earth. The light was poor and the rivulets on the glass distorted the outside world but her sight was good and, to her surprise, she saw two men pacing the lawn of The Circus, as if impervious to the downpour that assailed them. It was William and Belle, taking measured strides across the grass, marking out the terrain in preparation for building their tent.

As Mercy watched them, their forms drifting in and out of

focus through the panes, she became more and more certain that both were men she knew.

She placed her hands against the glass, rubbing furiously as if the act might brush away the water and give her a clearer line of sight—if only for a second, please only for a second! And then it came: a burst of rain against the window followed by a gust of wind that swept it dry, and ...

Her hands fell furiously on the latch as she fought to open the window. It had to be true. She could not be imagining it. Far down below, in the most fashionable city in the world, in a rainstorm that had gathered all its force from the other side of the Atlantic, must be her half-brother Pablo and his friend Belle Nash.

She tore at the catch, pulling it free and lifting the lower sash. She began to cry out even before the window was open, her mouth scrabbling for words just as her fingers were scrabbling for purchase.

'Pablo! ... Pablo! Mr Nash, please!'

The thunder roared again and the men looked up. It was not certain whether they had been attracted by her cry or the sound of the heavens.

'Pablo! I'm up here! It's Mercy. Pablo, please!'

At last, she prised the sash up and stretched her arms through the bars, waving them violently. Raindrops blew against her face and cascaded down her cheeks like tears. She filled her lungs with air and prepared to cry out again. A final effort to attract the attention of the men below. To secure her freedom.

At which point, she sensed a presence behind her. A smell of fried eggs and black pudding made her gag as a man reached out from behind, pulling at her hair and shoulder. She tried to fight but his strength was too much for her. Within seconds, she had been pulled back from the window and thrown onto her bed.

He was on top of her now, his hands bunched into fists that pummelled her face. She felt the blood flow in her mouth as her eyes swelled. She knew from experience what was coming. As he tore at her dress, she made one last try, and screamed out the name of her brother.

BELLE AND WILLIAM stopped pacing and looked at each other in alarm. No one else was mad enough to be out in the rain. And yet the voice, if only to Belle's ears, had been clear. Where had it come from?

'Pablo! ... Mr Nash!'

'Someone's crying out for us,' Belle shouted. 'I've heard that voice before.'

Inside an amphitheatre such as The Circus was, sound reverberates, bouncing from side to side, disguising its direction. Not knowing where to gaze, they stared at each other. The rain fell harder, the wind whipping through the air.

'Pab ... It's Mer ... !'

They both glanced skywards but the rain had stung their eyes. For an instant, they thought they had caught a glimpse of a figure, arms reaching through a barred window, but just as quickly she was gone.

Belle approached William in a sudden state of shock.

'Did you see that, Pablo?' he said, pointing up. 'Did you not recognise her? The voice!'

William, however, had not heard Mercy's voice as clearly as Belle had and was tiring of Belle's confusing him with Pablo Fanque. He reverted to formality, wishing only for the task of measuring the lawn to be completed without delay.

'Oi saw nothin', Mr Nash. The rain was in moyn oyes.'

'It sounded like ... it sounded like your sister, Pablo. Didn't you think?'

But of course William could not have thought any such thing. It was Belle alone who had heard the voice clearly, he alone who could have recognised it as Grenadian, he alone who could then have ascribed it to Pablo Fanque's sister. It was a huge assumption but, having made it, Belle was certain that he was right.

185

'It is the voice of your sister. I met her on the plantation, when you invited me to your home. You must remember.'

'Moy sister? Oi 'as no sister, Mr Nash.'

'By God, man, I speak of Mercy—torn from you in Grenada and taken to Jamaica. Your own flesh and blood.'

It was one falsity too many for William. He realised that, with the court case won, Belle's delusion had deepened.

'This must stop, Sir, 'ere and now. Moy name is William Darby and tha' know'st it!'

There followed a scream so piercing and so full of pain that it filled the air of The Circus and penetrated the surrounding streets: a sound that could freeze the blood or stop a human heart.

In Gay Street to the south, Gaia hesitated in her questioning of Miss Prim, her friend's distress paling into insignificance beside the cry of anguish they had both heard.

'The void,' whimpered Miss Prim, grabbing hold of her sheet in fear. 'The terrible void.'

At the same time, the sound of Mercy's torment reached the ears of bedbound Ernest Camshaft in nearby Rivers Street. As her scream faded, a tear of pity filled his eye for the unique misery inflicted on the world by the scum of humanity, and the chairman of the City Corporation breathed his last.

At Number 33, The Circus, by contrast, a contented smirk came over the unlovely face of the Hon. Cecil. He lifted himself off Mercy, who lay weeping on the bed, and having assaulted her physically now assaulted her verbally.

'I gave you fair warning: one more act of insolence and I would chain you to this bed. You disobeyed me and you will now suffer the consequences. Mrs Neech will bring up the chains for I, dear Mercy, am a man of integrity—*vir integritas impeccabilis*—and when I say I shall do something, I do it.'

NOTES

- The concept of a two-day, work-free weekend in England began in factories in Northern England in the early nineteenth century. Factory owners were persuaded that shortening the working hours of Saturday to 2.00 pm would allow the workers to return sober and refreshed on Monday mornings.

- Tom Shelton and George Maddox were prize fighters in the early nineteenth century. Other fighters of the era included Tom Cribb and the African-Americans Bill Richmond and Tom Molineaux. Boxing aficionados still talk of the Cribb–Molineaux world championship fight of 1810, which lasted thirty-five rounds and was won by Cribb in controversial circumstances.

- Traditional poultices were typically a heated mass of moist bran, flour and herbs. They were applied to the body and kept in place by a cloth, and were intended to draw out inflammation. The use of goose fat as a poultice for treating chest infections became briefly popular in the 1930s and 1940s, so Dr Griffith of The Paragon (a row of grand houses in Bath) was a hundred years ahead of his time in this regard, though in other ways more retrograde.

PART TWO
'THE SCUM'

The more I see of Mankind,
The more I prefer my dog.

Blaise Pascal

CHAPTER XVI

Post-Mortem

GUILDHALL CHAIRMAN ERNEST Camshaft is dead!' shouted the town crier, who had not had much to say for several months and was making the most of his opportunity. 'Guildhall chairman Ernest Camshaft is dead!'

Barely a person alive could recall Bath's City Corporation without Mr Camshaft as its chairman. The surviving councillors immediately decreed a week of mourning and solemnly issued a request that the Bishop of Bath & Wells conduct the funeral in the abbey. The bishop replied promptly that he could perform the service the following Friday.

Before then, there were still matters that required the attention of the living. As anyone who has suffered the death of a friend or family member will attest, it is an oddity of mourning that life must go on.

It was not necessarily disrespectful, therefore, for Belle Nash to suggest to Gaia Champion that she host their friends for Sunday tea at Somerset Place. Though the loss of the chairman was still a raw wound, there was much to discuss and none of it could wait. A tea party would allow them also to air and display their mourning clothes in solemn remembrance of the departed.

For men, the requirements of society when it came to mourning attire were straightforward: a dark suit sufficed when coupled with a black hatband, gloves and a cravat. For women, society's demands were more onerous. Throughout Bath, pungent mothballs were being removed from trunks holding dresses of black paramatta silk trimmed with harsh crêpe. These were matched by black hats and black jewellery.

Lady Passmore of Tewkesbury Manor, as was her style, had extended mourning attire to her resplendent chaise and four carriage. Its Indian red silk curtains, edged with gold brocade, were replaced. Similarly, the French embroidered white cotton net curtains and the red Axminster carpet were exchanged for black nets. Which was all very well but ...

'With these black curtains, I can't see where we're going,' said Mrs Pomeroy, who had joined her ladyship on the journey to Somerset Place. 'Where are we?'

'Somewhere on Sion Hill, I believe,' replied Lady Passmore, who had a strong sense of her position in life, whether social or geographical. 'Be patient, Mrs Pomeroy. We will be at Mrs Champion's house soon enough.'

Mrs Pomeroy, however, was *im*patient.

'Will she serve cake with tea? I can't remember if cake is served or not during periods of mourning.'

Lady Passmore was unamused.

'Thinking of your stomach again, Mrs Pomeroy, and in a period of mourning? Really, you can be most impolite.'

Mrs Pomeroy clutched at her belly.

'I cannot help it, Lady Passmore of Tewkesbury Manor. My stomach has an independent mind. I am more than upset at the loss of poor Ernest, of course, but my stomach cares not a jot.'

From the incline of the carriage, it was clear that they were travelling upwards but since Bath had so many hills, the likelihood of this being Sion Hill seemed to Mrs Pomeroy to be no better than one in eight.

'I need to look outside,' she said, leaning forward to a window. 'I cannot bear not to know my whereabouts.'

Quick as a shot, Lady Passmore raised a closed parasol and slapped down Mrs Pomeroy's hand.

'It is forbidden, Ma'am.'

Mrs Pomeroy stared at her ladyship in frustration.

'But why, Lady Passmore of Tewkesbury Manor? Why do we do all these things for those who have passed? Wear uncomfortable crêpe and bombazine. And change your carriage's fine net curtains for impenetrable black. Do the dead require this? It seems so unnecessary.'

Lady Passmore disagreed and settled back into her seat.

'You speak in ignorance, Mrs Pomeroy. At times such as these, we embrace the allegorical spirit. By using black curtains, and not knowing where we are on our journey, we identify with the dead who lie in limbo between Heaven and Earth. Or Hell, in some cases, although not in the case of our beloved chairman, of course.'

Mrs Pomeroy ceased her efforts to look out of the window and settled back in her seat. There was, after all, little else to do in the blacked-out interior and, for once, her ladyship had made a lot of sense. Life was easier to understand, Mrs Pomeroy decided, when perceived as a journey made in darkness.

Not that her stomach agreed with this conclusion for, with every turn of the grand carriage's wheels, its yearning for cake got more intense. Unless, it suddenly occurred to Mrs Pomeroy, it was not because her stomach wanted actual cake, but rather that, in the great story of life, cake also had an allegorical meaning. If only she could work out what it might be ... .

THE QUESTION OCCUPIED Mrs Pomeroy's thoughts for the rest of the journey until the horses drew up outside Number 24 Somerset Place. Their timing was perfect, for the other guests had already arrived and Lady Passmore was able to confirm her superior status by being the last to enter the small gathering. She pushed Mrs Pomeroy ahead of her and dabbed at her mouth with a black cotton handkerchief. She must not only be seen to be late but in a state of decorous heartache.

Freshly brewed tea was served by Gaia's butler John Pritchard and even though the pot was still steaming, Gaia judged that propriety required her to ask whether Lady Passmore found it acceptable.

'Are you sure that the tea is of a satisfying warmth, Lady Passmore of Tewkesbury Manor?' said Gaia, studiously.

'Yes, Ma'am, it is quite warm enough. Thank you.'

Her ladyship looked around the room at the other guests: in addition to herself and Mrs Pomeroy there was Belle, with his circus-loving Caribbean cousin Pablo Fanque. Gaia's young clerk Lucius Lush was also in attendance, to take notes, she assumed, rather than talk about his risible social almanac. Notable by their absence, however, were Phyllis Prim and Arthur Quigley. And the cake had not yet appeared.

'Does Miss Prim remain out of sorts?' asked Lady Passmore.

'At present, yes,' replied Gaia, 'but there is better news on that account. I visited Gay Street yesterday and, after much effort, uncovered the cause of her ailment. I intend to tackle this in the next few days, after which I am hopeful that Miss Prim will be back with us once more.'

This was good news but left hidden the identity of the ailment. Lady Passmore had blamed Miss Prim's demise on Belle's return to Bath and Belle was keen to understand the truth of it. He was unable, therefore, to rein in his inquisitive nature.

'And from what does dear Miss Prim suffer, if I might venture such an indiscreet question?'

Gaia did not answer immediately. It was clear that the last thing Miss Prim would want was that her indebtedness become the subject of chatter. Since even friends find it hard to respect confidences, Gaia decided to keep the matter private for now.

'Miss Prim has an ailment that is, ahem, specific to ladies,' she replied, closing the subject down with a half-truth.

'Ah. Well then. Let us say no more,' Belle said. 'The weather has been unseasonably wet of late.'

Belle noted that William and Master Lush were embarrassed on his behalf, and grateful that they had not asked the same question themselves.

It was at that moment that Pritchard returned carrying a simple sponge cake that was visibly ungarnished. He began to distribute slices on side plates, starting with Lady Passmore.

'Thank you, John. This is most welcome,' said her ladyship, grateful also for this diversion in their attention.

Mrs Pomeroy, who was next to be offered, took the side plate and studied the slice. To her eye, the ungarnished sponge looked naked without the sweet, moistening properties of jam and cream. She imagined that the parsimonious nature of the sponge was in keeping with mourning, although if that were the case, the cook could have gone one step further in the allegorical spirit of the week.

'A single piece, thank you, John,' she said, as the butler handed her the plate. 'Cake goes so well with tea, although I note that it's not black.'

'I do not follow you, Ma'am,' replied Gaia, who was not alert to the workings of Mrs Pomeroy's mind.

'I remarked merely that the sponge is not black,' said Mrs Pomeroy, pointing at the side plate. 'It's an ordinary sponge. I would have anticipated its being black during this period of mourning.'

There was silence.

'Indeed?' Gaia said, after a pause. She did not care for grief and was not *au fait* with the changing customs of society. 'I do apologise, Mrs Pomeroy. John, gather up the plates and ask Mme Galette to bake a black cake in double-quick time. It should take her no more than an hour and it should be ready when our tea is exhausted.'

'Yes, Ma'am,' replied the butler, now imagining the reaction of the cook and her choice of words on being asked to produce a black cake in one hour.

To the disappointment of all, and none more so than Mrs Pomeroy, the slices of cake were rapidly removed by Pritchard, who hurried away with them downstairs to the kitchens. Back in the drawing room, the time had come for the business of the day. To this end, Gaia turned to Belle.

Belle had revealed to Gaia that he had important news to impart and Gaia had wondered what this could be. She noted that his nervous state had worsened since the court hearing, as had his relations with the man whom she knew as Pablo Fanque. The supposed cousins sat on opposite sides of the fireplace, as distant as they could be within the close confines of the drawing room.

MME GALETTE, YOU are to rustle up a black sponge at the request of Mrs Pomeroy,' explained Pritchard, as he set foot in the kitchens with the uneaten slices of cake. 'According to our betters upstairs, black cake is more in keeping for a period of mourning. You have been given an hour to complete this more than urgent task.'

The diminutive cook, who was never short of an opinion and who had lost none of her Parisian heritage despite spending half her lifetime in Bath, placed her hands firmly on her hips.

'To bake *un gâteau noir* I have need of *le chocolat*. Mais we 'ave none *dans le cellier*. How am I to bake *un gâteau noir* without *ze chocolat*? Burn it?!'

Pritchard had a useful working relationship with Mme Galette, respecting her deeply, but they were not companions of the soul.

'I am not a cook, Madam, and cannot advise, but … '

'*Que se passe-t-il* upstairs? *Les aristocrates ont perdu leurs billes.*'

' … I would suggest that burning the cake is not the answer.'

Mme Galette's face looked hotter than her hot oven as she contemplated what to do. Her only dark colouring was beetroot juice but that would make the cake red rather than black, and a rather morbid red at that. Then she had a thought.

196

'I would not go there *moi-même*, Monsieur Pritchard, but I would *envoyer* one of *les garçons* into the coal cellar and tell him to find *un morceau de* coal, *le plus noir*. Meanwhile, *voulez-vous me trouver* that pestle and mortar on that shelf. *Ze* scullery maids are *toujours* putting it there *hors de ma portée. C'est* one of their *blagues stupides.*'

Pritchard did not question the cook. She had a plan and at that French *moment là* it was to be embraced. He reached for the pestle and mortar before searching out a footman to bring a piece of coal.

WHAT BELLE NEEDED to explain to the gathering was a matter of the utmost seriousness. It was also extremely difficult, for his evidence was far from definitive and he was not in agreement with the one other witness to the events.

As with most discussions, he eased his way towards the critical issue by first discussing one of less import, in this case the funeral of Ernest Camshaft. He offered his condolences to Master Lush, the chairman's great-grandson, and they discussed the news that the bishop had been invited to conduct the funeral service.

'Bishop George Monstrance. Is he not your godfather, Belle?' Gaia asked.

Belle acknowledged the fact.

'Georgie Monstrance is an upstanding man, though tempted by spirits both holy and unholy. When he has partaken of the latter, he is most often to be found under a pew, curled up with his beloved cat Horace. We must ensure that nothing of that kind happens in the days leading up to the funeral, otherwise we may find Horace presiding over the committal, rather than his master.'

Ignoring mention of anything so impolite as cats and inebriation, Lady Passmore ventured to add a comment of her own.

'On the subject of godchildren—and I share Mr Nash's condolences, Master Lush—it should be known that my niece, Miss

197

Daphne Passmore, was goddaughter to Mr Camshaft. Daphne is on a grand tour of Italy at present so will be unable to attend the funeral but I have written to her, asking that she light a candle in Mr Camshaft's memory in the *duomo* of Florence and for a mass to be said in his honour. It is the sort of thing that Roman Catholics like to do, and Italians in particular.'

Everyone accepted with good grace her ladyship's sharing of information, some even feigning interest in the absent relative they had never met. Then Belle took advantage of a pause in the conversation to bring the business of the day to a head.

First, he belatedly fulfilled his promise to Gaia to explain to Lady Passmore and Mrs Pomeroy the circumstance of his exile to Grenada. He spoke of how he had committed to travel to the Caribbean at his Aunt Sarah's behest and that Gaia's sentence had been designed to avoid far more serious charges being levelled at Herr Gerhardt Kant and Master Lush. On hearing the explanation, Lady Passmore sent a withering look Master Lush's way.

'Dear Mrs Champion,' she said, 'Mrs Pomeroy and I owe you an apology for past criticism. Particularly as we are now aware who was at fault. You should be ashamed of yourself, Master Lush. You are the cause of a four-year grudge which I now see was entirely uncalled for.'

Master Lush reddened but Belle saved him from further embarrassment by now introducing his intended topic of conversation.

With a solemn countenance, he described the visit that he and William had made to The Circus during the previous day's storm. He spoke of the broken words they had heard through the wind and rain, and his glimpse of a frightened figure at the barred window of Lord Servitude's house. Finally, having spent a sleepless night contemplating the facts, he revealed who he believed the girl in the room to be.

Lady Passmore was the first to express an opinion.

'It is an outrage that this girl should be held against her will.

And to think that I allowed myself to be courted by Lord Servitude in years past. Something must be done.'

It was natural, given her legal expertise and eminence as a magistrate, that Gaia should take the lead in asking questions. Unfortunately for Belle, she began by casting doubt on his suppositions, the better to apprehend the truth.

'If I may summarise the situation, you believe a girl of Caribbean descent is being held captive in Lord Servitude's house ... '

'Quite so. And that the girl is most likely Pablo's sibling, Mercy.'

There was a moment's silence before Gaia spoke again.

'"Most likely" you say? Not "most certainly"? Therein lies our first hurdle. Are the Servitudes to be arraigned for offences against a person unknown or against one whose identity is known to us? The latter would give us an easier path but does the evidence exist? Mr Fanque, may I turn to you? Mr Nash says that Mercy is your sibling and that you were with him when he heard her cry out. Are you of his opinion?'

William felt his spine stiffen. He had spoken at length with Belle about the girl's identity after they had returned from The Circus and knew what Belle thought. Here, under the eagle eye of Gaia Champion, he did not wish to challenge Belle's view but he was also a man of principle and did not wish to lie.

He had, of course, never met Mercy and his experience of events during the storm had been fragmentary. Assailed by wind and rain and thunder, he could not imagine how Belle had arrived at the firm conclusions she now presented.

Anticipating problems, Belle tried to intervene. 'If I recall, Ma'am, Pablo had his back to ... '

But Gaia interrupted him.

'Belle, let your cousin speak for himself. He is in far the best position to tell us if this girl is his relative. She is his half-sister, you say. Then he would be more attuned to her voice than you are. Mr Fanque, please let me hear your account of events.'

William chose his words carefully. His hands were shaking.

'Tis with regret, Madam, that oi 'as to express moy reservations. In truth, oi cannot corroborate Mr Nash's account. Oi did not get a real view of anyone at a window, nor clearly 'ear a voice. Oi 'eard a lot of thunder. Whether there was more, oi cannot say. Oi don't wish to disbelieve moy cousin, if he insist a girl is being held against 'er will. But whether the girl is moy sibling, or even from the Caribbean—that oi cannot say.'

Honesty, for once, was not a virtue. Whilst Belle looked deflated, it was the look of the others that struck William most painfully. They stared at him in amazement, as if it was inconceivable that he should not endorse Belle's claims automatically. Suddenly, he felt alone. It was as if he had engaged in an act of betrayal. But as who? As the Englishman, William Darby? As the once-enslaved Pablo Fanque? Or as a lone African, adrift in a Caucasian world?

He tried to justify himself but immediately felt even guiltier for protesting his innocence.

'It was comin' down with rain, Ma'am. There wuz a storm. Oi didn't see no one clearly. Oi can't be expected to confirm that the voice Mr Nash says he heard is moy sister just to ... to ... make loife easier for thee!'

Gaia raised a hand. She could see that the young man's emotions were disturbed. She spoke calmly.

'Nor would we wish you to, Mr Fanque, and thank you for your honesty. Meanwhile, if we are to help the girl that Belle thinks he saw, we need more evidence. Lord Servitude is not a man one confronts lightly. To do so could endanger the very person whose welfare appears to be at risk. Your sibling. Or whoever this girl may be, if in fact she exists.'

On this point, all were in agreement, which provided a sensible juncture for Gaia to call for a short break in the discussion. They could continue, she suggested, once the anticipated black cake had arrived.

'In the meantime, Master Lush will pour more tea,' she said, now looking at both Belle and William with concern. 'And let us engage in polite conversation.'

NOTES

* Mothballs, made from purified coal tar, were a wildly popular invention when created in the 1820s. Leading scientists of the age, including Michael Faraday (1791–1867), the godfather of electromagnetic theory, were involved in their creation. The original mothball, which can easily be mistaken by children for candy, only fell into disrepute when its principal ingredient, naphthalene, was found to cause nausea, vomiting, seizures and coma.

CHAPTER XVII

Confession in the Library

T HE TEA PARTY at Somerset Place did not become any
easier for William Darby. Seated opposite his supposed
cousin, Belle Nash, his sense of isolation grew worse when
Lady Passmore chose the suffering of slaves as her topic of polite
conversation.

'When I first became apprised of this dreadful subject, I wrote
a personal letter to Admiral Lord Passmore, my husband, in
Jaipur. I asked him, "Are we responsible for any slaves on our
overseas estates? I hope not, because I do not wish the Tewkesbury name to be tarnished by slave ownership. Besides, I have
quite enough trouble with my servants." He wrote back by return
and confirmed that the Passmore estates are slave-free. My conscience is therefore clear.'

As the question of slavery started to be discussed, Pritchard
re-appeared with a silver tray displaying neatly cut slices of a perfectly black sponge cake. Mme Galette had risen to the challenge,
within the allotted time, as had the cake, and Pritchard stood to
attention, looking quietly pleased. The French may have a reputation for being difficult, thought Pritchard, but they certainly know
how to cook.

'Congratulations are in order, John!' exclaimed Gaia Champion. 'I would never have believed it possible. A genuinely black
cake. How did Mme Galette achieve it?'

'I believe Mme Galette would regard that as one of the secrets of the French *cuisinière*,' replied the butler diplomatically, 'and not one she would care to disclose.' It was preferable to describing Mme Galette sweating profusely as she crushed a lump of coal in a mortar with a pestle, or her enraged expression when he pointed out to her that there was plenty of coal dust in the coal cellar, if that was what she had really wanted.

Pritchard handed out the cake, with no one daring to take the first bite, for who has ever seen a coal-black cake?

There was now a lull in the conversation, and that had to be filled for, as a rule, a tea party should never go quiet. To avoid such an occurrence, where the imparting of information and humour has been exhausted, it is acceptable to ask a question—an expedient that might otherwise be regarded as indecent to the point of being vulgar. Since Lady Passmore had already brought up the question, Gaia enquired, 'Mrs Pomeroy, did you own any slaves before the passing of the Abolition Act two years ago?'

It was terrible question, Gaia knew at once, and poor Mrs Pomeroy looked most embarrassed, as did all Gaia's other guests. Their only recourse was to eat as much cake as possible, as quickly as possible, whilst appearing oblivious to everything else, a procedure developed by society to cover precisely such moments of ignominy as this.

Gaia bit into the sponge, as did Belle, Lady Passmore, Mrs Pomeroy, Lucius Lush and William. The cake had an interesting, slightly grainy, dry texture that was not unpleasant. It was unusually crumbly, however, requiring all of them to wipe smears of powdery black crumbs from their lips.

Unfortunately, Mrs Pomeroy still felt obliged to answer the question that had been thrown at her.

'Have I owned slaves, Mrs Champion? Not that I know of, but I confess that I have not looked into the matter with the same diligence as Lady Passmore. Does slavery include children? The gardener often has his boys help with the weeding and they don't get paid with anything more than apple juice.'

Gaia wiped at her mouth again and was disconcerted to find that her mouth was even blacker than before.

'What is your opinion, Mr Nash, on the employment of children?' asked Lady Passmore, who also thought it best to keep the conversation going. 'Is it slavery to send children up chimneys, as we all do every three months, or to work them in factories, where their nimble fingers are so much better at fiddly work than the clumsy hands of adults?'

Gaia looked up and noted with alarm that everyone's lips and tongues had become unnaturally darkened by whatever mystery ingredient Mme Galette had used to perform her miracle. Mme Galette had done well to produce a black cake in an hour, Gaia thought, but it was not a miracle she would now wish to visit on her guests a second time.

'Slavery is indiscriminate,' replied Belle, who hated to be thought of as a specialist on the subject, just because he had spent four years in Grenada. 'Slavery affects men, women and children alike. Arguably the worst affected are children, whose liberty to be young and innocent is thereby lost for life. What was it Mr Blake says about the young chimney sweep?

> A little black thing among the snow:
> Crying weep, weep, in notes of woe!
> Where are thy father & mother? say?
> They are both gone up to the church to pray.'

Gaia began to panic. She could see that William had noticed the blackening faces around him, although 'Cousin' Belle and the other guests had yet to pick up on their transformations.

'What cannot be forgot is that all humans share the same right to be respected, regardless of the colour of their skin,' Belle continued. 'Yet Europeans exploit Africans, men exploit women and adults exploit children. Tis all the same game: the more powerful leeching on the weaker:

> Because I am happy, & dance and sing,
> They think they have done me no injury ... .'

As Belle got into his stride, Gaia attempted remedial action by catching Mrs Pomeroy's eye and pointing repeatedly at her mouth. Mrs Pomeroy, who had been delighted at the appearance of the cake and thrilled at her contribution to allegorical tradition, misconstrued Gaia's message. Instead of attending to her lips, she used her already blackened napkin to wipe her entire face, until there was very little left of it that remained white.

Meanwhile, Belle continued:

> ' ... and are gone to praise God & his Priest & King
> Who make up a heaven of our misery.'

To Belle's disappointment, his intoning of William Blake's poem was met not with applause, but with silence. Fearing his audience to be unsympathetic to the poem's sentiment, he turned to Lucius Lush.

'You'd agree, wouldn't you, Master Lush, about the need to provide Christian care to all?' he asked.

Master Lush, however, was distracted by the fact that his right hand, having delivered several portions of cake to his mouth, was now the colour of spilt ink. Belle turned instead to William.

'And do you have an opinion, Pablo?' Belle enquired, before helping himself to another bite of Mme Galette's peculiar concoction. The recitation of poetry had left him hungry; the ingesting of cake now left him discoloured—on his lower jaw, at least.

William stared at them all. Having followed the course of the most condescending conversation he had ever been exposed to, he thought hard about how he might compose a reasonably worded response. What he wanted to say, however, was simply too uncouth for present company. He therefore took the only other option available to him. In as dignified a manner as was possible, he rose to his feet and left the room.

WILLIAM SPENT THE following day in The Circus, directing his troupe in their efforts to raise the big tent. With a heavy mallet, he helped hammer into the ground the large stakes required to secure the guy ropes. And through the physical assault of metal on wood, he tried to expel some of the anger of the previous day.

'Stupid ... '

Thwack.

' ... stupid ... '

Thwack.

' ... stupid white people!'

Thwack.

The rest of the troupe were largely silent and unusually focused on the task in hand. They had never seen William so upset and were too nervous to ask him why.

'Begging your pardon, Mr Darby, or Mr Fanque, I should say, but you seem not yourself,' said one of the Ridley Brother clowns. 'I could tell you a joke if that would help ... '

'Oi'm not in the mood for jokes,' William barked as he raised the mallet above his head, his chest and biceps rippling. 'All oi wants is to get the tent up and then readied for our show.'

The prize fighter Tom Shelton, who was good at hammering in posts so long as someone positioned him correctly, said, 'But isn't time on our side, Mr Fanque? I understand that the opening night of the circus has been delayed until after the funeral of the late Mr Camshaft.'

This was true and it had only soured William's mood further. Having acquired the licence to perform, they were now having to wait upon the dead, William pointed out.

'Besides which, Mr Shelton,' he added, 'oi want the roof of this 'ere tent raised today and there's to be no arguing on the matter. The sides and seating can follow in due course but the roof must be up today.'

Raising a large circus tent is not a straightforward task. The two central poles, hewn from oak, must be fixed into the ground before the fabric of the tent is laid out. A system of pulleys and ropes then raises the heavy cloth of the roof up the poles. Once it has been pulled tight, the cloth can bear the weight of a man as readily as the slates of a townhouse. But the weight is immense, and it takes some pulling to get it up.

William was typically not inclined to take risks but, the moment the guy ropes were taut, he was climbing a rope that hung down from one of the poles. His arms worked faster than his feet and soon he was at the top of the tent and was squeezing through an aperture that gave access to the sky.

'Mr Fanque, secure yourself,' shouted the lass who looked after William's horses. 'It may not yet be safe.'

But William did not listen. He was on a mission. The height of the tent, he had calculated, was the same as the parapet of the surrounding houses. As such, it could provide him with a vantage point to see into the neighbouring top-floor windows. There was one in which he had a specific interest.

The tip of the pole was several feet proud of the tent itself. William, a skilled tightrope walker, was confident in his balance. Holding onto the pole with one hand, he leant out towards Number 33. He remained some fifty feet or more from the house but it was as close and as high as he could safely get. He trained his eyes on the barred window.

W HEN WILLIAM HAD left the drawing room of Somerset Place the previous day, Gaia had followed. Among the other guests, Belle attempted to join her but was sent back to his chair.

'Stay! You are all to stay here,' Gaia had commanded. 'And Master Lush, ring for a maid and ask her to bring warm water and towels so we can all clean this ridiculous cake from our faces. We look like a minstrel show.'

She had then hurried after William, doing her best to wipe her face clean with a sleeve of her dress. She caught up with him in the hallway.

'Dear Mr Fanque, please wait. I am distraught at what just occurred, and acknowledge my folly in drawing attention to a sore topic. It was injurious to your feelings and thoughtless of us all but I hope you will allow that it was also ... '

He had turned. There was anger in his eyes but mostly hurt.

' ... an innocent mistake?' he had said, finishing Gaia's sentence for her. 'Oi understands, Mrs Champion, that tha' callousness were unintended. But what a twisted world it be when a Negro, such as oi be termed, whose people have been traded, enslaved, tortured and murdered these last hundreds of years, be the one bein' asked to show understanding for ... for ... '

Gaia had felt helpless as William spoke.

' ... for the crass foolishness of the English,' he continued. 'If them as are in the drawing room are to be considered moy friends, what hope 'as oi against moyn enemies?'

Gaia had stepped forward and grasped William's hands, anguished that her own insensitivity and that of her friends had offended him. Worse, that she had failed him.

'Your enemies are my enemies too, Mr Fanque. And Belle's. I do not deny that we are fools and have much to learn about the conduct of our society and how to improve it. But we are wholly of your cause. I will not offend you again by asking for you to re-join the tea party but please accompany me to the library for a few minutes. I respect your honesty in saying that the girl, if there was a girl, might not be your sister—that must have been hard to confess—but you and I need to work together, and with a common mind, if we are to save the victims of Lord Servitude's cruelty.'

I T WAS THAT conversation that had impelled William to climb onto the roof of the circus tent, and having done so to march once more up Sion Hill to Somerset Place. It was late Monday afternoon and Gaia had informed him that this would be a propitious hour for them to confer a second time.

Though deep in contemplation, William walked quickly and within a few minutes was at the front door. It was opened by Pritchard.

'Please enter, Mr Fanque. Mrs Champion is expecting you. She asks that you join her with Lady Passmore of Tewkesbury Manor in the library.'

William accompanied Pritchard across the hallway to the library, the shelves of which were filled with leather-bound legal texts collected by the late Hercules Champion and a range of novels, natural histories and works of the ancients.

William stood outside as Pritchard announced his arrival. Unlike the drawing room, permission to enter the room of learning had to be granted. Whilst waiting, he could clearly hear the ladies' conversation.

Gaia was telling Lady Passmore, 'It has been a great relief to confide in you about Miss Prim. If I read the situation right, its owner is engaging in money-lending on usurious terms whilst purporting to trade in wool. For the former activity, she requires a licence, and such she does not have. I can therefore seek to close the establishment down.'

'I have long held knitting in low esteem,' Lady Passmore replied, 'but this brings it to a new nadir. You must do what you can, Mrs Champion, to set matters aright. Meanwhile, the person for whom I am most concerned is Lord Servitude's captive, and I must tell you why.'

Pritchard coughed to alert the ladies to his presence.

'One moment, John,' said Gaia. 'I need a couple of minutes more. Lady Passmore of Tewkesbury Manor, do continue.'

Her ladyship breathed deeply. Now that Gaia had shared a

confidence about Miss Prim's predicament, she had a secret of her own to reveal.

'Many years ago, Lord Servitude and I briefly courted. I knew him as Freddy at the time. We spent a week as guests at Cliveden, where he made clear his affection. Thank the Lord, I rejected his advances.'

Gaia nodded.

'Have you stayed in touch over the years?'

Lady Passmore lowered her voice, but not so low that she could not be heard by Pritchard and William.

'The last time we encountered each other was fifteen years ago in London. It was the occasion of the Hon. Cecil's tenth birthday party. I was staying at our house in Bedford Square, where I was joined by my husband's young niece Daphne, her parents having been posted to Khartoum. I took her to the party at the Serv-itudes's Mayfair residence.'

Gaia waited for her to continue.

'It was dispiriting and disturbing, Ma'am,' recalled Lady Passmore. 'The years had not been kind to Freddy, either in his appearance or temperament. As for his son, a more offensive child would be hard to find. Other children attending the party kept their distance, and so it was left to my niece to play with the young Servitude in the nursery.'

'It was good of her to indulge him,' commented Gaia.

'Not so, Madam, for when I entered the nursery to take her home, I saw what they had been up to. They had been playing with wooden building blocks and lead figurines. It left me with no choice but to forbid any future contact between them.'

'And what were they, these nursery creations? A house? A palace? A Roman temple?'

There was a brief pause before her ladyship answered.

'No, Mrs Champion. They had built a French guillotine and a replica of the Black Hole of Calcutta. Two children, one of them from my husband's family. I own that I was appalled.'

210

In the silence that followed, Pritchard took the opportunity to cough again, this time more loudly. Stunned by Lady Passmore's tale, Gaia took a moment to pick up on the signal.

'I do apologise, John, for the delay. Do we have a visitor?'

'Indeed, Ma'am. Mr Pablo Fanque awaits your presence.'

Grateful to move the conversation on, Gaia clapped her hands and rose swiftly to her feet. Lady Passmore, as befitted her status, remained planted in her chair.

'Mr Fanque is here! Let us hope he has good news. Please bid him enter.'

William did not wait for the butler to pass on the invitation. He strode immediately into the room and gave Gaia a small bow.

'Mrs Champion,' he said, before giving Lady Passmore a significantly deeper bow. 'Lady Passmore of Tewkesbury Manor.'

'Mr Fanque, please take a seat,' said Gaia. 'Lady Passmore of Tewkesbury Manor and I were just discussing the plight of the girl. Do you have news for us?'

William took a seat as directed, then waited for Pritchard to leave. The butler let himself out and stood guard discreetly behind the closed door.

'Oi cannot say for sure,' William replied. 'Loike we arranged yesterday, Mrs Champion, oi ordered the troupe to raise the tent this mornin'. From its roof oi could see into the barred window. The window was small but open, and it wuz dark insoide, yet oi could make out a girl—African, loike moyself, and in a condition of great distress.'

'Your sister?' asked Lady Passmore before Gaia could speak.

'Oi could not tell, Madam. Oi wanted to croiy out so she could see me but there wuz people coming and going in the street below me, and oi was fearful of endangerin' her further, for what oi saw was terrible. It seemed that the girl was ... '

William hesitated.

'Was what?' demanded Gaia, alarmed. Lady Passmore's account of the Servitudes's nursery remained fresh in her mind.

211

'She appeared to be shackled to the bed, Ma'am. Oi couldn't see clearly but through the open window oi believe oi could make out chains that rattled as she moved.'

Lady Passmore began to rub at her wrists, imagining herself in the girl's situation.

'This is worse than shocking,' she said. 'Slavery and incarceration? In England? Today? You must do something, Mrs Champion.'

'It is more difficult than you imagine,' Gaia said quietly. 'If I send the special constables to question Lord Servitude, it will give the hateful son time to spirit the girl away. The only alternative is to raid the property. But what if we are wrong? The scandal would finish us. I would be removed from my position and you, Mr Fanque, would be locked up on a charge of perjury. Dear Sir, I must ask you again: regardless of whether the girl is your sister, can you confirm that she is held captive and chained to a bed? If so, I can bring a charge of false imprisonment.'

William lowered his head into his hands and cursed his doubts. The distance between his vantage point on the tent's roof and the house made certainty impossible. Peering from fifty feet through bars into the dim light of the attic room, he knew he may not have seen what was there but what he—and all whom slavery had touched—feared to see.

Raising his head, he said, 'As an honest man, Ma'am, oi could not swear to it on oath. But what oi can do is gain entry into the house and foind out for mi'sen.'

'Break in, Mr Fanque?'

'Tha' put'st it hard, Madam. Let's say that oi'd use moy skills to effect entry.'

'No, Mr Fanque, I won't allow it. You cannot commit one crime to right another.'

At which point, Lady Passmore rose to her feet. It was not that she had tired of the conversation, as was usually the case, but that she believed she had an answer.

212

'I will do it.'

Both Gaia and William looked at her with expressions of amazement.

'With the help of Mrs Pomeroy, I will do it,' her ladyship repeated. 'Remember, Lord Servitude once courted me and I am a woman of position. I will ask for an invitation to his house and take Mrs Pomeroy with me. He will not refuse me. No one ever has. Whilst I am there, either Mrs Pomeroy or I will find our way to the top floor and locate the room in question. By such means, we will have the answer and appropriate action can be taken.'

'But Lady Passmore of Tewkesbury Manor, consider the danger,' Gaia protested.

'The risks are terrible great,' added William. 'Servitude is a monster, Tha' Ladyship!'

But Lady Passmore was adamant.

'I can and I will and I must. I will call on Mrs Pomeroy immediately and formulate a plan. Mrs Champion, please ask your butler to summon my carriage.'

Gaia and William both protested again but Lady Passmore's mind was made up.

'There is no going back. Lord Servitude and his offspring should have been exposed as demons long ago. As for our competence, the team of Tewkesbury and Pomeroy have deep experience in the dark arts of espionage, as we revealed in the Case of the Bath Soufflé. We will be quite safe. At a time of crisis, Mr Fanque, it is best to leave things to the professionals.'

NOTES
- The involvement of Lady Tewkesbury and Mrs Pomeroy in the mysterious arts of espionage can be read in full in the preceding volume in this series, *Belle Nash and the Bath Soufflé*.

CHAPTER XVIII

The Professionals

THE PROFESSIONAL CAN be distinguished from the amateur by virtue of having set aside time to learn a desired craft, honing the skills thus acquired and having equipment appropriate to the task. Neither Lady Passmore nor Mrs Pomeroy possessed any of these advantages, in spite of Lady Passmore's claims to the contrary.

Their one previous attempt to spy had been a night-time vigil outside a general store in Bath owned by a crook named Hezekiah Porter. Their efforts had failed, however, for while Lady Passmore had attempted to disguise her identity by keeping the curtains of her chaise and four closed, her precautions had not also disguised the presence of the carriage itself.

Her record of failure had in no manner dented Lady Passmore's confidence. Having committed herself, she duly sent a note to Lord Servitude inviting herself to tea and collected Mrs Pomeroy the next morning to begin their self-allotted task.

'At Number 33, we will be served tea as is the custom,' said Lady Passmore, on arriving at Mrs Pomeroy's house on Lansdown Hill. 'Then, at a convenient moment, you will ask to use the commode or the outhouse.'

Mrs Pomeroy blushed.

'Use the commode? You embarrass me, Lady Passmore of Tewkesbury Manor. Why should I do that?'

Lady Passmore glowered by return.

'It is a pretext, dear lady, to get you out of the drawing room. Then you can climb to the top floor and ascertain if this poor girl is indeed held captive.'

Mrs Pomeroy had doubts about the plan's efficacy and the apportionment of responsibility.

'That means I have to discover the girl without being discovered myself. Suppose a servant is set to keep an eye on me?'

'That is why you will ask to use the commode. I do not think that your use of the pot will call for monitoring, even in the Servitude household.'

'It seems that all the risk falls on me,' Mrs Pomeroy objected. 'Whilst you sip tea with Lord Servitude, I shall have to excuse myself while excusing myself, and slip to the top of the house. Suppose I am found out?

'My dear,' her ladyship retorted, 'one of us has to keep Lord Servitude distracted and I venture that my conversational wiles will prove the more compelling.'

Mrs Pomeroy knew from experience that there was no point in protesting. She did, however, eke out one concession.

'I accept the challenge, Your Ladyship, but if I am to undertake such perilous work, I must bring my Egyptian pussy, Kiwu, with me to Lord Servitude's house. Her feline presence will calm me.'

She reached down to pet an unusually large cat that was sprawled out at her feet.

'A cat! Whatever next?'

But Mrs Pomeroy stood her ground.

'I am adamant, Lady Pomeroy of Tewkesbury Manor. Either Kiwu comes with me or I shall stay at home.'

THUS IT WAS, late Tuesday morning, that two women and a large cat could be found in Lady Passmore's magnificent carriage. At the last moment, Mrs Pomeroy had also brought with her a large bottle of water and, much to Lady Passmore's displeasure, was already pouring herself measures from it.

215

'Drinking in a carriage, indeed! You have very common habits, Mrs Pomeroy.'

'You forget that I will need the commode,' replied Mrs Pomeroy.

Lady Passmore sighed.

'You won't actually be required to use the commode. It is merely an excuse to get upstairs. In fact, using a commode is the last thing you want. It will delay your efforts to find the girl.'

But by then, Mrs Pomeroy had already downed most of her bottle.

A tense silence followed, broken only by the purring of the cat on its mistress's lap. For the remainder of the journey, Mrs Pomeroy was occupied with visualising the interior layout of the target building. She imagined her hand gliding up polished bannisters to that mysterious point found in every grand house: the door that provides access to the servants' quarters.

But will the door to the servants' domain be evident to me? she wondered. Would her natural female intuition, that strange but most powerful of human instincts, lead her to it? In the dark of the carriage, she felt her hand creep forward on the imagined bannister, only for it to be slapped down by a parasol.

'Ouch!'

'Let that be a warning to you, Madam,' reprimanded Lady Passmore. 'Leave the curtains alone. We must remain in the dark until Chairman Camshaft's mortal remains are interred.'

Mrs Pomeroy rubbed her hand.

'I wasn't going to touch the curtains. I was rehearsing the task ahead—feeling my way to the girl's room.'

'Is that so, Mrs Pomeroy? Well, try feeling your way onto the pavement. We're here.' The carriage had drawn to a halt, propelling the cat to the floor with an undignified thump.

Mrs Pomeroy did as was instructed and stepped down onto the broad Welsh stone pavement of The Circus. Blinking into the daylight, she stared at Number 33 and up to the barred window.

Lady Passmore swept past.

'Don't dilly-dally, Mrs Pomeroy. We cannot attract suspicion.'

'Of course, Lady Passmore of Tewkesbury Manor,' replied Mrs Pomeroy, with the cat under one arm, and the hem of her skirt in her hand.

At the front door, Lady Passmore gave the bell a jerk strong enough to break a pheasant's neck. Moments later it was opened by the housekeeper.

'Lady Passmore of Tewkesbury Manor?' asked Mrs Neech.

'Indeed,' replied her ladyship, thrusting out her chest. 'Behind me is Mrs Pomeroy of Lansdown Hill, with her cat. Lord Servitude is expecting us. I sent a note yesterday evening inviting myself to tea.'

Mrs Neech opened the door wider. They were, indeed, expected.

'I am Mrs Neech, Your Ladyship. His lordship alerted me. Please follow me to the drawing room, where tea will be served.'

Lady Passmore entered the hall with Mrs Pomeroy and Kiwu. Inside, light from the flickering beeswax candles reflected off the gold-and-purple wallpaper. Portraits of deceased Servitudes hung on the wall. Ahead of them, the housekeeper led the way to a broad staircase.

Mrs Pomeroy hugged her cat tightly as they climbed the stairs, her thoughts now on the girl in the attic room.

'Hold fast, my dear,' murmured Lady Passmore. 'We are on our way.'

ALSO ON HER way was Gaia Champion who, having completed the day's hearings at Guildhall, was preparing to tackle Mrs Wellow's House of Wool. She walked up Milsom Street with a firm stride. Earlier at court, she had ordered an inn to be closed for watering its beer and had gaoled the publican. When she was in the mood, she gave no quarter. And Gaia was in the mood.

She swung into George Street and involuntarily licked her lips. Inside the shop, everything was as she had anticipated: wooden fixtures on the walls provided compartments for balls of coloured wool; a glass-topped cabinet displayed an array of knitting needles; and the air was perfumed with the smell of fleece.

Ahead of her, a lady customer was being served and Gaia took the opportunity to study further the shop's interior. With its high ceiling, it had an aura of a temple, albeit one dedicated to the honour of an even-toed ungulate. As such, it was not the first temple to be tainted by the practice of money-lending.

She heard the customer make a request in a fragile voice.

'And a single double-point knitting needle, if you please. The very cheapest you have. I lost mine only this week. I have searched high and low but it will not be found. I am very vexed.'

'Very well, Mrs Bellringer,' replied a woman from behind the counter, whose assertive tone announced her to be the proprietrix. 'I shall add that to your account. But I still require you to make your weekly payment. It is eight shillings now, I believe. I cannot entrust you with these new goods without your covering the interest on what you already owe.'

Gaia smiled as a large ledger was pulled onto the counter. This was an open-and-shut case of unauthorised money-lending.

'Oh, but I cannot be in arrears,' said the customer, opening her purse. 'I make the payments you demand but the sum I owe you always grows. Why is that, pray?'

There was silence as the payment was made. The proprietrix used a quill to mark a new entry in the ledger.

'Price of wool, Madam,' was the explanation. 'If you wish to object, I advise you to talk to the sheep.'

AT NUMBER 33, Lady Passmore, Mrs Pomeroy and her cat were shown into a drawing room characterised by ostentatious furniture and a further display of Servitude portraiture from past generations.

The largest canvas, by Thomas Gainsborough, was of the fifth Lord Servitude with his wife and four children; the offspring included a young Freddy gazing lovingly into his baby sister Anna's eyes, a pink sash tied round his waist. It was a model of family rectitude, with a Doric column in the background and not a slave in sight.

'They must bring their portraits with them from London,' observed Mrs Pomeroy to Lady Passmore. 'How odd to travel round the country with one's ancestors.'

'I venture that it makes them feel at home,' replied her ladyship. 'The Servitudes hold themselves and their wealth in high esteem.'

The two ladies took their seats as they awaited their host. Once settled, Mrs Pomeroy placed the cat on the floor and wrinkled up her nose. The room smelt of the previous night's port and cigars and had what she imagined to be the atmosphere of a Pall Mall club. Discarded newspapers were scattered on the floor, all turned to reports of stock prices and foreign commodities, and framed engravings of Servitude plantations were set out on mahogany Sheraton side tables with marble tops.

When Mrs Neech returned with the tea, Mrs Pomeroy's spirits were momentarily lifted until she saw that they had been offered a plate of dry biscuits rather than the cake she was hoping for. Staring in shock at the biscuits, Mrs Pomeroy missed the entrance of Lord Servitude and he in turn was singularly unimpressed at not being noticed.

'Please, ladies, don't get up,' he bellowed, seeking maximum attention.

Lady Passmore, of course, had no intention of getting up—she rose for royalty alone—but Lord Servitude's bellowing bounced Mrs Pomeroy into action. She rose to her feet as quickly as her hips allowed.

'Lord Servitude, it is generous of you to provide tea. I am Mrs Pomeroy of Lansdown Hill, and I am accompanying ... '

219

Mrs Pomeroy received a cursory welcome, for Lord Servitude cared not a jot who she was. Lady Passmore, on the other hand, received his full attention.

He said, ' ... my dear friend, Lady Passmore of Tewkesbury Manor, or may I presume to call you by your first name, as in happier times?'

Lady Passmore had studied Lord Servitude from the moment he appeared and was struck by what she saw. A hereditary trait of boorishness had infected a man who had been handsome in his prime. His once ice-blue eyes were grey and bloodshot. His proud jaw was now a cantilevered platform from which hung folds of skin above his distended gut. As for the state of his teeth ...

Lady Passmore drew in her breath, repulsed by the notion of any intimacy from her host. No one used her first name, not Mrs Champion, nor Mrs Pomeroy, nor yet her husband in his letters from foreign climes.

'No, Lord Servitude, you may not,' she said firmly and to the point. 'Our week at Cliveden has long since passed. I enter this house a married woman and decency must be respected.'

Lord Servitude laughed and Mrs Neech quietly tittered as she poured the tea.

'I like a woman who's hard to get, eh?' he roared. 'Sets a man a challenge. Never was a woman harder in the chase than Lady Passmore, so no change there. What do you say, Mrs Fontelroy? You said your name was Fontelroy, didn't you, Ma'am?'

Mrs Pomeroy blushed.

'Pomeroy, Lord Servitude,' she corrected. 'Of Lans ... '

'If you say so,' replied Lord Servitude, a glint in his eye. 'But to the question, Mrs Pommeljoy, as Mrs Neech serves us tea. Have you ever known a woman less accommodating of a man's advances than our beguiling Lady Passmore?'

Mrs Pomeroy shuffled in her seat awkwardly.

'I fear I am unequipped to fashion an adequate reply, My Lord.'

'When young, I was infatuated with your companion,' said

Lord Servitude, biting on a biscuit. 'We were guests of the Countess of Orkney for a week. I did all that might be expected of a suitor. Rowed her up and down the Thames each day. Performed favourite scenes from Shakespeare. Read her accounts of the latest sugar prices—and for what, Madam? Not even a whiff of interest.'

Lady Passmore remained po-faced. For her part, Mrs Pomeroy chose to support her friend.

'I am certain that her ladyship esteemed all your attentions most highly. I am reminded of ... '

She found herself, however, swiftly interrupted by Lord Servitude, who preferred the sound of his own voice to that of others.

'Saw her years later with a pretty niece at my boy's birthday party. I thought, by heavens, Madam Tewkesbury's matured nicely. Better than a fine wine. Or a cheddar. Or a nice cut of African biltong. Might give her another shot. Made my advances but ... blow me down, I got nowhere and fifteen years went by without another sighting.'

Mrs Pomeroy attempted levity.

'I remember fifteen years ago as if it were yesterday.'

'Then, out of the blue, yesterday evening,' the peer continued, 'the lady invites herself to tea and I think, what's going on here? Fancied she might be one of those slow burners, finally brought to the boil and ready for action—until,' he now turned his gaze to Mrs Pomeroy, 'I saw she had turned up with her praetorian guard.'

If it had been Lord Servitude's intention to rile his visitors, his plan succeeded. With her free hand, Lady Passmore slapped the arm of her chair.

'Freddy, be silent.'

'Hey-ho, the lady speaks!'

'You are right, Sir; I am not a woman easily won over by men. You were offended many years ago at Cliveden, and again at your child's birthday party. When I learnt that you were in Bath with your son, I saw an opportunity to mend fences. The Season lies ahead and we should put our pasts behind us. It is time for the houses of Tewkesbury and Servitude to be at peace.'

Lord Servitude smiled and noticed a stiffening in what might politely be called his resolve. Lady Passmore's use of his first name was a small victory, and one on which he was sure he could build. His task, however, was hampered by the presence of a chaperone.

It was with relief, then, that the woman with the cat surprised him by suddenly gulping down her tea and asking for the use of a commode. Rather than order up a chamber pot and a screen, he turned to his housekeeper.

'Mrs Neech will take you to an upstairs chamber where you can avail yourself of all you need. And do not rush yourself, Madam. Lady Passmore and I have much to discuss.'

As MRS POMEROY left the drawing room with the cat Kiwu under her arm, Gaia was leaving the House of Wool, her work substantially done. Unusually for a visitor to the shop, she was departing without any purchase of wool. Instead, she carried the large ledger that contained the record of the monies owed by Mrs Wellow's customers, and on which she charged interest.

Once the shop had emptied, Gaia had made herself known to the proprietrix, whose face had turned as white as a Cheviot sheep. The woman had protested her innocence but Gaia had retorted that there was only one way of proving the claim, which was to hand over her accounts. This could be done in private, in which case Gaia pledged to pay Phyllis Prim's debt, or in public, with the House of Wool being prosecuted, fined and shamed.

'Besides which,' Gaia had stipulated, 'there will be no more payment of interest by your customers; only the principal sum, less the interest they have paid already.'

'But in that interest lies our profit,' exclaimed Mrs Wellow.

'And that is the point. There is a real need for a wool shop in Bath, but it has to be an honest endeavour, not a racket. I shall inform you within the week how much each customer owes or, indeed, what needs to be returned to them.'

Mrs Wellow had had no choice and had handed over her books. Her task fulfilled, Gaia had been about to leave the premises when a final thought occurred.

'Within the hour you will send twelve balls of wool to Number 40 Gay Street with a bunch of cut flowers and a note, wishing Miss Prim well. If you wish to object, I advise you to talk to the sheep.'

C LIMBING THE STAIRCASE with Mrs Neech, Mrs Pomeroy reassessed the balance of risk. She had agreed to explore Lord Servitude's attic rooms on the pretext of using a commode, and she must not take too long for fear of arousing suspicion. At the same time, the water she had taken in in the carriage and the tea that she had added to her load in the drawing room now started to demand being let out. Her need for a commode was no longer a fabrication.

'Along this corridor there are several bedchambers. Any will do. Leave the door open when you're finished so we know which you've used. Unless you wish me to assist.'

Mrs Pomeroy wished to be rid of the housekeeper.

'Thank you, Mrs Neech. I can manage by myself,' she said curtly, and setting Kiwu down on the floor, she watched with relief as the wretched servant descended the stairs, to eavesdrop, no doubt, on her master's conversation.

Oh dear, said Mrs Pomeroy to herself. What do I do first? Despatch the contents of my bladder or search for the girl?

What Mrs Pomeroy should have done was obvious; instead, the thought of Lady Passmore's disapproving expression bore down on her, hastening her to set about the vital errand she had been sent to perform before attending to her more personal needs.

It was to her good fortune that the contemptible Cecil had

gone out earlier in the morning to buy a new hat, for the first room she passed was his bedchamber. She closed the door, to suggest to Mrs Neech that she had entered the room, and then continued along the corridor until, behind a third door, she found the staircase: narrow, uncarpeted and poorly lit by a miserable skylight.

Having checked that she was not being watched, and ignoring the growing pressure on her bladder, Mrs Pomeroy climbed the stairs. At the top, a corridor ran the width of the house. Recalling the location of the barred window, she turned right and tried the doorhandle of the furthest room. It was locked. Biting her bottom lip, she gave the door a light knock.

'Hello? Is anyone there?' she whispered.

There was silence. In the void, however, her bladder cried out for help of its own kind.

'I repeat, is anyone there? I believe you are being held against your will and I am here to assist you, if I can.'

There was a sound of clanking chains from inside the room, and then the voice of a weak and broken girl.

'Ma'am, I hear you. But who are you? I'm frightened.'

Mrs Pomeroy placed her hands on the door. She had agreed with Lady Passmore that it would be unsafe to disclose her identity lest the girl be forced to speak.

'I am a friend, my dear; that is all that I can say. What condition are you in? Are you hurt?'

There was a further sound of chains as the girl moved upright on her bed.

'Please, Ma'am, help me. I am bruised. I am bleeding.'

'Of course I will help,' replied Mrs Pomeroy, but she spoke too soon for, at that moment, she heard footsteps. Pulling herself away from the door, she flattened her back against the wall and looked down the corridor through the grey light. From below, came the voice of Mrs Neech.

'Madam, have you finished in there? Have you filled the pot?'

The question triggered more bloating in Mrs Pomeroy's bladder and left her with a decision to make. She could stay quiet, hoping that Mrs Neech would assume she was in the Hon. Cecil's bedchamber below and leave her alone, or ...

'Have you filled the pot, Madam? I can get you another one if you need one.'

... or she could go back down the stairs, claim to have got lost and go in immediate search of relief.

She whispered through the locked door, 'I'm sorry, my dear, I must go. But help will come. Have courage.'

'Don't leave me,' came the distressed response. 'You cannot leave me.'

'Oh dear ... '

Reluctantly, Mrs Pomeroy retraced her path down the corridor, descended the stairs and emerged some eight feet behind Mrs Neech.

Mrs Neech spun on her heels, cursing that she had ever left Mrs Pomeroy unattended.

'I do apologise, Mrs Neech,' said Mrs Pomeroy, as casually as she could. 'I brought my cat Kiwu up here with me, and then couldn't find her. I have been looking everywhere.'

'Your cat followed me downstairs and is now in the kitchen eating chicken.'

'How kind of you to take care of her so well,' said Mrs Pomeroy. 'And now I must take care of myself—urgently—if you would excuse me. Did you say there was a commode in this first room?'

NOTES
• In describing the Servitude family portrait, I suspect my uncle used *The Baillie Family* by Thomas Gainsborough as his template. James Baillie (1737–1793) acquired the Hermitage plantation in Grenada in circa 1755 and spent twenty years in the Caribbean, trading in slaves and developing his interests. In 1833, his heirs were compensated for the 'loss' of 1,821

slaves. Thomas Gainsborough, who spent a year living in Bath at Number 17, The Circus in 1759, painted the monumental Baillie Family portrait in 1784.

CHAPTER XIX

Crass and Insensitive

G AIA CHAMPION HAD arranged for Lady Passmore and Mrs Pomeroy to deliver their report in Somerset Place. Attending them was a triumvirate of men—Belle Nash, William Darby and Lucius Lush—and, in addition, Phyllis Prim, making her first outing in several weeks. Now free of debt, and with a new supply of wool, Bath's most admired knitter had finally made a recovery.

'Oh Miss Prim, you have suffered so,' said Mrs Pomeroy, embracing her friend. 'It is a pleasure to see colour in your cheeks once more.'

Tea was served by Pritchard, who then circulated a cake baked by Mme Galette. Lady Passmore fingered her slice with suspicion.

'Not black today,' she noted. 'I'm surprised, given that Chairman Camshaft's funeral is not for another three days.'

Mrs Pomeroy shuffled uneasily in her seat.

'It was an experiment not to be repeated,' responded Gaia. 'I advised the kitchen that a simple loaf cake would make the point equally well.'

Miss Prim accepted the modest slice that was offered to her.

'I have never seen a black cake, nor would I wish to. But talking of dear Chairman Camshaft, I am knitting for myself a black veil, using the veil stitch.'

'That is wonderfully appropriate,' said Master Lush, encouragingly.

227

The clerk's comment received harsh looks from all, for Miss Prim's monologues on knitting were not something that even the kindest heart would wish her to dilate upon, having done so too often, and at too great length, before.

'It is a unique stitch,' continued Miss Prim, now emboldened, 'developed for the very purpose of knitting a veil. My own use of the stitch combines ... '

Gaia firmly tapped her teacup with a teaspoon to break the thread of Miss Prim's monologue.

'Dear Miss Prim, how we hang on your every word! But this is not the moment. We must bend our gaze to the visit of our two intrepid spies to Lord Servitude's lair. Dear ladies, what did you learn?'

Seated on chairs and settees—with Belle and William once again on opposite sides of the fireplace—everyone leant forwards, agog, including a red-faced Master Lush.

Given her superior rank, Lady Passmore spoke first.

'We arrived together, Mrs Pomeroy bringing with her a cat as an accomplice. At a convenient moment, she made her excuses and departed the drawing room to find the captive girl. And so, I was left alone with Lord Servitude.'

'Oooah,' whimpered Miss Prim.

Lady Passmore raised her chin in response.

'He spoke of the week we spent at Cliveden during my debutante year. For seven days, he tried to seduce me by rowing me up and down the Thames, making insufferably lewd comments.'

There was a sharp intake of breath in the room.

'How awful,' said Gaia, speaking on everyone's behalf. 'What a dreadful ordeal.'

'It was a traumatic experience,' confirmed Lady Passmore, 'made the more onerous by his performance of choice passages from the Great Bard and his fascination with the latest sugar prices. He was a large man even then and as he stood up in the boat to declaim the more dramatically, I feared he would tip us into a watery grave. A successful relationship requires balance and I saw that he had none.'

The comment attracted universal agreement, and everyone looked to Lady Passmore to continue. To their surprise, however, the great lady had allowed herself to slump. Her shoulders sloped and her head drooped.

Gaia was quickly on her feet.

'Lady Passmore of Tewkesbury Manor, are you unwell?'

In response, her ladyship raised her gloved right hand.

'What I wish to tell you now, I have kept to myself some fifteen years,' she replied. 'I will only repeat it if you all promise me your complete discretion.'

All nodded.

'Absolutely, Ma'am.'

'You may count on us.'

Lady Passmore now slowly lifted her head.

'I should have learnt from Cliveden. It was the occasion of the Hon. Cecil's tenth birthday, and I had taken my husband's niece Daphne to the Servitudes's London residence. Like a fool, I found myself alone with Lord Servitude and it was then that he made his move.'

The mouths of her friends fell open.

'Oooah!' exclaimed Miss Prim.

'He ... ' started Belle.

'Dear God,' proclaimed Gaia.

' ... tickled you?' asked Mrs Pomeroy.

Mrs Pomeroy received a glower from Lady Passmore.

'I beat him off but this morning, when Mrs Pomeroy was absent upstairs, he made his intentions clear to me once more. He is all for a union between the houses of Servitude and Tewkesbury, if not in the church then in the bedchamber.'

All were stunned.

'How very horrid,' said Gaia.

'Most horrid,' agreed Belle.

'Exceedingly horrid,' remarked Miss Prim, breathing deeply. 'Why would he want to marry in a bedchamber rather than a church? Is he pagan?'

It was another question that Lady Passmore wisely left unanswered. Instead, she continued her tale of woe.

'On this occasion, unlike the previous, I played along with him as a means of providing Mrs Pomeroy time to fulfil her mission and, as soon as she returned, I insisted that we take our leave. But Lord Servitude has made his desires clear and I fear that he will pester me anew—and endlessly. He is an immoral monster and I feel greatly afflicted.'

Having concluded her speech, Lady Passmore managed to crank her chin back up to its natural position. Belle rose to his feet in response.

'Lady Passmore of Tewkesbury Manor, you did all that could have been asked of you and more. You are a fighter, Ma'am, a warrior queen in the mould of Boudicea.'

Her ladyship gently waved a hand in acknowledgement.

'I did my best, Mr Nash. I did my best.'

Belle then swept an arm through the air.

'In the name of Hercules, let us hope Mrs Pomeroy's story is similarly heroic. Did you find the girl, dear lady? Do not spare us the truth. We wait on your words enrapt.'

Mrs Pomeroy swallowed hard and not just because a piece of cake had just lodged itself in her gullet. By comparison, she feared that what she had to say would disappoint. She placed her hands submissively on her knees.

'Well,' she began, hesitantly. 'As Lady Passmore of Tewkesbury Manor has already set out, I was accompanied by my cat who, I should mention, showed great bravery by entering that horrible house, for the Servitudes's abode is not a happy home. We know that many slaves have died at their hands; I do not imagine they are any more caring of household pets.'

Her opening remarks were met with silence, except that

William began to drum his fingers. Whilst sympathetic to Lady Passmore and Mrs Pomeroy, he had only so far heard about an inflamed lover and a heroic cat, and was impatient to hear about the real business. Maybe what Mrs Pomeroy had learnt would allow him to resolve his differences with Belle.

'After being welcomed by Lord Servitude and partaking of tea, I excused myself and was led upstairs by the housekeeper ... '

'On what grounds did you excuse yourself?' asked Gaia, wishing to understand the stratagem.

'For the use of a commode,' said Mrs Pomeroy with a gulp. 'It was a pretext, but given the water I had consumed in the carriage and all the tea at the house, I ... '

Mrs Pomeroy hesitated. How she wished she were somewhere else at that moment!

'The girl,' said William. 'Didst tha' find the girl? That's what we all want to know.'

Mrs Pomeroy looked guiltily at him.

'I did. The housekeeper left me to my own devices and I took the stairs to the servants' quarters. It was there that I found the girl.'

There was an exhalation of breath. At last, a breakthrough! William leant forwards in anticipation.

'She was held in a room that was, as we suspected, locked.'

'And did you speak to her?' enquired Belle.

'Of course,' said Mrs Pomeroy. 'That was the purpose of the visit.'

'And what said the girl?' asked William. 'Did she state 'er name or predicament?'

These were reasonable questions but ones which prompted Mrs Pomeroy to dab at her brow with a handkerchief.

'The girl was clearly distraught and said she was bruised and bleeding. I told her I would help and would have spoken to her for longer but the dreadful housekeeper suddenly returned, forcing me to retrace my steps downstairs and explain myself. It was a

231

worrying few minutes but I explained my absence on the disappearance of Kiwu.'

Mrs Pomeroy stopped and showed no inclination to continue. She attempted a small smile but, unlike Lady Passmore, received no praise. Instead, she sensed disappointment and frustration, particularly from William, who had clenched his fists. She had clearly not done well enough.

As the hostess, Gaia intervened.

'For the avoidance of doubt, Mrs Pomeroy, did you not ask the girl for her name?'

Mrs Pomeroy twiddled her thumbs and looked at the crumbs of cake on a nearby side plate.

'I forgot,' she replied meekly.

'And did you not ask where she came from?' continued Gaia. 'An island from the Caribbean, for instance?'

O, if I could just hide amongst those cake crumbs, thought Mrs Pomeroy, before admitting that she had not.

Belle, who had remained standing, stepped forward.

'Did you at least enquire who she is—whether she is Mercy, the sister of Mr Fanque, or another?'

'I regret I did not.'

'Or whether,' cut in Gaia, 'she is being held lawfully?'

'No.'

Everyone sat back in their chairs, dismay etched on their faces. A gathering that had started with high expectations had become sullen and morose. In response, Mrs Pomeroy burst into tears.

'I tried my best,' she wept, 'but the awful housekeeper came back and I was desperate for the commode. It was only thanks to the cat that I had an excuse for ascending the stairs to the servants' quarters and ... and ... oh dear.'

If Mrs Pomeroy had been expecting sympathy or to be treated as heroic, as Lady Passmore had been, she was mistaken. The expressions on her friends's countenances darkened further.

'Oh dear, indeed,' said Gaia. 'I fear, Mrs Pomeroy, that not only have we gained no new information but we have also raised the enemy's suspicions. You did your best under trying circumstances but we may be worse off than we were before.'

A lull fell over the assembled company, eventually prompting Master Lush to wonder whether he might not have the key to reviving their spirits.

'Perhaps more tea would help,' he suggested limply, immediately regretting his words.

'Damn tea,' said Belle dryly. 'What we all need is a whisky.'

PRITCHARD ARRIVED IN double-quick time with cut-glass tumblers, a decanter of single malt Glen Garioch and a jug of water to hand. The need for a morale boost being universal, all those present took of a dose of the restorative liquid. Even Miss Prim accepted the benefits of a little Highland dew.

A word of warning: if drunk to excess, whisky can induce a flaccid state. A modest amount, however, can boost the creative mind and so, given Mrs Pomeroy's failure, it was agreed that whisky was exactly the right remedy. With their glasses topped up, Gaia restarted their deliberations and summarised their endeavours to date.

'We had hoped that our spies would return with definitive proof of a captive girl's identity, but they have not—although, to her credit, Mrs Pomeroy should be thanked for having established both her existence and her condition,' a consolation that made Mrs Pomeroy want to embrace Gaia and shed tears.

'Our dilemma is that the suspicions of the Servitudes have most certainly been raised,' Gaia continued. 'Mr Fanque: since the girl may be your kin, if not your sibling, I think you have the right to speak first. What should we do?'

The whisky had emboldened William.

'Were it moy choice, Ma'am, oi'd knock down their front door and throttle anyone as stood in moy way.'

'I understand that impulse, Sir,' said Gaia, 'but we should

avoid any act that might endanger her whom we wish to assist. If you failed in your effort, the girl would be spirited away and remain enslaved for life; and you, Mr Fanque, might be gaoled and even hanged for attempted murder. It is not a course of action that I could commend, although I appreciate the passion that lies behind it.'

Lady Passmore spoke next, taking the opportunity to disown her companion.

'As a consequence of Mrs Pomeroy's ineptitude, Lord Servitude may be preparing for the girl's departure as we speak.'

'Oooah,' whimpered Miss Prim.

Mrs Pomeroy shrank into her seat and reached for another whisky. That they might already be too late to save the girl was too terrible to contemplate, especially if she herself was the cause.

William, however, had some good news on this account for he had not been idle.

'Mrs Pomeroy, downt distress tha'self overmuch. Oi've arranged a rota among the circus troupe to keep a watch on th' 'ouse. If thems remove the girl, oi'll be told and then, boiy God, oi'll step in to save 'er.'

'And if the girl is not removed?' enquired Gaia, sensibly. 'Do we sit out the Season until the Servitudes depart? The girl could face months of seclusion and may not survive. Mrs Pomeroy learnt that she is injured and in need of attention. We must act quickly.'

They all peered into their glasses, as if the means to defeat their enemies lay in the amber liquor.

'The immediate issue,' said Belle, 'is not how to get into the house but how we get its principal occupants out. Without their commander-in-chief and his lieutenant at home, our chances of mounting a rescue would be immeasurably improved. Can we entice them away?'

'Could we claim that a python has gone missing from Mr Fanque's circus and was seen entering the building?' asked Master Lush, feebly. 'Or a lion, if he has one?'

'Oi 'owns no snakes and no loions, Maaster Lush,' replied William, stony-faced.

'Might Mr Quigley be persuaded to play his violin outside the house?' said Miss Prim. 'If it attracted a crowd, the Servitudes might join the throng.'

'Is there a contribution my cat could make?' said Mrs Pomeroy. 'Or Miss Prim with her knitting?'

'While the Season is on, could we invite the Hon. Cecil to dally in the park with a visiting beauty?' suggested Lady Passmore. 'We know that he has been brought from Jamaica to find a bride. If marriage were on offer, decency would demand that Lord Servitude accompany him, at least at their first meeting.'

But no beauty was known and the group fell silent. None of the assembled company appeared capable of crafting a scheme that would draw the two Servitudes out of their house for long enough for their captive to be rescued. Or could they?

'It is unfortunate that my husband's niece Daphne is in Florence and not Bath,' commented Lady Passmore. 'Were she here, she might promenade with the revolting Cecil, under the watchful eye of myself and Lord Servitude.'

While the others tried to think of more constructive notions, Belle's mouth began to flicker into a smile and then break into a broad, jubilant grin.

'You've cracked it, Lady Passmore of Tewkesbury Manor,' he said and threw the remnants of his whisky into the air. 'Lord Servitude wishes your two houses to be united and your niece Daphne is exactly the temptation that might woo him from his lair.'

'But Belle,' said Gaia. 'Lady Passmore of ... '

Belle was not listening.

'We can arrange an appropriate location for courtship away from the house. On the first occasion of their meeting, the potential lovers will be accompanied by their elders: that's Lord Servitude and you, Lady Passmore of Tewkesbury Manor, her aunt. This will leave the house free of both Servitudes and allow us to gain entry!'

'You are simply repeating what her ladyship has already said,' objected Gaia, 'but without acknowledging the fact that ... '

' ... my husband's niece is in Tuscany,' confirmed Lady Passmore.

Belle, however, waved the comment away. 'You are too hasty, Ma'am,' he smiled. 'It is true that *we* know where Daphne is; not so Lord Servitude and the Hon. Cecil. Nor have they seen her for fifteen years or watched her grow up. Someone of similar age and beauty could act her part and neither would be any the wiser.'

'But who?' asked Gaia. 'Even in the tightest of corsets, I am too old, and I warrant that Mrs Pomeroy or Miss Prim could not pass for twenty-five, either, wonderful though they are in other ways.'

'You are right, Mrs Champion,' Belle responded, 'yet there is one among us with the perfect attributes of age and beauty. A touch of rouge on the lips, a puff of powder on the cheeks and that person would be transformed into an irresistible object of desire,' and his outstretched finger moved round the room from person to person until settling on Master Lush.

Five pairs of eyes sized up the opportunity that the clerk presented.

'He's got the figure for it,' said Gaia.

'And the cheekbones,' agreed Lady Passmore.

Imagining the sound of wedding bells, Mrs Pomeroy offered to design the wedding cake.

'And I could knit the wedding dress,' offered Miss Prim. 'I've always wanted to knit a wedding dress.'

'Yes!' cheered Belle.

Poor Master Lush was struck dumb by what was being proposed and the blood rushed from his face. Belle's idea took advantage of him; it was not his fault that his features had a touch of the feminine but it did not mean that he should be treated as bait. Did not dangling him in front of the repulsive Cecil rob him of his dignity and treat him as a plaything? To fight subjugation by subjecting him to humiliation was morally inconsistent.

William was shocked too. For one thing, he considered Belle's idea absurd, whereas punching his way to the top floor seemed eminently practical. More fundamentally, he considered putting a young man in a dress for so serious a cause to be unfair to him, inappropriate and possibly titillating.

It was the frivolity of it all, he raged. What was it about Bath and these privileged people who would call themselves his friends?

'Oi don't like it,' he cried. 'Oi'm a plain man and don't know 'ow to put moy misgivins into words but it seems to oi that for all yewr claims and noble insights, yew remain bloind to the sufferings of others, if yew are willin' to heap more indignities on their backs.'

His audience was bemused.

'Is he talking about us?' asked Lady Passmore.

'I cannot think so,' replied Mrs Pomeroy.

William's patience now broke.

'Aaaargh! A girl's to be saved and yew talk of puttin' a man in a dress! Is everything a joke to yew? Have yew no foiner feelings? It's no wonder misery infests this world when yew paragons of virtue, cocooned in your Baath palaces, put your own amusement before all else. Tha' poor girl would do better slittin' 'er throat than wait for rescue by yew.'

Belle was alarmed.

'Pablo, calm yourself. The plan may work. Don't dismiss it out of hand.'

William slapped the side of his head as if to wake himself from a dream but to no avail. The veins in his neck pulsed in fury as he looked about the room.

'Oi can't believe oi'm hearin' such nonsense! Oi can't take no more. I've 'ad enough of it. No more tea. No more cake. No more whisky. No more cravenness. Mrs Champion, oi wants a moment with 'ee in tha' library. Another minute in this 'ere room and ... and ... oi'll use words oi'll immediately regret.'

William turned on his heel and marched out of the drawing room. Belle made to follow but for the second time in as many days, Gaia ordered him to stay.

'Don't!' she commanded.

Belle sat down, disconsolate.

'But it's a good idea to put Master Lush in a dress. Truly, it is.'

Gaia raised her hand to him.

'Silence, Belle.'

CHAPTER XX

Away with the Faeries

LUCIUS LUSH HAD been shocked by the pace of events. For four years he had enjoyed the uniform and trappings of a clerk of court. Suddenly, within a day of Lady Passmore and Mrs Pomeroy presenting their report, he found himself back at Somerset Place, stripped to his undergarments by three women who were sizing him up for a silk dress.

'I wrote to Lord Servitude this morning and received an immediate response,' explained Lady Passmore. 'A union between the Hon. Cecil and Miss Daphne Passmore is greatly desired.'

'And how is that to be achieved?' asked Master Lush.

He was answered by his employer, Gaia Champion.

'You and Lady Passmore of Tewkesbury Manor will promenade past their house, where Lord Servitude and his son will watch from within. If the Hon. Cecil finds you attractive, a vase of flowers will be placed in the window.'

Master Lush shivered and not just from fear and awkwardness. Near naked, he was cold and wished to cover up his body from the ladies' prying eyes, not that his body was without charm. His slim hips and thin waist would have been the envy of many a girl less well endowed. Belle Nash was right: with rouge on his lips and powder applied to his high cheekbones, Master Lush would be a dazzling beauty.

The young man now looked pleadingly at the third woman in the room: Gaia's maid, Mary. At least he might win the sympathy of the servant class, he thought—but in this respect he was mistaken.

'Master Lush is too old for pantalettes,' adjudged the maid. 'He's no longer a child.'

'You are right, Mary,' agreed Gaia. 'Long hose, stockings and petticoats better suit a damsel of his age.'

'Yes, Ma'am. But how many petticoats, I wonder?'

As Master Lush now learnt, this is a question that had vexed many a woman.

'What is your view on the matter, Lady Passmore of Tewkesbury Manor?' asked Gaia. 'I own that two petticoats will normally suffice.'

As on most things, her ladyship held a firm opinion.

'There is nothing worse than a limp frock. If in doubt, always add another petticoat.'

Master Lush was immediately made to don a petticoat, and then a second and a third.

'Add a fourth,' said Lady Passmore, with the benefit of her expert eye. 'Some girls are greedy for petticoats.'

Master Lush groaned with disbelief. When William Darby had demanded a private hearing with Gaia the previous afternoon, he had ardently hoped that the threat of being turned into Daphne Passmore had been dispelled. Yet on her return to the drawing room, Gaia had announced that Belle Nash's outlandish plan would proceed.

How had it come to this? he wondered. What could Mrs Champion have said to persuade Mr Darby of the merits of this mad scheme?

I T WAS COMMON when disputing with Gaia to be humbled within minutes. Under her rigorous cross-examination, watertight arguments sprang leaks like colanders. So it had been for William the previous afternoon.

William was a man who spoke from the heart and he had not

been able to hide his anger at the damage done to their prospects by the spies' visit to the Servitude house. Gaia had closed the library door and had allowed William to vent his rage.

'Not wishin' to be 'arsh, Mrs Champion, but tha' Lady Passmewre and Mrs Pomeroy have been reckless and inept.'

Gaia had motioned him to a chair.

'Take a seat, Mr Fanque. Reckless and inept, you say.'

William had nodded.

'Aye, Madam! Oi be a man of few words but t'is evident that their enterprise has been bunglin' and incompetent and wantin' and clumsy and bumblin' and maladroit and ineffectual and lackin' and inexpert and ... '

'Mr Fanque, Mr Fanque! Though a man of few words, you seem to have swallowed the lexicology of Dr Roget. Let us speak calmly, otherwise there is nothing to be achieved.'

'But how could Mrs Pomeroy have engaged the girl in conversation and not asked 'er name? She were at the door! She were right there!'

On a writing desk had stood a jug of water and several glasses. Gaia had poured a glass for William and handed it to him.

'Please sit, Mr Fanque, and take a glass of water and listen closely. We can speak openly here. What you say is true but incantations of rage will not progress matters. When it comes to the girl, our best chances are to act as a team. Accusations do not help.'

'They help if they reveal where we lack the skills to accomplish our aims.'

'That is a fair point,' Gaia had replied, 'and we must always be alert to our limitations. I am not against people speaking out in that respect, but on this occasion you were wrong. The plan might have worked had Mrs Pomeroy not been beset both by physical distress—for an aching bladder is no small aggravation for those thus afflicted—and by the hypervigilance of an over-attentive housekeeper. As for Mr Nash's idea, it is certainly bizarre, as many of his notions often are, and it may take advantage of Master Lush, yet it has merit. In a just and equal society, what matters is acquiescence, above all. We should not impose our plans on anyone who opposes them, and Master Lush was certainly not at once excited at being passed off as Lady Passmore's husband's niece. But should he recognise the greater good, do you then not think we should let it run its course? If it works ... '

'A moighty "if"! Maaster Lush in a dress!'

' ... it would free the house of the Servitudes and at a time of our choosing. But that is only half the task. And as you rightly pointed out, there is still the freeing of the girl, and you are the person best suited to the challenge.'

Whilst her observation pleased William, Gaia knew she had more to do, for William's preferred option—as evidenced by the clenching of his fists—remained brute force. Having been standing by the writing desk, she had now knelt at his chair and held his hands in her hands, as his mother had held his hands when he was a boy.

'I dare say much has changed for you since leaving Grenada,' she had said, comfortingly. 'You have been uprooted and now find yourself among a very queer lot, myself included. You have accepted us on trust but we are unknowns to you, and you have put your faith in us without truly knowing what we amount to. Much that you have seen must trouble you, and you have bravely kept it hidden behind a taciturn façade. Would it not lift your burden to share at least one of your woes? As a lawyer I am privy to many secrets; as a friend, you would not find me any the less.'

William had looked into her demanding eyes and had shaken his head.

'Oi thank 'ee, Mrs Champion, but some matters cannot be spoken of. These are moy torments. Moyn alone.'

Gaia had then stood up and stared back at him.

'Except that they're not, are they? They are coupled to another question. One that has troubled me since your arrival in Bath.'

William had watched as Gaia moved to a shelf of books, running her fingers across their spines as if to examine their titles. Then she had turned to face him.

'What is wrong with Belle? Like you, he is uneasy in his mind. He is returned from Grenada a broken man and his disposition worsens.'

William had nodded but remained silent.

'I shall be straight with you, Mr Fanque: I believe the answer lies with you. I do not doubt your honesty but I fancy there is something you are hiding, or that Belle is hiding that pertains to you. I see it eating away at you, and at Mr Nash. It is destroying you both, Sir.'

William had picked up his glass of water as if his thoughts could be seen floating on the surface. Instead, in the reflection, he had seen a face staring up. The face of Pablo Fanque. Startled, he had put the glass down.

'Oi promised Belle to keep a secret,' he had said, now shaking, 'and oi cannot give it voice. Too much is at stake.'

Then Gaia had returned to his side, kneeling once more and speaking in a firm voice. She was a woman accustomed to putting her point persuasively.

'Much as I admire you, Sir, and all you seek to achieve, Belle is my very closest friend. I love him perhaps as much as I loved my late husband and I will do anything to protect him. Of that you have my word. If there is some secret in which you are both complicit, and which ails you both, my helping him would surely help you both. Dear Mr Fanque, open your heart and speak your mind, and then maybe we can also save the girl.'

I T IS NOT easy for a man when he walks in female attire the first time. Scotsmen have their kilts, of course, but the kilt is the uniform of the warrior and Scots carry it off with military assurance. Burmese and Malay men wear their *longyi* and *sarong* with similar aplomb. But to compare those fine garments with the pleated, full-length frock that Master Lush was wearing on top of four petticoats belies the picture that he presented.

It was a cream cotton frock with a pattern of climbing roses. To go with it, the three women had found a very fetching wide-brimmed, pastel-pink bonnet.

'Do I have to wear a bonnet?' Master Lush pled as the final touches were applied in Somerset Place.

'Most certainly,' Lady Passmore replied. 'A bonnet not only protects the neck from Nature's elements but its brim allows you to be visible only to those by whom you wish to be seen. It puts you fully in control.'

'I don't understand,' said Master Lush.

'Like this,' explained Gaia, moving her head in the manner that well-brought-up girls are taught to do before coming out as debutantes. 'And like this.'

'Just so,' Lady Passmore confirmed. 'Now practise, Sir.'

Master Lush did his best but not to his tutors' satisfaction.

'You're jerking your head like a chicken,' her ladyship scolded.

It took a full thirty minutes of training before Master Lush was declared fit and ready to show himself in public. There followed a final pull on the corset, like the tightening of a horse's saddle, and an additional application of powder on the cheeks by the maid, Mary.

Lady Passmore then held out her arm.

She said, 'For the promenade around The Circus, I shall be your guardian. You will follow my instructions to the letter. When I say, "Appear coy and tilt your head to the left", you will ... '

'Appear coy and tilt my head to the left,' Master Lush replied, submissively.

'Very good. If all goes to plan, the vase of flowers will surely be placed in the window.'

'After which, I may be permitted to resume my breeches?' Master Lush asked.

'Not immediately,' Gaia responded. 'You will first go to Miss Prim's house in Gay Street, where Mr Nash will be waiting. He will advise Lady Passmore on the letter she will write. In it, she will propose suitable occasions for you and execrable Cecil to meet. I will then arrange for your clothes to be sent to Gay Street in the evening.'

'Can they not be sent now?' pled Master Lush.

His request was waved away.

'All in good time. I have court papers to read. With Guildhall closed on Friday for the funeral, tomorrow will be a busy day. Be off with you, Master Lush, and be comfortable in your frock. The horrible Cecil awaits.'

THE HORRIBLE CECIL did indeed await, as did Belle, who was sitting impatiently in the parlour of Number 40 Gay Street. With him was Phyllis Prim, completing the knitting of her black veil. For his part, Belle was composing missives.

His primary purpose for the day, as Gaia had described, was to assist Lady Passmore in fashioning her next letter to Lord Servitude and the proposing of suitable locations for subsequent trysts for the adoring couple.

But as he waited for news, Belle had also written a second letter, one destined for London. Drying the ink with a blotter and sealing the envelope with wax, he instructed the cook, Mrs Mulligatawny, to despatch it.

'Please, make haste to the post office, Mrs Mulligatawny. It must be delivered to London by tomorrow.'

'Celeriac,' she replied. 'Cannot the maid Millicent post it when she returns?'

'I regret not. None can be trusted save you, Mrs Mulligatawny. You are the soul of discretion and I dare commend my errand to your custody alone.'

'Carrots.'

The cook departed and Belle returned to drafting Lady Pass-

245

more's communiqué to Lord Servitude. The challenge he faced was its style: her ladyship's tone was by nature haughty but the letter had to be enticing. How could he manage the right balance?

From Miss Prim's chair, the sound of the needles—click-clack-click—momentarily ceased.

'What are you up to, Mr Nash, if I may be so bold as to enquire?'

Belle looked up and saw, in amazement, that Miss Prim's veil had grown in length by a foot in the past hour.

'I am imagining myself to be Lady Passmore,' he replied.

'What an odd pastime,' she said, continuing her knitting. 'You always surprise me, Mr Nash, with your many fancies.'

Click-clack-click.

'It is a labyrinthine fancy indeed, Miss Prim, and one that even Daedalus, sire of Icarus and Iapyx, might struggle to resolve! You see ... '

At that moment, the doorbell tinkled. With Mrs Mulligatawny gone and Millicent away gossiping, Belle rose from his chair. He checked the time on his pocket watch. It was too early for Lady Passmore to be back with Master Lush. If he knew the caller at all, it had to be William.

He had last seen his companion at breakfast, when their conversation had become fractious again. They were in agreement on the need to rescue the girl, but it was clear that William still had little love for Belle's plan.

Belle opened the front door and there indeed was William. They embraced but with no more warmth, Belle felt, than he might have derived from the embers of the previous night's fire. What would it take, he wondered, to fan the flames of love again?

'Miss Prim is in the parlour,' he explained. 'Let us avail ourselves of the dining room. It would afford us more privacy.'

The dining room was close by.

'How goes the circus?' Belle asked, closing the door.

William stood by a sideboard.

'Oi led the troupe and the hosses through their paces. We're feelin' confident.'

'Good. And what else?'

William had surely not passed by with nothing more to impart. It was clear to Belle that he was withholding something.

William shrugged his shoulders. He saw no reason to deceive.

'Oira Aldridge visited the tent. We engaged in a brief intercourse and 'e then invited me to 'is house where we had coffee and what he calls "cookies". Biscuits by any other name.'

Belle felt a tinge of jealousy. By reputation, Ira Aldridge could make strangers swoon. And what starts with a biscuit could soon grow into ...

'A chance encounter, then,' he suggested, banishing thoughts of impropriety.

William would not be drawn.

'Mr Aldridge and oi shared intelligence,' was all he would say. 'Oi may say more, as th'occasion demand. Till then, oi've come to enquire of Maaster Lush. Has your hateful proposal to disgoise him as Miss Paassmore been greeted with success? Is the Hon. Cecil ensnared?'

Belle started to pace the room.

'We will know within minutes, Sir. Our Miss Passmore is promenading with her aunt at this very moment. Did you not see them in The Circus?'

William shook his head.

'Oi dared not look, lest oi gave the game away. In moy heart, oi knowed tha' plan wuz mad and bad and dangerous, but oi promised Mrs Champion to let it run its course.'

The criticism irritated Belle.

'Mad and bad, you say. Then let me reveal more of my madness and maybe I shall set your mind at ease.'

He then told William how, once the Servitudes had taken the bait, he had identified two possible occasions for a renewed liaison between the despicable Cecil and Master Lush.

247

'And they be?' enquired William.

'The first is the funeral of Ernest Camshaft on Friday. If we can persuade the Servitudes to attend, there will be plenty of time to conduct a rescue in whatever manner you see fit. You see, I am thinking of you. It is an excellent plan, is it not?'

William gave a mocking laugh.

'Excellent? Tis worse than folly. Tha'art away with the faeries, Belle. A funeral is no occasion for romance—besides which, Maaster Lush is the great-grandson of the deceased, so 'e'll be expected to attend as 'isself. What's the second occasion tha've identified? It cannot be worse than the first.'

Belle had never had his plans questioned in such a manner. It seemed to him that William had gone from being a friend to an inquisitor. Nevertheless, he would keep his temper.

'The next occasion is on Saturday evening.'

William laughed again.

'Praise the Lord, oi won't be there to bear witness. Forgive oi for not bein' free to attend but the circus opens that evening.'

'Exactly,' said Belle.

'Well, do tha' worst. Once tha' com'st running back, tail between tha' legs, and tell me of tha' failure, oi shall be free to devise a realistic plan. The last thing oi wants on the opening night of the circus is ... '

At which point William's words ground to a halt. His eyes shifted warily to Belle. For once, the circus artist felt himself teetering on the tightrope.

'Tha' said'st "exactly", Mr Nash. What meant'st tha' boiy that? Please tell me tha's not plannin' to put moy circus in jeopardy. No, Belle. Tha' can'st not destroy the openin' night of moy dream.'

Belle attempted a smile. William had, indeed, second-guessed his plan.

'But what better occasion is there, dear Mr Fanque?' said Belle with bravado. 'I shall have Lady Passmore issue the Servitudes an invitation.'

248

'But the Servitudes 'ate the circus—the tumblers, the jugglers, the hosses. They showed that when they tried to break us in court.'

'But on Saturday night, Daphne Passmore will be the main attraction, not the tumblers or horses. The abhorrent Cecil and his father will swallow their pride to couple with a Tewkesbury. Is it not a brilliant idea?'

William slapped an elegant Hepplewhite sideboard with his hand.

'Brilliant? In what way is it brilliant?'

Belle had it all plotted out.

'As impresario, you can control how long Lord Servitude and the repulsive Cecil stay. You can dance on the horses until midnight if you wish. It gives you all the time in the world to conduct the rescue. It's perfect.'

William, however, looked aghast.

'Whilst oi leads tha' assault on the house, art tha' sayin'?'

'Indeed. That is your role.'

'But oi shall be in the ring! How dost tha' expect oi to control events in the tent whilst oi leads the storming of the house? Art tha' out of tha' mind, Sir?'

Unfortunately for Belle, William's critique was sound.

'Admittedly the plan needs refinement but do not be unkind,' said Belle, his confidence detumescing. 'As you say, you will be in the ring; maybe we can prevail upon the Ridley Brother clowns to lead the rescue in your stead, or one of your other talented artistes. Or ... or ... your new friend Mr Aldridge, the biscuit man. No doubt the tricks of magic that they perform in public could be put to use in ... '

His sentence, however, remained unfinished for at that moment the doorbell rang again. William crossed quickly to the window and looked out onto Gay Street.

'Let we talk more on this matter presently,' he snapped, 'if we must. For now, Lady Paassmore and Maaster Lush 'ave joined us.'

249

Belle brushed his hair with his fingers.

'Of course,' he replied. 'We must hear Lady Passmore's news.'

With their argument suspended, the two men left the dining room and entered the hall. From the parlour came the mechanical clatter of Miss Prim's knitting. Belle opened the front door and daylight flooded in, bringing with it Lady Passmore.

'Lady Passmore of Tewkesbury Manor, what a pleasure,' said Belle as her ladyship swept past. 'And, if I am not mistaken, the exquisite Miss Passmore, looking as pretty as a picture.'

Pulling his dress with him, Master Lush now followed, every inch a damsel in distress. It was clear that promenading with Lady Passmore had taken its toll. Master Lush placed a hand against a wall.

'Tea,' he said in a weak voice. 'I need tea.'

Belle blinked.

'I would, but Mrs Mulligatawny has ... '

On the far side of the hall, Lady Passmore spun on her heels.

'Tea can wait!' she declared, smacking the tiled floor with the end of her parasol. 'We did it!'

Belle's eyes opened wide.

'You did?'

'Yes, Mr Nash. The vase of flowers was placed in the window!'

'Truly?'

Lady Passmore smiled, then offered that rarest of compliments.

'I will allow you to shake me politely by the hand, Mr Nash. Your plan ... '

And as he extended his hand, Belle cast a wary eye at William. His expression did not insinuate that he shared Lady Passmore's assessment.

' ... appears to be working!'

NOTES

- Though Belle Nash was taking a risk in sending an afternoon letter from Bath for delivery the next day in London, it was not an impossible feat. Mail coaches provided a sixteen-hour express service running from Bristol to London via Bath. The mail coach also took passengers, although not in great comfort. In 1836, three passengers travelling from London to Bath for Christmas died of frostbite.

CHAPTER XXI

Just the same as Guilt

A LTHOUGH WEDDINGS ARE the more welcomed, there is
nothing like a good funeral to improve the soul.
Step back and consider. A marriage, if it fails, will
either be ruinous to the bride and groom or, if blessed, will highlight the failure of others. An inhumation, by comparison, uplifts
us all. The funeralgoer may honour the memory of the deceased or
gleefully greet the handcart that takes them off to Hell.

It was Friday, the day of the funeral of Ernest Camshaft, the
late chairman of the City Corporation. He was widely remembered for his good nature and generosity of spirit, and those
attending the service were happy to share memories, some of
which went back an exceedingly long way. Such was the case with
a pair of old ladies who occupied one of the central pews in the
abbey.

'Emily! said the first, bent double by age. 'We have not met
since last Christmastide but one, and Miss Walcott's funeral. That
was a chill day.'

'Miss Walcott's funeral was five years hence, Gwendoline,'
replied the other. 'It was a cruelly cold winter and my toes fell off.'

'So they did. Have you managed to replace them?'

'No. I now rely on those of others.'

There was a further dusting off of memories, a gentle laugh
about the chairman's famously poor eyesight, and his ability to
confuse gentlemen for servants and peers for paupers.

'I remember him handing Lord Darlington his shoes to clean!' joked a city councillor, joining the two venerable dames on their pew.

'Rumour has it that he confused our present lady magistrate for a man when authorising her appointment,' added a fellow councillor, as the gaggle grew larger. 'But thus is history made!'

'Talk of the devil. Here she is.'

Indeed 'she' was. Gaia Champion, dressed magnificently in a black dress that was full and resplendent, was walking her party up the aisle. With her was Lady Passmore, who for once was not accompanied by her perpetual companion, Mrs Pomeroy. Instead, by her side was a demure young woman wearing a modest frock of matt black paramatta silk, with black kid gloves and a hat to match. Behind a veil of demure black lace was a nervous-looking face.

It was, of course, Master Lush's face. Belle Nash had had his way and the poor clerk, though attending his great-grandfather's funeral, had accepted the higher moral argument for coming as Miss Daphne Passmore.

Given her seniority as magistrate, Gaia had arranged for a pew close to the front of the abbey. She motioned for Master Lush to enter first, followed by her ladyship, with Gaia positioned next to the aisle. Already seated on the far side of the pew were Belle and William Darby.

The two men had been in a side-chapel watching for the arrival of Lord Servitude and the egregious Cecil but they now suspended their vigil.

'Good morning, Miss Passmore,' said Belle. 'My condolences on the death of your godfather and great-grandfather. It's a complicated family tree you have. May I hope that you are holding up?'

Master Lush sat unhappily in the pew. He was full of regret at not being able to attend the funeral as himself and could only pray that none of his relatives recognised him.

'With the help of this corset, I'm holding up as well as could be expected,' he gasped. 'Indeed, without any effort at all except

253

that I find myself in great discomfort. I can hardly breathe and the paramatta silk itches worse than fleas.'

Belle discreetly felt the material for himself. It was, indeed, rough to the touch.

He whispered, 'A sacrifice worth making, young lady, so long as the Servitudes take up Lady Passmore's invitation. Her letter could not have been better worded, for I worded it myself! In anticipation, Gaia has reserved a place for father and son on the opposite side of the aisle.'

Master Lush scratched at his arm.

'You will have to point out the Hon. Cecil. I can barely see through this veil. Are you certain they're not here already?'

Belle half-lifted himself from the pew to scrutinise the church. Towards the rear of the abbey, he saw Mrs Pomeroy dabbing at her eyes and looking sombre as an undertaker. With her was Phyllis Prim, whose knitted black veil descended almost to her knees. He gave them a discreet wave before sitting back down.

'If they were, I think I should recognise them. It's not often you'd see a Tamworth pig and its runt in a church.'

Behind his veil, Master Lush ground his teeth. On the one hand, he wanted the Servitudes to come quickly so that their captive's rescue could be effected soon. On the other, he wished them to hold off, for fear of failing in his tentative impersonation of Daphne Passmore.

'If they do turn up ... ?' the clerk asked Belle nervously.

Belle explained, 'If they do turn up, Pablo will go straight to their house, where he will be joined by the pugilist Tom Shelton. Although their story is too ludicrous, the most implausible stories are often the most readily believed, for experience has least prepared us to question them. Following your own suggestion, they will claim that a vast fairground python—twenty-foot long and nine-inches wide—had escaped from the circus and was seen slithering into the house. If they are not believed, they will force entry anyway.'

254

Under his veil, Master Lush nodded.

Belle continued, 'Of course, I will join Mrs Pomeroy and Miss Prim, lest my presence on this pew antagonise our prey. As for you ... '

'I have been fully briefed by Lady Passmore,' Master Lush said, quivering. 'I will make the necessary hand motion to acknowledge the Hon. Cecil, whom I will then meet after the service. By that time I hope the girl will have been rescued.'

'It is our dearest hope too. But only if the Servitudes turn up.'

Belle again lifted himself from the pew. As the minutes had passed, his explanation of what the day might hold seemed ever more fanciful, for it was looking ever more improbable that the Servitudes would attend. And if they arrived after the bishop had begun the service, they would most likely prefer not to interrupt the proceedings and return home.

Suddenly, there was a rustling of papers and a movement of feet. In a human wave that rolled from the back of the abbey to the front, the congregation started to stand. Master Lush looked at Belle with alarm.

'Are the Servitudes here? Is that why people are standing?'

Belle shook his head in disappointment.

'No. It's the pallbearers carrying the coffin. And following behind is the Bishop of Bath & Wells. It seems, for today, that our best efforts have failed.'

ONCE IT WAS clear that the Servitudes had not been tempted to attend, Belle had picked up the order of service and focussed on the hymns and readings. His godfather George Monstrance, the Bishop of Bath & Wells, had crossed the transept with a jewelled crook in his hand. People had bowed their heads at the sight of the coffin. Belle had been struck that this was indeed a time for introspection rather than personating.

To the booming sound of the great organ, the bishop now climbed into a pulpit, with two ordinands on either side, dressed in vestments, holding giant candles. The sound of the organ died away. When George Monstrance spoke, he did so in the gently melodic voice that men of the cloth are taught at seminary school.

'Ernest Camshaft's love for his wife Audrey was deep and true to the day she died. His love for Guildhall and the City Corporation was also profound. Love characterised Ernest, and it is with love that his family and friends are gathered here today to bid him farewell.'

There was a general snuffling in the congregation as men and women dried tears and blew noses into handkerchiefs.

'As we walk through the valley of the shadow of death, let us remember how God's love conquers all. Holy Lord, may our hearts be filled with joy, not pain, at the memory of your humble servant. With joy in mind, I ask that you all stand and sing the hymn "There is a fountain filled with blood".'

'Love,' mused Belle, as the choir and congregation started to sing the hymn. 'What is it about love that so captivates the human mind?'

> There is a fountain filled with blood,
> Drawn from Immanuel's veins;
> And sinners plunged beneath that flood,
> Lose all their guilty stains.

Belle remained silent—he was not a man to sing in church; his love of the Church and of churchmen was half-hearted—but his subconscious ear picked up on the hymn's words.

'There is truth there,' he thought. 'Love will always be with us, whether we desire it or not. In that sense, it is just no different from guilt.'

BELLE REMAINED IN a meditative mood after the service had concluded and the congregation had decanted itself from the regimented lines of pews into Abbey Church Yard. In the yard, family and friends drifted around, meeting and greeting each other like ornamental fish in a pond.

Yes, thought Belle, how very like fish they were, lips touching lips and retreating, hands motioning like gills, the ladies suspended in their dresses, the men displaying in their Sunday best. How calm they all appeared, gliding betwixt and between, unaware of the sea monsters, the Scylla of Lord Servitude and the Charybdis of his son, who had opted to stay in their lair for another day.

After several minutes of watching the funeralgoers, Belle realised he had become detached from his group; indeed, that the group had dispersed. There was Gaia conversing with a councillor, there was Lady Passmore presenting her gloved hand to people of lower social rank and there was William chatting to Mrs Crust.

Gaia's clerk, disguised as Miss Passmore, stood alone. Deciding that Master Lush urgently required company lest he attract the attention of others in the congregation, Belle swiftly made his way to his side.

'Fair lady,' Belle said, 'like beauteous Andromeda, you have been abandoned on a rock by your guardian. But fear not, for your Perseus is here.'

Master Lush lifted his veil and heaved a sigh of relief.

'Oh, Mr Nash. How relieved I am to see you. Lady Passmore is off doing her rounds, and has left me to wait here. By her command, I am forbidden to talk to anyone, which is a harder charge than it seems. The Camshafts are a chatsome lot.'

'The travails of being a beguiling single lady,' reflected Belle. 'I strongly recommend that you return to your aunt. When you do, please whisper in her ear that we are to regroup in an hour's time at Somerset Place.'

Master Lush again raised his veil.

'In an hour's time? Not sooner?'

'Social niceties, I fear, must keep us here longer than I would

257

have liked,' Belle explained. 'But you will be able to disrobe once we are back on *terra firma*. Then we can discuss the next step.'

'The next step? Was this not sufficient?'

'I regret, dear Madam, that the Servitudes have not taken our first bait and that we must now rely on my second trap—of which more anon. For now, go to Lady Passmore lest you get pestered by an uncle.'

'Yes, Sir.'

Master Lush curtseyed, then headed to Lady Passmore, leaving Belle once more to survey the crowd. His fishes, he noted, had all moved. Gaia was now talking to the eminent physician Dr Sturridge and William was with Miss Prim learning the art of the pearl stitch. Belle was about to join them when he received a firm tap on the shoulder. Thinking it must be a forgotten friend, he turned expectantly.

His mouth fell open. Although he had never met the man, he knew who it was at once.

'Do I have the honour of addressing Mr Cookie? Mr Biscuit? I mean Mr Aldridge, Sir?'

The actor faced him with a withering stare.

'It is I.'

'And you were ... looking for me?' asked Belle.

The actor placed a hand by his mouth as if to disguise his words.

'Indeed, I am, Mr Nash.'

'Do you know me, Sir?'

The question prompted Mr Aldridge to emit a deep laugh.

'You are famous in Bath, Sir. Your voluminous cravat and bachelor airs set you apart.' Then his voice dropped to a whisper: 'And I believe we share a mutual friend: a Mr Darby, also known as Pablo Fanque.'

If Belle had been surprised at meeting Mr Aldridge, the actor's knowledge of William's identity bowled him over. William had sworn himself to secrecy.

'You know who Mr Fanque is?' Belle whispered back.

'And a good deal more besides, Mr Nash. Mr Darby told me that there's a girl in trouble and that she needs help. He also said that you have a foolhardy plan that will never work.'

Belle would have enquired further but suddenly, there to his left, stood William, with an alarmed expression on his face.

Belle could not hold back: 'The cat is out the bag, William! Mr Aldridge knows all! You have betrayed me!'

William grabbed hold of Belle's arm.

'Not 'ere, Belle.'

Belle hissed, 'Traitor, Sir. Sharing our secrets with a stranger.'

'I told 'ee, not 'ere,' he hissed back. 'And Mr Aldridge ain't no stranger. He's been to Astley's many a toime and knows moy name full well. Besides which, there's more important matters as requoire tha'n attention.'

Belle laughed a bitter howl.

'More important than honesty among friends?!'

Still holding Belle's arm, William pointed across the yard with an urgency that Belle had not seen before. With William on one side and Mr Aldridge on the other, Belle's blinkered eyes had no choice but to survey the other side of the abbey grounds.

'Who am I looking for?' he enquired.

'There,' said William. 'Yon woman with Lady Paassmore and Maaster Lush. She is the cause of moy alaarm.'

Belle nodded.

'I see a woman but do not recognise her.'

'You shall do soon,' said Mr Aldridge. 'She is a witch sent by Hecate.'

'Worse,' said William, who had startled to tremble. 'Her name is Neech, the 'ousekeeper to Lord Servitude. Mrs Pomeroy identi-fied 'er to me. And she come with a message.'

'Which is?' asked Belle.

William now flung away Belle's arm. Their companionship had cost him dear.

'Lord Servitude and th'abhorrent Cecil will attend the circus tomorrow, an occasion when oi cannot assist in the girl's rescue. Tha' foolish scheme will be her undoin', Mr Nash. Dear God, what's to be done? Somethin' must be done.'

NOTES
- 'To Hell in a handcart' is a phrase of uncertain origin but is likely to refer to the unedifying removal of corpses during epidemics such as The Great Plague of London (1665–1666) when the dead were transported to mass graves in wheelbarrows, rather than risk exposing valuable horses to disease.
- 'There is a fountain filled with blood' is a hymn written by William Cowper (1731–1800). Cowper, whose writing focused on scenes of everyday life, was described by Samuel Taylor Coleridge as 'the best modern poet'. Like Coleridge, he suffered from depression, spending a period in an asylum, and wrote this hymn after dreaming, and awaking convinced, that he was doomed to eternal damnation.
- Ira Aldridge's reference is to the Greek goddess Hecate, who orders the witches to congregate in Shakespeare's *Macbeth*.

CHAPTER XXII

The Trumpets Sound

N EVER LET YOUR enemy know what you are doing; it is
likely to be fatal.

Equally dangerous is the failure to communicate clearly to one's own forces, for who can forget the Battle of Karansebes
in 1788 in which drunken divisions of the Austrian army mistook
each other for enemy Turks? When the Ottomans arrived two
days later, they found 10,000 Austrian soldiers dead upon the
field.

The plan to rescue Mercy was similarly characterised by a lack
of communication between Belle Nash and William Darby.
Although they shared a common aim, distrust between them had
worsened and each was wary of providing the other with details as
to how their plans were unfolding.

After William had thrown off Belle's arm in Abbey Church
Yard, Belle had watched his companion deep in conversation with
Ira Aldridge. A short while later, Belle's perceptive eye had caught
William talking to Arthur Quigley, which was odd, given that Mr
Quigley spoke nothing but nonsense.

There could be but one conclusion: that William was devising
an alternative plan with neither Belle's participation nor his
consent. Come Friday evening, before they retired to bed, Belle
confronted William in the drawing room of Sydney Buildings.

'I know you and have watched you, Sir. You are laying your
own plans to rescue Mercy,' Belle said. 'You must admit me into

your stratagems so that I can assist—or least, neither fall foul of them nor endanger them by implementing those of my own.'

The answer was cold and stark.

'If oi did 'ave a plan, Mr Nash, oi wouldn't be seekin' help from 'ee. Oi knows 'ee and 'ave watched 'ee, Sir, and tha' well-meaning interventions would only do more haarm than good.'

'Harm?' said Belle. 'You are unfair. I only wish to save the girl —and William, the invitation to the abysmal Cecil cannot be undone. He and his father will be at the circus whether you wish it or not. All is in motion.'

All was indeed in motion but, as Belle now found, much more than he had reckoned and none of it of his own doing. If William had not damaged his pride enough, Gaia Champion now sent him a note, rejecting his offer to help with the dressing up of Lucius Lush as Daphne Passmore the following evening and warning him to stay away from the circus. Lady Passmore had determined that Belle's presence would unnerve Master Lush, and Gaia had agreed.

REJECTED BY BOTH his companion and his closest friend, Belle suffered a fitful night and dreamt of being an old nag put out to pasture. On Saturday morning, he opened his eyes to the offer of a cup of tea, but what appeared to be a gift from William turned out to be a bribe.

'This is unexpected, William. To what do I owe the pleasure?' Belle enquired suspiciously.

'Oi've sent word to Mrs Champion and them other ladies that oi'll let 'ee attend the show tonoight,' said William, in what seemed a conciliatory tone, 'but tha's not to sit close to Lady Paassmore or Maaster Lush.'

'I'm not? And why, Sir?'

'Thems' not to be distracted.'

So affronted was Belle that he almost returned the cup.

'None of you understands that success this evening depends

upon my plan of action!' he exclaimed. 'It won't work without me. I have help coming from London. A friend is arriving by coach who ... '

William was adamant.

'No, Sir, absolutely not. Oi've told 'ee already: *tha'* plan will not succeed. Whoever tha' moight be dependin' on, them'll not be needed. Moy circus opens tonoight and tha'lt not do nothin' to put it at risk. Tha' may'st come along but only to accompany Mrs Pomeroy and Miss Prim. Nought else.'

'You have some nerve, William! After all I have done for you!'

William was unmoved.

'Oi'll send Mrs Pomeroy a note on tha' behalf, askin' 'er to meet thee at Miss Prim's in Gay Street an hour before the show. As for the rest of the day, spend it as tha' will'st, but don't interfere!'

'I ... '

There was nothing, however, that Belle could do; William had chosen his moment well. Arguing in bed with a hot cup of tea in your hand is a challenge to any mortal, and by the time Belle had drunk the cup William had departed.

Alone at home and in a sultry mood, Belle rose and occupied the morning hours admiring his porcelain collection. He then inspected his silk cravats for moth holes, spent an hour working on a watercolour of his drawing-room fireplace and revisited a book of dried flowers that he had gathered whilst walking in the foothills of the Pyrenees. By afternoon, however, his frustration at life could no longer be assuaged.

'Damn it all,' he cried, slamming the book of flowers closed and looking at his pocket watch. 'I cannot bear it. Interfere, indeed! Let's see: the London coach will be in Bath within the hour. I shall walk into the city, take the air and wait for its arrival.'

Donning his coat, Belle left Sydney Buildings and went towards Queen Square, where ladies and men promenaded in the afternoon. His route took him past the Theatre Royal and the adjacent townhouse in which his grandfather Beau Nash had lived and died. Outside the theatre, he saw a group of people studying a notice that announced, 'With regret, tonight's performance of *King Lear* is cancelled.'

'Do we know why?' he asked one of the group.

'Mr Aldridge has taken unwell,' he was told. 'The theatre management is providing refunds and complimentary tickets to the circus instead.'

Belle listened with interest. It seemed strange to him that Mr Aldridge was unwell, for he had been in rude health the previous day at Ernest Camshaft's funeral. Indeed, had he not been required to meet the coach from London, Belle would have enquired further as to the actor's indisposition. However, his own plan of action—for let there be no doubt that Belle still had a plan—demanded his attention, and he strode onwards.

MASTER LUSH'S SPIRITS fell as Gaia's maid Mary strapped him back into a corset. Being dressed in a frock for the promenade three days earlier had at least been a novelty, as, indeed, was his being swathed in black for the funeral. On both occasions he had made a passable effort at acting a comely young virgin. He now feared, however, that his third pretence would prove his undoing.

'Don't be scared, Master Lush,' said Mary, trying to calm the clerk's nerves. 'You're prettier than ever, and so slim. I do declare, you've lost weight in the past two days, and there wasn't a spare ounce on you before.'

'I've certainly lost weight,' replied Master Lush. 'I can hardly breathe, let alone eat, in these clothes, so tight do you lace me in.'

'Well, let's get this dress on, and then I'll start on your hair and hands.'

Mary pulled a dress of shimmering yellow silk up and over Master Lush's shoulders, watched closely by Lady Passmore and Gaia. Under other circumstances they might have laughed at the sight of a man in a petticoat, but both wore expressions of the utmost gravity, the task ahead of them being so serious.

'Lady Passmore of Tewkesbury Manor, might I suggest you run through the requirements of the evening whilst Master Lush is being powdered?' said Gaia.

'We shall proceed to Lord Servitude's residence by carriage, arriving at fifteen minutes to seven o'clock. Under no circumstance shall we enter the house. Rather, I will send my coachman to the door to announce our arrival. We will remain in the carriage when Lord Servitude and the Hon. Cecil come out to greet us. Only then will we step down from the carriage and walk with them to the circus tent.'

Gaia approved.

'And what will you do, Master Lush, when the unutterable Cecil engages you in trivial but flirtatious conversation?'

Master Lush swallowed hard. He had received several hours of instruction.

'In the first, second and third instance, I shall giggle and look demure—like so,' he replied, cocking his head to one side and smiling sweetly. 'Once the circus performance has started, I may put a finger to my lips and say, "Shush, Sir," again whilst looking demure. If the unpalatable Cecil wishes to hold my hand, I shall accept.'

'But do not let the hand wander. Never let it wander,' warned Lady Passmore. 'And always remain demure!'

'Quite so,' Gaia confirmed. 'To manage a man's ardour, a lady must be ever demure.'

Master Lush, however, looked less than certain.

'I'm not sure such a demand is within my capability.'

Lady Passmore huffed.

'I have remained demure for over forty years. Surely you can manage an hour?'

'Follow Lady Passmore of Tewkesbury Manor's example,' Gaia insisted. 'Her experience in repelling men is invaluable.'

'But ... ' started Master Lush as Mary pulled a brush through his hair—'Ouch! I only mean that remaining demure for an entire circus performance may yet leave more to be desired. Will it be sufficient? Suppose he requires ... more of me? Oh, I do hope that Mr Fanque acts swiftly to free the girl. Do we know what his stratagem is? Is Mr Nash assisting him?'

Gaia answered, albeit reluctantly.

'Mr Fanque has a plan and that is all we need to know. As for Mr Nash, if he attends the circus tonight, it will be solely as a witness to events. But let none of that distract you. You must concentrate only on remaining demure.'

Master Lush let out a whimper.

'Please keep close by, Mrs Champion, in case I need help,' said the clerk. 'I imagine that Lady Passmore of Tewkesbury Manor will have her hands full.'

Her ladyship straightened her back.

'I have no intention of having my hands full, young man. That is the benefit of staying demure.'

Gaia was silent, preferring not to reveal that she would be staying at home on this momentous evening. The risk of attracting Lord Servitude's ire was too great, having already found against him in court; nor, as magistrate, did she wish to be present when William carried out his plan, for fear of appearing complicit.

'In Pablo Fanque we trust,' she whispered.

A T THAT MOMENT, William was doing what he always did in situations of stress. He was with his horses, in a field just above Royal Victoria Park. They were creatures who understood his mind and to whom he gave unconditional love in return.

'Come 'ere, Osei, moy man,' he said, stroking the stallion's neck. 'Tonoight's a big noight for thee and oi. There's a full house guaranteed and they'll be expectin' a show of moment from us. Art ready for it?'

266

The mares trotted over. A fortnight after leaving Astley's, they sensed that something big was expected of them this evening, with William poised erect on their backs.

William did not wish to disappoint them but neither did he tell them the truth.

'Ladies, good evenin'. Nzinga, behave tha'sen. Beatriz and Idia, yew look beautiful. Oi'm expecting great things of yew all. Promise not to let me down.'

Looking across the field, William saw two figures approach. It was Annie the stable lass and the unmistakeable form of the contortionist Ki Hi Chin Fan Foo. As they approached, he gathered the horses around him, hugging and kissing them one by one.

'Oi love yew. For your skill. Your bravery. And for carin' for me as much as oi care for yew. We look out for each other, don't we? Well, tonoight there's someone else as needs looking after. A person what none of us 'as met, but what requires our 'elp more than we can imagine. We cannot disappoint 'er. Yew understand that, Ladies, don't yew? That the girl must come first?'

'Enjoying a craic with the horses, now, is it?' said the contortionist, leaving the stable lass to greet Nzinga, who had trotted over to say hello.

'That's right, Mr Foo. A final craic with the family. Art tha' and the lass ready for tonoight?'

'Aye, so we are,' Mr Foo replied. 'I'm standing by to shimmy up the drainpipes of the house, so I am, and get on the roof, right enough, but I can't do too much after that. Me arms are made of rubber, Mr Fanque, not muscle like your own.'

William nodded and breathed deeply. The hour had come. He beckoned the stable lass to come over.

'Take 'old of the hosses. We must go. Oi needs to be on the tent's roof before the audience arrives. There's no toime to waste.'

267

I T WAS CLOSE to seven o'clock and, from the size of the crowd, it seemed that half the royal city was descending on the circus. There was a sense of joy in the air. The week of mourning for Ernest Camshaft was over and the pleasures of the Season could start to be enjoyed once more. And when it came to pleasures, there really was nothing better than a circus, one of those rare settings where adults could unleash the child within.

Under strings of festoon lights, an excitable throng had joined the queue to buy tickets, eager for an evening of fun. Members of the troupe sold fudge, liquorice, pear drops and toffee apples. One played a merry tune on that most modern of instruments, the accordion. The smell in the air was that of a marketplace—not of fruit, vegetables, meat and fish, but of entertainment!

As arranged by William, Belle had met Miss Prim and Mrs Pomeroy at Gay Street, where the latter had unwisely devoured most of a pound cake. After the short walk uphill to The Circus, Mrs Pomeroy and Miss Prim queued, then paid for their tickets and entered the tent, which was illuminated by gas lamps. Sitting down together on a bench, Mrs Pomeroy at once complained of the indigestion. Meanwhile Belle took the opportunity to greet townspeople whom he had not seen since his return from the Caribbean.

At a short distance, he saw Lady Passmore's carriage parked under a tree and wondered whether her ladyship and Master Lush were inside Number 33. Then he saw Lord Servitude and the re-volting Cecil exit their front door, prompting aunt and niece to emerge from the carriage. After a brief introduction and a tilt of the head from Master Lush—who looked resplendent, if nervous, as the maidenly Daphne Passmore—the group headed his way.

Like Gaia, Belle knew that the Servitudes must not see him, so he now entered the tent. On the far side of the ring, he re-joined Miss Prim and Mrs Pomeroy.

'I do apologise for leaving you, dear ladies. Are you sitting comfortably?'

'Not at all,' said Mrs Pomeroy, holding her bloated belly with both hands. 'The pound cake weighs two, I could swear, and I am swelled with wind.'

As Mrs Pomeroy's stomach rumbled, Miss Prim and Belle remained silent. The former concentrated on the intricacy of the plaited stitch, whilst the latter cast his eye about the audience.

Belle noted the arrival of Lord Servitude's party in the tent and the audible hum as the crowd became alert to his presence. With a conspicuous flourish, the peer ushered Lady Passmore to her seat whilst, to prevent mischief, Master Lush held onto the hand of the grotesque Cecil.

Belle scanned the tent again, this time looking for Gaia. To his dismay, he could not find her, and his heart sunk at the realisation that his closest friend would not be attending.

Why? he thought. On this of all nights, Gaia, why leave me alone? As grisly Charon did attest as he pocketed his obolus, to lose a friend is to lose one's soul.

He then looked to the red curtains that masked the back of the ring, from which the performers would appear. From experience, he knew how troupe members liked to peek out from the curtains to report back on the size of the crowd. At Astley's he had often seen Tom Shelton or a Ridley Brother there. Instead, much to Belle's surprise, a tea cosy momentarily appeared between the velvet and, with it, Mr Quigley.

'Look there!' said Belle to no one in particular.

'Where?' asked Mrs Pomeroy, whose stomach cramps had worsened by the minute.

'Has the show begun?' commented Miss Prim dreamily.

'Mr Quigley is sticking his head through the curtains,' Belle explained.

'Perhaps the silly man has joined the troupe,' suggested Mrs Pomeroy.

'God forbid,' snapped Belle. 'The circus has enough clowns already. He's ... '

Further thought, however, was drowned out by the sound of trumpets. The audience became a sea of expectant faces, all anticipating the pleasures to come. The trumpets sounded a second time, the curtains opened and through them somersaulted a dozen acrobats. Hard on their heels was a juggler with an arc of swirling clubs.

The pugilist Mr Shelton and the Ridley Brother clowns came next, followed by a boy holding the reins of two horses. Belle inspected them all. Notable by their absence were Mr Foo and, of course, William. But Belle knew from previous shows that a third blast of the trumpets would mark the impresario's entrance, and that Mr Foo would eventually appear.

The crowd whooped and Belle found himself clutching his knees in excitement. It had been close to a month since William had expressed his desire to have a circus, and now here it was. Together, they had made it happen. Whatever their differences, this moment was real.

The trumpets now blew for the third time. The troupe members in the ring stopped their performing, turned towards the curtains and held out their arms in a dramatic flourish to welcome their master of ceremonies: the Magician from the Caribbean, the magnificent Pablo Fanque. And in he strode, in a splendid woollen red-tailed coat, riding breeches, boots and top hat.

The audience gasped, in awe at the circus master's charisma, his certainty of touch, his command of the moment. Belle gasped too, but for different reasons. The man basking in the cheers of the crowd was not his companion, the Norfolk equestrian William Darby. Unrecognised by everyone else, the impresario commanding the attention of all was an imposter. It was Ira Aldridge.

O N THE THICK canvas of the tent's roof, between the massed audience below and the dark sky above, crouched the silent figure of William. He had been there for an hour, listening to snippets of conversation as people arrived for the show, and the sound of performers inside the tent honing their routines up to the last moment.

His keen ear had picked up voices he knew. He heard the twittering sound of Miss Prim, the anxious voice of Mrs Pomeroy, the bombastic preening of Lord Servitude as he laid siege to a resilient Lady Passmore, the smug platitudes of the unendurable Cecil as he teased terrified giggles from dainty Master Lush. And he watched Belle, outside the tent, doing what came naturally to him: going up to Bath's citizens and greeting them as if they were old friends, asking after their health and well-being. Whatever his faults, William recognised, Belle was a gentleman who considered others before himself.

Oi'm sorry, dear cousin, William had whispered to himself as the audience took its seats. Oi could 'ave divulged moy plan, but tha'd never 'ave forgiven me.

Then, as the trumpets sounded below for the third time—and Aldridge entered disguised as Pablo Fanque—William rose carefully, steadying his feet on the canvas. Once certain that he was unseen, he turned to the barred window of Number 33. A small candle flickered inside the attic room, insufficient to cast more than a dull light in the evening's gloom.

William adjusted his gaze to the top of the house, where he was cheered by the sight of movement. Mr Foo had successfully scaled the drainpipes at the rear of the house, had clambered over the roof and was now behind the low parapet that surmounted the front. With practised speed and deadly accuracy, Mr Foo unwound a length of string that was attached to a lucky horseshoe and then flung the horseshoe into the air so that it sped across the street and landed on the roof of the circus tent, falling neatly into William's hand.

Now it was William's turn. He took a coil of rope, one end of which he had tied to one of the tent's central poles, where it emerged through the top of the canvas roof. Removing the horseshoe, he tied the string to the other end of the rope, enabling Mr

271

Foo to haul the rope quickly back to the parapet. Once it was in his hands, the human spider lowered himself over the parapet, using his legs as grappling irons, and reached down to the barred window. Upside down, hanging by his feet, he pulled at a bar to test its strength and then secured the rope to it.

William pulled the rope tight, wrapping it around the central pole, pulling it again and again with a tautline hitch, until it no longer sagged. He wanted no mistakes for the most important tightrope walk of his life.

Holding onto the central pole, he now pulled himself up onto the tightened rope. His feet were bare, for better purchase. He then checked his waistband for two tools: a hacksaw that could cut through iron and a heavy hammer. Reassured, he let go of the tent pole and stepped out into the dusk.

The night was dark as he crossed the void between the tent and the grand façade of the house. He looked down: one slip and his neck would be broken; a single cry of alarm and the game could be up. Far below was the third member of the rescue team —Annie the stable lass who, acting as lookout, was holding herself flush to the tent below. William gave her a nod. All was going well.

What William did not notice, some fifteen yards distant, was a person rather broader than the stable lass hiding behind a poplar tree that bordered the lawn. He did not see, peeking out from behind the tree trunk, the same person's furtive eyes trained on him as he walked through the sky, or hear the voice as it whispered to itself, 'Has Mr Nash, I wonder, told anyone that I'm here?'

CHAPTER XXIII

And for the Encore ...

WILLIAM DARBY WAS a man used to keeping his nerve. Like all in the circus troupe, he was aware of the dangers of his profession and had suffered his share of tumbles while learning his skills. More painful than his bruised ribs, however, had been the sight of a teenage lad named Harry Cadman as he fell to his death from Astley's tightrope ten years earlier.

Blocking out that and other distractions, William stepped carefully along the rope until he had reached the cill of the barred window. Once there, he lowered himself into a seated position, his left hand holding onto one of the bars as his right checked again for the hacksaw and hammer. Only when he was set and prepared did he knock gently on the closed window.

Peering through the glass, the weak light of the candle revealed a small room and a bed. On the mattress was a crumpled sheet which, on closer inspection, hid a human form. As he knocked gently on one of the panes, the sheet moved to reveal the emaciated figure of Mercy.

She opened her eyes. Through the window she saw what she imagined to be an apparition—the face of her sibling Pablo lit by her own candle—and she began to cry, for she knew it could not be true, that it had to be a delusion born of hunger or the madness of thirst. She tried to crouch on the mattress, then lowered her head between her knees, her soiled nightgown clinging to her blistered skin. In her despair, she raised her arms to God, exposing the manacles on her wrists that chained her to the bedframe.

William's knuckles sounded at the window once more. Reluctantly, she looked up. It was the apparition again, Pablo staring at her, but this time with a finger to his mouth, and an urgent look in his eye.

She tried to look away but the cruel image drew her back. The thought that Pablo had come to visit her could only mean that her life was about to end: that he had died too and had come to carry her away.

But the knocking returned, this time insistent, and with it the thought that whilst ghostly apparitions may mock your misery, or convey you to the heavenly throng, they do not normally knock on windows. So, she turned her head once more to see if her sibling was truly there.

T HE RIDLEYS HAD played their part, in their giant shoes and oversized patchwork coats, walking the ring with a comic clumsiness that had the crowd roaring with laughter. How good it was to fill the lungs with merriment and recall that, whilst respect for the dead has its place, life is for living. There was not a sour face among any in the tent.

Except that Lady Passmore and Master Lush looked anything but at ease. While Lord Servitude made crude jokes about the clowns' anatomy, the bestial Cecil tried to explore Master Lush's nether regions. Fighting off his attentions with his hands, the clerk did his best to keep up the stream of nervous giggles which he had been told were a lady's best defence in the event of an attempted grope.

'So coy, Miss Passmore. So coy!' said the wretched son, egged on by Master Lush's protests.

Meanwhile, Belle Nash was unaware of the writhings and counter-writhings taking place on the other side of the ring. His mind was straining to understand what William was up to. It was clear to him that a rescue plan was in progress but what its details were remained hidden.

The clowns now departed to great applause and some in the crowd shouted for the horses, whose tricks and dancing were considered the highlight of any circus. In response, Ira Aldridge reappeared with his top hat in one hand and a coachman's horsewhip in the other. Beside him was a boy carrying brass cymbals.

The boy lifted the cymbals high in the air and then brought them together with a mighty crash, not once, not twice but three times. Belle had a keen ear. Somewhere outside, disguised by the clashing cymbals, he heard glass break.

'My lords and ladies, a thousand thunderous excitements still await your accompanying incredulous accolades,' proclaimed the impresario to oohs and aahs from the crowd, 'but first, as we prepare the horses, we have the honour to present a violinist of international renown—protégé of the Chevalier de Saint-Georges in Paris and pedagogue to hundreds of pupils, past and present, at our own Abbey School for Boys. Never before have any of Bach's partitas for solo violin been performed under the big top but here tonight, for the first time, Pablo Fanque's Circus presents the inimitable, the incomparable, the irresistible, your own—your very own—the astonishing Mr Arthur Quigley!!!'

There was a moment of confusion from the audience, many of whom knew Mr Quigley of old and did not think highly of his accomplishments. None the less, the velvet curtains parted and in strode the Abbey School's venerable music master, wearing a threadbare silk dressing gown for a coat and his favourite tattered tea cosy as a hat. In his hand was his prized Landolfi.

'Oh dear! Please not him,' whimpered a woman in the row behind Belle.

'He killed my son's interest in music,' commented another.

'Goodness me, Mr Quigley has joined the troupe!' exclaimed Phyllis Prim.

As for Mrs Pomeroy, the shock at seeing their musical friend in the ring had the beneficial effect of moving five ounces of pound cake through her pyloric sphincter and into her duodenum.

'That's a relief,' she gasped, burping.

'Don't speak too soon,' Belle cautioned, waiting for Mr Quigley to start. 'You haven't yet heard his performance.'

They were prescient words, for Mr Quigley's efforts to reproduce the notes of the frenetic *Partita for Violin Solo No. 1 in B Minor* in the same order that Bach had written them was excruciating to everyone's ear. It brought to Belle's mind Gaia Champion's description, at his homecoming tea party, of Mr Quigley making a sound like a demented jackdaw—or, as Belle had misremembered it, a hacksaw, which was a more accurate description.

NEVER HAD MR Quigley's Landolfi sounded so painfully angry but it was exactly the noise that William had wanted, for as soon as the screeching of the strings began, a hacksaw was exactly what he started attacking one of the window bars with.

Cutting through iron is never an easy task. Doing so suspended in mid-air on a rope requires the utmost determination. With rapid movements of the arm, his bicep acting as a piston, William drew the blade across the bar. Below, he could hear the crowd starting to protest at the dreadful noise of Mr Quigley's violin. As the sound grew, William knew he had to complete the task before the crowd's patience fully expired.

Having used the hammer to break several panes of glass during the crashing of the cymbals, William was able to work the hacksaw at its full length. At last, the bar gave way as Mr Quigley reached the end of the first partita, but a second bar would need to be removed to gain access to the room. William took the opportunity of the hiatus in Mr Quigley's performance to wipe away the sweat on his forehead. Then, as the Landolfi began to explore the challenges of the third partita (passing over the second as insufficiently dramatic), the howl of the violin resumed, and so did William.

After a few more minutes of exertion, to his great relief, the second bar came free. He reached through the broken glass to release the latch of the sash, then cursed, for he had misjudged the act. A shard of glass had remained in the frame and now sliced through the flesh of his left forearm, a stream of blood mingling with his sweat.

William tore the sleeve from his shirt to bind the wound. Removing the offending shard, he returned to the window and pushed up its lower half. A moment later, he found himself perched on the window cill, unable to enter because of the fragments of glass on the floor.

'Pablo,' said the girl, looking up in wonder. 'Is it truly you?'

So, Belle Nash had been right all along, said William to himself: he did resemble Pablo Fanque and the girl was indeed Pablo's sibling Mercy. As to the question she had asked, William chose not to give a direct reply. This was no time to explain his true self.

Instead, he said, 'Sister, oi be 'ere to free thee. But there's still mortal danger and we must make 'aste. The Servitudes are not far away so tha' must be brave and follow my every word.'

'But Pablo,' Mercy interrupted: 'you sound so strange.'

'Oi can't explain now,' said William, extemporising. ''Tis my England voice. Now throw me the sheet, quick.'

She flung it, and William dropped down upon it and then used it to sweep clear the floor. Next, he crossed to the door and listened for sounds of disturbance in the house. There were none.

Turning now to Mercy, he reached for the candle and inspected the handcuffs and chain. Had he had enough time, the hacksaw might have been sufficient but at that moment, the circus crowd decided it had had enough. Mr Quigley's diabolical solo performance was more than it could bear and several members of the audience threw shoes at him in the hope of knocking his prize Landolfi out of his hands.

William would have to work faster and he gritted his teeth. With Mercy's hands tightly cuffed, there was only one option.

'Place tha'n hands on the floor with the cuffs on the boards,' he directed. The chain was attached to an iron rod three inches long which joined the cuffs. 'Look away now, Mercy, and don't tha' flinch or that'll lose tha'n hands. Promise me.'

Tears flowed freely from her eyes.

'I promise, Pablo. I will be brave.'

'Tha' must trust me. Tha' must trust tha' brother.'

With her head turned, William removed the heavy hammer from his belt. Crouching like a panther, he raised the hammer high into the air and then, with all the fury and strength he could muster, swung it down towards Mercy's hands.

NOT SINCE HE had kissed fair Desdemona on the lips in London had Ira Aldridge witnessed such mayhem at a public entertainment, although on this occasion it was fully justified. A troop of vixens in labour could not have made a more dreadful sound than Mr Quigley with his violin. With the crowd in uproar, he only hoped that William had completed the task of sawing through the iron bars and freeing the girl.

The situation in the tent was made worse by the ancient music master's mistaking the collective howls of disapproval as cries of elation and the flying shoes as well-earned bouquets. In Mr Quigley's mind, he had reached heights unimagined by Bach and believed the good people of Bath wanted more. Had the burghers of Leipzig ever given their Thomaskantor the ovation that he was now receiving? Had they ever stamped their feet in ecstasy as the circus crowd was doing now? It was, he decided, his greatest performance since he had played the solo from Haydn's *Violin Concerto No. 1 in C Major* to British troops storming Tipu Sultan's fort in Bangalore in 1791.

'Lovers of music, do not fret. I will play an encore,' he declared, bowing deeply as he soaked up the applause.

'Please don't. My ears are bleeding!' cried a man from the back.

'Arrest him. Put him in Pulteney Gaol!' shouted another, whose wife had fainted.

Mr Aldridge waved his hat and cracked his whip in an appeal for calm. Mr Quigley, however, was in seventh heaven.

'As an encore, dear friends, I shall play *Ave Maria* by Franz Schubert forwards, then backwards, then forwards, then back ... '

Not since the Massacre of the Innocents had such a cry of distress been heard. Fearing a stampede, Mr Aldridge had no choice but to intervene. He grabbed Mr Quigley by the collar and seized his prized Landolfi.

'You are all safe!' he shouted to the audience, cracking his whip. 'See, My Lords, Ladies and Gentlemen, I have the violin!'

His swift action worked, soothing the crowd like balm upon the skin. Slowly the audience settled back into their seats. There was, after all, the remainder of the programme to enjoy: the dancing horses, an amazing contortionist and tumblers and acrobats galore.

'It is evident that Mr Quigley's playing has pleas'd not the million,' roared Mr Aldridge, improvising Shakespeare. 'Perhaps 'twas caviary to the general—I cannot say, for I have no ear for music—but it is clear, Mr Quigley, that you have strutted and fretted your hour upon the stage and should be heard no more!'— a judgement that bought great cheers that Mr Quigley wholly misinterpreted.

'But they want me to play again!' he appealed to Mr Aldridge.

'No, we don't!' the whole of the front row shouted in unison.

'Mr Quigley, they really do not,' confirmed Mr Aldridge, holding the violin at arm's length.

If Mr Quigley had been a child and Mr Aldridge his master, this display of authority might have been enough. But Mr Quigley was not a child. In his own opinion, he was a maestro, and no maestro should ever refuse when the crowd bays for an encore.

'Give me back my instrument, Sir,' Mr Quigley demanded. 'It is not yours to take away. It's my Landolfi. I have to have it back. You're a circus man and know well the danger of disappointing the crowd. I cannot let them down. They will never forgive me; and they will never forgive you.'

'We will, we will,' called the crowd, and a woman who looked like the late Jane Austen called out, 'You have delighted us long enough! Let the other young ladies have time to exhibit,' which made near neighbours of Bath's most celebrated writer laugh out loud.

Mr Aldridge decided it was time to stand his ground.

'Take your bow, Sir! It is time for the next act.'

Mr Quigley, however, did not take his bow and, as the two men faced up to each other, the crowd in the tent fell silent. Would there be fisticuffs? As pugilists go, Messrs Aldridge and Quigley seemed mismatched, but one must never underestimate an octogenarian diva, especially one wearing a tea cosy for a hat.

'Did you not hear the applause, Sir? These are my people.' He pointed in Belle's direction. 'There, for instance, is my dear friend Councillor Nash, recently returned from Grenada. Beside him is Mrs Pomeroy from Lansdown Hill. And with her is Miss Prim, the city's greatest knitter, who has given up her evening to hear me tonight. You cannot deny them my encore, surely?'

Perhaps for the first time in his life, Mr Aldridge was lost for words and Mr Quigley, sensing that he had the advantage, looked around the ring for more acquaintances.

'Behold the eager faces,' he declared. 'My dear friends Lady Passmore of Tewkesbury Manor and the delicious Master Lush, dressed rather amusingly in a frock. You would not deny them too?'

While Ira Aldridge searched for an appropriate riposte, Master Lush squirmed and blushed, first from embarrassment as

300 pairs of eyes focussed on him, then with increasing terror as the wandering hand of the nauseating Cecil pulled away from him.

'Father, Father,' the stomach-turning Cecil cried aloud, clambering to his feet. 'I recognise this creature now. This isn't Miss Passmore. It's the clerk from the magistrate's court. But why? Why would Mrs Champion's clerk be dressed in a frock? And why have I been holding her hand?'

It was a question that the ever-astute mind of Lord Servitude now analysed at expeditious speed. He looked first at Lady Passmore and then across to where Mr Quigley had pointed out Belle, Mrs Pomeroy and Miss Prim. He thought back over past events and quickly hit upon the answer. Immediately, he, too, was on his feet.

'My boy, we have been snared. They are plotting to release your wretch of a girl! That's why they've invited us here—to get us out of the house. Mrs Neech was right to be suspicious. Hurry, Cecil, we must return without delay!'

At which point, matters progressed apace. Lord Servitude and the contemptible Cecil tried to push past Lady Passmore, but Lady Passmore had never in her life been pushed past before and stuck out a leg to block their way. This gave Belle time to race from his seat. Although he remained unaware of how William intended to rescue Mercy, he knew that every second counted. He ran across the ring and, as the Servitudes descended the gangway, grabbed hold of the slave-abusing son.

'Let go of me, Sir. You have no right to touch me,' yelled the Hon. Cecil, struggling to break free. And, indeed, he might have broken free, for he was as slippery as a worm, had not the fighter Tom Shelton now decided to practise his art.

'Not so fast, Mr Servitude,' he said, running up, and threw out a giant fist, which caught the odious Cecil in the face. Lord Servitude's repugnant scion slumped to the floor while a bloodied front tooth flew across the ring and landed upright on the ground, a tiny gravestone to misbegotten privilege.

A yard distant, admiring Tom Shelton's demonstration of Newton's Second Law of Motion, was Belle.

'By Heracles, the snivelling son lies slain.'

With a handkerchief, Mr Shelton wiped the blood from his knuckles.

'The son will live,' he replied. 'Now where's the father?'

It was a point well made. Whilst felling the offensive Cecil, they had allowed Lord Servitude to escape. If only he could be seen, but he was lost in the crowd, many members of which, shocked by the display of violence, had also made haste to leave the tent.

Belle's eyes scoured the panic-stricken scene.

'He's there!' he suddenly cried, pointing to an exit of the tent. 'Quick! He must be caught! Pray God that my Pablo and dear Mercy are safe!'

NOTES

* Though I can find no record of the tightrope artist Harry Cadman, I suspect my late uncle was referring to the steeplejack Robert Cadman (1711–1739). Cadman pioneered an early form of zip-wire utilising a wooden breastplate that had a central groove. Whilst adept at walking up ropes, he was more famous for sliding down them. Cadman attracted crowds of thousands as, strapped to the breastplate, he 'flew' from the tower of Lincoln Cathedral as well as off Dover cliff and across the adjacent harbour. He died aged twenty-eight years when a rope broke under him. He is buried at St. Mary's Church in his hometown of Shrewsbury; it was from its sixty-eight-metre spire that he learnt his art of rapid descent.

CHAPTER XXIV

The Present and the Past

TWO MINUTES EARLIER, William Darby's blow with the hammer had been firm and true. The rod connecting the cuffs had broken and Mercy's hands, though each still wore a metal bracelet, had been freed of the chain and were no longer shackled together. William had led her to the window to check outside. The pavement had remained empty, although the roar of disapproval from the crowd at Mr Quigley's threat of an encore had reached a crescendo.

'Listen closely, sister,' he had said to Mercy. 'There be a toight-rope what runs from yon window to a circus tent outsoide— oi'll explain whoy later. We must cross the rope together. Then us'll be safe.'

She had looked at him as if still in a dream.

'But how?'

'Oi will go first, like a toight-rope walker. See! Tha'll follow and cloimb on moy back. We'll make the crossin'. Tha' must have trust, Mercy. Have faith.'

He had leant out of the window and whistled to the stable lass below, indicating that she was to fetch the horses Osei and Nzinga. The lass had then run back to the big tent to where the horses were tethered.

Then William had swung his legs and torso through the window so that he was sitting outside on its cill. He had motioned for Mercy to join him. There was just room for them both. For a

283

moment they had breathed in the cool night air, then he had given further instructions.

'This is 'ow we'll do it. Oi'll stand on this 'ere rope with moy arm against the buildin'. Put tha'n arms over moy shoulders and tha' legs around moy waist. Hold me toight but stay as still as tha' can'st. In that way will oi carry you to th'other side.'

'Like Saint Christopher?' she had asked, as a means of dispelling doubt.

'Just loike Saint Christopher,' he had replied, kissing her on her cheek.

He had stood up slowly, placing his feet carefully on the rope. With an arm against the wall, he had signalled Mercy to climb onto his back. She had done so and he had been shocked by her lightness.

'Have faith,' he had told her. 'We can do this, tha' and oi. We can escape this nasty world.'

In the corner of his eye he had seen Annie the stable lass return with the horses. They needed to make speed but speed was also their enemy. He could not afford to rush. Each step had to be placed carefully because each step was a step to freedom. Don't go too fast, he told himself. Remember Harry Cadman. Respect his memory. No distractions. One step at a time. Only ever one step at a time.

They had reached halfway across the tightrope when the crowd inside the tent had fallen silent.

'That sounds better,' he had thought. 'Whatever the problem were, Mr Aldridge 'as it under control.'

WHICH WAS AS far from the truth as it was possible to be. It was at that precise moment that Tom Shelton was landing a punch on the detestable Cecil's nose, setting off shouting and panic among the more genteel members of the crowd, and prompting the rush to get away.

And now, three things happened simultaneously.

The usually unflappable Nzinga, frightened by the mayhem, reared up and broke free from the stable lass's grip. The lass did the sensible thing: she held the cooler-headed Osei's reins tight and let Nzinga go.

Mrs Neech, who had decided that the earlier cries of dissatisfaction from the circus tent were worthy of investigation, appeared at the front door of the house and saw her master, among the crowd, running towards her.

And William, for all his skill and training, allowed his focus to be distracted by the mayhem below. With Mercy clinging to his back, he missed his footing and fell forward, and the two of them would have plunged to the ground had not one of his outstretched arms fouled on the tightrope, snagging him painfully under one armpit but breaking his fall.

He screamed in agony as Mercy, locked to his sweaty back, began to slump to his waist.

'Hold on!' he beseeched, as the two of them swayed.

'I can't!' she screamed, sliding further.

'Can'st tha' grab the rope instead of me?'

'No!' shrieked Mercy. 'I'm scared. I'm slipping. Help!'

In desperation, William stretched behind himself with his free arm, reached around the back of Mercy's slim waist and clamped her more firmly to him. The rope cut deeper into his other armpit and he knew that, with the torture so great, he would soon have to let go.

The drama in the air was matched by drama down below. As William ached in pain, Lord Servitude looked up at him and Mercy and willed both of them to fall to their deaths.

'I espy a Negro above us,' he called grandly to Mrs Neech, 'making off with an item of our property: look how his high wire leads back to one of the attic rooms in my house.' And then, calling out to all who were watching, he added, 'Stand back, everybody, and let them fall: it will be a just punishment for a debased crime.'

At the same moment, Belle Nash rushed out of the tent with Tom Shelton, only to be transfixed by the sight of Lord Servitude clearing a space and two human beings in the air above him, floundering as if from a gallows tree, a sight he had witnessed several times in Grenada when riding past the Servitudes's plantation—the epitome of evil, blood on the leaves, blood on the roots, the lifeless corpses of the enslaved who, having lost their fight for freedom, were strung up for the crows.

'It cannot be!' he screamed in terror. 'Pablo! Mercy!'

Mr Shelton was not similarly transfixed. Though his knees were weaker than in his youth, he ran towards the space that Lord Servitude and Mrs Neech were keeping clear.

William saw him come and wondered how long he could hold onto Mercy before she fell.

'Hurry, Mr Shelton, and catch the girl—quickly!' he called out, and to the stable lass, who was still fighting to keep control of Osei, 'Ready the 'osse, Annie.'

Lord Servitude prepared to block Mr Shelton's path, expecting that between the two of them, he and Mrs Neech might do enough to make William and the girl land hard on the ground.

And so they might have done, had assistance not arrived from an unexpected quarter.

Behind the poplar tree, a visitor from London had bided her time, waiting for the moment when her help was required. It was Mrs Nonsuch, the doughty manager of Jaunay's Hotel. Invited to Bath by Belle, and forewarned by him of the dangers that might lie in store, the lady had brought her bowling stick with her and her trusty iron hoop, long capable of despatching an assailant from fifty feet.

Her head held low, and her bowling stick in hand, she now whacked the hoop towards Lord Servitude. The latter, his eyes fixed eagerly on the dangling figures of William and Mercy, was completely unaware of its advance. The iron hoop cracked into his aristocratic legs, shattering his kneecaps and making him buckle

286

and fall. Rushing up, Mrs Nonsuch performed the historic Non-such *coup de grace*: with a mighty blow, she brought her bowling stick down on his head and knew at once that he would trouble them no more.

'First blow for the abolition of slavery and those who milk it,' she muttered, 'and that includes *you*,' she added, swinging round to find Mrs Neech attempting to attack her from behind. 'I think you keep house for Lord Servitude,' she said, felling the house-keeper with a single backward smash of her fist. 'Not any more.'

With Lord Servitude out of the way, Mr Shelton was able to occupy the space directly below his beloved ringmaster.

'Let her go, Sir,' he called up. 'I'm ready for you. You can drop her now.'

'No!' screamed Mercy, but William let go, trusting in his colleague, and less than a split second later, Mercy was safe in the arms of the aged fighter.

Relieved of her weight, William felt suddenly buoyed and hauled his mutilated body along the rope, dropping onto the roof of the tent, then sliding down the fabric to the ground. From there he leapt onto the horse, Osei, that the stable lass was holding and, within a moment, had galloped back to Mr Shelton's side.

'Pass me the girl, Mr Shelton,' he ordered. 'No delay now.'

'Are you sure, Sir? We can keep her with us. She'll be safe with the troupe.'

William shook his head. He had made up his mind two days' before and had no intention of suddenly changing his plans.

'No, Sir. Oi thank 'ee with all moy heart for saving the girl's fall but she must now come with oi.'

William reached down for Mercy, who was barely conscious, and Mr Shelton lifted her gently onto the back of the horse. Seating her on the saddle in front of him, William held onto her with his uninjured arm. With the other he pulled at the reins and prepared to kick his heels into Osei's sides. Then something made him stop.

Belle, his head spinning in confusion at all he had seen, stood before him, bewildered. The two men stared at each other, before Belle stepped forward.

'You have her, Pablo,' he declared. 'You have saved your sister. And you're both alive! But is she all right? You must take her back to our home. Or to Somerset Place, where Gaia can wash her. She must sleep. She must rest awhile and you must dress your wounds ... '

William's eyes filled with tears as he shook his head. He was not to be dissuaded, even by Belle.

'Oi is sorry, dear cousin, but 'tis not to be. I must take Mercy home.'

And with that he urged Osei forward. The stallion needed no encouragement and moved through his paces from a canter to a gallop, carrying William and Mercy around The Circus towards the downhill slope of Gay Street. They sped past Miss Prim's home and past the neighbouring house where Belle had once lived.

Belle ran after them, but the distance—like that between the present and past—widened.

'But Pablo,' he cried. 'Mercy *is* home. She's with us.'

When he reached the top of Gay Street, Belle caught one last glimpse of the horse in Queen Square but then it was gone. And with it the man he loved.

'Pablo! Fair Pablo! You cannot leave me. Pablo!'

Except that his companion could. And, despite Belle wishing otherwise, had. It was a point reinforced by a voice he recognised speaking from behind.

'They have gone, Mr Nash. Accept it, Sir. Events happen. Life creeps in this petty pace from day to day. It is a tale told by an idiot, full of sound and fury, signifying ... nothing!'

Belle turned and found himself face to face with Ira Aldridge, dressed as the impresario.

'Accept it?' Belle stuttered. 'Pablo was my life and I shall not be told by you, Sir—a man who calls a biscuit a cookie—to let him go.'

Mr Aldridge remained calm, for he understood that Belle was a man in distress.

'Do not be angry, Mr Nash. I tell you to accept it, not for my own purposes but because Mr Darby has requested it of me. He sends you a short message.'

Belle took a step backwards.

'Which is?' he asked, his voice breaking with fear.

'That whilst he cares for you, he has decided to accompany the girl back home to Grenada where she can be re-united with her true brother. With regret, Mr Darby will not be returning.'

Belle looked at the actor in disbelief.

'But how? There is the circus to look after and he has little money. The whole enterprise will close without him and he cannot survive on his own.'

To Belle's surprise, Mr Aldridge laughed.

'Circus people are used to looking after themselves, Mr Nash, and William Darby believes the interests of the girl take precedence. As for funding, you are not the only patron in Bath.'

Belle felt the ground open up beneath him.

'But that he should leave me!' Belle wept. 'That I should count for nothing!'

Mr Aldridge stepped closer. He spoke in an uncompromising tone.

'Mr Darby came to you when you wanted something from him and he wanted something in return. That transaction is now complete. So wipe the tears for ever. Now, Mr Nash, the shepherds weep no more. Henceforth thou art the genius of the shore!'

The compliment provided no succour.

'Your poetry ill suits my aching heart,' said Belle, clutching at his chest.

'I speak only as I find,' said Mr Aldridge. 'The poet normally says more pithily what we poor mortals struggle to express. Mr

289

Darby is off to fresh woods and pastures new, and you must too. But if you wish for less poetic words, then understand these. Privilege may be the white man's coin but it cannot buy you love. Move on, Mr Nash.'

Belle recoiled.

'You speak to me, Sir, as if I were the Devil.'

'You need not sound so wounded, Sir,' said Ira Aldridge, whose patience for Belle's anguish was exhausted. 'You claim to be virtuous, as do many in your world, but still tolerate the mass who do us harm. And I would advise against self-pity, Mr Nash. As ever, the answer lies within. Understand that whilst you are not an evil man ... '

'Nor am I,' replied Belle weakly. 'I'm sure I'm not.'

' ... neither are you as good as you would wish to be. And though you suffer, many suffer more. Much more. Think on't and goodnight, Sir.'

And with a flourish, Mr Aldridge made his exit from the stage of Belle's life. His speech was done; his one-night role as Pablo Fanque was at an end.

With the gaslights above the front doors of houses lighting him as he went, the celebrated actor walked away, passing through circles of light until at last, in the distance, he disappeared.

Belle Nash, an audience of one, fell to his knees. For the second time in as many minutes, he had seen the image of the man he loved—Pablo Fanque's image—desert him. It was too much to bear. His broken spirit lay dashed on the pavement, its fragments scattered beyond the reach of his outstretched hands.

Into the void. Into the void!

NOTES

* My uncle borrows two phrases from *Strange Fruit*, a protest song with lyrics by Abel Meeropol, sung most memorably by Billie Holiday in 1939.

Southern trees bear strange fruit,
Blood on the leaves and blood at the roots,
Black bodies swinging in the Southern breeze,
Strange fruit hangin' from the poplar trees.

- In this and the previous chapter, Ira Aldridge quotes both from *Hamlet* and *Macbeth* when addressing Mr Quigley, and from Milton's *Lycidas* when talking to Belle.

A PERFECTLY SHORT
EPILOGUE
IN ONLY ONE CHAPTER

CHAPTER XXV

Tea, Whisky and Wine

P EOPLE OFTEN MISUNDERSTAND melancholy, fearing that it might be infectious or lead to social decay. In his youth, Belle Nash had been told by his elders to 'snap out of' whatever torment it might be that ailed him, as if the happy man should have no occasion for sadness. Such advice was both insensitive and ignorant.

To his friends, Belle appeared an ebullient man. They talked of how he joked and of the pleasures that he took in life, unaware that the barometer of his emotions went from high to low or that a melancholic soul can also sometimes enjoy good humour or the sweetness of the world. As all melancholics would acknowledge, when in a good mood they will laugh at their miserable nature.

But find a melancholic in desolation ...

It came as no surprise to Gaia Champion to learn that Belle had retired to Sydney Buildings with instructions that he was to receive no visitors. Of all his friends, she understood him best and judged that time must pass before she sought to intervene—not that Belle was wholly unattended. She had a maid from Somerset Place deliver daily provisions, and equally frequently sent her clerk, Lucius Lush, to check on his well-being.

'There is no improvement,' Master Lush said on the third day. 'Mr Nash has not washed or shaved since the departure of Mr Darby, as we know him now to be. He wishes for no society but to be recluced. I greatly regret that I have no better news to convey.'

Friends made efforts to visit but the front door of Sydney Buildings remained closed to them.

'He's without a footman or a housekeeper to show him my card,' Lady Passmore had complained, standing on his doorstep with Mrs Pomeroy and Phyllis Prim. 'What is one supposed to do when there is no lackey to answer a door?'

'I've knitted him a cravat to cheer him up,' Miss Prim had commented.

'And I've bought a slice of his favourite pie from Mrs Crust,' Mrs Pomeroy had said. 'I fear I shall have to eat it myself, lest it go to waste.'

The circus had opened on a Saturday night. Gaia waited until the evening of the next Wednesday before she made her move. There was something about a Wednesday, the tipping point of the week, that seemed right. So it was that, in the early evening, she undertook the thirty-minute walk from her home in Somerset Place to his home in Sydney Buildings. On the front door of Belle's home was pinned a note on which was written in large letters, 'No Visitors. Stay away. Your Presence Is Not Wanted.'

Declining to pull the bell but simply opening the door and entering uninvited, Gaia made her way to the drawing room, which was dark, the window shutters having been closed. Master Lush's report that Belle had cut himself off from the outside world had been true. Gaia waited in the corridor to allow her eyes to become accustomed to the gloom and then stepped cautiously forward.

In the drawing room, she could see her friend lying motionless on the chaise longue. Before seating herself, Gaia decided to pull back the shutters and open the window. Fresh air was needed to counter the stale smell that hung about the room.

She saw Belle look up.

'You knew, Madam. That's why you weren't at the circus.'

She hesitated and worked on opening the window before answering.

'I persuaded Mr Darby to reveal his identity to me last week. He also told me of his intentions. So, yes, I was forewarned that he would take Mercy to Grenada, there to reunite her with her brother.'

'And to abandon me,' Belle added.

Gaia turned from the window.

'That was his business,' she said carefully. 'I did not try to dissuade him, nor did I disclose his resolve to you. As for others, no one else was aware.'

'But why, Gaia? He meant everything to me. I wonder that you call yourself my friend.'

Gaia moved away from the window and took a seat by the chaise longue.

'You know me well, Belle. I did not stay quiet for no reason. My argument was that the man you love is Pablo Fanque; that however much you desire it, William Darby is not that man; and that the interests of Mercy were paramount. It was clear that she had to be accompanied home to Grenada—not an errand that you had expressed any intention of performing, while Mr Darby conceived the plan and determined to do it. That impressed me. In addition, Mercy will now know the truth of Mr Darby's identity and not be beholden to a falsity, as you have been.'

Belle was unconvinced.

'And who, pray, met the cost of the voyage? And who will save the circus troupe that is left without employ?'

Gaia fell quiet for a moment. Whilst Belle may have barely moved for the past four days, his mind had not been inactive.

'Before coming here, I pledged not to lie to you,' she said. 'I made an offer to pay but, at his own request, Ira Aldridge covered the expense of the journey to Grenada. As for the circus, there has been a collective effort to raise money for the troupe. Again, I have been involved. A group of ladies who knit owed me a favour and they have earned twenty pounds selling their wares for the cause.'

'Including Miss Prim?'

'Indeed. She knitted mittens in the shape of shackles in tribute to the cause. Mrs Pomeroy organised a cake sale, and Lady Passmore ... '

Belle lifted himself briefly.

'So all my friends have betrayed me. And I have lost my beloved Gay Street to boot. All joy is lost. I have no purpose left in life.'

It was a harsh critique and not one that Gaia would accept.

'That is a sensational and graceless statement, Belle, and not one you would make if you were of sound mind.'

It was a riposte that elicited a sardonic laugh.

'Of sound mind, you say,' he whispered. 'There's little enough hope of that, for you see before you a broken man.'

Gaia edged forward in her seat.

'I don't think that is true,' she said, regretting her earlier remark.

Belle's head hung low.

'But it is. Twice I have found love, only for it to be a chimera and one that I cannot slay. Why is that, Gaia? Either love is false or I am false—my mind, I mean. I need to recognise the truth about myself and accept that I am unloved—to look in the mirror and see not the debonair man I wish to be but the deluded wretch I truly am.'

She stood up from her chair.

'I'm going to open the shutters of the other window. It's daylight outside, Belle, and you need a candle in here it's so dark. If you want the truth, you're a picture of melancholy.'

He looked up at her as she let in more light.

'That is because I *am* a picture of melancholy. I am melancholic by nature.' Then, holding his head in his hands, he cried, 'Oh, the void! The merciless void!'

Wise Gaia, however, did not react to Belle's anguish. A woman of sound mind, she decided a diversion was required instead.

'What shall we chat about, then?' she said, changing the subject. 'We have hours to spare. Shopping is all the rage, I hear. It's what everyone is talking about in the city: they say that tea parties are becoming a thing of the past. We should visit Jolly's department store, which opened last year. It has wonderful fabrics and you could re-upholster your chaise. Or you could get a dog. I think you'd value a canine companion. Many dog owners swear by them.'

'I'm not in a swearing mood,' he replied dryly.

Gaia clapped her hands lightly. She was not giving up.

'If we cannot agree on your future, let us talk about your past. Not of Gay Street; enough of Gay Street. But your green-and-salad days. Tell me about your mama and papa.'

Belle stared at her, wondering in what direction her light banter was headed, for Gaia's conversation was never wholly innocent.

'What of them? They're dead.'

'That I know. But where did they live? Your childhood home in ... '

'They lived in Frome,' he said, with a degree of suspicion. 'Not far from Bath, but proximity did not mean closeness.'

'By which you mean ... ?' Gaia asked, pleased to have diverted him from talking about melancholy and of others' betrayal to talking about himself.

'My governess and teachers were closer to me than my parents. To them, I could talk about everything—except about the most important thing of all.'

'Which is?' she persisted, feeling she was on the right path.

'About whom, and how, I love,' he sighed.

She nodded. This conversation would not be easy but it was necessary, if Belle was to be saved.

'My parents were fine enough people in their own way, admired by the citizens of Frome. I do not gainsay their goodness and decency. But I was alien to them, an errant child; nor could

299

they do what all parents should wish to do. They could not feel my needs, nor reach out to comfort me.'

'They were remote?'

'They did not mean to be. They cared for me, in their way, but did not understand my nature.'

She paused.

'Are you certain?'

'I am certain. You are a person of great wisdom, Gaia, but ... they ... .' He hesitated. 'Few understand the curse of the bachelor. The bachelor stands alone in the world. He has no family. He has no support. You doubt the frailty of my mind but look at Mr Quigley, whose mind was broken by the death of his companion. In solitude, there is no solace.'

The answer was too painful.

'Belle ... '

'No, Gaia,' he insisted. 'Respect my answer. The best of us are defined by others, which is how it should be. Do not be offended by my saying that you were defined by your husband Hercules, for he in return was defined by you. I looked at your marriage and envied the love that you shared. That love formed you as surely as a potter's hands transform clay into a bowl.'

She half-smiled. She should have guessed that her encouraging of Belle to analyse himself would soon turn back on her.

'It's true that Hercules and I lived for each other.'

'It is no wonder, too,' Belle continued, 'that for years I have searched for a person with whom to share my life so that I, too, might be defined. And there's the rub. Who am I, Gaia? I am alone and without form. Unmade, except by my own fantastical mind. I have no shape. No one has shaped me. Nothing has touched me. It is as if I don't exist. The fact is, without love, I am nothing. I am a void.'

She shook her head.

'Belle, as your friend, I know that is untrue.'

But he was deaf to her.

300

'Indeed, I am worse than nothing, Ma'am, for I sought love in the recesses of my foolish imagination. William was never Pablo. And neither man was meant for me. Now do I reap the consequence of my delusion. It is a fitting end.'

His head slumped forward once more.

'This is melodrama, Belle. Worthy of Ira Aldridge.'

He did not respond and Gaia did not know what to ask next. Casting around, she picked up his earlier invitation to talk about herself.

'After my dear Hercules died suddenly, I was lonely too, as you will recall. Cholera had taken his life and all but destroyed my own. But eventually there was something that returned meaning to my world: friendship. The friendship of the ladies, of course, but most of all *your* friendship.'

It was sufficient to get Belle to raise his head.

'Kind of you to say so, Madam.'

'Not kind. True. And as a bachelor, you may have understood my loneliness more than others. But also, as I recovered from Hercules's death, you also appreciated my determination to stand on my own—as a woman. You supported me when others simply sneered. "A woman magistrate? How ridiculous."'

It was now Belle's opportunity to ask questions.

'Has it been worthwhile? Has the lady pioneer no regrets?'

For a moment, Gaia looked at the ceiling.

'I will admit that life was not easy during your absence in Grenada. But worthwhile? Yes. As a widow, I have had more time to think than is normal, whilst being a magistrate has provided daily insights into the mind and motivations of humankind. From this, I have drawn a conclusion.'

'Which is?'

'Which is that while life may leave much to be desired, it is all we have, and is therefore better seen as a gift than a burden, for any life is better than no life, for life always has something while no life is truly nothing.'

301

It was an answer that began the slow task of lifting Belle out of his melancholic state.

'That is true,' he conceded. 'Tell me then: whilst I was in the Caribbean, was that the only conclusion you came up with?'

'Can you better it?'

'I can add to it. That friendship is easier than love.'

Gaia smiled. The corner had been turned.

'I can add to it too,' she said. 'That life is a good deal less interesting when you're not around. Hiding yourself away for the past four days, you won't have read a newspaper or heard the gossip. The news of the Servitudes's crimes has reached London and they are pilloried by all. Along with broken kneecaps and cracked skulls, their reputation lies in tatters ... '

'Broken kneecaps?' interjected Belle. 'I'd rather it had been broken necks. You think that a little rough stuff and social opprobrium suffices for their crimes of enslavement, rape and murder?'

Gaia shook her head for Belle spoke the truth.

'No, but it was a defeat for the Servitudes nonetheless and all thanks to you. And to William Darby, of course. And Mrs Nonsuch of Barbados. I'm glad I never played at bowling with her! It was clever of you to invite her to Bath.'

Belle smiled. The mention of the West Indian dame brought his mind back to where, in truth, it had been marooned these past several months. To Grenada.

'But mostly thanks to Pablo Fanque,' he said.

Gaia moved and knelt by the chaise longue, so that she could hold her friend's hand.

'Yes. None more so than Pablo Fanque.'

They were silent, paying their respects to a man whom Gaia had never met but, through others, knew well.

'How do you think history will treat the Servitudes?'

'As bigots and charlatans of the worst order,' said Gaia. 'They will be objects of derision, despised by generations to come.'

Belle nodded.

'I am much relieved, Ma'am, to hear you say so. And what of us, Gaia? Will history remember us?'

She squeezed his hand, and from Belle's drawing room in Sydney Buildings, they looked together at the view of Bath across the flood plain of the River Avon. In the middle distance stood the magnificent spectacle of the abbey.

'This is one of the finest views of Bath. It makes me feel as if we are floating in the sky.'

He looked at her.

'My question still hangs, Gaia. Will history remember us?'

'I suspect not,' she declared softly. 'We shall drift into blissful anonymity, Belle, which is how it should be and what any sane person should desire. Along with tea and friendship, of course!'

He nodded.

'Talking of which,' he said, swinging his feet onto the floor, 'why don't we go down to the kitchens and work out the mysteries of the stove?'

'Or we could stay up here and take advantage of the whisky decanter,' suggested Gaia.

'Or I could investigate the wine cellar. There are several cases of fine claret just waiting to be opened, all four years more mature than when I last pulled a cork. Don't tell William but I considered them wasted on him.'

Gaia laughed. She had resolved not to cry until her friend had been rescued from despair, but now allowed tears to gather in her eyes. Leaning forwards, she hugged him in a warm and strong embrace.

'You see, it takes only a moment's consideration for a world of near-infinite possibility to emerge. Tea, whisky or wine? Let's have them all and drink as friends until dawn. It's good to have you back, Belle.'

End of Volume 2

303

ACKNOWLEDGEMENTS

A FTER PUBLISHING VOLUME 1 of *The Gay Street Chronicles*, it was pointed out to me that I had failed to mention in the Acknowledgements to that book my late uncle, Dr W.B. Keeling, whose research and manuscripts are the heart and soul of this series of books. My first thanks, therefore, go to him and to all amateur historians who seek to plug the leaky colander of times past.

Now pushed into second place is my editor Dr Stephen Games, still an insomniac, who with his quill will cross out sill for cill, stating the latter to be more in keeping with the period.

I pray that I have treated the brutal subject of racism with sensitivity, given the politically satirical template of the chronicles. I would like to thank those who have kindly given their time to read and comment on the novel in its various drafts: Biyama Kadafa, Jessica Oura, Christopher Rodriguez, Alasdair McWhirter, Sanj Bhopal, Immanuel Ameh, Gary Griffith, Nick Thorogood and Robert Hobhouse, among others.

Once more, my thanks to my family. The support of my siblings, their spouses (and beyond to my fabulous nephews, nieces and cousins at various levels of removal) has been wonderful to receive.

Similarly to old friends. I have been struck by the warmth of schoolfriends who not only, in their generosity, bought Volume 1, but read it and enjoyed it! Particular thanks to Mark Davies for his love and support. Also to my English teacher, Mr Venning, for his kind words. It was an honour to be your pupil, Sir!

My heartfelt thanks to all the authors and book reviewers who have endorsed the series so far. Also to booksellers (a shout out in Bath to Toppings & Co., Mr B's Emporium, The Oldfield Park Bookshop and Waterstones) for their support. I have shed tears of gratitude sufficient to require a mop—so thank you.

And last, but never least, to the readers. Other than for my own well-being, I write for you and hope you have enjoyed *Belle Nash and the Bath Circus*. There will be more volumes to come— I am not yet halfway through my late uncle's manuscripts—and I welcome you warmly on Belle's journey ahead.

Notable titles from EnvelopeBooks

www.envelopebooks.co.uk

Belle Nash and the Bath Soufflé

WILLIAM KEELING ESQ.

In the first volume of *The Gay Street Chronicles*, bachelor Belle Nash attempts to navigate bigotry and corruption in Regency Bath without compromising the nephew of Immanuel Kant or the legal talents of Gaia Champion.

BB1

Postmark Africa

MICHAEL HOLMAN

Made an Amnesty Prisoner of Conscience while he was under house arrest as a student in Southern Rhodesia, the author went on to document Africa's emergence from colonialism as Africa Editor of the *Financial Times*.

EB1

Why My Wife Had To Die

BRIAN VERITY

There is no known cure for Huntington's disease, a wasting condition that sufferers acquire from a parent. In this painful account of how their lives were wrecked when his wife started to show the same signs of it as her mother and brothers, the author vents his rage at society, lawmakers, health services and the church for not grasping the need, as he sees it, to legalise compulsory sterilisation and assisted dying.

EB9

Non-fiction from EnvelopeBooks

www.envelopebooks.co.uk

My Modern Movement

ROBERT BEST

London's Festival of Britain in 1951 marked the belief that Modern design was visually, morally and commercially superior. Robert Best, the UK's leading lighting manufacturer of the period, thinks the dice were loaded. This is his memoir.

EB8

A Road to Extinction

JONATHAN LAWLEY

When Britain colonised the Andamans in 1857, the welfare of its African pygmy inhabitants was of no concern. Nine tribes died out. Dr Lawley now assesses the three remaining tribes' prospects and the legacy of his grandfather, who ran the colony in the early 1900s.

EB2

From Bedales to the Boche

ROBERT BEST

Bedales, the progressive boarding school founded by J.H. Badley in 1893, instilled values that sustained many of its pupils through the rest of their lives. Robert Best recalls its influence on him as an enthusiastic army recruit in 1914 and, from 1916, in the Royal Flying Corps.

EB3

Fiction from EnvelopeBooks
www.envelopebooks.co.uk

A Sin of Omission
MARGUERITE POLAND

An emotionally intense novel, set in 1870s South Africa at a time of rising anti-colonial resistance. The book focuses on the tragedy of a promising black preacher, hand-picked for training in England as a missionary, only to be neglected by the Church he loves. Based on a true story. *Winner of the 2021 Sunday Times CNA 'Book of the Year' Award in South Africa.*
EB6

Mustard Seed Itinerary
ROBERT MULLEN

When Po Cheng falls into a dream, he finds himself on the road to the imperial Chinese capital. Once there he rises to the heights of the civil service before discovering that there are snakes as well as ladders. Carrollian satire at its best.
EB5

Frances Creighton: Found and Lost
KIRBY PORTER

Love demands trust but trust is a lot to ask for victims of abuse. Having been bullied by two teachers in Belfast as a boy, Michael Roberts suppresses his childhood pains until the death of a girlfriend years later forces him to revisit lost memories.
EB7

The Train House on Lobengula Street
FATIMA KARA

An anguished but life-affirming novel, set within the Indian community in Bulawayo in Rhodesia of the 1950s and 1960s, about the capacity of women to gain the same advantages as men in the modern world while remaining faithful to traditional Muslim values, and about the cruelty of white oppression. Warm and passionate writing.
EB12

Lagos, Life and Sexual Distraction
TUNDE OSOSANYA

A collection of twelves short stories, mostly focused on Lagos—the commercial capital of Nigeria—but with two dedicated to the plight of people living in northern Nigeria, under attack from Islamist insurgents. The book reveals what a typical Nigerian does to keep his or her dreams alive and shows the tensions that exist between different generations, sexes, social classes and ethnicities.
EB13